Yria Dane

Yria Dane

Julien Kade

For my Mom.

Thank you for being my biggest supporter.

Chapter One

My name's Biertempfel. Satordi Biertempfel; and much like any man from Annecy, I look like your average Joe, just another buck with brown hair and blue eyes. Speaking above-board about my image, well, sorry to disdain you, but there's nothing swank about it. Most days you'll catch me clung in suspenders clipped to the waistband of my trousers. Depending on the day, I'll wear a starched shirt with pin stripes; other than that, I like solids; usually white, but here and there I get bold and try colors. So saying that, seems what's mentioned is the average style dress for men around here.

On a unique note, unlike my fellow man in these parts, I never married. Have I met my darling damsel, the one to be my reining consort? Could be, but then again, I'm just guessing. I'm not eager about marriage, nor am I stalled by the thought.

Being thirty-nine, I'll say and be frank, it doesn't hurt me to accept my path, how it's gone. I'm just fine with no band braced upon my ring finger. It makes me no less a man. I might be without a wife, but it's not to say I'm alone. I've got my steady girlfriend Deja; she's thirty-six, and all I need at this time.

My life may sound simple, but my work's hard. Thirteen years ago my brother and I went into business. Less than often, the junior Biertempfel runts got into trouble for snooping. We were the bloodhounds of our day. We found anything out, knew all the business and obscurities of our town. No one was safe. We meddled and poked our way into shit. We were two amateur sleuths, Marin and I.

It seemed forth on, from that starting day, way back in our youth, Marin and I knew our skills would become an occupation. Here we are currently among the year and our operation stands firm. Marin and I own a nice little building along the main street. It's nothing to brag about, but still, we're both happy. Our sign's not hard to catch. Big letters stretch across the front window that read Biertempfel Brothers, Private Detectives.

We're not lowlife schmucks with no brains and false claims. We take our work seriously, whatever the matter. Marin's forty-one. Despite that he's older, he's kept his place as my business partner, not some bossy chum directing orders to his little brother.

Unlike me, Marin's married. He has a pretty wife named Cerissa, who's ten months younger than I. She's a considerate lady, kindhearted and sweet. She and Marin have been together sixteen years and mar- ried eleven. They have a nine-year-old son, Paien, then Zuri, their sev- en-year-old daughter. Though, being kids, they're pretty decent squirts.

From 1939-1952 Marin and I've worked hundreds of cases; everything from cheating spouses to runaways and missing persons. We've done it all, or so I think. Marin bickers we'll tackle something irregular someday. He dreams of that period when we're presented a case that's totally unlike our standard norm. Mind you, being in business as long as we have, cases are always the same ole same. Seems my brother's just out of his mind and growing bored with his work.

Currently Marin's on a case of his own. He's on his four day link of tracking his client's wife and new lover, some young swain from Savoie. The wife, Mrs. Audric Badeau, had been married twelve years when she decided to abandon her husband and young daughters. When she met Christoph, the new flame in her life, he was working along the canal, lifting crates from a dinghy. Her foot ironically got caught up in rope before she fell into his arms. The incident must have literally swept her away. Before long they were secretly meeting. The first time she laid him must have ignited a fire. Apparently Christoph had more vavoom than Audric. Christoph's stamina and lasting endurance had captured his lover. It was Christoph's animal efficacy which led Mrs. Badeau astray. Now it's been my brother's job to go find her.

Me, on the other hand, I'm free of a case. I wrapped mine up just this past week. I've now got time on my hands as I wait for another. I sit at my desk and await the punching toll of my telephone, which doesn't seem to be doing much of nothing. Here I am alone, while Marin's out on work. My ashtray's overrun with butt after butt. A half glass of pommeau rests in my sight. A mixture of apple juice and apple brandy, mahogany in color, and aged thirty months. It's a smooth swallow and, of its flavor, I'm fond.

The silent stand of this room is unbearable. No one to talk to, so I just stare at the pallid ceiling, with nothing to do but count foursquare boxes from left to right. When I grow bored enough, I'll take a nap. If I hear a clang at the door, I'm summoned to wake. It wouldn't be professional to let a possible client see me sleep. Soon as that clink breaks, I'm alert and sitting straight.

Unfortunate for me, it's a slow day in the office. In this moment I'm staring at my phone, begging the damn thing to ring. I'm the type man who needs to be out on the streets collecting information and tracking some truant. Sitting here doing absolutely nothing just drives me insane. Just like before, I'm sitting, counting boxes left to right. It ain't much amusement, but it's something to do. As I number the thirty-fourth tile of ceiling, I hear the pleasant reverberation of my once hushful phone. It's about time, I say. I'm ready and willing to work into action. As not to sound eager, I calmly answer my phone, "Satordi Biertempfel."

The man at the other end responds by saying he's in serious need of help. I then ask him to define the situation. The man boldly states it's not anything to be relayed on the line. My curiosity elevates. "Then how can I help you?" The man stands silent for a good thirty seconds, then I hear him again. He asks if I know the location of Frenchman's Tavern. After remarking yes, he gives instructions he directs me to follow.

I pull forth a white tablet and scribble upon it. I circle Frenchman's Tavern and a name the man gives me, Haulmier Guloe.

I hang the phone and prepare for my mission. I'm unsure what I'll be getting into, but I know it's my choice to withstand the chore or not. I quickly eye my blazer from behind my chair. I know first impressions always stick with a client. It's better I look appropriate than appearing a scab who's unkempt and not clean.

Before leaving, I grab my glass of pommeau and guzzle the remainder. After slipping my tablet into my chest pocket, I make sure my pen's tucked in place. Concluding I'm ready, I depart through the door, prepared for my quest.

It's a fairly sunny day; warm, but not hot. I look around, discerning the fact, Annecy's one gorgeous place, I must tell you. We're lucky having the most stunning scenery of any city, with a mazarine lake and aerial Alps in range of our vision. You'd not see a more wondrous place than what you'd find here.

Outside my building there're a group of kids tossing bottle caps atop the sidewalk. Apparently it's keeping them busy as I brush alongside. I'd had tossed them a franc had they known I walked by. Instead, I stretch farther along and step to my car, a 1950 Grand National Roadster. Sable, I call her; my black beauty, a true hard body. If anything has my heart, it's my slick metal lady. No woman contests to Sable's grace and flashy exterior.

I seat myself within my wheels knowing Frenchman's tavern isn't far, a few blocks at most. It'll be a short ride, then I'll be off pursuing my business.

As I'm arriving to my destination, I see the tavern in sight, a narrow building, square in shape and small in size. Before treading forth, I obtain my tab from my pocket, with intentions to spy the name I'd been told to come find, Haulmier Guloe. I knew it was like that, or at least something close. I recount the name once more in my mind, then start toward the door while feeling ever confident.

The clangor of the bell tolls as I enter the room. I look around to a bunch of men's faces. I ease toward the bar, steadily peering upon the one man pouring drinks at the counter. To me he appears young; he don't hardly look twenty, but I guess as age goes, it can sometimes deceive. Watch, this babyfaced chap's probably in his mid twenties, yet I can't help thinking he's some brash teen who's working a bar. This boy with his dark hair and tough looks should be training for fights. He looks like a boxer, a lightweight, at least.

He asks, "What'll it be?"

I tell him, "I'm looking for Haulmier Guloe. You know where I'll find him?"

He eyes me a second, scoping me over. "You've business with the man?"

"Possibly," I say. "He here?"

"At the end of the bar. The one sitting solo."

I nod quickly and carry on my way. If the man I'm viewing's Guloe, he seems pretty harmless. He's not a stick figure; rather the man's kind of solid. He's most likely to be in his early forties, with brown hair on his head that's yet to start balding. I notice right off his suspenders aren't clipped as they hang down beside him; typical sight for a man who's laid back, laxing the day's load from his shoulders. Before taking a seat, I address the man by relaying speech, "You Haulmier Guloe?"

He looks to me with inspecting eyes, then gets it. "You must be Detective Biertempfel?"

"I was given word you'd expect me."

He relays to me sit, to take an open seat, and as I was guided, I sit alongside him.

"Artus," he yells. "Fetch this man a drink."

The man behind the counter approaches, standing tall before me. I look to his eyes, saying, "Scotch on the rocks." While I dig for my mon- ey. Guloe directs I put it away, that the drink's on the house, however many, so I respond with a nod, then gulp my first swig.

Guloe eases forth in his chair when he leans in to tell me, "For reasons I couldn't spare details over the line, it's best we speak private." His voice then quietens. "I'd have involved the police, but my matter's too risky. I have no intention to expose illegal business that would close down my bar."

"Yours?" I ask, with a curious stare.

"I own Frenchman's," Haulmier explains. "I have for some years. This building's my life, it's my pride. Aside from that, the reason I brought you. I've had goings-ons which have caused me some trou- ble. It's best we move to a vacant room and be absent of ears." I follow Haulmier toward the basement before he turns to Artus. "No one goes down, not until we've come back."

We get to the basement which is full of scattered crates and equip- ment. I look around quickly as I take in the sight. "What trouble you in? What leads you to thinking you might use my help?"

Haulmier inhales a deep breath before he takes to my side. "I must have you understand, whatever's said mustn't be involved with any arm of the law."

Though, Guloe hasn't stated the predicament he's in, seems this man's deeply involved in some trouble. I refrain from further speech to analyze his verbalization.

"You're a private detective, Mr. Biertempfel. Not some suited narc. I'm trusting you'll do as I say."

My nostrils flare as I take in a breath. I don't want to appear unsettled or troubled as I retain my composure, but seriously, Haulmier forces my wince. I decide to explain, "Should this situation involve some fellow you want tracked and you wipe that man out, then I'll tell you now, I can't help. Another thing. I'm not a hitman. I don't kill for hire. Those are my rules."

Guloe explains, "I'm certain, Mr. Biertempfel, you and I can talk business."

"Be it a clean case, most likely I'll take it."

"It's for your judgment to decide, Mr. Biertempfel. If you're at ease with the circumstance, I'm sure it'll work. I guess it's time I cut to the facts. The person I'm needing you to find is my daughter."

I draw forth my tablet of paper and begin taking notes. Haulmier continues. His daughter is Ambrielle Guloe, an imprudent seventeen-year-old with a history of prostitution.

Just four days ago Ambrielle skipped town, carrying a massive stash of stolen loot she'd taken from her father.

Haulmier claims he'll be exact on what happened. He confesses his tavern doesn't make nearly enough to pay bills. When realizing he was in a financial mess, Haulmier determined he'd do something about it. He says he needed to make money and it had to come fast, even if it meant going under the law. He confesses before me, upon this second, his illegal involvement with absinth. He tells me it's made under the roof of this tavern, within a walled basement room, and is then traf-ficked to loyal contacts throughout the city. It's been this leading de-mand that's making him money.

Haulmier attests to his doe having been concealed within a safe in this room. Not minding the money chamber on a constant basis, Haulmier figured his loot was secure.

The day Ambrielle left, Haulmier claims his daughter had been acting strangely. She made several repeat trips to the basement, but each time she'd come up, she had nothing in hand. Haulmier claims now he knew what she'd done. As not to be caught, he imagines Ambrielle lifted a window, then set the loot onto the ground. Once outside, Ambrielle tread to the side, picked up her sacks of plenty, and fled with the funds.

Haulmier never heard a word from his daughter. Like usual, on prior days, Haulmier figured Ambrielle had gone home. This leaves me to wonder whether their relationship was good, or perhaps there'd been trouble? Seems their line of communication had been nothing but muted, so I'm left to ask, "Were you two on good terms?"

Haulmier clinches his teeth. I know because I see his jowls protrude and fill in size. He takes a moment's time, then relays his answer, "In the least. Ten days a year we get along."

I think for a minute, then interfere in his business. "What's the reason for that?"

"I don't support her way of life, Detective. These words may be harsh, but my daughter's a tramp. She's a run through with men. A handled whore, spreading her legs for petty cash and coins."

I look to my notes, then decide on a question. "Where's her known residence?"

"Well, she was living with her mother and me. We had hoped we could change her. Though, she lived in our home, we couldn't decline her from the filth of those streets."

Okay, I think. I like my job, it's what I do; but when I'm hired for a case which involves prostitution, I'm easily unglued. It isn't difficult to get knocked off in the wrong side of town. Bad people, boozers and drug fiends of all kinds associate to the areas, these locations I'm going. I can pray that I'm wrong that, that's not where I'll be, but speaking from my gut, I can honestly say these places will soon catch my drift.

I envision Ambrielle returning to one, if not more of those offensive reserves, those spots she's known and has frequented often. I know not to ask Haulmier, but I do anyway. "If I were to take this job, where's the one likely place I'd catch sight of your daughter?"

"She rents rooms along her district. Roach-infested hole in the walls. Rancid places. Dens of stench."

Just as I figured, I'll have to fit in, present a guise, and become a lowlife. I've done this sort of thing before, but I'm always uneasy. I nev- er know what I'll walk into, or worse off, who I'll encounter. Will there be trouble? You bet there'll be trouble. For resting on the other side of town's the ugly streets of Annecy. A few times I've encountered a blade at my back. I've been robbed, I won't lie. Those streets are rough and, the men, even tougher. Unfortunately, I like the thrill of concern pes- tering my mind. It's this strange inhabitation that keeps me forgoing. So yeah, I'm a little weird, maybe unorthodox, if you will. I get upset by unease, but thrive off its thrill.

It's my job to probe and direct an interrogation, and it's my client's responsibility to answer back with the truth. Right now I've got infor- mation, but I'm needing more facts, so being who I am, I arise with a question, "Your daughter got any kin, any family she'd go to?"

Haulmier quickly returns with his answer; nobody. She's got no one, he tells me. I mark possible relatives off my list. Next, my question concerns an apparent boyfriend, if any.

Haulmier rubs his forehead, seeming stressed by my poll. "I wouldn't know. Probably. Maybe many. I can't say for sure."

"You have any pictures? At least one photo to show me?"

"Maybe in my wallet?"

Guloe lowers his hand to the back of his pocket. He draws forth a leather billfold that's crinkled and worn. Inside, he hunts through an amassment of business cards, folded notes, and small portraits, then hands me a print.

"That'd be my most recent snap of her. It's probably a year old, maybe more. She looks the same. Still has those flowing strands of am- ber waves cast down to her shoulders. Her eyes are soft blue and her skin's pale. And she takes after her mom, with her petit five foot, four inch stature."

I've taken note of everything Guloe's said. It's enough to throw me on track. I haven't agreed to be hired, but I feel I've settled the consent in my mind.

Haulmier braces his eyes upon me as he breaks into question, "What do you think? Is this a job you can handle?"

I evade him momentarily and stall him a moment, or perhaps several seconds. I ogle my notes, then return to the picture, leaving him to suspect that I've not yet decided. I press my lips together, then moisten the folds. Haulmier's waiting patiently, or perhaps he's intolerant and ill with concern. I can't read him quite clearly. His composure's solid, which puts me off track, so I await him to break into sweat. It's offbeat, I confess, but I do this to clients. I need to see it's as important as he's making it out. That first break of excretion shows desperate demand.

It's an odd inspection, but this simple test will prove that he's honest.

I give Guloe a second more, then spy the perspired tears which have formed on his head. It's now time I catch him off guard, so I say to him quickly, "Seems you know where your daughter's at. Maybe not the exact location, but you're aware of her district. Had you given thought into looking yourself?"

As though it's unnerved him, Haulmier promptly snaps at my question, "I dare not step foot in those places. Those foul, filthy trails, plagued by disease and vile infestations. Those locations I'd not tread if you paid me."

"Well," I say. "If I do this, you'll just need me to find her? And no intended harm once I do, is that your word?"

"There's no way I'd hurt my daughter, Detective. I could get angry and yell, but I'd never strike out. I'm not that kind of man. Ambrielle's my daughter. I just want her home. I don't sleep when she's away on those streets. I worry. I need assurance she's safe."

"What about the money?" I examine Guloe. "Hadn't that been the reason for summoning me?"

I await Haulmier's comment, which is slow in coming. Finally he acknowledges it'd been his intention, but confesses now it's her safety that minds him. He says if she hadn't spent the loot, he'd demand it all back; and if she did, he'd be at a loss.

I look to Haulmier, then conduct a reply, "It's time we discuss my fees. I charge fifty-five francs each day that I work. I'd report every night with information regarding your daughter. I prefer to meet in person, here if possible, to convey our discussion. As for payment. I demand my day's earn at each nightly encounter."

"Fifty-five francs a day seems steep for a man with no money."

"For the places I'm going, I'd have the right to charge more. Take it or leave it."

Haulmier responds no word, but instead, breathes heavily. He walks to the window he suspects Ambrielle used to slip money. I inspect the back of his head as I leer at his stillness.

"Hey," I say. "You need time to think this over? I can come back tomorrow."

Quietly he continues to stand, then swiftly he turns my direction. "I'll make my decision today. Let's return to the bar."

I follow Guloe along the stairs before we enter the taproom. We trace our way toward our chairs where we find ourselves settling. Haulmier inquires if I want another drink. I nod and laugh briefly. "It's on the house, right?"

He steps behind the bar, ices fresh glasses, then spouts liquid bliss. He returns to his seat as I'm firing my smoke.

After acquiring my drag, I point to my pack. "Care for a stick?"

Sure, he tells me, so I let him select.

"How long you imagine it'll take before you're finding my daughter?"

"If she's in town, as you suspect, a few days."

"And you're a sure thing?"

"If you trust me, Mr. Guloe, you can trust that I'll find her."

"When can you start?"

I peer out the door, into the shade of night. "The day's half gone, so I'd be starting tomorrow."

"Why can't you start now?"

"I'd charge you half pay."

"And tomorrow your fee would be set at full price?" I nod in agreement.

Guloe gulps his last swig of scotch. He relays to me, get started tonight. "Report tomorrow following your shift, duty, whatever you call it."

I draw my tab from the depth of my pocket. "I'll need your contact information."

Haulmier relays the bar's number, then the one for his house. "Phone the tavern. If you don't reach me, try my home." He walks to the back of his bar and pulls forth a locked bin. He's retrieving my money, then hands me my earnings. "Your night's pay."

I push my empty glass toward the counter as I stretch to my feet. "You mind me keeping this picture?"

Apparently he don't, 'cause he says, "It's yours till she's found."

I slip my earnings into my wallet, then I tap on the counter. "I'll be in tomorrow."

I say goodbye, then head to the door. I spot Sable before the curb where I parked her. I slide through the hatch, trigger her engine, all the while summoning her comely purr. I relish that thunderous roar. It's an enthralling tone breeding envy in male motorists all over. I drift the street knowing Sable's my girl and not some benighted sap's.

Currently it's eight past nine, and decidedly I think I'll head to my business. If I'm in luck, I'll see Marin's meandered back, but as I pull to our building, I don't see his car, so rather, I park in his space. I leave Sable along the curb while I tread to my office. Inside, I find myself standing before an unframed mirror. If I'm to walk the foul streets of Annecy, I better look the part. Lucky me it's a warm night. I remove my suspenders and set them along the top of my table. I loosen my shirt, leaving it to slack in an unbounded position. After undoing several buttons, I allow my undershirt to show through. I tassel my hair by messing it up. Once acquiring the look I desire, I pour me a glass of pommeau. I cheers myself, saying, "All hail the case. Here's to staying alive."

I look toward the mirror, responding, "Time to hit the streets, you schmuck." Though, that's not who I am. I only figure it'll lend some air to my ego.

I prep myself for the filthy streets. You've got to be wise, I say to me. Deviously smooth, sharply and keen. I'll gamble my wits, my cunning intelligence, to support my shrewd hauteur.

It's now twenty-three minutes past nine. I know I'd not be wise driv-ing my Sable along the wrong side of Annecy's tracks. I wouldn't risk her to some hoodlum who's wanting to swipe her the instant I'm stepping adrift. I'd not attempt it. I'm not dumb, so I decide I'll walk. I finish my pommeau before I find myself off, but just before, I slide a blade to my pocket, so I now feel prepared. I'm feeling inclined to hit the streets with my crooked scheme. I go, assuming the part of a lowlife.

Chapter Two

I've walked alone to South Road, one of the bad streets in Annecy. It's cluttered with boozers and beggars, eagerly pinching passers for an expected franc. Had it not been the effect of liquor, then half these cads are mental. I spot several now needing putting away. One man I'm passing sits upon the curb, yelling to an imaginary goat he calls the Billy devil. He's freaked the horned *bouc* will take his soul. Had it been real, there's no need that I'd doubt it. I'd hail one less louse on the street. The man's creepy, insane, and wacky, and I still hear his screams, though I'm now far from his step. If he hasn't unsettled me, perhaps the next will.

I continue my pace without looking back. I maintain my eyes in a straightforward position before an uncomfortable encounter pulls them astray. I sense someone's adrift as my neck hairs become stiffened and stand from my skin. I decide to confront the pesky trouble that's riding my back. I turn aside to encounter a man sniffing like Fido at the rear of my shirt. "Hey," I'm yelling. "Get out of here. Go find yourself a hydrant."

The man continues as I push him away. In seconds he returns like an irksome mutt, annoying my nerves and boiling my veins. "I thought I told you to get. Brush off, man, before you find yourself hurt."

The man responds, "You smell fresh, boy. All good and clean. You be careful. Broods here would tear you apart."

The man turns and strolls away, not minding me again. Had he laid one hand in my space, he would have found himself pricked by my blade.

I continue down South Road and hang a right onto the next foul street. I find myself at the corner of Harbour Ridge Avenue where I'm viewing more black sheeps than before. I now approach some manic loon, wielding a bible and preaching some blabber. Seems he believes a prophecy based on illusionary inaccuracies. What it is, I'm not yet aware.

He steps forth, laying his load of bogus yak. Some crap he says. The dead will rise and, when she does, a bloodline shall suffer. He's another needing admittance and locking up. I don't say a word, but I quicken my pace and stride in long steps. Appears my encounters may be working me up and upsetting my peace.

Just one block to go and I'll be at the red light district. There're roach dens all along these streets, but those I seek will be scouted along the main strip. I'm nearly reaching the end of this noisome avenue when I happen upon some nutty woman with crazy hair and shallow eyes. I don't know whether she's singing a song or reciting some sonnet. Whatever it is, it's ghoulishly peculiar.

Once again I find my hairs on end. I brush before her when she livens her speech to a most critical tone. The woman lifts her head and stares to the sky. It's then I hear her words more clearly; dreadfully, I feel. It's as though this witch has cursed me. Her words linger like an enduring steam, polluting my breath. Drawing her eyes upon me, while speaking through a scratchy modulation, she conveys, "If Yria Dane be by or here, don't deem on her to disappear. Once the words are spoken right, you've conjured up this spook of fright."

Okay, I've completely decided this woman's a quack, not just physically scary, but mentally as well. I tread faster and move from her sight; the farther away, the better I feel. But honestly, I'd give anything to return to my home. Least there I'd know I was safe.

Suck it up, Satordi, I tell myself. Endure the happenings of this night. You thrive off thrill, remember that. You've tread this walk umpteen times. Like those before, you'll do it again.

Finally I've made it to the main strip. I wish I could sigh a breath of release, but I know I can't. There're still many screwballs around to sharpen my guard and heighten my sight. I dare not drop my head and display defeat. Keeping solid and maintaining composure will keep the creeps away, I hope.

My first stop will be to The Easy Way Inn, an obvious slogan, granted its name. It's a rundown rent room servicing a mess of floozies to trailing men. Only dirt-bags and horn balls get sighted here.

I pace through the door, gazing. Within the tramp shop are half-dressed sleazes, throwing forth their invitations, each anxious to lure me upstairs. I wasn't paid to screw these skimpy broads and wispy whores. I'm here on business.

I walk to the counter where some scuzzy chump's greeting my step. "Take your pick," he tells me. "Whatever you want. My girls do it all. Bondage, fetishes, special traits, whatever's your call. You want plea- sure from more than one, they're here for your service and eager to go."

I lean onto the counter, asking, "You got a girl by the name of Am- brielle?"

"You looking for hot times, are you? I should've figured you'd be into beat and choke."

"Don't judge a book by its cover. It's liable to surprise you."

"Course not. I'd never consider."

Some scank walks up, rubbing my shoulder. "Forget Ambrielle. I'll show you good times, however you'd want them."

"No thanks, sweetheart."

"Come on, baby, how about you reconsider? I'll do all Ambrielle does and I'll add a tad more."

I redirect my focus to the man before me. "Is Ambrielle available or not?"

"You want her that bad, mister? But sure you do. Walk on over to The Blossomed Rose, across the street. Last I heard, she was working there."

I turn from the man and step into pace. As I tread, I hear him speak, "You're an eager one, hunting Ambrielle. Well, I say, you must have her name reserved on your prick."

I forget his babble as I'm heading away. I return to the streets where I'm walking among scattered boozers and loopy freaks. The Blossomed Rose is roughly thirty steps off, so I hike to the curb and I'm peering both ways. As I'm crossing, out from nowhere, a man's running up. He begins screaming constant blather upon my ear. "Can you sense it? Can you sense it?" he screams. He jerks his head in a robotic motion as I'm brushing away. My attempts are scarce when once again he comes upon me. "Can you sense it, that strange feeling in the air? It's her. It is. She stirs about."

"Listen, chum, I don't know your deal and it's not my care to. Now walk along."

"Don't think I haven't warned you." He's poking my chest. "Bodies will drop and, whence they do, there'll be blood on your hands."

It's nonsense this dullard talks. He's out of his mind. The stench from his clothes can consciously imply the fumes on his breath, even if I hadn't smelt them.

He follows me like a lost dog and I'm getting angered by his unwant- ed presence as I begin to shout, "Shoo, man. I don't like being followed."

"But you need me. I'm the only one who'll attest your innocence."

"You're crazy, fool. Get out of my sight."

"The name's Ghislain. I'll be here when you need me."

The man turns around, disappearing from view. Thank God. Thank God! Another second, I thought I would stick him. I continue my way when seeing The Blossomed Rose just ahead. This is it. The girl's got to be here.

I enter the door and, unlike The Easy Way Inn, this place displays class. My first stop had been a junky den with half-baked broads in raunchy dress, or the lack there of, I should say. Here the women dress sensibly. They're not standing in drapery that leaves nothing to the imagination. These women are in satin gowns and decently clothed. On another note, they appear proper and coy.

I further my stroll to approach the front desk. As my step advances, I spot the debonair resting comfortably within her velvet chair. She's a mid-aged lady, with few wrinkles. Her green eyes are light and her brown hair's been pulled in a bun. Considering, I'll take this woman as mannerly and kind, but I'll confirm my educated judg- ment is merely a guess.

"Good evening, sir," she speaks pleasantly to me. "Can I interest you in one of my girls?" She's now flashing a smile. "If not, I'd be glad to assign you a room for the night."

A lovely woman approaches and interrupts my response. "Lady Ancelin, we need sheets in room twelve. The cupboard is bare. There were no shrouds I could find."

"I'll fetch some fresh laundry. Just let me tend to this client." Lady Ancelin redirects her eyes upon me. "Have you enough time to decide what you'll need?"

I take not a moment to convey my reply. "Ambrielle, if she's working."

"I do apologize. She's no longer with us."

My eyes widen. I had hoped to hear better, but instead I'm side-tracked by an acknowledgment I hadn't considered. "She's not?" I stand dumbfounded, without any thought.

"She picked up and left a few days ago."

"Any idea where she's gone?"

"Well, sure, dear. She stays with my sister." Lady Ancelin casts her head to the side as she studies me over. "She must have been a favorite of yours. But I must say, I've never seen you. Have you come here before?"

"I haven't, ma'am, no. I'd been acquainted to Ambrielle when she worked at The Easy Way Inn."

"Must have been many moons ago. Ambrielle hadn't worked there in nearly a year."

"Had she lived here?"

"But of course. She kept a room upstairs."

"For how long?"

"Only the times she wanted. Ambrielle came and went."

"Where else had she stayed?"

"Poor girl. She's been between homes. Sometimes her parents', other times here."

"You mentioned her at your sister's?"

"Well, yes, as of now." "For what business?"

"It'd been no secret. Even my girls could say she wanted away from her dad."

Haulmier didn't lie, I see. Ambrielle took the money as said. I'll have to find the girl soon before she's fleeing this town. I pat Lady Ancelin's hand. "I'd be joyed to see her again. Simply viewing Ambrielle would brighten my day."

Ancelin remains hesitant a moment. "Ambrielle stays in Grenoble, at The Petal and Stem. My sister's Madame Voletta. She runs the bordello."

I thank Lady Ancelin, then once again find myself on the street. I head back to Harbour Ridge Avenue, where I unfortunately encounter the crazy woman with wild hair, still crooning her dreadful villanelle. As she accounts the poem, its rhythmical creation gets ever more creepy. She says, "Yria swore she would not rest and conjured up the perfect hex. Curse ye be who brung her pain. Damned to hell, she'll speak his name. His sin is hers, she takes in bane. Those who beckon, she'll furnish strain, whence she scouts his bloodline's name."

Course, at this point, I find myself highly unsettled. There's something about this superstitious verse which brings me to quiver. Chills ride my skin, though there's no breeze to produce it. I'd give anything to escape this hell hole, anything. I'm regretting now I didn't drive Sable. If only she'd carried me here. I know I'd been concerned for her safety, but now I'm wishing I'd been more halfhearted.

Maybe I'd be wise to act like I don't hear these things around me. Tune it out. Keep your head straight and your feet forward. I'll be away from here soon, but soon isn't quick. Not quick enough, I'll tell you. I still have several blocks to walk. About two before I'm fleeing these execrable tracks, then I'll be on to pleasant streets and feeling secure with my safety.

Here I am, alone. Many sidewalks I've traveled, just me and my thoughts. It's a lonely position, but one which I take. It's not always easy. Sometimes I find myself in places like this. These are unfavorable streets, producing vile citizens and harrowing impressions. The commonsensical populace of Annecy know better than to dawdle here. Maybe one day I'll be part of that crowd.

I'm upon the corner of South Road when I encounter a sharp pain being slapped to my back. The agony's unbearable as I fall to my knees. I look to detect some young mental cad. Within his hands are connective metal links. He forces a swing when trying to belt me upon the top of my head. I think fast and roll from his way. The chains slap the ground as I stand on my feet. I wasn't looking to spill no blood tonight, but the thought occurred only if I were to bump into a situation where I'd be defending my life. I'm not hesitant as I pull the blade from my pocket. It reflects in the young man's eyes as I begin my series of screams and shouts, "Do it again, creep, and you'll be carved like a turkey. I'm not shouting steam. You'll be sent to a crypt."

The young man backs step by step. Now readying his aim, he casts his links to the air. I twist my arm, knotting the chain and removing its slack. I rage to the cad as he's backing away, "What's your plan now, punk? Seems you're all out of breath."

The kid drops what portion of chain he had, throws his hands to the air, then takes off running as he scrams from my sight.

Turns out that chum was nothing more than a scaredycat. What nerve he had was to take me off guard. He thought I'd stay down with that blow to my back. Had I dropped and not gotten up, he'd have robbed me for sure.

I peer to the side, behind me, then forward. After taking these seconds, I slide my shank to my pants. What a night, I got to say. No way another could be crazier than this. I've seen it all; a man conversing with a devil goat, one who thought he'd been birthed from a dog, another preaching a dead woman's rise, and a crazy woman versing some mentally deranged words. So yeah, I'll be glad to be away from these streets.

Twenty minutes later I arrive at my business. I fire a light before chasing my key and take a drag of my cig. Inside I smell the stale air as I'm treading through. It's a familiar scent which inhabits me. It's nice to come back and be in one piece. Regarding my happiness, I'd have prob- ably kissed the darn floor had the damn thing been clean.

I rest in my chair and toss the pad from my pocket. I scribble the brothel's name Lady Ancelin had given, The Petal and Stem, which will be found in Grenoble. I raise my head to the clock. The time's 11:53. Wondering now, I ponder whether I'd find Haulmier at his tavern, though I'd rather go home and crawl into bed, I do realize my work must come first, therefore, I'll live by that motto. I decide my plan, head to Grenoble tomorrow after I've woken from sleep. I then debate I'll have no time to see Haulmier once morning arrives. My luggage needs packing at least by tonight. I suppose I'll make my attempts and head to the tavern. Before going, I rub out my cigarette and fish for my keys.

Chapter Three

After arriving at the bar, I ask Artus to fetch me a tall glass of water. No more booze tonight. I've had my fill. I don't have a problem like most scum in this town. I know to say I've exceeded my limit. I don't get teased or screeched. The boys here respect my request and give me no bother.

Luckily I find Haulmier's still here. He's taken his seat as I reveal my report, but as not to divulge every piece of information, I decide to hold off on a few things Lady Ancelin said. I'll be honest, however, on one vital thing; Haulmier has the right to know of his daughter skip- ping town.

After relaying the news, I witness Haulmier's mouth droop in shock. I decide to reveal my approaching absence come morning. "Un- til I've gathered enough facts, I won't be back. I will, though, be calling to fill you in on my finds."

Knowing I'm tired, but still with things to do, I exit the tavern. I'll now head home and pack my luggage. Least then I won't have tomor- row to do it. It'll be a long day, so I hope I'll get rest.

Chapter Four

It hadn't been the annoying signal of my alarm which roused me. Instead, it's the warm sun bathing my face, as well as its extending streams spiking my eyes. I peer to my clock through slit slight to perceive the time. It's a quarter till seven. So unsuited is this moment that I could drift away another hour, but the unnecessary incentive to rise drives me from bed. I couldn't fall into slumber even if I tried. I'm alert and fully enlivened. Had I planned to retreat to my covers, I'd have defeated the initial purpose of sleep. My body would lie provoked and revived. Rather, I do as my body directs. I leave the comfort of my sheets and step from my bed.

Walking to my dresser, I pull forth a pair of socks. I then move to my closet to scope my starched shirts and lazed pants. After selecting my attire, I travel to the bathroom. I brush my teeth, wash my face, then comb my disordered hair. Later, I regress to the bedroom, gather my luggage, then head through the door.

I carry my personal possessions to Sable's trunk, then backtrack to my home for a hasty morning meal. I'm not much for cooking. I don't sling my grub to a pan and allow it to fry. Instead, I gather two bagels, smear them with butter, then fix me some fresh roasted brew. Quickly I hesitate on filling my mug entirely. I'm too afraid of spilling scalding ink inside Sable. Should it slosh and spatter, not only would my car become a sticky mess, but the likes of me as well.

I pace toward the ingress, clinching an uneaten bagel between my teeth. Retained in my hand, I steady my mug of liquid vigor, all the while minding the lock on my door.

Seems I'm ready to set out for my journey. I glide to Sable, then pass through her door. After securing my mug in its rest, I devour the last of my food and lean comfortably into my cushion. I realize I'll be sitting awhile, and during that time it'll be my ass that's benumbed. So I position my rear, making certain it's comfy.

I galvanize Sable's engine as her comely purr reacts on key. She breathes deeply through a thunderclap before I set her loose, and off I go with my metal baby, blazing down the street.

I lower my driver window and sling my arm on the door. As the air rolls in, it breezes through the cleft, sweeping my face and messing my hair. To live on the open road would be pleasing. Maybe once I'm retired it'll be something I'll do, just cut out; let the road take me wherever place it goes, and if that's lost, I wouldn't care. It'd be a gaiety adventure, one I'd have myself.

Chapter Five

Following a seventy-five minute drive, I pull into the city of Grenoble, unknown to where I'll go. The hour's still early as it's nearing 8:20. Businesses are just opening, least some, not all.

Damn me, I should've stayed home, stolen extra rest, then ris- en later. I see I've embarked my adventure too young in the day. I've got nothing to do, with nowhere to go. I suppose this happens when I'm coupled with strive to get where I'm going. What's to do? Drive around? Kill an hour? Should I journey back toward Annecy? I'd be insane to waste my gas. Besides that, I'd be boosting Sable's odometer.

Rather than risking another trip between towns, maybe I'll pose as a tourist just traveling the area, but oh, the thought makes me cackle. Then again, there're places to see and things to be learned. Might as well tour the town for whatever joys it does offer. I suppose I could gawk at buildings and pace through the markets. Maybe if I'm lucky I'll find Dej a nice gift, whatever token it'd be.

I miss her during my times away. I grow lonely and sad not seeing her face. Half the time I feel we're worlds apart, though my impression's rightfully false. I'm surprised she hasn't taken a new man and named him her lover; then again, I have no knowledge she hasn't. She could've since I'm not around to be aware. I hate the thought to which I'm now thinking. I feel pestered. In an attempt to feel better I can think of my brother. He and Cerissa are married. She's never gambled their vows, though my brother's away most time. Cerissa has Paien and Zuri. Maybe that stops her from going astray.

Now my merriment lessens. What do I have? I'm not married. I haven't any tots or sprouting runts who've been reared from my loins. As I've said before, I'm not eager about marriage, but seems now the thought looms in mind. Maybe I should consider asking for Deja's hand? I feel certain she'd say yes. I know what a lovely wife she'd make, and moreover, what a happy husband I'd be. Guess I'll have this to pon- der. While in Grenoble, I think I'll look at rings.

Julien Kade

I station Sable before a mass of large buildings along the main street. Seems a fair place to be parking my ride. I see no suspicious cads or feral creeps. Had I, Sable's wheels wouldn't be parked where they're at. I can leave her peacefully along the curb without worry.

I peer upon the buildings before me. I spot a pastry shop, then deli, followed by the cheese mart, wine stock, and bread store.

Farther down's the gift goers division. Mount side by side is a perfume mart and soap stand. Next door's a place to buy fabrics, linens, and textiles. Near that's The Candle Box, where Grenoble's pillars and tapers get crafted. A stone's throw away are men's quarters, I like to call them. The specialties include all types of fun crap. I eye the blacksmith and locksmith. On down the way's a gunsmith and, I'm believing, should I be right, the bladesmith's next door. Nestled with them's the paint shop, hardware store, and an alluring spot to buy tobacco, pipes, and cigars. Had I needed a quick fix of Toby, I'd have headed there, but I know my supply's good to last me.

If I paced on down I know there'd be more to see, but instead I stand in place, searching for a jeweler. I might be wise to turn around and scope the shops behind me. Then there, on the small stretch of street, I eye the weeny building, Shining Diamond's, Gems and Jewelry. Next door's the flower shop and candy store, ironically synced together to serve those decreed by infatuated hearts and enamored souls. As I'm easing on, I'm realizing, I'm one of those besotted fools.

I'll admit I don't know Deja's size, but if I found the right ring, the one to deduct my respire, it'll be the one of my choice, for it I shall buy. Accordingly, should Deja accept my proposal, I'll make sure the ring gets trimmed to the breadth of her finger.

I navigate through the doors of the jewelry shop and begin browsing the lengthy exhibit of glass displays. With many to opt from, I see my time will be spent inspecting ringlets. I can pass the minutes and, if I'm lucky, an hour; then later I can head out and hopefully find Ambrielle.

Chapter Six

The Petal and Stem, which Satordi shall later find, is an adoring cheateu, dating back to the seventeenth century. This majestic estate consists of sixteen rooms. It was built by Gralam le Magne, for his wife, Maura.

The mansion had been kept in the le Magne clan for generations, until the nineteen-twenties, when Alesta le Magne decided to sell for personal reasons. Upon the first sight of sale, there'd been many well-to-do prospects who'd considered the place, but the lucky buyer had been a congenial woman by the name of Voletta Bruel, later to be known as Madame Voletta, a warm hearted matriarch, who, like her younger sister, Ancelin, is a respected lady of her town.

Akin to her sibling, Voletta, too, has green eyes and brown hair. She adores beauty and stately surroundings, which beckon her refined taste. Her appetence is displayed throughout her home and place of business, and all who partake in her brothel are swept away by its lofty bravura.

We now approach the present time with a young girl declaring, "Madame, the dishes, they've been washed, dried, and returned to the cupboard."

"Through already? Well, you do work quick. And if you wouldn't mind, the parlor plants are appearing wilted. I keep a watering tin in the kitchen, below the sink."

In respect, the young girl tilts the slightest bend of her head as a means of understanding.

"I must confess my adores, Ambrielle. You're such a sweet peach."

"Thank you, ma'am," this youthful courtesan acknowledges. "Will that be all, Madame?" Ambrielle awaits her response, then heads to the kitchen.

Just as the matriarch declared, there'd been the watering can perched below the basin. Seconds later the maiden returns to the sitting room to hydrate the plants and shriveled flowers. After doubling back to the cookery, she settles the tin within its place beneath the sink.

Feeling thirsty, Ambrielle pours herself milk, then returns to Voletta's side. "A drink for you, Madame? Some wine?"

Miss Bruel pats her hand upon the couch. "Come you, child, relax you now."

"But the laundry, ma'am. It hasn't been tended."

"We'll have enough linens to last through tomorrow. Unless our display of clientele boosts growth by tonight."

Ambrielle prepares to rise from the couch, but Voletta grasps toward her wrist and pulls her back down.

"Sit, darling, sit. I've no intention to work you to death. You've al-ready been such a wonderful help, making sure food's prepared and the laundry's been kept."

Ambrielle looks upon the light wrinkles crinkling Voletta's face, then pulling her eyes up, peers deeply into the woman's green saucers. "You know I don't mind."

"You fill my shoes well. Even at your tender age. Tell me, sweet peach, shall I progress once you've gone?"

"I'm certain, ma'am, you'll get by without me."

"Confident, you are, but this hurdle's not easy," Voletta's respond-ing. "I've had many memories in this place, wonderful, beautiful mem-ories, and all with my girls."

Ambrielle draws on Voletta's joyance. Thinking it'd take the lady's mind off her leaving, Ambrielle pleads, "Tell me, ma'am, what be these reminders?"

Voletta smiles. "It's been nearly thirty years I've kept here. Rooms were maintained, well, from that first day. Few girls stayed a year, oth-ers stayed many." Voletta's smile crinkles as her happiness winds down. "Sadly, time and again I watched as they'd leave me. Eventually, new damsels came along, ringing my bell. But of all them, you'll be the one I'll miss most, darling girl."

"That's most kind, Madame. I shall miss you as much."

"When, oh, when are you leaving? Rather, I'd have you malaise my heart now instead of scrupling it later."

"To speak fairly, ma'am, seems I'll be around another two days. Al-ready I've saved forty francs to make my departure."

"Then I shall send you with food and drink."

"I'll gladly accept your sincerity, Madame. Your gratuity's noble. I'm grateful to have it."

Voletta pats the young girl's hand. "I feel you're one of my own, Ambrielle. My girls mean a lot, and I see they need care."

"You're a good woman, Madame. You supply their needs. I know not a soul failing to return their admirations to you."

"I feel it's my job to do right by them. Though, I may have contributed too much for my sake. I can't say I've known other harlots whose lives have been better."

"To speak on truth, ma'am, you've obliged their every whim. Even overindulged on demands. I must say, you keep them quite pampered."

"That they are." Voletta breaks to laughter. "I've spoiled them into rotten brats. Be it my fault. I mustn't be coaxed into catering their every request. I tell you, though, I've never been able to beg one girl into doing the things you have, Ambrielle. They think it's unsuitable, those mollycoddled waifs. I could do to them as they've done me. I could find myself pleading, but the trash would never find its way to a can. My girls, they get all they ask, want, and need."

Ambrielle spies a butterfly fluttering past a bay window and goes to observe it. She watches it land upon a flowering bush to collect it some nectar; then, ever gracefully, it draws together its stunning blue wings as the young courtesan declares, "I'm sure if you showed a little inflexibility, you'd clip their requests. You're aware Constance has four strands of pearls, yet she woos you for more? Understand, ma'am, no matter how much you give, they'll never find it's enough."

"For a girl your age, you speak wiser than most. I've felt greedy in my want to keep you, but I know the importance of your desire. You're wanting your mother and sister. Acknowledging that, I couldn't be selfish. I understand it's been days since you've seen them."

Ambrielle finds herself lost in thought as she's attending the *fenêtre*. "I'm glad they're out. Lord knows I've prayed for their safety, but these days seem like years, and I'm missing them greatly."

Chapter Seven

Thirty minutes have passed as I stand inside Shining Diamonds, Gems and Jewelry. I ogle two rings which have ensnared my attention. Both are uniquely entrancing, therefore each would make an exceptional addition to Deja's hand, but the hard part of this conclusion is deciding which band. I find it's not easy and I feel I've grown flustered.

A sense of temptation plays through my mind. Buy both. Though, the thought is absurd, I find me considering. I'm reduced to moron- ic thoughts. Am I this stupid? But honestly, what's the best way of re-solve? I could present both and see to which Dej is drawn most, but oh, yes, I know, my thoughts are outlandish. And my measly attempts to bargain are illogical, costly, and purely, unwise, I may add. If only I could settle. I take a moment to contemplate. How is it most gentleman do this? Between two rings, how is it they pick?

The jeweler stands before me, probably irritated with my inability to elect the right choice. He stares calmly, then relays a few words, "I'm sure the lady to be would be swept away with whatever you pick."

Still feeling irritated, I'm deciding I'll ask, "How would you choose?" He tells me, with assurance, the right ring will speak to my heart. I hold both as I examine them closely. "I still can't decide." I'm now twisting them as he views my annoyance. "Isn't there an easier way?"

"Well, son, how bout closing your eyes?"

The goal's to allow my hand to guide me to the one it's most drawn. It might be crazy, but I'm for it. So, acquiring a breath, I contend on shutting my eyes. I take a moment before allowing my hand to roam freely. I'm unknown to whether the jeweler has mixed them, but if he has, I like his intent.

All right, I acknowledge, I'll have one fair shake at this, so I'm hop- ing to grab the appropriate ring for Dej's heart. I progress to the count- er, feeling anxious and nervy. Before grabbing a band, I hold off a good minute. I shuffle between the two ringlets, soaking the vibes from the air. I repeat this method several times when noticing, with my extremity's above one, my hand's feeling hot. I take it as a sign. Now moving my palm toward the counter, I grasp for the object and, keeping my eyes clinched, I raise my hand to the air. "This. This one's the one."

The jeweler draws near and I release him the ring.

"Quite a stunning selection, sir. Your future wife shall be proud."

I feel more anxious than ever. I have to see! Which had I chose? I release my eyes from their grip and, presented before me's an impressive, 14k white-gold ring, with twenty-two single cut diamond inlays; a brilliant piece, simply striking. If this isn't perfection, then tell me what is. I'm feeling elated. No, ecstatic! If I'm like this, I can only imagine Deja's reaction. I know I've chosen right.

I follow the jeweler to the cash register, where he's ringing me up. I pay him cash, then await what I'm owed.

"Congratulations, sir," he acknowledges me happily. "I wish you much luck."

"This is it," I respond proudly. "I can't go wrong."

I stretch toward the door before making my way out to Sable. I ease to the driver's side where I slip through the entry. I'm responsi- ble knowing I shouldn't leave Dej's ring where someone might find it. Its safety is crucial. For what it means and, for the amount I paid, I'd be dumb to leave it in sight, so, decidedly, I'll place the bag within my glove compartment. I release the hatch, then bury the sack beneath trivial possessions and needless papers.

I look to my watch, checking the time. It's twenty-two minutes past nine. I feel it's yet early to be heading to The Petal and Stem. Know- ing this, I'd be smart to embark my drift at least by eleven.

I sit, debating what it is I'm to do. A few minutes later I'm feeling an attack of hunger pestering my gut. I acknowledge the bagels I'd eat- en hadn't been enough. I'm now left with an appetite which yearns for more food. I peer through my windshield, looking for a hash house or grease joint. It isn't until I'm gazing toward Grenoble's deli that I spy café *L'blendery*. Being in the mood for hotcakes, I decide to head there.

I transcend through the door when I'm greeted by Aglae, the hostess and owner. She has a tender disposition, kindly and sweet. She asks my preference, counter or booth? I'm figuring a booth would suit best and within one I'm seated. Once lounged, Aglae presents a menu. I scan the bill of fare, but it doesn't take long to find what I want. "I'll have the buttermilk griddle cakes, a side of bacon, and a large juice."

"I'll put your order in and be back."

"Can I get a coffee, too, please?"

While Aglae attends my request, I pull forth my wallet to extract the photo I got from Guloe. I'm still not understanding how an innocent looking girl robs her old man, then has no concern for his care. I'm wondering, had Ambrielle planned on running away to marry some man? What other reason had she had to have done what she did? Hopefully, by talking with her, I'll have better understanding. As I'm study- ing the print, Aglae approaches.

She sees the photo and comments quickly, "Oh, sir, your daughter, she's beautiful."

Unaware she's mistaken, I explain, "She is that, but the child's not mine."

Aglae blushes as I've corrected her thought. "I apologize. I figured she was yours."

I begin to laugh. "That's quite all right."

Feeling comforted by my reply, Aglae then smiles. "Your order's up shortly. You care for jam or syrup?"

"Syrup. Oh, and butter, too, please."

"I'll fetch that and be back with your plate."

Once again I'm alone at my booth. I tuck the photo of Ambrielle away, then Aglae returns, carrying my breakfast. She bids me good eats as I butter my cakes.

The first bite of food's now entering my mouth, it taste satisfactory, and my crave is now roused. Before long I find myself governed by my gluttonous desire for pleasurable foods. In heaping bites, I'm scarfing my grub, and to those around me, it most likely appears I haven't eaten in days. Much to myself, my taste buds are happy and my tank is content.

Most people assume I'm eating too quickly. Take Marin's wife, for example. Cerissa's a phenomenal cook, even chef quality, if I may. She flings it like the best of them, yet that doll's underpaid. Anyway, before I steer off subject, Cerissa's usually on my case, saying I never take

Yria Dane

enough time to savor my meals. She has it in her to believe I chew once, then swallow quickly. I can honestly say her thought's not a foot to the truth. Cerissa lacks in realizing I take big bites, but then I'm grinding them slowly. I like to chomp every ounce of delicious flavor and let those extracts soak through my palate. When I've grazed my food into mushy slop, I swallow my fare, then prepare to cram more.

I don't overindulge as a sin. Truly, I just like exceptional food with excellent flavor. So, am I really at fault if I enjoy what I eat?

I consume my remaining bacon with my final bite of hotcake. Feeling full, I rub my gut to relieve my bulging paunch. Doing so, I've inflamed my indigestion as it rises through my mouth. I belch quietly beneath my breath, or so I think. I spy the herd of feasting folks. Seeing no one's staring makes me believe not a soul has heard me out.

I push my barren plate along the table with my depleted mug and vacant glass, then, glancing at my watch, I notice the time. It's twen- ty-eight minutes past ten when, across the way, I see Aglae. I decide to wave with the shake of my hand. She notices quickly and comes to my side, asking could she fetch me more drink. Rather, I refuse, so she's attending my bill as I'm tossing her tip.

Chapter Eight

I've been driving fifteen minutes with no luck of finding The Petal and Stem. I'm unknown where to go, or if I'll even find it. I should do right and inquire some local, but would that shame them, me inquiring that place? I can continue, unsure where I'm going and probably never making it. I'll give myself ten more minutes. If I'm without luck, then, yeah, I'll quest for some help.

I turn down a street, spotting a handful of people attending their lawns. They look to me with inspecting eyes and judging minds. Seems likely these folks know all, and all who reside here. They're probably suspicious of my scarce face and uncommon car. I'm trawling slowly, I'll admit. While scoping their houses, I'm inspecting for signs. I see my meddling glance is unnerving to those watching. Their brains prob- ably suspect me a sneak-thief. To ease their vexation, I begin waving and smiling briefly. Seems it's working as I'm spotting friendliness ex- pressed on their faces.

I'm halfway through the street when I see a young man, profess- edly my age, give or take a few years. I'm debating whether to call his attention and solicit his aid. If I do, it better be now before I'm passing him by. Resting my shoulder among the cleft, I ease my head through the breach. "Sir," I say. "Excuse me, sir? Would you know where I'd find Madame Voletta?"

I spy him in the distance clearly scouting for intrusive neighbors. When concluding none, the man steps to my car with bolting pace. "*Le Pétale Et Tige,*" he whispers.

Thankfully I attain his speech and, in knowing, it's the French translation of The Petal and Stem.

"You'll find her there," he carries on. "How'll

I find it?" I grin.

"Ride this street to the end. When you've come upon the inter- section, hang left. Go three blocks till you see Flourished Lane. Once there, hang right. *Le Pétale Et Tige will* be on your left."

I acknowledge, "Are there signposts or logos?"

"No. Residence unaware suggests it's a boarding house."

I understand the man's direction, but I'm shot to pieces on how I'll find it. I look to the man, perplexed. I'm confused. "How'll I know it without markers?"

"The purple lilac trees throughout the front lawn. Nestled behind is a magnificent white house. You'll know you've found it when you've arrived at that setting."

"Okay, sir. I appreciate it." I pull myself into my cushion and nod quickly. I decline the street, keeping the man's direction in mind.

Barely into a three minute drive, I find myself coasting through Flourished Lane. Just as the man mentioned is the magnificent white house, with lilac trees glorifying the lawn. The place is a picture perfect postcard; an absolute spot for an artistic eye. The presentation's warm and welcoming, a peaceful retreat or lifelong escape. Madame Voletta's done well by the sight of this place.

It's now 10:56 when I decide I'll climb the stairs. Standing with my posture straight, I attend the door and await its toll. Twenty, maybe thirty seconds later a mid-aged woman acknowledges my call.

I release my speech. "Good day, Madame, I've–" She cuts me off.

"Sorry, sir, services won't start till tonight."

"But I've come–" She does it again.

"If you wish, I'll arrange you with someone you may have for later."

"That's quite all right. I–"

"But the girl you'll want might not be available. It's first come, first serve."

"Madame. Madame, no, that's not the reason I've come."

Voletta pulls the door behind her. "Sir?"

"Please, do you have a minute? Could we speak?"

"Be it of what, dear?"

Without hesitance, I say, "Ambrielle Guloe, ma'am."

"Ambrielle? Well, whatever the matter concerns me as well." She refrains near the door. "Does your pleasing face include a fair title?"

"Detective Biertempfel. I've come from Annecy."

"Detective? Well, I best stay respectable." I'm then accepted by her smile. "We'll go to the parlor. You'll take a seat there."

I stretch to the couch where I recline on top of cushioned pads. I'm offered a drink, but I pass.

Amid a teak table's a crystal plate containing eclairs and lady fingers. After watching me, Voletta grants my permission. Never being one to pass delectable treats, I happily welcome her requisition.

Sooner than later I spare details for my being here. I tell her I was sent on part of Haulmier Guloe.

Not aware why she's done it, Madame Voletta gasps upon my delivery. Stunned by her response and, evidently viewing her discouragement, I ask why my words bring bother?

She eludes my question while asking her own. She examines me by imploring whether I'd return Ambrielle to her home. I keep our discussion straight, remaining honest. I tell her it's Haulmier's intention his daughter returns.

I watch her shake with disagreement. "There's no way, on your accord or hers. And for myself being responsible for the girl, I couldn't allow her attainment. I'm sorry, Detective, but tell that man, Haulmier, there's no sense in you trying. Ambrielle's staying here."

I must say I'm completely shocked with this statement. While analyzing Madame Voletta, I'm sensing some troubles. In better understanding her, I ask why there'd be no reasoning in the girl going back.

She tells me, if I inspected Haulmier, I'd learn for myself. Feeling irritated, I inquire, "Do you know him?"

Voletta acknowledges that it's only through stories which Ambri- elle shared.

I'm confused and getting nowhere. If there's something I'm to understand, it's best it's revealed. I look toward the debonair. "Well, then, will you divulge what you know?"

I sense she's nervous to speak. I know because she's sweeping her wrist. Any unconscious movements as these are dead giveaways. One just has to know the signs, then he can spot them quickly.

I await Voletta as she breaks into words. "Haulmier isn't a being of delightful enjoyment. With that, I've said enough, so that'll be the extent of my snitch. Please understand, things Ambrielle divulged had been private. I feel it's my duty to keep them confined."

"You're merely being fair, ma'am. I'll respect your acclaim."

"If there're things you wish to know, it's best you speak with Ambrielle. If she finds you're admissible, she'll allow you the facts."

This could be harder than I thought, trying to speak with this girl. What's to say she'll grant me her truths? She could take one look at me and order me off, but I wouldn't leave, no. I'm determined. So looking into Voletta's eyes, I'm asking, "Is she present?"

"She is. I'll gather her now."

I notice an ashtray along a side table, and as Voletta's leaving, I pull it toward me. Now firing my smoke, I draw in the first puff.

Four drags later the Madame reenters the room. Toward her back's Ambrielle. Then, turning aside, Miss Bruel says to the courtesan, "This pleasant gentleman's requesting your time. I'll let you alone now."

I remove myself from the couch. "Ambrielle, hi. I'm Detective Biertempfel." I'm stretching my hand with hopes that she'll shake. She does, but says nothing. Sensing her apprehension, I assure her with ease, "There's no reason for fear. I promise we'll get along nicely." I draw forth my notepad, prepared to document any facts she'll confirm. "I just have a few questions."

"You may ask what you want, Detective. I know why you've come," Ambrielle confesses as she falls to a chair.

"Then you must know your father worries and awaits you back home."

"That man has no care for me," she sadly expresses, "and if you believe I'll go back, I'll confess it's not so."

I see I'm presented a challenge. So, questioning her statement, I ask, "What's so bad it deters your return? Could you not face him because of the money?"

"Hmm?" Ambrielle looks confused, like she's unknown what I say.

"The money you'd stolen."

"He said I stole money?" Ambrielle looks toward me through moistened eyes. "I can assure you, sir, that I've not done."

"That's not what your father spoke."

Ambrielle chokes when trying to speak. "That man, he's no father of mine." The young girl sniffles while wiping her eyes.

I see she's filled with much hatred and hurt. "Apparently he's done something to make you deny him."

"That man's done a lot, giving reason I not like him."

"The money then you claim you'd not stolen it?"

"I've never stolen a franc from that man. Never would it have crossed me, the thought. It was my money, my savings he'd taken."

The plot thickens, I concede. The questions is, who's to believe? "How was it he'd stolen from you?"

"He'd work me, and when my monies came, he'd rip me off. The earnings I had were never my own."

"What're you saying? He'd work you at Frenchman's?"

"There, the streets, anywhere."

Whoa, whoa, whoa, I think. "Your father admitted to not liking your life. Are you saying he lied?"

"It was Haulmier who forced me to tramping. It was never my wish. My aspirations were never approved by that man. Rather, what he saw was a pretty face and tight body. So theorizing he'd make money, he sold me to men."

This isn't the conversation I'd expected to have. I feel saddened for Ambrielle, if she's telling the truth. "The aspirations you had; what had they been?"

Ambrielle seems distant and sorrowed when I arise with the question. "For years I've yearned to practice ballet. I'd see myself on stage, in a theater, and I'd perform for an audience." Ambrielle wipes a flow of tears from her face. "Haulmier said my dreams were ridiculous, that I hadn't the talent."

"Instead, he forced your lifestyle and made you neglect your ambition?"

"I'm merely stating the truth. Fact is, I've been roughhoused. You name it. Burnt, cut, beaten, choked. It's no good a life. I wanted out the first day. Haulmier sold my chaste to the highest bidder. I was an eight-year-old girl. I was only a child."

My heart aches as it sinks in my chest. Ambrielle's words have sickened my core. "You truthfully admit not wanting any part of it?"

Clearly she expresses her reluctance and hatred for the beast, the man she calls Haulmier. As an honest fact, I feel she's not lying. But I'm still left with questions, uncertainties.

Frankly, parts of my mind remain obscured, even confused with the truth. Had she been forced, or had she elected to do it? I'm tempted to ask, "How was it you began work at The Easy Way Inn?"

"Haulmier. It'd been his instruction, though I fought to not do it."

"And so you picked up and left?"

"The place was horrible. I nearly died to get out. All that ever came through were demeaning, rude jerks. Hostile bums, they'd all been."

"What about other places you worked?"

"I suppose it's the truth you want? Fact is, sir, Lady Ancelin saved me. It was a night I was to work at The Easy Way Inn. I'd been running late, a few moments, not many. From nowhere the owner came. He caught me outside. I was dragged to the rear of the cathouse, where he proceeded to rape me. I'd been beaten bad when Lady Ancelin heard screams. She came to my rescue with her pikestaff in hand. Luckily for me she pelted him off. Following that, I was taken to The Blossomed Rose. There Miss Bruel nursed me to health. Following my incident, I'd been advised not to return to that bawdy filth across the street. Lady Ancelin offered a job to which I accepted and, after two weeks, I began my work there."

"What about Haulmier?"

"He knew nothing of my business. Far as he knew, I was still working at The Easy Way Inn."

I then inquire, "Did you keep a room with Lady Ancelin?"

Ambrielle affirms the truth. She tells me she'd stay a few days, then return home; that way Haulmier couldn't gain any suspicions. She says had she not, Haulmier would have eventually gone looking for her, expecting his money and demanding her home.

She accounts her attempts on trying to leave town, but confesses she'd been without luck. More questions arise while I sit here and listen. It's my job to pry and I'm planning to do it. "Where's your mother been through all this? No mentioning of her's been acknowledged."

Ambrielle speaks simply, "My mother left. She had to, sir." I hadn't been aware. Haulmier never discussed this.

The girl goes into detail and discloses her story. Lady Ancelin had been aware of Ambrielle's discrepancies at home. Ambrielle claims Miss Bruel bought a train ticket so the child could meet her mom in Marseille. The night before Ambrielle was meant to leave, she packed her luggage, then snuck it across town. Ambrielle now reveals she'd forgotten to pack the most important piece of her trip.

The following morning, while attending the train station, Ambrielle realized she was without her ticket. When returning home she says Haulmier had been waiting with it in his hand. Angered by his daughter's attempt at departure, Haulmier shred Ambrielle's escape to salvation.

If things had gone as planned, Ambrielle would have been the first to arrive at the destination, and her mother, several hours thereafter. Ambrielle states her mother boarded the later train, believing Ambrielle was already en route to Marseille.

I nod at Ambrielle's disclosure before I surface a question. "Had your father been aware of you and your mother's arrangements for leaving?"

"No. He knew nothing of it."

"When had he realized your mother was gone?"

"That day. It'd already been turning dark around nine. My mother was expected from work around five. When she hadn't returned, Haulmier grew suspicious. He confronted me. I told him whatever scheming my mother had had been made on her own."

"Had he believed that?"

"I tried my best to convince him. When asking where I planned to journey, I was aware Haulmier hadn't looked at my ticket. I knew to protect my mother and her whereabouts, I needed to lie. I told Haulmier I was going to Switzerland, but knew nothing of my mother's plans or where she was heading."

Wanting to take note of Ambrielle's mother's name, I request her announcement, yet the girl seems unwilling. After gaining her trust, she presents me the name; Yasmina.

Following her reply, Ambrielle kindly requests that I not relay any part of our speech. Feeling obligated by her trust, I'm promising her words shall remain between us. I then ask if she's still considering her travel.

Ambrielle acknowledges this plan is her wish. For me to fill in more pieces, I arise with this question, "Why had your mom left?"

"She despised Haulmier. He forced my mother into doing things she hadn't wanted. Not only have I suffered by him, she did as well."

"So it was for those reasons she left?"

"If you were a battered woman, sir, forced against your will, wouldn't you?"

"I suppose." I then watch Ambrielle. She strokes her hands as she's appearing troubled. What could be the cause? I wonder. Clearly, I witness, she stirs with unease.

"I must confess, sir, I've not been completely honest. I'm uneasy admitting this."

I cut her off. "I won't scold you for withholding new facts."

"Then grant me your word. You have no intention on finding my mother."

"I have no reason."

Ambrielle waits a few moments before she's ready to speak, "You probably don't know about Holland. She escaped with our mom when they left for Marseille."

A sister? Well, now, this is a rising development.

"My mother, afraid Haulmier would do the same to Holland, found enough chivalry to take her away. She'll be eight her next birthday. The age I was when my innocence was taken."

The thought of an innocent child being forced into such abhorrence makes me angered and queasy.

"I don't want my sister facing things which I've lived. If she can have a better life, I want her to have it."

"Well, you've certainly shared a lot. And so being, what's been said shall not be shared with your father."

"What of me, sir? What'll you say?"

"I'll tell him we spoke, but I'll not disclose where you're at or planning to go."

"Is this a vow which you promise?"

"I don't make vows I can't keep."

"Then I hope your sincerity's as true as your word. You have no idea, sir, the damage you'll bring should your statement be false."

After finishing my notes, I focus my eyes to the room, and gazing toward the corridor, I see Madame Voletta, standing solely beneath the wood frame.

"Excuse my interruption, but I have to attend to some errands and, Ambrielle, I'll need you to help."

"Certainly." The young maiden's nodding. "Detective Biertempfel was about to take leave."

I watch the debonair ease toward the young girl, holding paper in hand and perhaps several francs. "Darling, would you mind stopping by the butcher, then market?"

"Ma'am, I don't mind. I'll leave soon, if you like."

"The faster, the better. And don't forget the basket when leaving." In this day and time people know, if you want vegetables, you better bring your own creel. The stands offer nothing, no help whatsoever. It's part of life here in France. It's how we live.

As Madame Voletta converses with Ambrielle, I stand from the couch. "Well, ladies, I thank you for your cooperation and time."

I shake the debonair's hand, then nod briefly. Peering from the corner of my eye, I spot Ambrielle and within seconds she's upon me.

"Sir." She extends her delicate hand.

I shake and nod, then wish her my best. Upon my departing remark, I turn to the mistress and her junior peer. "Enjoy your day, ladies." I proceed from the house as its door is now closing.

I imagine, strolling away, Voletta stepping round to her fledgling attendant, their words distant to my ears as their conversation arises. Being separated by an impermeable entree, I'm no longer accepted into their discussion, on account, it's no longer mine to be hearing.

Madame Voletta gently brushes away several strands of hair from Ambrielle's face. "I must know, how much information had you disclosed, dear child?"

"Madame?"

"Had you told everything?" Voletta asks with concern.

"I spoke the truth, ma'am."

"And the abortion?"

Ambrielle hesitates not a moment and responds, "I hadn't relayed the embarrassment."

"You did what's best. Had you not, I'd have told you. Come, child, to the kitchen. Inside, girl, inside."

"What of the store, ma'am?"

"You'll go later." Madame Voletta then motions. "Come along. Come along. There are important issues we need to discuss."

Ambrielle positions herself at the table while Voletta pours wine. "Madame. Madame, you seem bothered. Have I done something wrong?"

"Course not, Ambrielle. But must you know, I'm plagued. That detective fellow. I sense that man's brought me worry."

"Of what?"

"He knows too much, child. You, your mom, of Holland. If he goes searching, what is it you'll do?"

"Madame, he promised. He swore not."

"But, Ambrielle, dear, you don't know what conversations he'll have with your father. More certainly, child, we don't know what Haulmier might pay him to do."

"The man made a vow. I attest to believe it."

"Honestly, my sweet, I don't feel I trust that meddling poke."

"I thought he'd been quite likable. Had I been wrong?"

"Sometimes in life, dear, we've trusted people who weren't deserving. That man had me feeling strange. And while you attended your discussion, I phoned your Aunt Reinella."

"You did what, ma'am? But why?"

"Feelings, Ambrielle. I have feelings. You need better protection than what's offered here. I want you kept from harm's hand, not cast off into it."

"But I'm to leave for Marseille. What of my mother and sister?"

"And you'll get there, child. But right now you'll stay with your aunt. Trust me, my girl, take my instruction."

"I haven't the money for travel. How'll you expect me to go?"

"Detective Biertempfel will suspect you're in Marseille and search for you there. Once things settle, you'll join your mom and Holland."

"But, Madame, the money; I haven't enough."

"Let that be the least of your worries. You're going, Ambrielle, should I have to pay."

"Madame, no. No, I kindly refuse. I won't let you cover the expense of this trip. It's not your position."

"I love you, Ambrielle, and I don't want you hurt. You're going and that's it."

"Then allow me to work for my share. If you don't, ma'am, I'll refuse any charity."

"You're very just. Must you serve duties, I won't stand in your way."

"And when do I leave?"

"Your aunt expects you tonight."

"Tonight? Tonight, ma'am? But packing! I'll not have the time."

"I'm sure you'll have plenty. Now head to the store. We need food for tonight or no one gets fed. And can you fetch me a paper?" Madame Voletta gathers her car key, then finally her creel.

Ambrielle looks to the key with much hesitance.

"What is it, my girl? You look doubtful, I see."

"I'm shamed to say, ma'am, I've no experience with driving."

"Don't worry on that. I'll drive us, my sweet."

Across town Miss Bruel drives the streets of Grenoble like a dainty fair lady. Though, being careful and cautious, her snail-like pace is considered unsuited by additional motorists.

Finally, pulling into a parking space, she puts an end to the engine. "I figured, Ambrielle, you'll go to the vegetable stand while I visit the butcher."

The young girl opens her door, then stretches her feet to the pavement. She then foots toward the perennial mart, which is serving an amassment of fruits, locally grown vegetables, fresh herbs, and sprouted greens.

Ambrielle peers to her list, eyeing the tally of produce she's been sent to come buy. Near her, she spots a crate of potatoes, then gathers seven for her creel. Shopping around, she finds onions and, gently beside her spuds, she sits two. Then, brightly colored carrots catch her attention. Ambrielle grabs a bunch, then continues to pace. She goes on to select four tomatoes, a stalk of celery, and a half dozen ears of corn. As she's nearing the counter, she steps to the herbs. Seizing the remainder of her list, she collects fresh basil, thyme, and rosemary.

Ambrielle's approaching the cashier and warmly acknowledges, "Good afternoon, Mr. Mercier."

Mr. Aramis Mercier's an amiable gentlemen, nearing fifty. He's been in the business of fruits and vegetables since the moment he first walked. The timely stand's belonged to his family for three generations. He's been in charge of the ancestry market more than twenty years, where he works alongside his teenage sons, Blas and Sebastien.

"Good day, Ambrielle. I see Miss Bruel's sent you to town. You've found everything you need, I suppose."

"I did, sir."

"Good." He grins. "And how might Voletta be? Well, I haven't seen Miss Bruel since last she came in."

"She's just fine, sir, just fine. She's down a ways with the butcher."

"Tell that kindly lady to stop in, won't you?"

"Absolutely, sir. I'll let her know."

"You haven't yet gathered her gazette, have you?"

"I was on my way now. Would you like I get you one?"

"Got mine this morning, thanks. Read what I wanted," Mr. Mercier relays. "Why don't you take it? Give it to Miss Bruel. Save you some change."

"That's most kind. I know she'll say thanks."

"Well, all right, little lady. You be off and have a good one now."

Ambrielle heads to the car where Voletta's been waiting. The young maiden opens her door to take a seat. "Back already, ma'am? Do you have all your bags?"

"Butcher Boileau, the kind man, carried it all to the car." Voletta laughs. "My muscles, so weak, I wouldn't have made it."

"Well, least you had aid and, if not him, his son."

"That boy of his was inquiring about you."

"He had?"

"I told him you were visiting. He's thinking about stopping in to-night, but I said you'd be leaving. Anyway, he says hi. How's Mr. Merci-er? You saw him, I take?"

Ambrielle grins. "He sent you his paper."

"Oh, really? How kindly of him."

"He'd like to see you, Madame. Told me himself."

"Did he? Well." Voletta's now blushing.

"Yes, ma'am. He's asking you stop in sometime."

"Well, I imagine I'll spare him a visit."

Miss Bruel starts her engine and, ever cautious as before, takes through the streets, driving slowly as possible, though as respected as she is, folks still get bummed with her snail-like pace.

Eventually Voletta pulls upon The Petal and Stem as Ambrielle's responding, "See yourself inside, ma'am. I'll get these bags."

Voletta looks to a mass of wrapped meats infesting her car. "Not by yourself. There's too much. I'll not leave without helping."

"I insist not. I tell you, I've got it. Now traipse forth, Madame. I'll get these myself."

"You'll do no such thing."

Ambrielle's tilting her head aside. "Hard-headed, ma'am. You're hard-headed."

"Mustn't I be?"

"You've no business toting groceries in such miserable heat."

"You're afraid I'll faint?"

"To speak honestly. But I pray you, put me at ease. Go recline in your chair."

"It's a shame I hadn't birthed you myself. You'd have been the per-fect daughter. Well, I'll gather some help, then see you inside." Madame Voletta walks to her door, opens the frame, and yells in, "Ladies! Hello! Come help with the groceries. Come on, girls, pull out from your rooms."

Sophia, one of Voletta's nightly seducers, meets the Madame be-tween the corridor of the hallway. At nineteen, she stands tall at 5'9", with golden blonde hair and brown eyes. As kindly as she is, Sophia cordially states, "I'll go."

"Least one of you offers," Voletta begins to yell again. "Ladies! One more of you! You better hear when I'm shouting. Come on, come on, get off those lazy rears. And don't be giving no grief!" Voletta waits, but no one comes. Ah, heavens. They act like a moment of time's forever to spare. A name then pops through her mind. "Zal! Zaline, come you. Get down here. If you're not out in five seconds, I'll have you make dinner!"

Zaline comes rushing from her room. She, like Sophia, is a nightly seducer, but unlike Sophia, Zaline's got an attitude that needs some adjusting. Zaline arrived at The Petal and Stem two years ago, at the age of sixteen. Standing 5'6", she's a raven-haired beauty, with fair skin and grey eyes. "Yeah, yeah. I'm here."

"Good. Move on, girly. Ambrielle's out front." For whatever rea- son, Voletta peers to Zal's feet. "Be more decent than that. Slide on your shoes before you go out." Voletta then turns aside and walks to her kitchen where she begins stocking the freezer with meat. Within minutes Ambrielle treads behind her. "Leave the rest for Zal and So- phia. They're not incapable of work. You've done enough. Take a seat and unwind." Voletta gathers a lead crystal pitcher from her fridge and pours two glasses of cold, quenching tea. "There you go. Help cool yourself down."

Zaline enters the room, carrying an arm full of wrapped meats when, suddenly, she spots Ambrielle at the table and quickly begins griping, "Who gave you permission to sit? You should be helping, not resting your feet."

Voletta turns to the grumbling girl. "Cut down on that whining. I told her she could."

"Why's Ambrielle get to sit when Sophia and I are stuck bringing these? Mind you, the two of you bought them."

"Zal, finish your job without boasting complaints. It'll show you're less fussy."

Knowing she'd been defeated, Zaline acknowledges, "Yes, Ma- dame." Now heading from the room, she mumbles softly, "It should be me sitting, enjoying tea."

Voletta overhears and lends some advice. "If your intentions were not to be heard, Zal, I suggest you stay silent."

"You couldn't have heard, ma'am. I'm not in the room."

"I may be old, but I still have my hearing."

Zal meets Sophia in the hallway, where an accumulation of wrapped meats stands in her way. "This everything? You brought it all in?"

"I did my bit. It's yours now."

"Hey, wait, you could help, you know?"

"No, Zal. I lugged it in. The weight's yours. I'm through."

Becoming flustered, Zaline remarks, "Fine, you snot." Then quickly an idea sparks her mind and her disposition soon changes. "On thought, tell Janely and Maribel they can come pack the freezer. Should they refuse, tell them it's Madame's orders."

"You're crooked. All right, I'll go tell."

Zal returns to the kitchen carrying a stack of wrapped meats. Soon after Maribel and Janely enter, then silently begin stocking the freezer with beef, lamb, and chicken.

Maribel's another of Voletta's girls. She has deep red hair and pale blue eyes. And like Sophia, Maribel's also nineteen.

There's also Janely. Having lived here three years, she's one of Voletta's oldest girls. Janely's twenty years of age, with auburn hair and unusually green eyes which strike those who see her.

"It's nice seeing a little help. Even better, there's no need I be asking." Miss Bruel smiles, all the while feeling proud.

Janely, sensing she's been set up, now directs, "Sophia said you inquired."

"Really, she did?" Voletta turns to Zaline. "And I wonder from whom she got the incentive? Have you any idea, Zal?"

"I'm caught, aren't I?" She flashes a quick cheesy grin.

"Wouldn't be the first time."

"And you wish I'd learn, right?" Zal then turns to Ambrielle and, in a rather bold manner, directs a bantam question, "So's your crotch still discarding that icky mess? I mean, what's it like, having an abortion? You leak stuff, right?"

"Zaline, I tell you now, hold your tongue," Voletta riles. "I'll not have you probing in that."

"What? I'm curious is all."

"It's a touchy subject. Don't be bringing it up now, you hear?"

Ambrielle acknowledges, "It's all right, Madame. She knows no better."

"At her age, dear, Zal's matured enough, she should know. She's aware what you've been through, and to ask such a question is shameful, I'll say."

Zaline makes a bashful face, then apologizes to Ambrielle and Madame Voletta for her wrongful inquiry. "It shouldn't have been asked."

"No, it shouldn't have, but least now you're sorry. Ambrielle has to pack so I'll be with her upstairs. I'd appreciate you three tending to dinner."

Trotting through her chamber door, Ambrielle precedes to her bed. Taking a seat upon the firm mattress, the young girl peers to Voletta in tears. "I'd give anything to stay. This room's my home and this dwelling, my shelter."

Voletta seats herself beside the depressed maiden while cupping the girl's head. Despite her attempt to give comfort, Ambrielle continues to languish. Tucking the sobbed girl's face upon her shoulder, Voletta tries to nurture Ambrielle's disheartened grief. "How I hate to see you go. Though you've been here only days, I feel you're my family."

"If it wasn't for you and Lady Ancelin, my life would be wrecked." "We want, Ambrielle, for you to be with your mother and sister. You deserve a better life, not one of sorrows."

"I promise you, Madame, I'll always come visit."

Voletta sits with the young courtesan as she holds her awhile. "Well, peach, shall we line up your luggage and get you your things?"

"Only because I must." Ambrielle steps toward a closet where she gathers two trunks. "The night stand, ma'am, has my undergarments and bedgowns. And the dresser, a few pairs of socks." Ambrielle removes several hangers of clothes from the closet. Among them are wiggle, lace frock, and swing style dresses. She packs them away neatly, then returns to her wardrobe. Upon the floor are three pairs of peep toe pumps, black for most days, white for others, then red for days of immodest expression. "This seems to be about it, ma'am. Other than cosmetics, my belongings are packed."

"Hadn't you brought hats or scarves, child?"

"No, Madame. I haven't any."

"Every fine dame deserves a fashionable hat. I'll not allow you without one."

Madame Voletta treads to her elaborate room which is compiled into a posh quarter fit for a queen.

Within her bearings sit a shabby, ash blond settee, a rare piece carved from rosewood and upholstered in the mid nineteenth century. Upon both sides are matching chairs for additional sitting, and standing mid-room's Voletta's bed, a stunning four post, covered about with magnificently chiseled etchings.

Fancy leather trim and wallpaper hat boxes stack off the floor near an admirably aged dresser. Voletta searches through her possessions until finding the right piece. Within her hand's a citrine scarf arrayed with salmon roses and Kelly green leaves. She carries the wrap to Ambrielle, where she's presenting it gladly.

"I've held on to this for more than a decade. Its representation reflects The Petal and Stem by these resplendently stained flowers. It's a gift, Ambrielle. May you always remember this place and its Madame Voletta."

Ambrielle breaks down to tears. "I'll always remember you. There's no way I couldn't."

"Then so be it with you, my sweet. I'll help you carry your luggage. When you're ready, it'll be by the door."

"I wish I could tuck you away and just take you with me." Ambrielle smiles. "But I know the rest of the girls are needing you."

"Always visit, whenever you can." She hugs Ambrielle. "I suppose it's time we step to the kitchen. Hopefully those girls aren't creating no messes."

Ambrielle begins to blush, then smirks ever slightly. "We offered no guidance, just left them to cook."

Voletta pulls a train case from the bed, then precedes downstairs. Aside from the door, she sets the luggage against the wall. Ambrielle comes from behind where she stacks the last trunk upon it.

Miss Bruel's now whispering, "Let's sneak in on the girls, see what they're up to."

The two stand before the cookery, watching silently and observing the others.

"Maribel. Maribel, stop! You don't have the flame high enough!" Zal screams.

"It's fine what it's on. Stop yelling at me."

"Move aside. Come on, get out of my way. It's clear you're not sure what you're doing." Below the cooking pot, Zaline ups the fire.

"Zal! Zal, no, you'll have it boil over!"

"It'll do no such thing."

"Bring the flame down. Bring it down! Won't you listen?"

"Hello, stupid! Potatoes boil faster when the flame's high."

"Fine. But when starchy waters spill, you're cleaning the mess."

"God you're lame."

Maribel, now flustered, releases her steam. "Aw."

Zaline, now provoked ever more, asks, "Why must you be such a damn brat?"

Janely, who's sitting quietly, without any fuss, is watching Maribel and Zaline as they go back and forth. Becoming irritated by her house-mates, Janely turns to a radio and desperately searches for music.

As she settles within her seat, Janely notices the pot of potatoes boil over. "Zal, Zal, your boiler stews over!"

Zaline screams as she runs to the range. "Crap. Crap, this mess. Someone, come help."

"Don't look at me," Maribel adds. "I told you it'd happen."

Zaline turns to her second mate, pleading, "Janely, be a dear. Come spare me some aid."

At this point Madame Voletta enters the room. "And how're the apples of my eye making out?"

"Could be better." Zaline throws forth her lip. "It'd be wise you not leave this to us the next time."

"But oh, I'd say you've done a fine job."

"We weren't cut out for this. We can barely get by."

"Oh, Zal, stop bellyaching and tell me, what are your plans for these?" She raises the lid from the boiler and looks to the reduced lump of spuds.

"Mash them. That's what you do, right?"

"You do know these are ready, Zal? You'll turn them to mush if you let them go longer."

Zaline snaps, "Maribel should have said something. She thinks she knows everything."

"I'm sure she tried, but you better make it a lesson to listen, Zaline. Drain them, then get the masher and start squishing."

"I can't use a spoon?"

"Zal, no, you need a potato masher." Voletta peers upon the stove. "There it is. And what else has been cooked?"

Janely waves her hand. "I'm making roasted chicken. And Maribel's in charge of the vegetable mélange."

"Good work, girls. I'm sure you've put your hearts into this."

Sophia comes into the room. "Whose train cases are those? Are we getting new tenants?"

"They're mine," Ambrielle acknowledges.

"You're leaving?"

"Sometime tonight."

"But you've just arrived. You can't be leaving." Sophia puffs forth her bottom lip. "It saddens me, Ambrie. I've grown to like you."

"I've promised to come back. I'll be seen here again."

Sophia smiles, then peers to the other girls. "I see Madame's put you to cooking."

"Luckily you weren't here. She'd have asked you as well," Zaline sassily acknowledges her housemate.

As to put Zal in her place, Sophia responds, "Isn't it strange how some things are worked out?"

"We've come this far on our own. And rather than yourself, we'll have the bragging rights. Sorry, Soph, you were sorely excluded." Zaline finishes the potatoes, or least she thinks she has.

"Not quite yet, child. You're still needing milk and butter." Voletta then edges to the table to take her seat. "Has anyone seen my paper?"

"Behind you, by the radio, ma'am," Janely admits. "I'd been reading it."

"Anything good?"

"Just the face page."

Madame Voletta's unfolding the paper and, upon the cover's an emotional headline, Eleven Year Mystery Continues To Baffle Young Woman.

> **Orisia Laroque, elder sibling of Yria Dane, continues her desperate search for her missing sister.**
>
> *The 3$_{rd}$ of August 1941, Yria Dane, then twenty-two, was reported missing by her father, Gabriel Laroque. Mr. Laroque became concerned for his daughter once learning she hadn't returned to her Annecy home following an evening with her sister and friends. After more than a year into his daughter's investigation, Gabriel Laroque passed away, suddenly. He was succeeded into death by his wife, Sandrine. Following Gabriel's death, his eldest daughter, Orisia, took lead in the search for her sister. "I'll look everywhere till I've found her. Hopefully somewhere she'll see I'm still searching." Following her heartfelt statement, Orisia asks that the citizens of Rhône-Alpes lend their help however possible.*

"How sad. This poor girl," Voletta states loudly. "After all these years, she still looks for her sister. How awful. I know the girl will never be found."

"What, Madame?" Janely inquires.

"This missing girl, Yria Dane. Her family thought she'd been taken from Annecy back in forty-one."

Ambrielle questions, "What happened?"

Voletta appears puzzled. "No one knew really."

"Maybe she's alive, do you think?"

"After eleven years, I'd feel ill to believe it." "How sad for her sister." Ambrielle frowns.

"Janely. Janely, distract yourself. Check the chicken," Maribel's directing her.

Janely removes herself from the table to peer into the stove.

Maribel instructs, "Might be best you took it out."

"How'll I know it's done? Can you tell?"

Maribel stands beside Janely. "I'm no expert, but it seems that it's ready."

After it's been removed from the stove, Voletta gazes it over with a fine eye. "Looks baked and tawny. Go ahead, leave it out. Sophia, round the others. Tell them to be here in under an hour. Then, Ambrielle, I suspect I'll take you to the train station before The Petal accepts business." Voletta then realizes how poorly that sounded. "I'm sorry. I know that's forcing you off."

Ambrielle smiles. "Your apology's not necessary, ma'am. I know to be out before sun fall."

Voletta grows saddened. "Hearing you say that heavies my heart. Feels like I'm kicking you out."

"For my sake, Madame, cheer up and be happy." Decidedly, Ambrielle walks to the radio and increases the volume. "There's music. We must dance! Pull yourself up, Madame."

Ambrielle tugs upon Voletta's dress while dancing the jive, and though they aren't professionals, they do their damn best. The rendition soon follows to Maribel and Sophia. They quickly step into the bop while keeping pace with the tune. Last to join is Zaline and Janely. Their preference is the twist. It's an effortless routine which comes to them simply.

Voletta has eleven other girls in the house, but sadly for them, they're missing the fun.

Expressions ring lively as the kitchen fills with festive laughter, and it'll be a moment of memories these six women will contain in their minds.

Chapter Nine

After a seventy-three minute drive, I've arrived in Annecy safe, sound, and in my Sable. I find no need to journey back to Grenoble. As far as I see, Guloe's case has completed its end. I find no further motive to pester Ambrielle or pry in her business. What she told was enough for my reason.

At this moment I imagine I'll head to the office, see if Marin's in, and confirm how he's doing. The old chap's been gone plenty long, so I hope he's returned.

Cruising down the street, I spot his car before our building. God bless him, he's back. I'm excited. Maybe overly thrilled? I pull forward with Sable, then park in her spot. Not wanting to forget, I dig through my glove compartment and retrieve Dej's ring. Boy, once Marin catches sight of this, hell, won't he be shocked? I know my brother believes I'll never marry. I find it's time to change that thought when flashing this. I'll now shift through the door and spy his reaction.

Just as I'm stepping through, I see Marin stretched at his desk. His long legs spread to his workspace, with his feet propped on the lectern. At the back of his chair rests his head, with both arms nestled behind his brown hair. Quickly he spots me. "Hey there, sidekick. You've been absent, I see."

I laugh it off. "Not nearly as long as you. How've you been, brother?"

"Fair enough. Where you coming from?"

"Grenoble. Had some dealings there, but I'm back."

"You working a case?"

"Not anymore," I've concluded. I tread to my seat where I recline comfortably. "I'll tell you, though, I thought I'd be longer."

His brows raise to my comment. "Seems you'd been wrong." "Yap. Yap, I sure was. How bout you? You wrap your case?"

"Who knows? I'm beginning to think my client knew nothing."

I flash a quick smirk. "Were you chasing ghosts?"

Marin acknowledges the possibility wasn't slim. He says he found no trace of Mrs. Audric Badeau, or her so called lover, only known as Christoph. Marin says he carefully checked the lodging houses and residential quarters of Savoie. When getting nowhere, he went to Realtors, requesting information. Through his inspection, Marin says no names surfaced in match to Mrs. Audric Badeau, and not knowing Christoph's surname had dampened his search. Following no luck, Marin decided to abandon his investigation. He met with his client this morning, telling him the hunt had been over and had come to an end.

Marin says he apologized for not being able to complete the task, and doing what felt right in his heart, Marin refunded half the cost of his client's request.

"There's nothing more I could do," my brother's explaining. "I had to be honest and I showed that I was."

"What's your call now? You awaiting a new case?"

"If additional information's gathered, I told my client I'd try again, but to tell you, Satordi, I'm feeling burned out. I need time to recoup. Maybe take a vacation?"

"Hell, you know I hate sitting in this office alone. You've sat two weeks with no work. Least visit, I'm begging."

"Solve you."

It's not set in stone we'll always have cases. "Forget vacationing. Come chill out with your kid brother."

"Oh, I don't know. We'll see. Then again some time with Cerissa would do me some good."

"Come on, think about it, yeah? I mean, hey, I'm almost certain we'll have no new cases for at least seven days."

"I see what you're trying to do. I'll think about it."

I grin to his comment. "I'll work should I need to. You, you just relax, do whatever."

"Whoa now. I said I'd think about it."

"Well, I've already made your mind for you."

"You couldn't have left me do it? Oh, hell, who am I fooling? All right. Remember, though, any clients come through, they're yours to handle."

"Agreed. But, ah, should I get an assignment, you want to come? Could be fun. You'd do nothing, of course," I try to persuade him.

"You never stop, do you? Wait till then and we'll see."

I pull a velveteen box from my pocket with means to shock Marin. "I've got something."

"What, jewelry?"

"Open it," I say.

Marin reveals the contents and stutters in shock. He waits for his stupor to settle, then begins throwing questions. "What'd you go off and do? Satordi, tell. This ring, it'd been your business in Grenoble, wasn't it?"

"It was the least of my business. So you think Deja will like it?"

"Do I? This baby's a beaut. If you haven't won her heart, I'm sure this will," Marin goes on. He can't believe I'm finally deciding to settle down. He laughs momentarily, then continues, "I never envisioned this day. My kid brother's bought an engagement ring. Remember," he tells me, "once you've taken the step, there's no turning back."

"I'm not planning on it, Marin."

"So let me in on your news. When's the proposal?" "When the time's right and the day's going steady."

Marin nods and smiles. "Make Deja happy. That's all I advise."

"The day I propose, it has to be special. You know, like a fairy tale. Women gush with that stuff."

"Imagination, brother. That's all it takes. Now if you weren't journeying to Grenoble for the ring, what had you going?"

I explain to Marin I'd been hired to track a man's daughter. I go into detail and define the situation, everything from the instant we met to the moment I encountered the girl, Ambrielle.

"You're sure the girl hadn't lied? You know kids that age tell damn good stories."

"She seemed genuine enough. I detected no dishonesties. Body language showed no impressions of lying. Her statements concerned me enough, I believed her."

"I'm hoping you're right and didn't get wool pulled down on your eyes."

"Well, then if her words were made up I'd probably not known. Sometime today I'm to visit her father. Imagining, I can only envision how put out he'll be."

"You found the girl, right? That's what he wanted."

"It'd been a two part deal, Marin. I just didn't take her home, is my fault. Hell, I couldn't help but stall when she said what she did. Would you?"

"Regarding her safety, I'd have left her there, too."

"Seems for the fourth time in thirteen years, I regret seeing my client. I know already he won't be happy. To say calmly, Marin, I'm dreading to go."

"You've a way to handle this?"

"Only one. Pray I'm smart. I don't need to trip and screw this mess up." I go on explaining, "I promised I'd not betray Ambrielle."

"Well, if her father's how she said, course then you'd have to." I'm stretching to relieve the developing aches in my muscles. "When you leaving here?"

My brother responds, "Shortly."

I realize soon I'll be leaving as well. "Guess I'll be heading to my client so I can deal his shit."

"You want me coming with you?"

"And make him think he's paying double? Go home, Marin. Be with Cerissa and the kids."

"You going to Deja's then after?" "If I make it out of Frenchman's."

As a concerned sibling, Marin tells me to be safe while I'm gone. I'll not be a great deal from home, but still, I know my brother; he worries.

Chapter Ten

It's 3:14 when I pull before Frenchman's. I feel my unsteady nerves churning my gut. To tell you, I hate moments like these when my insides feel flipped. I know I'm worried. Maybe even too much? Thinking about it, I'll confess what it is. It's the dread of cuss words Guloe's likely to shout. I'll see his anger slip in till he's releasing his swears, and if he's boiled enough, he's liable to force punches.

If I'm to propose to Dej, I don't want lacerations or bruises covering my face. I now slip into thought. Hey, doll, I'm busted up, but it won't be forever. I'd then present her the ring. Be mine, sweet darling. I want us to marry. Yeah. I fall into laughter. How fairy tale would that be? That's real dream-like, truly some vision.

I pull myself from my blundering state. Maybe I'm wrong and this talk will go smoothly. Well, however it goes, it's best that I'm ready. Concluding now, I step from my cruiser. I quickly peer to my watch, keeping check on the time. I breathe, then into Frenchmen's I walk in search of Guloe.

The bar's pretty empty, except for three men. The third at the count- er's the tavern's drink slinger, otherwise known as Artus. So, keeping my back straight, I walk to the counter. "Hey, pal, I need Haulmier. He in?"

Artus is drying a glass while eyeing me over. "Back already, mister?"

"He available?"

"In his office. I'll find out if he'll see you."

I take a seat and, before long, my fingers go crazy and start tapping the counter. Am I just anxious, or are my nerves showing haste? Cool it, I think. I take a full breath when the bartender's appearing.

"He'll be with you. Want a drink while you wait?"

Oh, of course, I think. "I'll take a pint and a shot of whatever."

"Very well."

I look around. "Got any nuts?"

I await Artus when he slings me a bowl. Soon he returns with my mystery shot and a pint of cold beer. Feeling thirsty, I guzzle my drink.

That's the quencher; the best dang hops this earth has to offer. I then distract myself. What's this damn shot? I quietly wonder. One way to know certain; I slam it like water. I'm now tasting heavy fumes upon the weight of my breath. The flavor's intense, with a damn good kick presently burning my throat. It's devil's piss, I'm convinced, genuine bourbon at the height of its proof.

Guloe steps forth as I fire a smoke. "Enjoying yourself?"

I find my response quickly, "I damn well better be."

"I'd been expecting a call, Detective, but I see you're in person."

"Funny thing, isn't it? I considered I'd be gone a day or two longer." "I'll acknowledge that, yet you've returned in under twenty-four hours. What happened today?"

"I traveled out of town as I said."

"Surely you found Ambrielle?"

"Indeed, as you'd asked."

"Then tell me, Detective, why's she not here?"

I'd already predicted this question from him. Haulmier's not stupid, he knows what to ask, but, to protect Ambrielle, I must be selective on the things I'll confirm. I've conjured up lies to feed to his face, so with hope I do pray my untruths seem convincing. If not, there's no telling what's liable to happen. It's a play it crooked, straight, crooked deal. Make Haulmier believe I'm sure what I'm saying. Rules abide. Leave nothing on the lines or even between them. Leak no confessions, unless I find reason.

Guloe knew nothing of Grenoble, where I'd gone. I hadn't told him before nor will I be telling him now. I run through a crooked sequence that enters my mind. "Ambrielle's safe, I want to assure you. She stays at a shelter in Mâcon, run by a church."

"You're sure of this?"

God I'm thankful to be a fast one who thinks. I'm speedy to say, "I met Father Bovie who'd taken her in."

"Then I'm grateful for him. And will this Father Bovie be sending her home?"

Okay. This is where things get tricky. Do I tell him the truth or continue my lie?

"My daughter, Detective. Will she be coming?"

"Our talk was extensive, sir. I explained her your wishes."

Guloe narrows his eyes. "But?" he then asks.

Of all words he'd thrown to me this? What'll I say? Seems time's come to concoct a plan for this story. I think a second, still hoping my play will keep me on track. "Ambrielle mentioned ballet. Father Bovie said if she'd settle herself and stay out of trouble, he'd see to it she obtains the practice she's wanting."

I feel deep rooted jitters following my lie. Oh, man, I hope Guloe's not in lean of suspicion. Continuing my act, I carry forth to explain, "It'd been the both of them, Ambrielle and Father Bovie, who talked me into allowing her to stay. I acknowledge this wasn't part of your wish, Mr. Guloe, but I suspect your daughter's life would be better if she stayed in Mâcon."

Guloe's turning red. I see that he's angry. So he tells me the deal, "You were to find Ambrielle and return her home safely. Now hearing your dismissal, I can only ask but one thing. Have you returned with my money?"

"According to your daughter, Ambrielle made it clear, she hadn't taken from you, sir."

"Now just a God damn minute! I may not have pictures of her doing the deed, but I damn well know it'd been done by her hand, the tramping thief." He crinkles his lips and wrinkles his nose. "I can imagine what things she's said. And in figuring so, she's put me to blame."

Guloe goes on to explain how Ambrielle's respect for him dwindled once she entered her teens. "Like most youths, she didn't like rules. And it was a certain fact, she did as she pleased. As much as I've tried, I had no say in her life. She wouldn't apply to my rules or take any guidance." Haulmier continues, claiming his daughter's untruths. "Lie, lie, lie, that's all she's ever done. Such things she's said to make me look bad. She thinks she's grown, ready to be on her own."

I'm beginning to wonder what he meant by untruths, but before I can ask, he readily divulges, "I love Ambrielle, though she does hate me. Hell, I wouldn't doubt her telling you I forced her to tramping. Anything Ambrielle might say to shame me has most likely been said."

I've come to the thought, who's to believe? I have Haulmier with his story. Is it probable? Maybe. On the other hand's Ambrielle, convincing as she was, though it might have been an act to betray me. I'll confess she was certainly good had she been carrying on as a saddened young girl who'd been flailed by ill maggots, to which she included her father.

"You believe I should think everything your daughter's said had been composed as a lie?"

"Let me ask you, do I appear as a man who'd force his daughter to an ill-spent life?"

"I would think not. By law, anyone involved in such serious allegations would be facing some trouble. I'm certain you know this."

"Of course I do, but aside from that, I'm thankful you've found her. Knowing she's not working in some bug-infested den does bring me relief, but the money she'd stolen, which I tell you she did, has depleted my savings. Understand, Detective, I need whatever's left. My rent here is due in another two weeks. Without money, my tavern will parish."

I look at Guloe with a stone solid face. "Say your daughter lied about not taking money. What makes you believe she might probably still have it?"

"I'm under no assumption she does. If she's without, must you know, I'll assign her a job. Nonetheless, it'll be her checks that I'm after. You may not like what I'm to say, Detective Biertempfel, because I find it's against you, but I'll tell you once more, I demand her return."

I take the last puff of my smoke while pondering my thoughts. Ambrielle. I repeat her name in my mind. I envision our talk, even revive her conduction. Remembering, I recall a pleasant youth, courageous, yet timid and, though she was nervous, she bravely recapitulated her alleged mishap. It'd been that thorough recount which I felt was sincere, but now I wonder. Do I regard her as factual, or had she faked every word?

At my ear's Haulmier saying his daughter's a liar. I suppose in good judgment Haulmier's speaking truths. After all, the man hired me. Had he not had good reason, he wouldn't have sought my comply. Nevertheless, Haulmier's aware he's in trouble should I learn his claims were all false. What scab would risk his own ass by hiring a detective when, still, that scab knows he himself is not lawful?

I've briefed my thoughts. Now I break into question as I look to Guloe. "What ah, what kind of work would you find her? Something here in the tavern?"

"You crazy? Of course not in here. It's a bar, for Christ's sake. Rath- er, I imagine she'll take a job with her mother. Yasmina works in town, at The Spice Box."

Yasmina, I reminisce. Ambrielle mentioned her name. With Haul- mier not knowing I'm aware of his wife, I can quiz him for facts. "Yas- mina? That's ah, that's your spouse?"

"Well, yeah. Had you figured I'd say something else?"

Once again the plot thickens. Ambrielle claimed she'd be on her way to Marseille to see her mother and sister. Could that have been a lie? Time to feed him more questions. "Could your wife, would she be able to secure a job, Mr. Guloe, for your daughter?"

"Indeed, absolutely. The owner, Sylvie, she's good friends with Yasmina."

Is that so? I then arise with a statement. I tell Guloe I'd like to speak with his wife. He quickly agrees. I must say this situation's be- coming entirely too tempting. Should I meet with Yasmina, as Haulm- ier claims, it'll go to show Ambrielle of course, lied. "Your wife, could I find her now at the shop?" I await his response. "And you'd be okay with me stopping there for a visit? I'd feel better personally knowing arrangements could be made in regard to your daughter."

"That's perfectly acceptable. Yasmina will be working till five." All right, then. I take note of the time.

"Does this mean you're again on the case?"

I confess, "It seems so."

"But of course. Of course you are. And your fifty-five francs, I have your pay here."

I break down the drill and surface my lie. "In an hour, maybe two, I'll leave for Mâcon. Be expecting a call should any info arise. I can't promise this apprehension will go smoothly, or at the haste which you're wanting. Rest surely, however, the girl will be back."

"Fair enough, Detective. Take whatever time you'll be needing."

I finish my last swig of beer when I step from my seat. "I suppose we're done. If I find reason to call, I've got Frenchman's number as well as your home's."

"I'm sure you'll be reaching me one place or the other."

I salute Haulmier with a two finger wave when I embark my departure, then, peering at the bartender, I throw him a nod. See you around, I say in my head.

Chapter Eleven

Madame Voletta stands alongside a cabinet, reseating clean dishes as she sets them on shelves. "You girls made me proud today. For once your attempts served to cook a good meal. Maybe I'll see more of this in forthcoming days?"

"I wouldn't mind," adds Maribel.

Zaline acknowledges, "You would if you didn't have help."

"I'd do it, Zal. Besides, working with you's a nightmare."

"Girls, girls, be nice to another. I haven't the patience to listen to this."

"Madame?"

"Yes, Janely, what is it?"

"The leftovers, ma'am; I'm unsure where to put them."

Voletta eyes the measly portion of scraps not eaten. "Slop those remains on a plate, then set it out back, on the porch for old Bleu."

Janely shakes her head. "What's old Bleu?"

"Had you worked the kitchen more, you'd been aware we had a dog. The twiggy stray's in need of food."

"Oh, poor creature. Won't you let the thing in?"

"Janely, honey, I haven't the room for a pet. Just mind him out back."

Janely opens the back frame, curiously peering into the lawn. Beneath thick hedges she spots a *Bouvier des Flandres* in the shade of smog-gray. Sensing the unimpeded entrance, Bleu dashes through the grassland to seek Janely's side.

The young courtesan snuggles into the woolly tail-wagger. "Oh, Madame, you must let him in. He's just too darn cute. Look at this face."

"Janely, my sweet, if we allowed him inside, the task of getting him out might be a hard job. Do understand."

"Just five minutes?" She's pouting her lip.

"If that fuzz-ball runs stray and starts scenting our--"

"He's a good boy. Look at him, ma'am. He's just wanting some love."

"Oh, all right. Let the fuzz in."

Janely pats her knees as she exclaims with excitement, "Come on, Bleu. Come on, old fella, you're free to come in."

"Five minutes, Janely, and he's yours to be tending."

"Isn't he just the sweetest? Look at these eyes, both big, brown, and loving."

The girls attending the kitchen make way to old Bleu and seize him with snuggles.

"Can't he stay, ma'am? Ma'am, please?" Zal is begging. "I'll bathe him, give him baths," adds Maribel.

"I can take him for walks and tend to his brushing," states Sophia.

"And me, ma'am, I'll feed and give him water," acknowledges Janely.

"My-my. Listen to yourselves."

"Please, ma'am, please," Zal continues begging.

"Oh, I don't know. A dog in the house?"

"Look at him, ma'am, he's wanting to stay," Janely implies.

Voletta's inflexibility begins to wear down. "You each promise to tend to him? And when I say tend to him, girls, I mean day and night."

"Yes, Madame," they say in unison.

"Then I'm telling you girls, the moment you're not caring for Bleu, he's out of this house." Voletta can't believe the random words that have succeeded her mouth. What have I gone and done? she thinks. Well, it's too late to take back. "Sophia, discern the others of our dog." Madame Voletta peers to Ambrielle, who's poised at the table. "The hour's tread out." Her head sinks. "I'll be missing you shortly."

"Please, Madame, be strong."

"These days, they've been too short for us, peach. And though stating that, it's within my heart I wished you'd arrived sooner."

"I'm greatly saddened, ma'am, with my having to leave. I'd stay if I could. I enjoy being here."

"I know, my dear petal. It's been my pleasure having you."

"Madame, Madame, the day; it's getting late. I suggest I should go."

Voletta looks on sadly. "Then I'll see you to the station and wait with you there."

"When, Madame, do you suppose I'll arrive?"

"Somewhere around six and a half hours. You've got a long jour- ney ahead, so be prepared for your travel. I've fixed a basket of things you'll take with you to eat." Voletta sifts through its contents. "Fruits, a loaf of bread, and a jar of quince jelly."

Ambrielle smiles warmly. "How kindly you are."

"And your pay, dear, I have it here."

Ambrielle notices the wad of stash in her hand. "Madame, but, ma'am, you've given too much."

"You take what I've given. You'll settle on that."

Ambrielle nods and whispers softly, "I'll not bicker, then."

"Your train's set to leave within the hour." Voletta peers to Zaline. "Zal, be of use, gather Ambrielle's luggage. Carry her trunks to my car."

"Certainly, ma'am," the usually gutsy hussy says without hesitance.

Voletta nods at Zal, then continues with Ambrielle. "Gather your stole, child, and bring it to me."

Ambrielle returns moments later.

"Bow, dear, so I can tie this round you." Voletta sits the cloth upon Ambrielle's head. She tucks away strands of unrestrained hair, then pats the girl's face. "Look how pretty." Voletta guides Ambrielle to the sitting room. "Come, child, step to the mirror."

Ambrielle stands before the polished metal where she peers at herself. "Oh, Madame, Madame, how fetching it looks. I feel like a lady."

Voletta stands behind the young maiden, leniently caressing her shoulders with care. "With your stunning red coat and tasteful rose stole, I'd say you look grand, absolutely divine."

Zaline enters through the front door. "The trunks, ma'am, I've got- ten outside."

"Very good, Zal. Gather the girls. It's time for them to say their farewells."

All of Madame Voletta's courtesans come to bid Ambrielle their goodbye. Many tears are shed for the fact of her leaving, even Zaline, who, most the time's rather hard to get along with, displays the reality, even she, too, can cry, but her tears are short-lived, either by her own choice or the girl's simply fake.

Chapter Twelve

Following a lengthy discussion, with plenty of comments, I step from the spice shop with a heedful concern now pestering my mind. I take note of my thoughts, at the conjuring of things to which I do wonder. Had that been Yasmina to whom I had met? Seems my doubts are suspicious and in question of facts.

Ambrielle looks nothing like Yasmina, not through her face, nor in her stature. Additionally, both Haulmier and Yasmina each have dark hair. Ambrielle's clearly amber, I've taken no doubt. During my visit with Yasmina, I undeniably noted the woman was tall. Remembering, Haulmier once acknowledged his daughter's slight standing. He said, unmistakably, she was sixty-four inches, knowing assuredly, this, indeed, had been a statement released from his mouth. He told me, quite clearly, I'd even made note, his daughter, like her mother, is, too, short.

There's no way these two women are, indeed, the same height. Could it have been a simple mix up, obliviously made by Guloe? I guess I don't know.

Like yesterday, I realize I'll be en route to Grenoble, and though I embarked there this morning, I'll have to tread back. No need for pack- ing my luggage; it's still in my car.

My mind now races with things I'm to do. Supposing, I'll head to my brother's, tell him the news, and hope I get dinner. If he's up to join in my formidable task, chances are he'll trek with me to accompany my travel.

After several minutes of cruising the road, I pull to my brother's and suppress Sable's rouse. Following my steps to the threshold, I press the door's bell and, in seconds, Marin meets me as the tune dinger trills.

"Reach your step, little brother." "I'm

not disturbing you, are I?"

"Good grief, no. I told Cerissa you'd probably be by. Step on in. You have a surprise in the kitchen."

I'm reaching the feed room, relished with glee, and in a moment of standing, my merriment swells whence I peer through the foyer. There,

I see my darling, my Dej, staged near the counter, adorn in all pink, from the ribbon tying her gold, silky hair, to her coral dress, down to her cream and rose heels.

"Deja, sweetheart, honey, I thought you'd be home?" "A

little bird phoned me." My love gives a smile.

I kiss her face a few times. "I've been meaning to see you, but the job I've been on keeps my hours busy."

"Hmm. Marin tells me you were out trailing crooks."

"Got to do it sometime. Anyway, what's going on with my number one gal? You been all right?"

While I carry forth, Cerissa spontaneously prevails, everyone to the table.

My sister-in-law's setting out plates, and with her face leering down, she speaks to my brother, "I haven't time to gather the kids. Be off from your rear and bring them downstairs."

Cerissa's intention's to have her husband meander upstairs, but my brother who's sometimes inactive, for his own reasons, leans his head to the foyer and screams from the room.

"Paien! Zuri!" His voice cracks the air. "Dinner time, you two."

Above, on the wooden floorboards ahead, I hear the parturient bustle of their small scanty feet.

My brother breaks into laughter. "You'd think they'd gained weight since the last time you saw them."

"I considered they fell from their beds." I laugh back.

"I wouldn't doubt it, those two. So tell me, your client, had he recede you with ease or blustered your ear?"

As I'm to partake in my accounts of today, Paien rushes through the kitchen and leaps to my lap.

My nephew's a skinny little thing like his sister, but I'm never to tell him, 'cause I'd make him mad. He's a cute little guy, nonetheless, and I'm ever thankful for that, 'cause it's not his father he looks like. Rather, he takes after Cerissa, with his sunny hair and hazel eyes.

"Hi, Uncle Tordi. Guess what? I've got a loose tooth. Look, I can wiggle it with my tongue. Mama thinks it's gross."

"Paien, not at the dinner table, sweetie. We're getting ready to eat."

He explains to his mother, "I just wanted to show Uncle Tordi." Paien fidgets within my lap as he turns to me, whispering, "Mama don't like it much. It upsets her weak tummy."

I watch as Cerrisa's leering her eyes. "Paien, where's your sister?"

"Ah, ah, she was behind me. Want me to find her?"

"Honey, no. I'll have your father go. Marin. Marin, get Zuri. Tell her it's time to come eat. And no yelling through the door this time, please."

My brother doesn't listen. He pokes his head through the foyer and proceeds to scream out, "Zuri!"

I begin to laugh loudly. Had he lowered his eyes several inches, he'd have seen she was there.

"Hi, daddy."

I break further into laughter when my brother peers down. Stunned, he views the sloppy mess on her face. "What?" He's cracking up. "What's this stuff on you? Zuri, is that your mama's makeup?"

"Maybe," my niece incompletely confesses.

She'd taken Cerissa's rouge, using it to paint near every inch of her face. Cream blush smears across her small saucers, onto her weensy cheeks, and to her teensy lips. Only real features visible are her small blue eyes. Other than that, her coppery hair is still clean unless, somewhere inside it, she's streaked it with eye paints. Seeing her, that can't be far from the truth.

"That's ah, quite some job you've done. Go show your mother."

Zuri passes me as she creeps to Cerissa. "Hi, Uncle Tordi."

"Hey, there, squirt. You off to a pageant?"

"We'll have one in my room. Will you dress up?"

As nice as it sounds, I explain, "I don't think I'll have time today." She pouts her small lips before I can finish. "But," I respond, "Deja might be willing after dinner. Won't you ask her?"

"Will you, Aunt D? Will you dress up with me?"

Deja smiles warmly, but I know beneath that gracious simper she'd like to subdue me. Reason is, Zuri likes to imagine herself a makeup artist and anyone caught has to undergo alterations. If Zuri's denied, the little bean sprout whines all night till she's missing her voice.

Marin looks at me, his face all aglow. "Thanks for not dropping my name into that." He then looks to my lady. "No offense, Deja, that you'll pose in my spot."

"Oh, that's okay, Marin. Your day's coming."

Deja gets up to help Cerissa while Marin and I embark conversation. I've gone over my earlier accounts, telling my brother I'll once again be hitting the case.

"You'll be leaving tonight?" he asks me.

Of course, I nod. "You ah, feel like coming?"

"You're wanting company, aren't you?"

"I don't need it, but I thought it'd be nice."

"You'd fight me until I said yes. So I'm guessing I'll go."

"Really? I'm not having to beg?"

"Long as we're in your car and you're paying for gas."

Oh, bless him. I had hoped to not beg. Really, I wasn't looking forward to driving myself. My trips can be lonely and, when I'm without company or simple confabulations, I grow pretty sad. Had I known my coaxing him would have come so simply, I'd have inquired him sooner, but I'm finding peace now since he's agreed to go with me.

Chapter Thirteen

Voletta sits beside Ambrielle, upon a cast iron bench of deft artistry. An expanse of lacework and grapevines stretch through the settee, which is positioned before a small-scale building.

The undersized terminal's composed in off-white, with chocolate stipples detailing its shape. Several round top windows obverse the anterior. In all, eleven eyelets reach throughout the station, with duet frameworks installed at each end.

A small addition of people are advancing the building, where inside they'll tread through to wangle their tickets.

Voletta and Ambrielle perch in their bench, ahead the tracks, where rails of flat bottom steel lay supported by timber upon ballasts of crushed mineral.

Voletta comments, "It's a good night for travel. It's peaceful and still."

Ambrielle breathes in a warm breath. "Too bad I can't bring you with me."

"I know, child, but your Aunt Reinella will be happy you've come. It's a good place you'll be. My sister's told me what a fine soul she inherits."

Ambrielle becomes entranced as she envisions Reinella. "She's a fine woman, but her brother, he's different. When, I've asked, had he become so adverse?"

"Your father, you mean?"

"So vile, he is." Ambrielle's eyes droop. "Madame, you don't suppose that man had ever been decent?"

"Some people, my love, are born rotten into this world. Chances are he eventually spoiled."

Ambrielle's hands are cupped in her lap as Voletta reaches forth to pat them.

"Think not of him. His vision sours you."

"I'd need a hypnotist to rid his face from my mind." Ambrielle sinks with depression.

Like a loving mother consoling her child, Voletta reaches upon the maiden to tenderly brush at her face. "I think with a little effort upon your behalf, it'd be a task you can do. However way you'd choose to free him, you'll find the results healing."

"Where'd I be without your guidance?"

Voletta thinks not a second as she pays her reply, "Hopefully safe and en route of your journey. Speaking of which, I see your train down the railway."

"Already? Time's approached us too soon. I feel my words aren't yet finished."

"Oh, my petal, God's given enough to say what's been said. Be grateful we've had these moments to share. Now up with your trunk, child. I'll attend you to your coach."

A flock of people whish forward, bustling to board the train. The majority are civil, regardfully aware of the additions around them, and certainly it's been these mannerly beings who proceed, paced and slow; but less than half are disparaged, out-and-out rude. Their pitch cores show concern only for themselves, their advantage, then note nothing more.

Ambrielle stands in line waiting to board. "This is it. Just a few steps and I'll be drawing away."

Voletta takes the young girl in her arms, then sends her forth from embracement. "Keep yourself safe, peach, and may your freedom progress you."

Ambrielle mounts the train, then for the final time turns to recollect Voletta's image. "Madame, Madame, I'll miss you." She weeps from the steps.

"You be safe and, here, my little rose, your luggage and basket." Voletta refers to the goodies she'd earlier collected. "Come visit when you can. I love you, dear girl. You have a safe trip."

Feeling, though, she's lost her only child, Voletta returns to the iron bench she and Ambrielle shared. There she allows her heartache's expression as she cries to her hanky. And though this moment's one of true sadness, Voletta acknowledges it's a choice made to protect precious lives.

Chapter Fourteen

The evening has departed further along in the day and, though I had devised on withdrawing from my brother's much sooner, I'll gladly confess, it'd been before Marin's assent to come join me. Nonetheless, we remain in his house, visiting and palavering with our wonderful kin, but soon, at some point, these merry moments will have to fall short, merely on account I'll be hindering its progress.

I decide the right moment when our present discussion attempts to wrap up. As not to linger and wait for another, I rely my departure along with my brother's. "It'd be nice to continue this visit, but Marin and I, our time's found its finish."

"We don't want to hold you boys back. You need to hit the road. Anyway, Satordi, I'm glad you stopped in."

"I usually try." I smile to Cerissa.

"Might I mind you that'll be my husband you're taking. Promise you won't drive crazy, all fast and not thinking."

I make my vow, "I'll have him returned in one piece."

"Well, then you relate that to Deja. She wouldn't stand it if you died in some crash."

Whoa, whoa, I think. "There's no need for that thinking."

"I know your driving, Satordi, especially at night."

I step to my in-law. "Damn it, woman, have faith in my travel." I draw her in and wrap her in hugs. "Marin will be fine, and I know I'll be, too."

"Just you mind your driving tonight."

"Ease up, honey. I will." I then peer below when I notice the squirts. "How bout a hug before leaving?"

I spot Paien in his attempt to trail forward. "Are you going to die in a crash?"

"No, boy, not me. That's just your mama's annoyed thinking."

"So you won't?"

"Let's hope I don't," I express to him softly. "Besides, your dad will be with me. He'll keep me on track."

"Dad's good for that. That's why he's older."

"Well, okay." I stumble in laughter. "I'm sure you're right." I pat his thin shoulder. "You be good, midget." I look to my niece, who wears Cerissa's shawl and black pumps upon her small feet. "You having a good play date?"

"Aunt D and I dressed up," she exclaims. "Then we had a party with brownies and tea." The little thing leans to me whispering, when, innocently she asks, "Can Aunt D stay over? We'll make a tent, her, mommy, and me."

"What about Paien? He might want to join."

"He's got stinky feet," she politely responds.

"Oh, does he? Well, maybe he'll wash them before entering your hut."

"Does that mean Aunt D can stay?"

"Fine by me, but you better ask her." I look to my brother who stands at my side. "You got your things? You ready to go?"

"Just waiting on you." He's pretending I'm the hold up, but I know that I'm not.

I spot his feet, those shoeless large feet. Least he's got socks, yet his footwear are missing. I plan not to tell, to see if he knows. I laugh beneath my breath and stare through him dully, as not to seem heedful of his lacking perception. I can only presume, in his advancing age, it's his mind that leaves slowly. Better it be that than his bladder, which, one day, too, shall fail him come time.

I advance to Deja, the one female love of my life, besides my flashy hard frame, to which I call Sable.

"You know when you'll be back?" my gal asks.

"Stay patient, my love, you'll see me again."

"I feel I'm already missing you."

Flattered by her outspoken honesty, I smirk quickly. "I haven't gone yet."

"But you will."

"Hang in till I'm back. I'll have us something special in store." I kiss her soft lips. "Stay here tonight. Be with Cerissa and the kids. Zuri wants you. Don't break her small heart."

"I know. I've already decided on staying."

"Well, I'm behind on time. We need to get going. See you when I'm back."

Incautiously, I gaze to my brother, then to his shoed feet. Last I knew he didn't have loafers. The ole chum must have finally suspected something. Maybe that goes to say his memory isn't deprived as I earlier considered?

Marin and I hit the exit. My foot slides through the frame as I'm walking outside. It's now something irregular catches my sight. Resting with his backside before the first step sits a lone man. He turns quickly when hearing the door. I stride forth, screaming, "Hey, you, lazy scum, get off these steps. Go on, buddy, shoo. Get out of here."

"I've come, sir, come to warn you."

"Are you unsighted, creep? You don't know me."

"You're Satordi Biertempfel. I saw you yesterday on the street, pacing solo, remember? Listen, that strange feeling in the air's come back. I've figured—"

"You're screwy, you know? Just scram, man. Beat it."

My brother eases forth, not knowing to be calm or afraid. "Satordi, who's this man?"

"Just some stray, come from the wrong side of town. Don't worry, I'm having him leave."

"Don't you understand?" the man interrupts. "She stirs the air."

"You've had one too many drinks, pal. Be off before I'm calling the cops."

"You're not understanding me! You need to learn. Just a minute. Sixty seconds, please."

"I'm giving you ten to get out of my sight, bub. Don't waste your time."

"You're involved in something large. You don't know it, but you are. And you." The man points to my brother. "You'll need help. Listen to me! Listen, please."

"Your seconds are up, fool." I turn to my brother. "Marin, call the cops."

"Gentlemen, you see, I'm going. But I tell you, upon my departure,

Julien Kade

be careful what you touch. Don't be seen. You might find yourselves suspects".

The man saunters the dim street, disappearing along his way; then, emerging from the still silence, I hear him say, "My name's Ghislain. Remember that. I'll be around when you need me."

Sure, I'm remembering him, I think. He'd been the loopy bum who'd run upon me on the street. Never had I figured I'd be seeing him again. Something's surely wrong with the clod. He'd gone again, blabbering about shit, strange shit. Who's this woman who stirs the air? Probably a figment of his imagination, least one his drunken mind has created, but why's he following me? How'd he know my brother's house?

Considering the danger he may be, I took note this time of his dress. He wore dingy grey slacks with a sloppy blue shirt and, over that, a smoky wool coat. Thinking now of his age, I'd say he's somewhere around forty-five, at least. His chocolate hair was rather shaggy and in need of a trim. Surprisingly, he wasn't too tall. Maybe 5"7' or 5"8'"? If I ever, ever spot him here again, or God forbid, Dej's, I'll put him in jail, mark my word.

I turn to my brother when greeting his words. "You mind saying what that's about?"

"To hell if I know." I can't support that slopsucker's claims. His words meant nothing. How could they? He made no sense.

My brother's now speaking. "You don't know that fellow from Adam?"

"I first saw him yesterday," is my simple response. "Other than that, I don't know the man." I continue my speech when I begin feeling trou- bled. "I don't like him showing up at your house, Marin. I don't feel leaving the girls and kids here is right. Crap, man, call the cops. Have them send a patrol unit to camp out tonight."

I come to start the car after sending Marin in his house. Quickly, in an instant, I take notice of the passenger's seat. An ensemble of junk sits, supporting its structure. With two gripping hands, I pick the mess up. I fling it to the back, where half the shit slides to the floor. Marin seats himself following my tossing of objects. Had he squat sooner, he'd have sat on my hand. Truly not an encounter I'd have wanted. Marin's ass in my grasp would have been wrong. I cringe to the thought as I uphold the grim vision.

Marin states, "There's a car on its way. Should be getting here shortly."

"They'll be here all night? They said that, right?"

"It's been affirmed. Oh, and, thanks for cluing me in on my shoes."

"What?"

"You thought I didn't notice. I did. I saw you peering."

I boldly state, "Had you not noticed me, would you have put them on?"

"I'd have walked to the car in my socks and not known." My brother gleams. "You weren't planning on saying a word to me, were you?"

"No, brother, not really. Well, maybe after we got a block from your house."

"It'd have been your consent for making me feel foolish."

I smile slyly as a car pulls alongside us. Within the street's the dispatch Marin summoned. I roll down my window and shout to the driver, "Be on the watch for a man trailing these areas. His tower's slight. Hair's brown and shaggy. And he has a dreggy coat, grey in color."

The officer's acknowledging, "Sounds like a drifter."

"I'm pulling out. You can park in my spot."

I straighten the wheels slightly as my car's creeping forward, then, finally, we're off, Marin, Sable, and me.

I worry, however, not only is Marin's wife in the house, but so are their midgets, then Dej, who, out of kindness, is staying with them tonight. If anything happens to any one of them, I'll go looking for Ghislain and rough his ass up, if I'm not partial on killing the bum, which I'm liable to do.

Chapter Fifteen

After eighty-three minutes of driving, I come upon Flourished Lane and hang right. At the left of the street I spy the magnificent white house nestled behind trees of lush lilacs. Parking alongside the curb, I behold the ever breathtaking brothel that rests beneath reaching streams of moonlight.

Turning to Marin, I find my brother asleep in his cushion. "Hey." Marin grumbles lightly in response to my voice. "You plan on sleeping the whole time?"

"Huh?" He wakes and flutters his eyes. "We here?"

"Just pulled in." I wait a moment as he livens his stir. "You up now?"

"Well, I guess."

Marin's trailing aside as we hike to the house.

I'm first in line to stretch to the door. Behind the frame I descry merry voices conversing happily in laughter.

"Have we arrived at a party?" Marin inspects.

"Sounds it."

I reach my fist to the ingress and knock loudly. As quickly as I thrash, a spy window slides open and from behind are two eyes inspecting me, then the voice of a woman transmits through the air.

She says ever softly, "Affirm the phrase."

Phrase? I think. I find myself stunned. I know no code words to get ourselves in. Knowing I can't respond to her beckoning, I simply divulge, "I'm Detective Biertempfel. I've come inquiring Madame Voletta."

The window slides shut, then given a half minute, a mature woman approaches. Her eyes peer through the slit viewer when she requests why I'm here. I'm acknowledging, "I must see Ambrielle, ma'am."

Once again the window slides shut. Following its sudden closure, the door starts to open. Standing between the frame, I view the debonair. Kindly, she wonders, "I assumed you had no further business here."

"I thought wrong, Madame. I apologize."

"Well, my business is underway at this time, sir. Rather, you follow me to the kitchen, but quietly, please. We'll ensue our talk there."

Marin and I are politely welcomed into the parlor, then led away as we're brought to the kitchen. Once inside I'm noticing the Madame inspecting my brother. It's then I envision in moments her speech and direct to my assumption, I discover she does.

While keeping her eyes on Marin, she determinably questions, "You're Ambrielle's father, I acknowledge to take it?"

Before he could make his announcement, I do it for him. "No. He's Marin Biertempfel. The man's my brother."

"Is this true?" she asks him.

"For thirty-nine years that truth has been so."

Voletta continues to look him over. "Forgive my distrust, but you have an ID to prove who you are?"

Upon her request, Marin reaches into his back pocket. After battling his wallet, he culls the leather billfold in hand. Inside, Marin extends his fingers to his detective ID.

His title now rests within the hands of Voletta, while she intently scopes her eyes at the text. "You boys in business together?"

"Mannerly speaking, since thirty-nine," he answers.

"A family affair, then. Won't you men come settle at the table?"

We take heed of the offer and before long I explain why I'm back. "I apologize, but you must understand, I can't leave without her. It's my duty to take Ambrielle to Annecy. I have orders."

Voletta sits quietly, disharmonized by my mission. "This purpose of yours, it can't be done. Ambrielle's away sick as we speak."

I inquire, "Away, where?"

Time to resurrect a good lie, Voletta conceives quietly. "At the clinic. She'd been complaining of pains."

"And when was she taken?"

"Oh, don't know, honestly. I never minded the time."

I'm becoming frustrated. I draw forth my tablet, along with my pen. Then, breathing deeply, I try to gain ease. "This clinic you speak; where can I find it?"

Voletta finds the question has placed her in a predicament. She knows very well Ambrielle hadn't gone to no clinic, least not today. What's there to say? Voletta ponders, then continues, "Candle Wick Road, where I dropped her."

I take note, then poll, "Anyone got the time?"

"Mmm, 9:32, sir," the debonair announces.

"Well, the clinic would be closed now." The thought then hits me. How could Ambrielle be at the clinic? I begin to speculate Voletta's lying. I decide to declare her so. "Why don't you tell me where she's at? Really at?"

"I've said already, she's at the clinic."

I oppose to believe that. I explain, "There's no one to oversee patients now."

Unlike her modest speech, Voletta chooses to communicate boldly, "It's one of those dirty little secrets, if you catch what I mean. Payoffs come all hours. You have enough, you'll get sedation."

"If you're lying to–"

"It's where she was taken, but--" Voletta stalls herself suddenly.

"Go on. What you were saying?"

"I've seemed to forgotten."

"Oh? Well, okay, seems it wasn't important. What is, though, is me coming be back if I don't find the girl. My brother and I, we'll be on our way."

Marin and I make it to the front door. Strangely, we aren't accompanied by Voletta or any of her girls, so we step forth and depart by ourselves.

My brother's querying me the instant we're gone, "Why were you so rude those last minutes?"

"She was lying, Marin. I wanted her aware that I knew."

"You're sure?"

I rush to explain, "She'd been amiss after *but*."

"Goodness, she's an old woman, Satordi."

"Well, in case, she'll suppose our return, had the woman been lying." I seat myself in Sable and unlock my brother's door. "Get in. You're open."

I'm questioning rather Ambrielle was actually in the house, and for what reason had I been lied to, if she was? What sort of rebus dealings are they conducting to keep me away? I've already seen Ambrielle. Why hadn't I been allowed to again? Something's going on and I'm needing to get to the bottom of it.

Chapter Sixteen

It's been an exhausting drive looking for Candle Wick Road. One of the most difficult parts of this job is having to scout streets in cities you've no familiarity with. It's like my head's been screwed backwards and my eyes are withdrawn.

My brother finally shouts as I'm passing some marker, "That's it. Go there."

Having a second pair of eyes is always great in positions like these. I advise Marin upon our arrival, "Lay low, brother, and stay in the car."

"Ah, Satordi, really?"

"Hey, should my plans fall through, I'll be needing you to pose as someone."

"Role play? Hey, sure. Whatever you're needing."

"Keep your ass here and stay quiet." I advance to the prevention clinic where, inside, I'm meeting a nurse. "I'm from the Poison Control Center." I'm presenting my well faked ID I've had many years.

"Poison Control, at this time?" she polls.

I prepare my lie. "We've had a situation at the center. Seems three of your patients called, complaining of vomiting, visual changes, and dizziness, following their abortions. We're wondering rather your anesthesia's been contaminated?"

"Well, I, I mean, I don't know? How awful this is."

"I'd like to sample the drug being used. Also, I request speaking with your current patients who are here."

"Certainly, sir. We have four now in rooms. Walk this hall. When you find the eighth door, head in. That's our holding room."

"Had all these women requested anesthesia?"

"Sir, yes. Oh God, they did." She becomes panicked.

"It's all right, ma'am. Calm down." I'm trying to ease her. "I'll interview the four, find out how they feel. And the phial, if you would, bring it to me when you can."

I head on my way, searching for room eight. My intentions are to find Ambrielle, but who knows what luck I'll be having? I see the shad- ow of beds behind curtains of white fabric. I approach the first, drawing the shutter away lightly. A woman looks up and is inspecting my stance. "Hello," I speak softly. "I'm checking in, making sure you're okay." She nods a simple yes, but relays nothing. "Make sure to tell the nurse if you're feeling otherwise. You can return to your rest."

I continue my search until I've reached the last bed. To my fore-knowing, not a single soul had been Ambrielle. Damn Voletta, that lousy broad. How dare the woman screw me. Beneath quiet breaths I'm seething and yelling, Voletta lied, and straight to my face. What sort of respectful matron is she?

I see the nurse approaching now and considerably, it's time I cool my silent rage and draw forth a calm state. I tear a sliver of paper from my tab while responding, "No one's complained of symptoms, nor had they exhibited signs of poisoning."

The woman slopes in relief. "Oh, thank God. We sure didn't need a lawsuit coming our way." She modestly giggles in relief and hands me the phial. "May I ask, how do you test this?"

Luckily I have brains and can make people trust me. As miscon-strued as it seems, what I do's for good cause. So no, I'm not as bad as you think.

Within my pocket's a dram of water. I realize it's an uncommon item, something strange which I carry, but I've had it for years. I couldn't even say why it's with me. All I know's I just have it. "This little paper." I show her. "Should it turn orange, we'll know there's a problem." Yeah, that's reasonable enough. Anyway, what good does she know? I do a quick dip, then withdraw the wet paper. After nothing appears, which I deceivingly knew wouldn't, I kindly imply, "Seems you've nothing to fear, ma'am." I shake my head. "It's not the medication."

"Then might it be a bug?"

"Could definitely be. I insist you check your patients, see how they're feeling. Release them if they state no complaints. I must re-turn to the center, to start my report." I spot a trash, then toss the dipped paper.

"Thank you, sir. Thank you for coming."

"Happy to have done so. Have a good night now." I tread from the building and foot to my car. Inside, Marin waits patiently.

"Need me now?" he's asking.

"Nope, it's been handled. We're heading back."

"So you'd been lied to?"

"Yes. Yes, I was. And damn me, I'd known it."

After a number of minutes passing through several streets, I'm once again parking my cruiser. Like before, Marin and I stride the steps of The Petal and Stem. Feeling angry and misinstructed, I'm ready to rip off Voletta's head. How dare that bag lie. While taking in thought, I pause. Ha, well, guess I'm one to talk. I downright lied when saying I was from Poison Control. I see I'm no better.

A woman's answering my knock, and like before, a spy window's sliding and an acknowledgment requested. Affirm the phrase, I'm hearing. Damn this shit. "Suckers and whores," I react. "Get me Voletta!"

The door opens with a young woman welcoming me, and with myself barely through, she quickly tries shutting the ingress. "Not so fast." I reach around to the half shut frame. "You see him?" I snap. I motion my head. "Come on, brother."

"Sorry, sir, sorry. I thought it was just you."

"Learn to look first. Now where's your Madame?"

She leads us to Voletta's room, and acting with proper accordance, she awaits patiently when knocking. "Madame, there's a man who requests you."

In rear of the entrance I hear Voletta's voice, "I'm decent, dear. You can open it."

Inside, Voletta's poised behind a magnificent walnut, roll top desk, penning her name on papers. "Please, sir, won't you step in?" As Voletta curves in her chair, she asks, "How could I help—"

I cut her off before she can finish, "Told you I'd be back."

"Detective Biertempfel," she acknowledges.

"In flesh, and I've got a few words for you, woman."

Voletta peers at the young girl refrained near her door. "It's all right, Zal. Be on your way, child."

I step forth, trying desperately to withhold my anger. "You lied, straight to my face. Why? Why're you protecting that broad?"

"I–"

"Where's Ambrielle? God damn it, woman, tell me."

"Detective. Sir, I've no clue where she's gone."

"Cut the crap, lady. If you're not telling me what I need within the next second, I'll have Marin going through every last room in this house." I watch the wrinkled biddy as she peers to my brother. "You think I'm kidding?"

Voletta knows to stick to her lie. "I dropped her at the clinic. Following that, Detective, I can't say where she's gone."

I give question, "Was she planning to leave?"

I see Voletta's anxiety when she unconsciously pats her knee. "Not to my knowledge, no."

I state boldly, "You know what, lady? You're lying. And you wouldn't want me losing my temper now, would you? I'm pretty damn vocal. Think of the clients you'd be losing tonight."

"Really, sir, I know nothing."

"I'm not accepting that. I'll find Ambrielle without you. Good night to you, Madame." I step from the room in outrage. Behind, Marin lingers at my back. We try to escape the hall when the young woman who let us in calls us beside her.

"I have the information you're wanting." She motions my brother and me as we're being led to her room. "Got money, mister? I'll tell you everything."

What Voletta didn't know was Zaline had eavesdropped on her private discussions. As I conversed with the dishonest Madame, Zal stood beside the door, listening in. "Why would you help me?" I ponder.

"Funny." Zal laughs. "Money buys you anything. Besides, I wasn't fond of Ambrielle."

"You swear on the information?"

"Every bit."

I reach to my pocket and throw a decent amount of francs to her bed. "Talk."

"She's on her way to her aunt's, somewhere in Bordeaux."

So Voletta had lied. I knew it. I knew. "What's this aunt's name? You recall?"

Zal thinks while racking her brain. "Reinelle? No-no, Reinella.

That was it."

"Got a last name?"

"Give me ten more francs and I'll get it," Zal explains.

"Five, and it's a deal."

"Yeah, all right. I'll do it for five." She leaves her room while Marin and I await her return.

"You believe this girl?" my brother asks.

"She's our only rat at this point."

Zal returns with an answer. "Ladou."

"Tell you what, I'll toss you two more if you tell me she visited the clinic today."

"Hell no, mister. She was here."

I'm learning every word of Voletta's was nothing more than bogus yak. "There was an abortion, then?"

"She had one, all right, days ago. She didn't want the news reaching her father."

"Of her being pregnant?"

"No. The abortion."

I'm just learning now of this. Considering what Zaline said, I'm supposing Haulmier hadn't been aware she was with child. Seems the girl wanted to keep her sins quiet. "My brother and I, we'll be out of your hair."

"You're sure you wouldn't like something else? I'll work you twenty minutes if you toss me ten more."

"I've got better things to be doing."

"Your brother, then? Looks like he'd be up for a round."

"Marin's married. Leave him alone."

"You're killjoys, you know that?"

"There're many men in your parlor, sweetheart. Go rub against them." I make way through the door with Marin behind. We charge the stairs, then ease to the porch.

"Could you believe that?" Marin questions.

"You better be game for this trip, 'cause I'm not driving home."

"These hours with you are going to be bliss. And if it ain't, you better make it." My brother then smiles.

I smirk back. "Remember, I'm getting paid, not you. Whatever shit you put up with won't be rewarded."

Marin jokes a short bit. "That's a smack in my face if I ever did feel one."

I love my brother; he's a perfect reflection of how I can be. "You nut. Your door's open, get in."

So I see we're going to Bordeaux. That's quite a distant drive and I'm hoping we'll make it. Luckily we've both bought our lug- gage, and I'm sure us boys will be taking a rest stop somewhere into our long journey.

Chapter Seventeen

It's the wee hours of the morning when Ambrielle arrives at Bordeaux. She disembarks the train and heads near the station. There awaiting her lighting's none other than her aunt, Reinella Ladou. She's Haulmier's older sister, but just by two years. Reinella's a fair-hearted woman with a pure soul and fit manners. Also to her description's her dark hair and brown eyes.

Stepping forth, Mrs. Ladou heartily declares to her niece, "Look at you! Oh, look, how beautiful and grown." Reinella snuggles in warmly when giving a hug, then, backing petty inches, she pats the girl's face. "Ages. Ages it's been since you've graced me a visit."

"How good it is to see my sweet aunt. And Uncle Odo. I don't see him. Had he not come?"

"Odo's home, darling, resting. He's been down with a headache."

"Then surely I'll look forward to seeing him later."

"By then he'll be fine and ready to see your sweet, lovely face. I'm still so proud you've come, Brie."

Reinella carries the luggage her niece couldn't take, and after twelve steps, they arrive at a 1946 red Pontiac Torpedo. "I've you a warm bed waiting back home."

"After my long travel, I'm ready to sleep. I'm so tired. I nodded on the train, but was too afraid to rest long. But anyway, will I see Pensee, or she not yet awake?"

"She was out like a light last I checked. I'm sure, though, you'll both enjoy good times while you're here. Well, even to tell you, she's been so excited with you coming. She's just so happy."

Pensee is Odo and Reinella's only child, and though Pensee and Ambrielle are alike in their age, Pensee's quite different. On the contrary to her cousin, Pensee's maturity hasn't seasoned just yet. She lacks all her cousin acquires. Truth is, however, Ambrielle's lifetime encounters forced her maturity, possessing her with a mental development beyond her young age, not to mention the physical encounters she was forced to partake.

In their similarity, Pensee, like her cousin, has amber hair, but a shade lighter and inches shorter than Ambrielle's. Her eyes, unlike her relative's fair saucers, are deep denim blue, with hints of grey color.

Chapter Eighteen

After earlier arriving at her aunt's, Ambrielle cast herself to a bed, where it took no more than five minutes before she fell into slumber. She's been sleeping now for several hours when Pensee approaches the berth with intentions of waking her resting filiation.

"Brie," her voice carries lightly. "Brie. Hey." Pensee climbs onto the mattress, all the while poking her slumbering kith. "Hey, dilly-dallier, it's time you waken. Are you deaf? Ambrielle!"

Quite imaginably, the courtesan shoots forth from bed. "What? What?" Her eyes blink rapidly.

Pensee slips into laugher following the passing sight. "I'd not imagined you'd be in such fluster."

"You about startled me to death. A smidge louder and I'd have peed the bed." Ambrielle falls back to her pillow.

"Good thing you didn't. Anyway, mom sent me to wake you. Well, go on, get dressed. I told mom we'd see a show later."

"A movie?"

"Haven't you ever gone?"

"Not since I'd been a small child."

"Golly, Brie, it's time we change that. I'm taking us to see *The Days Of Sin And Silence*." Pensee makes spooky sounds to emphasize her response. "Some psychological thriller. Mom says it's intense."

Ambrielle moves from her bed to dress. "Don't leave me to wonder. Tell more."

"It's about a family, and one of them's harboring some dirty, dark secret. Each member begins suspecting the other. And as each tries to unravel truths, they eventually fall dead."

Ambrielle's responding, "Some plot." She then approaches a sad thought. "Last time I saw a movie I was with my mom and dad. God, that's such a distant past. But those were good days, if I ever had any."

Pensee comes back quickly, "I didn't mean to stir you, Brie. Anyway, there's a showing at 3:00. You feel like going?"

"Yes. We deserve a good time, don't you think?" Ambrielle's smil- ing warmly.

"It's planned then. Move along. Dad's been waiting to see you."

Ambrielle trails Pensee as they walk to the family room. Inside, Odo and Reinella sit before their mahogany cabinet, which contains a radio/record player. Premiering is a most recent episode of their favorite game show. Together the duo plays along, hoping to out-skill the other.

Odo's first to spot Ambrielle as she comes through the room. "Well, I declare! Reinella said we had a visitor."

Odo Ladou is probably, if not, the most likable guy in Bordeaux. His congenial manner has won him many friends. He's a right neighborly fellow and helper to all.

Ambrielle becomes tickled by his excitement. "It's lovely to see you. Aunty said you'd been with a headache."

"I'm great now, seeing you're here. You're not too grown you can't give your old uncle a hug?"

"I'd never deny your hugs, sir. They've always made me warm." She steps to embrace him. "How lovely it is to be seeing you."

"Quite the matter, indeed." Ambrielle stands back as Odo observes. "You were a mere ten years of age last we saw another. My how you've grown."

"That I was. I'm praised you remember."

"Well, bless your little heart, I do."

Reinella interrupts, "I fixed you girls sandwiches. I don't want either of you twigs to starve, so go eat."

"Are you and Uncle Odo coming to the movie later?"

"No, sugar. We've already been. Besides, we figured you girls, you're grown. You don't want us with you."

Pensee announces, "Mom, don't go into that. It's not we don't want you, but Brie and I, we'd like time by ourselves."

"Exactly as I said. You're both grown. Wouldn't want you embarrassed having your old mom and dad with you."

"Cut that out. Movie's at 3:00. We'll be leaving before then, so I guess we'll go eat."

"Oh, Pensee. Honey, come back. I've almost forgotten. You had a package come. Sweetie, what on earth have you ordered?"

Shock crosses Pensee's face, so she inquires, "What package, mom?"

"It's on the stairs. I'd put it there so you'd see."

Her daughter makes an awkward face. "I hadn't sent for any package. You're sure it's mine?"

"It's addressed to Miss Pensee Ladou." Reinella's grinning warmly. "You're the only one in this house by that name."

"Hmm, true. Well, I couldn't imagine what it'd be."

Ambrielle's following her cousin toward the stairs, teasing, "Maybe you have an admirer? Could it be he's sending you things? Who is he? Come on, say; I won't tell."

"Really, Brie, I haven't any idea."

"Who is he? Just tell."

"I'm serious, Brie. I really don't know."

"No lie? You're honest?"

"Promise you." Pensee's now shaking the box. "What's in here?"

"Is there someone you like?"

"Not really." Pensee begins to blush.

"Your cheeks say otherwise. It's okay if you don't want to say his name."

"Let's take our food upstairs and open this." Once in her room, Pensee sets the parcel carefully upon her bed. "Think it's breakable?"

Ambrielle shrugs, but soon she inquires, "You recognize the writing? Can you tell whose it is?"

Pensee raises her brow when she laughs. "I think it's my mom's. No, not really. I can't say."

"Maybe it is? There's no return address. If it's your mom, then she knew not to put it."

"If that's the case, she wanted to keep me tied with suspense. But why would she do this? It's not my birthday."

"Well, if it's not her, then you've got an unknown package from an unknown sender. You're sure you haven't any suitor?"

Pensee admits, "I don't, Brie. I don't."

"Well, if you say. But stop wasting time. Aren't you curious to see what's inside?"

Pensee carefully pulls a line of masking tape from the top of the box. After tugging both cardboard flaps, she reveals a considerable portion of newspaper. Then, taking it away, she exposes a rather strange gathering of objects.

From inside, Pensee retrieves a medium-sized ironstone basin containing two equally sized oranges and a pair of red tapers. She then sets them beside herself. "Who'd send this?" Miss Ladou studies the commodities while appearing perplexed. "What's to be done with all this?" She thinks a good moment. "Why'd anyone waste money to have this mailed? I can't even say what it's for."

"There's no note? Fish in. Give it a look."

Miss Ladou peers toward the bottom of the box and, reaching her small hand within the parcel, is pulling a retrieval of parchment notes. Now drawing them near, she begins reading quietly. A silent stand then fills the room and, noticeably being offended by the text, Pensee shoves them to Brie. A fixated concern attends her troubled eyes. "Get rid of them. Be rid of them now. Throw them out. Please, Brie, do it."

"Why? How come you're acting like this?"

"I'd rather not say. Just get rid of them."

Ambrielle analyzes her cousin. "You're upset."

"Upset, no. I'm scared. What I read were directions."

"To where?"

"Not directions like that. Rather, they're rituals. Incantations. They can't be found in this house."

Ambrielle beams as she's becoming enthused. "Magic, then? Like witchcraft, you mean?"

"I guess. I suppose. I haven't much care to know, really." Then, looking to Brie and, with an odd smirk, she directs, "Don't tell me you're curious."

"Of course. The strange and unknown is interesting, I think. Would you mind I read this?"

Pensee draws the letters from her cousin's grasp. "Brie, come on. Don't get caught up in this stuff."

Ambrielle snatches them back. "Don't worry. I'm just wanting to read."

"Damn you and your curiosity, Brie."

Unconcerned for cousin's upset, Ambrielle begins the first page silently.

> *For centuries and decades, before my time*
> *and even yours, people told stories around*
> *the world that were bore from specks of*
> *truth. They reach through generations,*
> *stretching successfully along their course,*
> *but through their reining span in time,*
> *tales often lose their trace of fact. From*
> *their retells told throughout the ages,*
> *persons find they alter stories, to declare*
> *them new or up-to-date, but there will always*
> *be one story, a bereaved tale to stay unchanged,*
> *and that's the yarn of Yria Dane.*

Ambrielle acknowledges, "This hasn't anything to do with spells."

"That's the first page. Are you forgetting there's more?"

"I'm just saying. Would you be mad I continued?"

"I'd rather you not. Brie, really, don't read anymore."

"What harm could it do? Like it or not, my curiosity wins."

"Fine. Fine. I haven't the authority to stop you."

Ambrielle returns her gaze to the parchments and, much to her cousin's discomfort, begins reading aloud, "When the moon is high and in sight of your window, flow your basin with running water. Then, carefully, without spilling, set it upon your floor. This will serve as your doorway. In regard to the tapers, position one at each end of the dish. These symbolize the depiction of blood and flesh. And last, but important, your oranges. In front of your bowl, place them aside, leaving one with its skin, while the other, peeled. These represent the body in physical and nonphysical form. Once your candles are lit, you're ready to begin. Read the poems supplied in the order they're given." Following Ambrielle's completion of the top page, she acknowledges her cousin, "I guess these others won't speak of romance and wonderful places?"

"I don't like it, Brie. This fills me with fear."

"You're about to jump through your skin. You've worked yourself up. Don't. All will be fine."

"Can't you stop? Be done with this, please."

"Calm your nerves. Don't have a fit. I'll read to myself."

Ambrielle carries forth with the text, but does so respectfully so her cousin can't hear.

> *Yria Dane was walking home when, in*
> *the wake stalked Guillaume Rhoe.*
> *He held his hand before her face*
> *and made her smell the drug's embrace.*
> *As she woke inside him home,*
> *she found her body skinned to bone.*
> *Now gagging on respired breaths, the*
> *panic settles within her chest.*
> *Mr. Rhoe then took his knife*
> *and rammed it through her sky-blue eye.*
> *Twisting, turning, whirling deep,*
> *he dug with pleasure when she shrieked.*
> *Then, popping out across the floor,*
> *roamed her eyeball from its core.*
> *Yria swore she would not rest*
> *and conjured up the perfect hex.*
> *Curse ye be who brought me pain.*
> *Damned to hell, I speak your name.*
> *Your sin is mine, I take in bane.*
> *Those who beckon, I'll furnish strain,*
> *whence I scout your bloodline's name.*

Shocked by the context, Ambrielle finds herself speaking, "Who'd write this? It's sick. This woman, is she real?"

Pensee relays without hesitance, "I think we should go to the cops."

"Cops, no, Pensee, I can't. They're probably looking for me."

"What do you mean? You're in trouble, aren't you?"

"I ran, Pensee. I ran away."

"It's your dad, isn't it? He's hurting you; is that why you're here?"

Ambrielle wants off the topic. Anything pertaining Haulmier, she can do without hearing. So, instead, she redirects her attention to the papers.

"Damn it, Brie, just put those down."

Ambrielle's cracking half a smile. "I can't. I have to know more."

"But, of course, you do."

"Don't worry. I won't be reading to you." Ambrielle lends her eyes to the last page.

Yria Dane's a gruesome sight,
feared by those who'll know her might. A
frightful specter looming near.
When clutched by veins, you'll cry for air.
Within the capsule of her eye,
you'll see the socket bleed, surprise.
If Yria Dane be close or near,
your flowers wilt from certain fear.
Wasting slowly, parched of life,
their colors fade apart your sight.
Should Yria Dane be near or by,
regard your pet that drifts affright.
Should it cower, or try to hide,
fear the wrath that lurks outside.
If Yria Dane be by or here,
don't deem on her to disappear. Once
the words are spoken right,
you've conjured up this spook of fright.
This dwelling phantom of inky night

> *will brisk your bones, then taste your life.*
> *And, as you breathe your last inhale,*
> *mind your kinship's blighted fact,*
> *bloodlines pay for kindred acts.*

Pensee peers to her cousin while upholding a question. "Ever heard the ghostly myth of that woman who appears in a mirror? Bloody Mary Worth, she's called. This Yria Dane, is she like her, you think?"

"An urban legend? Come on, Pensee. Those things aren't real. They were fabricated to scare people. Created, Pensee, to amuse bored youths."

"I can't agree. I think she's real."

"Well, don't, 'cause she's not."

"Gruesome Dane."

"What, Pensee?"

"Her name."

"Oh, so now you're naming this imaginative spook?"

"The last poem said it. It said what she is."

"Gracious, Pensee, you're out of your mind."

"I'm not out of my mind. And you sent me this, didn't you?"

"I didn't send it. Why would I?"

"To mess with me, of course."

"Really, Pensee? You think I'd do this?"

"Wouldn't you?"

"You know me better than that. Anyway, how is it you know folklore?"

"Reading."

"What, books?"

"No, a magazine. *Bizarre International.*"

"This sort of stuff scares you. Why is it you read it?"

"Who knows? I've wondered myself."

"I don't get you. I could try, but I can't."

Pensee laughs at her cousin. "I'm different, that's all."

"So, have you done it, mentioned Bloody Mary Worth?"

"No. Are you suggesting we should?"

"Well, I'm curious. But we've got Yria Dane. We could try her instead."

"You're really wanting to? Why?"

"I just want to know, Pensee. What if she's real?"

"Then we'll meet her, I guess."

"But you're afraid."

"The story's what scared me. How she died. What was done. And her suffering. It's like I felt each second of pain."

"It's no more than a story, so why be in fear?"

"I don't know."

"If you don't think anything will happen, then it can't."

"Then it'll all be in fun?"

"Like a game. What do you say? Want to give this a try?"

"Hmm, well, it might be exciting."

Ambrielle hears quiet chirps softly rising from the corner of her cousin's room. "You've got a bird?"

"Oh, that? Yeah. That's Kiwi."

"Kiwi?"

"My canary. She's under the cage cover."

Ambrielle walks to the medium-sized coop alongside her cousin as Pensee uncovers the pen. Inside, a pea-green bird sits perched on a twig, with small green plants of fresh bloomed foliage.

Ambrielle smiles with delight. "Pensee, you did this? How neat."

Pensee chirps to her small feathered friend. "Hi, Kiwi, you pretty bird." She then scoops feed into a small bowl, then latches the tiny clasp. "I was thinking, Brie, we could walk up town and maybe get milkshakes before the show?"

"Pensee, I don't know? My monies are tight. I've got to get to Marseille with what little I've got."

"Don't worry. I was planning on asking dad for some cash."

"Will he give you enough, you suppose?"

"We're talking about my dad. Of course he'll give money."

Ambrielle's growing ever excited at the thought of a milkshake, which, in past years, had been an unsighted delight, a treat in which she hasn't tasted in so many long years; and the same caressing beatitude's shared with her conscious surmise of a movie.

Chapter Nineteen

Marin and I are sitting at the booth of some quant café and we're finishing lunch. After arriving in Bordeaux at 5:40 this morning, my brother and I reposed until noon as we slumbered through breakfast. Of course, when waking we found ourselves starved. After gathering things from our room, we left the motel and, having hit the road quickly, we searched for a meal.

Considering Marin nor I have been to Bordeaux, we had no absolute clue to where we were heading. Tolerably, we stretched through the road before we found ourselves here, in this quaint little shack. It was to our attempted endeavor we came in to town and, happily, I might add. Seems we'd unknowingly embarked the right path. With our stomachs now full, we're bulging with glee, but no more resting our piggish guts and taking ease. We're aware we have work, so we rise from our seats.

"Guess you have no idea where we're heading?" My brother looks to me through shallow eyes.

"What I don't know, I always find out."

"Ain't it good to be you?"

"Actually, yeah. There's a phone booth outside. I'll check the directory."

I leave the café and head to the call box. Now stepping inside, I snatch the directory. My eyes spy upon names. I read several Ladou's, but none named Reinella. I realize my only option's to be calling them all.

Marin, now leaving the building, comes my direction. He stops near the booth, while rolling a toothpick around in his kisser. I wave him closer and, as he comes to me, I shove him the phonebook. I direct him to read numbers when, finally on my fourth call, Reniella acknowledges.

"I'm with the phone company," I say. "Several lines are down. I'm just checking your service." After hanging the phone, I gaze to my brother. "Whose name's that under?"

"An Odo Ladou."

Following his deliverance, Marin conveys the address and, me, yeah, I'm having to jot it all down.

We climb to my car, but before unlocking the hatch, I spot the passenger door unfastening for Marin. "No. Ah-uh! You know not to be leaving her open. Don't do it again."

"I didn't know, brother. I didn't know."

"Mind it next time." We drive around a short while when Marin spots the street we've been searching. "In the glove box are name plates. Take two. Pin one on."

My brother questionably responds, "What sort of scheme you got us doing?"

"Something you'll like. Grab them mustaches, too. I've got us some hats."

"Where's the rope and club?"

"Not funny, Marin. Go around to the trunk. Find the box of cologne."

"Cologne?"

"God, brother, you're a dim-wit. We're salesmen, you nit-twit."

Marin's shaking his head. "Don't you have a vacuum? A blender? A juicer, at least?"

Looking toward my brother, I impulsively say, "Behave or it's your ass getting sold."

"You're bound to have something better than this."

"Drop it. But when inquired, and, I do mean when, you act in accordance. You hearing me?"

Marin spies my new title. "Clearly, Vallis. You got a last name?"

"God, gees. St. Clair. You happy, Benrey?" I spied his tag, too.

"That's Mr. Benrey Duchelle. We sound like an old pair of bums, if you think of it." Marin giggles childishly. "What's our business?"

"Just be savvy and clever. Play your roll and don't stumble."

Marin follows me to the house and, deliberately, I've left him to serve as my carrier. It's mischievously I begin laughing in my head. How's that load weighing, brother? Conceiving, in thought, my hands wish to rest, yet they've attributed no labor. Empathically I must be feeling his plaint. Guess it's sympathy pain, you call it.

I ring the bell and wait on an answer. Within moments a lovely woman is greeting my stance. "Good day, ma'am. We're sales representatives from *Leurre Parfumerie*. I'm Vallis St. Clair and this is my assistant, Benrey Duchelle. Our company's contrived a fresh line of fragrance. Could we interest your time and show you these, miss?"

"Certainly, gentlemen. Certainly. Come on through. I'm Reinella, by the way."

She leads us through the front entrance, into the family room, where she offers us seats.

"Won't you grab you a chair as we're preparing our things?" I re- quest her.

Marin stands beside me as us eggheads pretend we know what we're doing. I begin the incentive. After opening the display, I'm retrieving three bottles. "All right," I exclaim. "Here would be the newest aromas to our collection." I take a handkerchief, drop three beads of scent to the cloth, then begin waving it through the air. "This first one's Chanternay. Its top notes are cinnamon and tangerine, with a mid note of nutmeg and base notes of ginger and rosewood."

Deeply Reinella breathes in the air around her. "Mmm. Mmm-hmm. I like that very much. It's quite pleasing."

I hand Mrs. Ladou the fragrance, while I say to my brother, "Mr. Duchelle, please, sir, will you prep the next sample? I'd like to give our prospect some time with the Chanternay."

"Absolutely. Madame, our second introduction's Zybara. I'm sure you'll find it's fetching. It's a favorite of the wife."

Marin grins through a cheesy cast, the slick bastard. He gathers a hanky, then trills several drips onto his tester.

As he waves it upon air, he presumes what to say, "The introducto- ry essence is a lovely orange scent. Its heart notes contain juniper and geranium, then closes with exciting hints of clove and vanilla."

Following my brother's completion, I readily supply the next scent. After my presentation, Mrs. Ladou acknowledges her fondness of all three. "Each would make exceptional gifts, especially for my daughter and niece. But decisions. You make this quite hard."

"We'll make this simple and let them choose. I'm sure they'll find what they like," I mindfully imply.

"But they're gone, Mr. St Clair, that's the problem."

"Would they be returning shortly?"

"Hmm, not for awhile." Reinella eyes the fragrance collection. "I do like these, however. Why don't I just cut the hassle and take all three?"

"Wonderful, ma'am. And I'll tell you what, how bout I give you all three for the simple price of two?"

"Well, that's an offer I couldn't pass."

I write Reinella a bill of sales, then hand the lovely woman her receipt.

After wrapping things up, Marin and I head from the house as we devise our next plan.

"Well?" my brother asks.

My response is simple, as it's all I can think. "We'll camp here, keep an eye on the house while we wait for the girls."

Really, what other idea could I have? We've come all this way. We can't be leaving, not just yet. It's cost me gas and it's taking my money to get where we're at. So, yeah, we'll sit in Sable. We'll wait around. Let's just pray we're not on each others nerves as we hang loose for this while.

Chapter Twenty

Ambrielle and Pensee have returned home in time for supper. While approaching the steps, they haven't noticed the empty space once retaining Satordi's car. Ten minutes before the cousins' arrival, Marin and Satordi decided to head out and find a quick meal. Their agreed objective was to depart long enough to find food, fill their deprived guts, then hastily return to their place of observation. What they didn't deem was the possibility the cousins would return before them, but since it's happened, Satordi has no way to know his person of interest has slipped past his sight.

After dinner Pensee lounges in her room, while Ambrielle attends a warm bath. Following her heated dip, Ambrielle retreats to her cousin's chamber. Then, upon an instant, both girls find their gaze inspect- ing the strange assets which had been sent to the house.

"What are you thinking? You want to tempt it?" Ambrielle questions.

"Suppose something happens. Something bad, maybe?"

"What could happen?"

"There're probably many things to suggest." "Then we don't do it. You're uncomfortable."

"I didn't say I wouldn't want to. I'm just unsure, is how I'm feeling." "Do we do this or not? I mean, your parents are sleeping. Now would be a better time than any."

"If we're heard, then what?"

"I doubt they'll hear a thing." Ambrielle lends her attention to the bowl. "So, how bout you run that with water? I'll set up the floor."

During Pensee's absence, Brie decides to peel an orange, as it'd been directed in the letter. She tosses the stripped skin to a trash, then sets the bare fruit alongside its cloaked mate.

Upon her return to the room, Pensee asks, "All right, the bowl. Where's this thing going?"

"The floor, here, by these citrus. We'll need those tapers off your bed. And I'm still needing matches."

Pensee steps from her room while Ambrielle's situating tapers. She positions one at each end of the bowl, then awaits her cousin patiently.

Pensee comes back and is peering at her ceiling. "Should I shut out the light?"

Ambrielle shrugs, then responds in accordance.

Pensee tosses a booklet of matches. "Light the candles, then. I'll tend to the light."

It isn't until the room's been switched to darkness that the chamber becomes illumed with the obvious glare of yellowing-blue flares.

"This is looking like witchcraft, Brie."

"It's harmless. It wouldn't have been sent if it wasn't."

"But I'm feeling shaky and I feel my stomach's in knots."

"Those are your nerves. You're fine. You'll get through this, just breathe."

"Oh, okay. Where's the poem?"

Ambrielle's holding the paper. "Guess we read aloud?"

"Quietly, though. I don't want mom or dad hearing."

Never once has Ambrielle or Pensee imagined the grim possibilities that might be produced, but, still, the girls sit closely, knee to knee, with their verbalizations prepared.

> *Yria Dane was walking home when, in*
> *the wake stalked Guillaume Rhoe.*
> *He held his hand before her face*
> *and made her smell the drug's embrace.*
> *As she woke inside his home,*
> *she found her body skinned to bone.*
> *Now gagging on respired breaths, the*
> *panic settles within her chest.*
> *Mr. Rhoe then took his knife*
> *and rammed it through her sky-blue eye.*
> *Twisting, turning, whirling deep,*
> *he dug with pleasure when she shrieked.*
> *Then, popping out across the floor,*

roamed her eyeball from its core.
Yria swore she would not rest
and conjured up the perfect hex.
Cursed ye be who brought me pain.
Damned to hell, I speak your name.
Your sin is mine, I take in bane.
Those who beckon, I'll furnish strain,
whence I scout your bloodline's name.

Unbelievably, to the girls, nothing happens. So, upon their perch they settle contently. It's during this time no grotesque phantoms appear. No repugnant scent of sulfur rises in the room, nor had any sparking flames reached high from the candles. Instead, the room is calm and still as before.

Though Ambrielle's comforted by peace, an inch of her is partial- ly displeased. Deep within, Ambrielle quietly prepares to watch what bizarre occurrences might take place before her. Had she been aware, Ambrielle might acknowledge it'd be just moments before the first transcendental encounter would make itself known.

The manifestation, though metaphysical and challenging to minds, is a simple betiding, though there're no overdoings of paranormal activity, like that of loud thuds or blown doors, what's happening is still nerving, maybe worse to endure.

Above the basin of resting water, passing down, drill brilliant beads of scarlet drops from the air. The blood trickles a steady fifteen inches from the ironstone washbowl, then audibly slaps against the aquatic pool, fanning along its claret color and staining the once pellucid waters.

Pensee and Ambrielle watch out of horror and disbelief; then, looking upon each other, their eyes meet with shock. The air soon stirs with a turbulent chill, causing pimples to rise on once temperate skin. Both girls return their gaze to the altar. A second sight emerges. It'd be in this time the cousins become evermore daunted. With no reason to explain it, the coated orange sheds its bitter-tart skin, as if shucked by sightless hands. Small shriveled veins emerge through bare flesh and swell with flows of rushing blood.

The room soon returns to average warmth as the coldness declines. It's this instant the girls deliver the succeeding poem.

Yria Dane's a gruesome sight,
feared by those who know her might.
frightful specter looming near
when, clutched by veins, you'll cry for air.
Within the capsule of her eye,
you'll see the socket bleed, surprise.
If Yria Dane be close or near,
your flowers wilt from certain fear.
Wasting slowly, parched of life,
their colors fade apart your sight.
Should Yria Dane be near or by,
regard your pet that drifts affright.
Should it cower, or try to hide,
fear the wrath that lurks outside.
If Yria Dane be by or here,
don't deem on her to disappear. Once
the words are spoken right,
you've conjured up this spook of fright.
This dwelling phantom of inky night
will brisk your bones, then taste your life.
And, as you breathe your last inhale,
mind your kinship's blighted fact,
bloodlines pay for kindred acts.

Following the sentence closure, the flames of both candles shoot high into the air, then return their standard height. As quickly as this happens, a second sight occurs. From the wax, thick globs of what appear as human flesh passes from the tapers and flops to the floor.

The girls become sickened by the ghastly sight when their mouths droop from repulsion. Outside the window, loud gusts of wind beat the house with violent blasts. Atop Pensee's night stand, near her bed, a bouquet of blue irises start to wilt, then, wasting slowly, their vitality parches and their brightness departs.

Inside her pen Kiwi's taken with panic. Her small feathers puff as she flutters her cage. Sadly, following her fright, the tiny bird succumbs to an overworked heart and falls dead in her hutch.

Through watchful horror the cousins stall their breaths when Pensee's closet doors release violently. Within the darkened walk-in ris- es a cushioned voice. It gradually increases when, becoming resonate at last, to decipher words.

"For centuries and decades, before my time and even yours, peo- ple told stories around the world that were bore from specks of truth. They reach through generations, stretching successfully along their course, but through their reining span in time, tales often lose their trace of fact. From their retells told throughout the ages, persons find they alter stories to declare them new or up-to-date, but there will al- ways be one story, a bereaved tale to stay unchanged, and that's the yarn of Yria Dane."

Emerging from darkness steps the silhouette of a woman. Aware she remains obscure, Yria brushes her hands in whooshing motion, all the while increasing the light within the room.

It's now, by trepidation, Ambrielle and Pensee view her awful form. A stretch of fiery-red muscle cover the entire range of Yria's body. Lacking all, not one sheath of skin composes her structure. She's a nightmarish vision for the girls, godawful and bloody.

Moreover, her eye, the right's clearly missing. The empty sock- et's been gouged to nothing, yet weeps trills of blood. Taken by Yria's woeful frame, the cousins become stiffened with fright. Their bodies, like stone, are unmoveable and bogged down in place. Their hearts pound fiercely in their throats, choking what had once been easy breaths.

Yria steps to the youths with unceasing speech. "Mind your kin- ship's blighted fact, bloodlines pay for kindred acts."

Rising from Yria's body reach a profusion of roaming veins, slithering through the air like skinny snakes. Pensee backs away in a hurried rush as the prowling vessels spread out to her skin.

Ambrielle finds her intonation, setting loose a burst of screams. She forsakes her frightened cousin and struggles to crawl beneath the bed. Within the opened space Ambrielle abandons Pensee to fend her lonely self.

Puncturing through Miss Ladou's flesh, Yria's veins advance through her body. Miss Ladou's bones become brisk before her blood's ingested. Yria's vessels then soak every drop of Pensee's life, draining her through phlebotomized death. Yria retracts her invading veins as the final gulp of vital fluid's been extracted. During their recession, clar- et fluid spritzes the room, staining the floor, walls, and bunk.

Beneath the bed frame Ambrielle witnesses a stiffened Pensee pass to the floor. The courtesan's eyes then widen and her body trembles. In an uncalculated move, Ambrielle impulsively frees herself. She sees no sign of the phantom corpse that once roamed the room.

Now sliding herself beside Pensee, the young girl bewails through her tears. The realization of her cousin, dead, brings shock to her sight. Turning the inflexible body aside, Ambrielle spots numerous punctures upon the whole figure. At closer view, trails of veins peep through the deceased girl's flesh like slender worms. Upon inspection, Ambrielle gloats at the pitiful, afraid look on Pensee's face. The dead girl's nostrils rest frozen in widespread flares, her eyes vast with fright and her mouth dilated in the fixed position of an unheard shrill.

The sight petrifies Ambrielle as she's dashing away. Within the hallway she bursts into an onset of screams. It's through her calamity and grievous weeps she wails, but her call goes unheard, so she advances to a room. Without knocking, she hurls through the door. In a rush Ambrielle accesses the bed. "Aunty! Uncle! Pensee I fray to say, she's cold on the floor."

Ambrielle stands shocked as the room remains silent. No words surpass mouths, not Reinella's or Odo's. It's then the young woman soundlessly questions, why won't they waken? Her concerns deepen and her mind further troubled. Lightly shaking upon her aunt,

Ambrielle tries to rouse her, but attempting no motion, Reinella lies still. Hesitant and scared, Ambrielle struggles to speak, "Aunty? Aunty, please." Now turning aside, she quests for a lamp. Her hand soon encounters a turn-switch, and upon an instant, light irradiates the room when, decidedly, Ambrielle's drawing back covers.

Frozen in dismay upon her bed, Reinella lay. Molded upon her face is the same pitiful and afraid leer as her daughter. Her body, like Pensee's, also contains holes and veins.

To her right, lying sound at her side, lolls Odo, expired from a stroke of bad luck. Unlike Reinella, it'd been his heart which gave out.

While staring upon her deceased uncle and aunt, Ambrielle achieves an unhinged state. Fear becomes her and takes her in stride. With the tragedy and shock of everyone's death, Ambrielle finds herself shifting to panic. She thinks to call the cops, yet refrains quickly. Leaving the room, she heads to the kitchen. Pacing and probing, she contrives what to do. Voletta, she thinks. Peering the room, she spots a mounted phone. The dazed, frightened youth rushes to the rotary dial. She waits several seconds as the line embarks rings, then, at the other end, she's received with a greeting.

Ambrielle wails to the receiver, "Janely. Janely, I need Madame Voletta. Put her on, quickly." In these mounting seconds she waits, nerved and anxious.

Voletta picks up seconds later. "Ambrielle? Dear, what's wrong? Janely says you're crying."

"Ma'am, ma'am, I, I, I–"

"Slow down, dearest. What's happened to you?"

"Everyone here, everyone, ma'am, they're dead. I must leave. I must."

"Dead? Dead of what? What's happened, child?" "She killed them," she yells.

"Calm down, peach. Calm down. You're alone, is that right?"

"They're dead, and that'll soon be my fate. Madame, please. I'll be arrested. I'm scared."

"Leave. Take a train. Head somewhere safe."

"No money. I'm broke. I don't know what to do."

Voletta thinks momentarily. "I hate asking, child, but are you willing to hike?"

"I'll have to."

"Then find your nearest kin."

"Ah-ah, Biarritz. I have a cousin."

"Biarritz? Let me think, child."

"Of what? We haven't time."

"That's roughly two hours from you. Could you tempt it, you think?"

Ambrielle's voice shakes. "I rather come to you."

"Child, you can't. That detective, he's searching. Gather your things. Leave nothing behind, but get something to protect you. And whatever it is, make sure it fits inside your coat. You'll want to be safe."

"Madame, I'm frightened."

"I know, peach. Be strong, though, I'm telling you. You're fit to get by this."

Ambrielle sniffles several times to the phone. "I wish I hadn't left you."

Noticing the distress in the young maiden's voice, Voletta express- es, "I'd hold you if I could, but the phone's all we have. Time's passing quickly. Gather yourself, girl. Be ready to leave."

"Please, Madame, remain hushed to what's happened."

"What of the bodies, dear?"

"Someone will find them. In days or a week."

"Stay alert to the news and be yourself safe. We'll talk again soon."

Ambrielle rushes to her room and gathers her luggage. Luckily, she hadn't unpacked. She slips into her coat, then ties her scarf around her head. Upon an instant she remembers Voletta's advice, carry something for protection. The thought burns her mind.

The maiden chases away to the kitchen and she's hunting through drawers. Following seconds of rummaging, Ambrielle finds an ice pick. She slides it into her pocket where it's wholly concealed, then, turning to her luggage, Ambrielle finds herself thinking it'd be impossible to take all this. I'll need to cut down.

She undoes the latch to one case. Inside, she pulls out her possessions, strewing them along the floor. Unlatching her second case,

Ambrielle fits only her most needed property, stuffing and cramming the carry-all full. After fastening the catch, Ambrielle decides what to do with the remaining trunk and tangibles. Just a mere amount of belongings are cast to the floor, things including toiletries, gowns, heels and slips.

Knowing she and Pensee were about the same size, Ambrielle decides to sneak her slips and nighties into her cousin's drawer, but to do so, she must enter Pensee's room, a challenge she's unsure to attempt. Ambrielle, however, realizes she's already been in view of the body.

Upon entering Pensee's room, Ambrielle takes deep breaths before cautiously returning to the sight of demise.

Upon the floor Pensee lie, a victimized girl whose life had been too soonly arrested. Trying to avoid the dire sight, Ambrielle keeps her head to the air when rushing to the dresser. After tugging a drawer, Ambrielle presses in her intimates. In follow, she shoves the chest back in place.

Not long after, she finds herself returned to the kitchen, eyeing her empty luggage case while concerned where to put it.

Quickly feeling rendered, Ambrielle sinks to the floor. Her eyes gaze the room in low position. Suddenly, to her relief, she spots a solution. Beside the refrigerator Ambrielle's locating a door. Certain it's the basement, she removes herself from the tiled floor, then pro-ceeds to the frame. After switching on the light, Ambrielle takes flight downstairs. She finds the right spot to cast the truck and abandons it to the room.

Knowing her business is done, she retraces her way to the kitchen. Just as her step's surpassing the floor, the anterior door tolls. Concerned for who's here, Ambrielle grabs her case while dispatching ideas.

Meanwhile; outside...

Marin and I stand before the Ladous'. This'll be our first attempt on seeing rather Ambrielle's home, following our return from the grease joint.

My brother redundantly stares upon me. "Won't you let it rest for tonight? You see there's no answer."

"But I'm determined. Someone better open this soon."

"You've rang the bell. No one's come."

"Then I'll ring it again."

"This is a waste, you know it?"

As Marin bickers about my perseverance, I reach to the knob, turn it a twist, then ease myself in.

"Satordi! Satordi, what're you doing? That's breaking and entering."

"Door's unlocked."

"You're crazy, you fool. You'll get us arrested."

"Chill, okay? I've got this. You coming or what?"

Marin narrows his eyes, implying his disturbance. "This isn't how we're to do things."

I advance through the corridor, looking around. The house glows with the brilliance of light, yet I spot no souls neither standing nor sitting. The place is quiet, almost too quiet and, it's disturbing my ease. I'm experiencing dread as an odd sensation caresses my spine. I'm unknown to why it's there, but tiny nails scale my back like climbing spurs, chilling my skin and raising my hairs. Something doesn't set right, or at least that's what I feel. Could this be my intuition warning me? I have yet to know.

I walk farther through the layout while declaring my presence, "This is Detective Beirtempfel. Anyone home? Mrs. Ladou?" I stand my position, but hear no response. "Is anyone home?" Like before, nothing. I turn to my brother. "I'm moving upstairs."

I leave Marin behind as I'm venturing to the upper floor. I'm top- ping the landing when I'm spotting three doors, all wide open and gleaming with light. Advancing the first entry, I find an empty room. I follow on to the next. Peering through an ingress, I notice the body of a girl in her teens. Hastily I rush in and trail alongside her. Presently my hands are upon her, feeling the cold expand from her skin. I needn't be a doctor to claim this girl dead. All indications affirm she's a stiff and has been for some time.

I take in closer view of the body, all the while becoming perplexed and impeded. What I'm detecting has no plausible means to justify its reason; holes; holes, everywhere, and I'm undecided to what might have caused them. Only a preposterous claim would explain this. Maybe a feast among vamps? But, really, do such legends exist? Typically two punctures are found. But this body, she has far too many holes. They're too numerous to count. I decide to call in my brother, see what he thinks. "I have no means to explain this. Anything cross you?"

My brother kneels to his knees to inspect the riddled figure. "Completely drained, she is." Marin takes his pen and is poking upon a scrounger emerging from a breach in the skin. "Parasites. Worm-like parasites, these are."

"Those are veins, brother."

"But pulled through the flesh?"

I explain to Marin, I haven't yet journeyed onto the third room. I take it to mind, the final one must be the main bunk. Maybe there I'll find Ambrielle, either dead or committing some crime.

Upon the mattress I find Mr. and Mrs. Ladou both cast away in eternal sleep. From Reinella's head and, probably on down to her toes, are the same wounds I found on her daughter, their faces, pathetic, even scared beyond awe; and like the previous room, blood's been freed to the wall, floor, and bed. What could have done this? I wonder.

I hear Marin's voice, so, decidedly, I return to him and report the two bodies. "Girl's parents are dead. Seems, too, Ambrielle has gone missing."

"Don't go rushing out just yet." Marin points to the floor. "That stuff, you see it?" My brother refers to candles, a bowl, and cast papers.

"Unless it's important, I don't care to see."

"Oh, I think you'll want to. Seems we've stumbled upon some devilry here."

"Now just a minute. Are you declaring Miss Ladou had been a witch?"

"Could have been, maybe. If not her, then your girl. But definitely something's gone on here."

"Well, don't you be touching none of that."

"Too late."

"It's a crime scene, and you're grabbing evidence."

Marin lays forth his hands with what's in them. "These papers were all I touched."

"Still, it was a stupid move. Give me those. You know we can't leave 'em." I take the spattered papers and force them to my pocket.

"Least read them."

After following his advisory, I look on with shock. "Yria Dane? I know this. Where do I know it?"

Marin reveals, "She was taken in forty-one. Newspapers picked up on the story."

"Ugh-uh. No. That's not how I know it."

I stall in my tracks and begin thinking deeply. I then retreat to my thoughts, to that investigation I did for Guloe in Annecy. I close my eyes while recounting that day when arriving on the foul side of town. First was the man conversing with a devil goat, then one who thought he'd been birthed from a dog. Who was next? Who was next? I rack my brain. Ah, the man preaching some dead woman's rise. What was it he said? What words had he spoke? Think, think, think. Think, damn it, think.

I'm hearing my brother as he tries to interrupt.

"Quiet, Marin. I'm thinking." I brush him off and return to my thoughts. Okay, it was simple. Something simple that coot said. She will rise and, no, that's not right. The dead will rise when, damn it, no. What was it? I give my mind a moment, then acquire the line. The dead will rise, and when she does, a bloodline shall suffer. Could the man have meant Yria? This presumption has me wonder.

I look through the second paper and perceive its last verse. Those who beckon, I'll furnish strain, whence I scout your bloodline's name. It's an eerie coincidence. I feel I know it. I sense a chill upon my spine.

"Satordi? Hey, brother, hey. We can't be found here. We need to get going."

I disregard him. My thoughts retract deeper. There'd been a fourth person, I remember; the crazy woman with wild hair. Yes-yes, I recall. I do recall. She was mental, that lady, and spoke of strange words. Those words, yes, I've heard them and I've seen them just now. I pass to the third paper, searching. Finally, frantically, I have the verse in my sight. It strikes me like I've never been struck before. If Yria Dane be by or here, don't deem on her to disappear. Once the words are spoken right, you've conjured up this spook of fright.

"Satordi!"

"Go, Marin. Leave me in thought."

"Two minutes, brother, and I'm walking out."

Though I love him, he's hectoring me and I'm becoming quite pissed. Forget him, I think. Returning my eyes to the paper, I take note of its final words. And as you breathe your last inhale, mind your kinship's blighted fact, bloodline's pay for kindred acts. "Here we go again with bloodlines," I whisper.

"I told you two minutes." Before leaving, Marin peers toward the body one final time. "Suppose that girl of yours did this?"

"I've wondered."

"What's your plan for the bodies? Leave them to rot?"

"I'll have it handled. Go to the car. Wait for me."

I follow Marin downstairs, but we part separate ways. He takes stride to Sable while I amble the kitchen. I didn't want to tell him, but I'm at loss what to do. With Ambrielle again gone, how the hell will I find her? I haven't any leads. My confidence grows thin and my mind's feeling conquered.

Seems my only choice will have me calling Guloe. I told him before Ambrielle's in Mâcon, staying at a church shelter. Furthermore, I'll have to feed him truths, then force in a few lies. I remove his number from my pocket while I traipse toward the phone. Now may not be the time to call on account of this crappy situation I'm in, but I'm left with no option.

I await his answer, then vocalize my predicament. I go on explaining how Ambrielle's no longer in the place where I said, that she's picked up and left, that she heads for Bordeaux. "Does she have friends or relatives there? I need to know."

"I have a sister, Reinella Ladou. She lives that way."

"Is there anyone else?" "Our niece in Biarritz."

Possibly, could this be where she's fled? I begin taking notes. "Who's your niece should I be forced to go find her?" I scribble a name Guloe gives, Desta Zerbib, along with an address.

After hanging the phone, I'm considering the bodies. I wouldn't want some scab leaving my family to rot had he known they were dead.

I decide I'll call the police in a prank-like fashion. Hopefully by doing this they'll have some incentive to head to this house.

I dial the number, allow dispatch to answer, then give the line brief time before hanging up. I go on to do this four times. Finding my concern's completed, I quest to my Sable. As I'm positioning my rear into the nest of my seat, I tell Marin we're to head to Biarritz, where we'll finish our business.

Chapter Twenty-One

Ambrielle hurries along a darkened street, wagging her luggage beside her. In desperation she peers around, searching frantically for an approaching car. However, instead, the road's idle with traffic. Since vacating the Ladou house, Ambrielle's seen but two lonely cars traveling the retired night, only to pass her pleading thumb. She continues her weary journey hoping to encounter a befriending motorist. Finally, in her pray for help, a young man assists her.

He pulls alongside the curb where he stalls in his car. "Hey. Hi. Where you heading?"

Shyly, Ambrielle acknowledges him, "Biarritz."

"It's about an hour from where I'm going, but I can take you that far." The young man unlocks the passenger door, then respectfully opens it for his maiden traveler. "I'd be happy to take you. What's your name, miss?"

Again, she shyly states, "Ambrielle."

"Nice to meet you. I'm Rui."

Rui is a thirty-year-old bachelor from Mont-de-Marsan, where currently he serves as locksmith. Though charming and mellow, Rui's mildly timid, but this wavering side isn't seen by Ambrielle. Instead, Rui accomplishes everything in his power to make his guest feel at peace. "You got business in Biarritz?"

"Oh, um, I'm making my way to my cousin."

"You plan to stay long?"

"A few days, mostly."

"My parents reside a few hours from where I live. I should be a better son and see them more often. It's been some time since a visit."

"I'm sure they miss you." Ambrielle gleams warmly. "I'm wanting be with my mom and sister later in my travel. I just hope I'll make it to them."

"You sound uncertain, miss."

Ambrielle smiles redundantly. "Things have been rough. Who knows where I'd be if you hadn't picked me up?"

"I was raised a gentleman. I'd never leave any lady on the street, no matter her deal. Some can, but not me."

"I imagine you learned from your father?"

"Well, he always says, could be your mom or sister out there, and my mom would say, could be your wife or sweetheart, too."

"I see they've raised a good man."

Rui begins blushing beneath the streaks of moonlight filling his car. "You're not planning to hitch on through to Biarritz?"

"Mmm, I'm needing to, actually. Hopefully I'll find another driver tolerant as you."

"Well, miss, we'll be in Mont-de-Marsan in another fifteen minutes. Is there some place I could drop you?"

Ambrielle digs into her pocket, feeling around at what little money she has. "Is there a bus station nearby?"

"Not too far off."

"If it's not out of your way, I'd appreciate it."

After a mere eighteen minutes Rui comes upon the desolate transportation stop. Ambrielle removes herself from the car before thanking her driver. Wagging her luggage to a near bench, Ambrielle proceeds to sit. She then waves to Rui, who partakes his departure.

Now alone with the company of night, Ambrielle peers to the street. Moreover, to her drought of knowledge, Ambrielle realizes there's no telling what time the next transferring vehicle should progress to her site. So, unattended, the young woman sits, patiently waiting through each moment's lapse. Following a brief period, Ambrielle grows fatigued and nestles within the confines of her shelter. Another course of time advances when a car's spotted along the intersection. Ambrielle decides to pass her attempt for a ride, feeling it would better suit herself if she waits for the bus.

Thank God Ambrielle chose this decision because the car crossing the traversal just happens to be Satordi and Marin, who, not perceiving Ambrielle, glide by her, unknowingly.

"You believe this, Marin? We've been driving a good hour and have seen less than a half dozen cars."

"Because people are wise and they know to be sleeping. Why not press the gas a little harder?" Marin then looks to me with glossy eyes and yawns sharply. "I'm tired, brother. Remember, I'm not as young as you."

"You have two years on me. That ain't much to fuss about. Jesus, brother, at forty-one, are you really washed out?" I'm in doubt, then again, that's Marin. He's tired too often. "Stretch along. Take a nap."

"Wake me when we're there."

I decide to joke. "I'll leave you sleeping in the car while I attain a room and bed."

"Prick."

"That a boy. That's the first harsh word you've said all night." Marin tweaks his head as it rests on the prop. "Blah-blah-blah. You're disrupting my peace and quiet."

I break into laughter. "Getting feisty now, are you?"

"Quiet. I can't sleep with you crowing."

"How bout getting me a smoke before you're off nodding?"

Marin utters complaint, "Will you hush then?"

"Grab me that smoke." I turn the radio, switch it through channels, then rest it on some mellow tune. After capturing my cigarette, I ease down my window, causing the breeze to pass through the breach.

Meanwhile, Ambrielle remains alone at the station. Hoping, she prays, the bus finds its way to her soon. Should it not, she'll be forced to hitch. She's open to the thought, yet she hates the idea.

Following fifteen minutes, a car pulls up and, behind it, the bus, barely trailing its rear. The car goes to pass, but the bus, applying its brakes, ceases. The gliding door sets motion as Ambrielle travels through. The vehicle's sparse. Seated souls are few and far between. Besides the male driver, four others have journeyed the lonely road. All are wearily dejected and reclined in deflation.

Ambrielle strides to an empty perch where, for the next hour, she'll repose into slumber.

Chapter Twenty-Two

I've just arrived in the beautiful seaside town of Biarritz. What an admirable place, I think. I imagine bringing Deja. How she'd adore it, my darling; the stretching length of beach, the magnificent coastal buildings, not to mention the sight of the Atlantic right here at my face. This resplendent location's become my utopia. Don't think Anncey's not beautiful, it sure in the hell is, but there's something about Biarritz, something which evermore draws my attention to this sea-faring town.

I'm not here to sightsee, unfortunately. Instead, accurately stating, I've business to attend. Sadly, desirable Biarritz will have to hold off till I'm here with my lady, whenever that'd be.

Feeling, though, Marin's missing out on these much acclaimed sights, I decide to wake him. Be him mad if he wants; I only wish my brother to see this.

"Ugh. Eh." He grunts in disgust of my request. "Don't rouse me. Not now."

"Biarritz, idiot. We're here."

Being that it's dark, Marin has no strain when opening his eyes. The instant he perceives this awesome vision, his jowls droop in awe. "Ah, wow. What a town. How bout we pick up and move here?" Marin presses his face to the window. "Annecy could do without us."

"Reminds me of when we were kids. Remember all those summers ago when mom and dad took us to Le Havre?"

"This place, it's spectacular. Le Havre, mmm, no, not so much."

"I meant the ocean, you sag."

"Then make your meaning clear."

I pay him no heed as I say, "How about helping hunt this street?" I hand him my note pad.

"Slick bastard. I see your intention for waking me now."

"Well, you are up."

"At your convenience."

"Easy, brother, don't be bitter."

"That's been done for."

"Huh?"

"Thirty-nine years ago, mom came from the hospital carrying her buttercup. Figured that meant I was getting a sister. Instead, no, there you were."

Quickly I add, "You were two. And well, not very smart. How do you know I wasn't expecting an older sister? Instead, there you were, my ankle-biting brother beast."

Marin barrels in laughter, so deep he starts coughing. "I didn't like you. Really, I didn't. My only way to deal with you was to make you cry."

"You were mean, you were."

"You hadn't been much better. Pulling my hair, you did, then squeezing my nose. And don't make me bring up those times you threw up on me. You deserved what you got."

"I guess between us, we were bad, but you more."

"Be happy we're not in diapers." Marin then shouts as we're passing up streets, "Whoa, hey, that's your road, blockhead. Slow it."

"You could have blared sooner. Now I'm having to turn around."

"Something goes wrong, it's me having to hear it. Been the same since we were kids. I'm not surprised. You're still unchanged."

"Are you nagging, whining, or mewling?"

"Hmm." He smirks. "I guess all three."

"So you're nag-whine-mewling?" I peer to Marin. "You'd have to be. You're a nag-whine-mewler." I grin ear to ear, happy by the formula- tion of my making, though it is comically inane. I'm a Tomfool, I know, I admit it. Ha-ha. *Bon mot.* As you envision, I'm laughing.

Marin snickers mildly. "Guess you'll be submitting those to the dictionary, I suppose?"

"I ought to. I should."

"Sure. Absolutely. But in the meantime, keep dreaming and take that spot before you lose it. Park, brother, there."

I look to the empty gap and wonder, will Sable fit? I'll have to showplace skill by easing her into this confined rift. I hope and pray Sable will meet the requirements. Steadily, I go, gliding back. It takes many tries, but finally I straighten my cruiser along the stone curb.

"That building, that's where we're heading." I point. "Mind the door when opening her. I don't want Sable scratched."

"Haven't scuffed her yet."

"You've known better. Keep on that."

Along the street are expansions of white condos. A multiplicity of tall buildings have been perfectly staged into this stunning context. Whether an apartment or home, I could live here.

Peering to Marin, I find I'm not the only one to be awed by wishful thinking. Almost, it's as if I hear his thoughts, though he's speaking no words. Through Marin's eyes his unremitting yearn is observed. I see his desire, strong like mine and burning fiercely. If he's to relocate and does so first, I'll find myself reduced to depression. I'm eager to benefit one obtainment, one thing to which I'll possess before him, and this dream is Biarritz.

Marin and I head on foot to the address ahead. I'm unsure how Desta Zerbib will react, or if at all she'll allow us in. Should Ambrielle accompany her, I sense difficulty passing even a single step through the door. I'll say now I'm in no mood for doltish cops, nor will I be willing to get escorted away by some goon.

I knock on the barrier, awaiting response; then, looking to Marin, I shake my head. "This is taking too long." I knock again, then again. Though my patience is dissolving, I uphold myself. During my wait, Marin and I acknowledge the raucous now emerging behind the closure. "Someone's there," I say. More clatter's heard. Before long clawing takes to the door, followed by fretful whimpers of a discomfit dog. Its strung-out yowls aren't easily ignored. Quickly I reach the knob. Damn thing better give, and so, following a twist, the ingress gives way.

Directing my eyes to the floor, I see a stripling white pup, no bigger than a cat. It hurries to greet me before I step foot through the frame. My discernment is caught by the garnet-red liquid, to which, at some point, had been misted upon little Fido's fur.

I kneel, taking closer view. "What's this, small fuzz?" By my proximate inspection I find myself all too familiar with this type of bespatter. Not even a fool would consider this sauce. No-no, it don't smell of tomatoes. Turning to Marin, I convey, "I sense dread filling me" The dog rushes off as I ease my way in. "Pray someone's alive.".

Speedily, I reach within my coat, urgently hunting my blade. Along, through the room, I caution my stride, keeping tabs on all corners. As I'm lurking toward the den, I spot it, this sight, and from the view in my eyes, I can't say it's human. I stand beside my brother, spying it, this gruesome thing. Moreover, it has no knowledge we're here.

My most accurate description of it, what I'm seeing, brings to mind the consideration of an unsheathed body. By that, I mean, without flesh. Whatever it is, it's a bloody, glossy mess. Additionally, to further shock, this creature-thing has, well, I wouldn't know what to call them stringy threads? And rhythmically they dance apart from its body. Being so frighteningly taken, I hadn't even noticed the receded torso till now.

Upon the floor's a young woman, mid-twenties, possibly, sprawled along the supporting surface. Above, the unnameable stands. As I'm widening my eyes, its threads strike the deceased one's flesh, bizarrely penetrating her sheath, like small drills. I don't know whether to move or remain still. Then, wondering if the woman could still be alive, I quickly act upon impulse.

Like a trained blade thrower, I pitch my knife. It spins in circular motion toward the unnameable. However, this thing, this creature, whatever, seems to have enhanced hearing as it's detecting low swoops. It retracts its threads quickly, while turning to face me. I credit now the body's female as I'm viewing skinned breasts. Though, whether human, I couldn't say, but now having spotted me, the terror swiftly contorts into a backbend and, grasping its hands around its ankles in an impos- sible position, it takes off, walking abnormally through a wall. Blood ex- pands along the barrier, leaving the distorted shape of its figure. Almost as if the confinement's acting as a sponge, it slurps back the blooded deposit, leaving no profile of the just sighted spook.

Marin screams, "What in Christ's name, brother? What have we seen?"

I stand. My heart pounds my chest as I look to my brother. "Was it real?"

"Like hell it was. Let's not wait around."

"I have to know, Marin. I have to know what that was."

"Don't be a fool. You stay here, you'll die."

"Don't think about budging. I need you. You're helping me."

I rush alongside the dejected torso, and fleetingly, memories of the Ladous' come to mind. These holes I see riddling this vessel. Desta's face and the frightened look which I spot, everything, reminiscent of what's already been seen, and, like them, this girl's been drained. Know- ing, without doubt, I've seen their killer, I can no longer suspect Ambri- elle. Presently thinking, I do ponder, where is that girl? Then it comes to me, I've no time to be thinking conclusions. I distract my thoughts to examine the girl's cousin.

"It's just like the other scene, every bit," I tell Marin as I point to the floor. "The bowl, candles, the oranges."

Marin perceives spattered papers near the body. "Give you one guess what those are."

Knowing what he's about to do, I yell, "Don't touch. Don't touch them."

Of course, bending to his knees, my brother analyzes each leaflet. His eyes then rise to mine. "You got word to explain this?"

"Ironic."

"What should be done with the body?"

"Isn't our concern. Let the cops figure this shit out."

Marin pulls himself from the floor. "She's someone's daughter, Sa- tordi. Anyway, the cops, don't expect they'll get this."

"What do I care?"

"This could be the case of our lives. What we've been wanting! I've said we'd tackle something irregular one day. This is it, buddy."

"We have no training for this. Damn it, Marin, what we saw wasn't human. We don't investigate preternatural phenomena, we don't."

"Then who's left to solve this?"

"Someone — anyone, but not you and me. This isn't for us."

"Why's it not? Just change how you're thinking."

"No, Marin."

"Whatever's happening, it's going on for a reason. Satordi, you know this. We're already involved. Why not let us stick to it?"

I feel my brother's comments have led me to anger. "I should have left you behind."

"Really?" Marin shakes his head. "You're a real piece of work, you know?" He shoves me. "You're the one, and, I'm not mistaken, who asked me to come. Had I known how impossible you'd get, I'd have gladly stayed home. Your problem brother's your attitude. You're a brute and you know it."

"Make yourself invisible, Marin, and close your mouth as you do it."

"Throw your keys. I'm going to the car."

Never will I again say, Marin, tag along. It's best we stay apart. Fighting's no good. I'd rather get along than tear off his head. He's my brother. We're supposed to have the others back, but, at the moment, it's not seeming so. Marin's right, I'm a brute as he termed it. As far back as I remember Marin's never carried a chip on his shoulder; it was me, always me. I'm the street-brawling badass, not him, but enough of that. I've got me a body to deal with, the fourth one today. Suppose I'll do as I did at the Ladous', prank the cops till they come. It's my only solution to getting Desta found.

I lurch through the house, searching for a ringer. I start becoming restless when I can't find a damn one. What was it, did Desta not believe in telephones? How insane and hard to believe. This puts a damper on my scheme. Only place I haven't checked is the bedroom. I almost feel an unwillingness to go because I doubt I'll be finding a phone, but there's a voice within my head telling me, try. Not to ignore my conscience, I head through the chamber. I find myself rummaging throughout Desta's possessions in an attempt to track the tele. Then, wallah, there it is; behold me, it shouts. I imagine yesterday, today even, Desta tugging the phone to her bed, where, currently it's resting.

I bet this girl had a sweetheart, and if I'm right, for fact, she did, she's long dead to him now. As I'm advancing my hand to the ringer, I hear a voice set clamor to an adjacent room. Well, damn. I believe Ambrielle's arrived, finally, and how shall I imply my being here? I can't creep upon her, that'd be an unsuitable approach, possibly resulting in cardiac arrest. Knowing I'm not that deficient, I won't try. Instead,

I walk to the den where I find Ambrielle cast to her knees, crying. I stall between the corridor, and to acknowledge my presence, I simply clear my throat. The reverberation emits the unclogging of phlegm. My affect's ignited Ambrielle's curiosity when her eyes dart my direction. Shock has filled her, I see. My being here's completely unexpected, but as it's so, here I am. "I hadn't meant to alarm you."

Ambrielle's eyes overflow when she shouts, "What're you doing here? Are you following me?"

"It's my job, miss."

"My cousin's dead. Have you no sincerity? Get out!"

"I'm afraid I can't. Even with your orders."

"I want you out. Out. Get out!"

"I've come a long way. I'm not leaving."

She snaps, "How long have you been here? Was my cousin already gone when you came?"

"I imagine she was, or near to it, at least. There's nothing to do here. She's gone."

"I want a moment. I want some time alone."

"Certainly. That's fine. I'll be in the kitchen."

Unheedingly I'm watching Ambrielle through an opened foyer, where my eyes are steadily upon her. She sits alongside Desta, wistfully clutching the dead girl's hand. Her heartache, a sight depressing enough, it's weakened my insides. I'm not one to be emotionally stroked, but this time I'm affected. Simply viewing her throe strains me. I guess, after all, I'm like you; I'm human.

After concluding her time with Desta, Ambrielle makes her way to the kitchen, lingering with melancholy.

"I'm sorry," I tell her, like that's going to perk her, but least she sees I'm concerned.

As if Ambrielle's staring into space, she says, "I hadn't seen her in years. She didn't even know I was coming."

I don't deal with conflict on emotional levels. I never know the proper words to respond. Call me a jerk. All I know is, "It'll be all right," is all I can say.

"But it's not. Death follows me whenever I go."

"It's not something you did. You're not responsible."

"I just think everyone would be alive had I not come to them. How's that not my fault? I'm the cause they're all dead."

"I know what happened in Bordeaux. You weren't the cause and you're not the cause here." I get caught by distraction when spotting Marin meandering to the kitchen. He saunters through the anterior door and is heading my way. Ambrielle hears, but is unable to see him.

After advancing our way, he valiantly questions, "Why're you still here?"

Alarmed, Ambrielle turns around quickly. "Who's that? Who's he?" I say, to calm her, "Don't be frightened. That's my brother you're hearing."

"Haulmier hired you both? But of course. Of course, he did. Why can't you leave me alone?"

My brother regardfully stares upon Ambrielle, but his voice is directed to me. "Found a live one, did you?"

I nod toward the girl. "Meet Ambrielle."

"Your client's daughter?"

I peer to the young maiden. "You'll come with Marin and me. We'll get a motel. You'll have a room, food, whatever you need."

"No. I won't. I can't go." "I'll make that decision."

Ambrielle quickly interrupts, "You can't take me. I'll be dead and gone before you make that attempt."

"Surely you wouldn't."

"You don't know what I've endured from that man. Haulmier's a loose cannon; he's corrupt and disgraced."

"If I listen to your claims, would you consider coming?"

"I have no reason to see him. None. Unfortunately you're determined to take me. I'd need protection. Please, I beg, don't leave me with him."

I nod clearly. "If it's protection you're asking, I'll need to hear your whole story. I have to know what's got you afraid."

Ambrielle looks hesitant, but finally agrees.

"You'll be all right." I look around, knowing time wastes away, "but we need to leave here." I scope my brother. "Get her to the car."

Ambrielle interjects, "Please, Detective, let me stay with you."

"Marin's a good man. You'll be safe. I'll be along shortly."

I trek to Desta's room where I'm grasping the ringer. After my fourth prank via the cops, I hang the tele and simply walk out. I presume they'll come and, maybe so, they're on their way now? Course I'm not sticking around to find out.

Chapter Twenty-Three

It's been an hour after leaving Desta's condo when myself and my passengers have declared our need for food. Having not eaten in a long while, we share a common complaint; the growling ache filling our guts. It's late, so finding a place has proved somewhat inaccessible. I feel I'll find nothing, but then I spot *Le Palais Rose*, a well-to-do restaurant serving a lengthy menu of highly-priced meals. If we weren't so damn hungry I'd have coaxed us to leave, yet being the only place open and, our stomachs in yearn, we decidedly stay. Our orders have been placed and, impatiently, we await our hopefully swelled plates.

During our downtime I converse with Ambrielle, hoping to extract hidden information she might be withholding. "Following our discussion at The Peal and Stem, I'd talked with your father. He's led me to assume you've been lying. Whether you are, I haven't decided."

"I've only stated truths, sir. I've no reason to lie."

"Your father remains firm you'd stolen money. If this is true, you need to confess."

"I've never stolen, not from anyone. I'm not a thief."

I look to Ambrielle's eyes when a feeling comes to me. I trust to accept these words which she's spoken. My gut hankers me to have confidence in what she says and I think I do, but should she be playing me, she's a damn good deceiver, because I'm not detecting a single impres- sion that's led me to doubt.

It's time I take this further. I wish to know how honest she is, or if she is, for that matter. I scheme to test her truths as I dig to her core. An abashing question regarding Ambrielle comes to mind as I dare its attempt. "During your time at The Petal and Stem, you had an abortion?"

She seems taken off by my poll. "Yes. An unwanted child. We'll leave it at that."

I see our food has arrived as I'm about to give question. The waitress says nothing. She's tight-lipped and detached when handing us plates. I distract myself from this unfriendly bitch as I return my leer to the girl. "Whose baby? Someone from the brothel?"

Ambrielle becomes irritated. "I had it tended to. He can never find out."

"Your boyfriend? Some regular? Help me to know, Ambrielle."

"Don't debase me with this."

With prostitution that sort of mishap's likely to happen. She knew prior to her engagements the possibility of spawning a child. So why's she enraged by shame? My only thought comes to mind. "It was that prick, the one from The Easy Way Inn. He got a hold of you, didn't he?"

Clearly the girl's peeved by my probing. I'll let her alone before her temper sparks.

I move to my next inquest. "You want to at least tell me what happened at the Ladous'?"

Ambrielle's quick to respond, "I saw things you couldn't believe."

"Let's compare visions."

Ambrielle shakes her head in confusion.

"Marin and I've encountered something."

"You saw her?" "Who?

What?"

"Yria," Ambrielle says, simply.

I reach to my pocket, pulling forth the papers taken from the Ladous'. I push them across the table in view of Ambrielle. "These seem familiar?"

The young maiden darts her eyes to the text and, observantly, I watch her pupils expand.

"You're frightened. Why?"

"They're dangerous, those papers."

"I only see words."

"No, no. I tell you, they're bad. They bring her."

"Yria?" I ask. "How so? I've read them. I haven't been hurt."

"There's a box. It must be delivered to you."

"Box?"

"The one Pensee got. It had a bunch of weird stuff. Candles and things. We also found papers. Directions, instructions."

"You did what they said?"

"We were only curious. How were we to know what would happen?"

"From where was this box sent?"

"We didn't know. It had no return address. Even the sender's name wasn't there."

"That's a damn shame. It would have helped if we knew who it came from."

"Desta got a box. I saw the items at her house."

Speculating, I ask, "Does someone have it out for your family?"

"I couldn't think. Except for your client, we're good people."

"Then who's this Yria Dane?" "I tell

you, sir, I don't know."

I turn to Marin. "You've got a vague idea. Who was she?"

"Just a woman who went missing in forty-one. Her body hasn't been found. No person resembling her has been seen. She just vanished. She, ah, has a sister. Older, I believe."

"What about her? The sister?"

"The Laroques were from Annecy, was all I knew. Why? You changing your mind on this?"

"Seems possible, I'm considering. Ambrielle's in danger, I think." I look to the girl. "I fear your life's at stake."

"Can you help? I'm alone in all this."

"I don't mean to sound awful, but I'm not sure." I ponder my thoughts, then scan through the text. "You know the name Guillaume Rhoe?" I point to the leaflets.

Apparently, as it states, he's the one who killed Yria.

"I don't know him, no. His name's never been mentioned."

"It's imperative we find out who he is. I think you're related and we need to know how. Unfortunately, the only person I can get answers from, you don't want to see. Regardless, I'll have to go to him. I suppose I'll quiz Haulmier when I find the right entry."

Ambrielle comes to realize, "I'm cursed and so's he. My mom, my sister, we all share the same fate. Sooner or later we'll have that box sent to us. They'll need to be warned, but mom and Holland are away in Marseille. Do I go?"

Now wait a sec. I'm becoming confused by something. If that was Ambrielle's mom in Annecy, how could she be someplace else? "You're sure your mom and sister aren't home?"

"Why'd they be there?"

"I met your mom in Annecy. I've seen her. We spoke."

"Detective, my mother and sister left. I told you that, honestly."

Something fishy's going on. If the woman in Annecy wasn't Yasmina, who the hell is she? "You swear?"

"On my life. Whoever you met. Whoever you saw, she wasn't my mother."

Images flash through my mind. The lady in Annecy had no resemblance to Ambrielle. There's absolutely nothing to compare the two. My thinking then shifts. "The box. It seems to always know where you're heading. Either appears before or while you're in the presence of relatives."

"Pensee received the box while I was there. And Desta got hers before I ever stepped foot through her door."

"That turns my concern to your mom and sister. If they're in dan- ger of receiving a box, there's no way I could permit you to travel. They could be exposed. If you're sincere on ensuring their safety, you'll come with us to Annecy."

"What if that madman talks you down? You'll return me to him."

"You're free to live where you want. I won't stop you. But for the meantime, consider staying with my gal. You'd have a place to stay till you're safe to go freely."

"How'll I know you're not sending me back to that creeping filth?"

"Listen, I'm going to tell you something I told your father. If your involvement with prostitution hadn't been your choice, but was, in fact, his, I could throw him in jail. He could be wearing striped dingy duds. You wouldn't need to worry."

"Could I add to that?"

"You have evidence of other crimes?"

"Rape."

"Haulmier raped you?

"Why do you think I ran? Soon as I arrived in Grenoble I had my abortion. Madame Voletta paid the cost. I didn't have it."

I feel outraged. How could a man rape his own daughter, then get her pregnant? I'm liable to have stabbed him if he was sitting alongside me.

Following a lengthy absence of Marin's infiltrations, he decides to speak. "Did he have knowledge of you carrying his child?"

"No, sir."

I inquire, "Had that been the valid reason for you leaving Annecy?"

"Part. My mother finally found enough courage to get herself and her children away from his house. Within a week she planned our trip to Marseille. She hid every bit of money she had."

"And was she aware of your problem?"

"She knew all about the pregnancy. Mom spoke with Lady Ancelin about getting a loan. She didn't have enough for the train tickets to get to Marseille. Mom said she'd wire Ancelin's money soon as she could."

The day they were to leave, Ambrielle explains she messed up when she'd forgotten her ticket. She said all she could think was go back to The Blossomed Rose and inquire Lady Ancelin, who told Ambrielle she could remain with her till she thought what to do.

"So you hadn't made it to Marseille with your mom and sister?"

"Well, because of my ticket, no, but Ancelin talked with Voletta who agreed to let me stay at The Petal and Stem. Following my arrival, she drove me to the clinic and paid to have the deed taken care of. A few days later I was supposed to leave for Marseille, but then you showed up, sir, and Voletta got nervous."

"Have you kept in touch with your mom?"

"No, sir, but the Bruel sisters have. Ancelin phoned my mother, telling her she was sending me to Voletta's. Following that, my mom was informed I'd be heading to my aunt's, then after a few days I'd be on my way to Marseille."

"I'd really like if you'd consider staying with my gal, Dej. You can call your mom, let her know you're all right and will join her at a later time. Your father will have no knowledge of your presence in Annecy."

"What'll you tell him? You realize he'll be angry I'm not with you." "I'm pretty good at making things up. I'll say whatever I need to keep him off my back."

Marin interrupts, "My brother may be an ass at times, but I assure you, when he gives his word, he means it."

Ambrielle peers to me following my brother's remark. "You promise I'll be safe?"

"That's my priority. But I need to know that you trust me."

"I'll trust you when you've proved yourself true."

"I understand that. Then we'll head out this afternoon. Right now we need rest."

I flag down our god awful waitress. The woman hadn't once come to see if we needed our drinks topped or to ask how's our meal. This place may be classy and all, but the service is a real hoo-ha. I get the check and, to my disbelief, the woman speaks, first time since taking our orders. She tells me she'll take the bill once I'm ready.

Knowing I don't want to stay a moment longer, I say to her, "Wait." I peer at the check as I'm reaching my pocket. "Here, it's exact. Don't come back," I speak in a disgruntled tone.

Of course she says nothing when strolling away. Damn unfriendly bitch. I think. People like her need etiquette lessons. Let her reap what she sows. The aloof broad gets no tip.

"If everyone's finished, I'd like to go. I'm tired and it's late."

Ambrielle reaches to her pocket. "What do I owe?"

"Nothing."

"I have money."

"Keep it for when you go to Marseille." The
girl smiles warmly. "Thank you, sir."

I return my smile. "It's no trouble. Can we get out of here now?"

When trailing to Sable, I throw my brother her keys. "Don't dent my lady. It'll cost you."

"I'm driving?"

"You've got the keys, haven't you? Get us to a motel."

After driving twenty minutes, Marin spies a tattered roadhouse along the main street. "This place all right?" he asks.

"It's probably unkept, but I don't care. I'm just needing a place to crash."

My brother parks before the office. "You going?"

"No, you are. Get two rooms, a single and double. Preferably side by side, if you can." Marin steps from the car when I'm yelling, "Don't let them talk you into nothing fancy."

As Marin goes off, I recline in my seat. "You all right back there?" I ask Ambrielle.

"Just tired, sir. I don't mean to be bringing this up, but you're sure you can help? I'm in fear, Detective. Yria's after my family, it's apparently so."

I mumble, "Finding a way to stop her's the only solution. I'm not sure how that'll be done yet. All I know's I'll need time."

"What is she? Have you given that thought?"

"Many times. Although, I can't say I've accepted an answer. The most bizarre theories cross me. Tell you what, though; before my encounter, I'd have thought beings like her were impossible. Guess it took something strange for me to wake up."

"I suppose we've learned this world contains odder things than we knew." Ambrielle sits silent as her mind races with thought. "Detective, the box, those notes; could have been chain letters?"

"Why would you think that? Obviously chain letters are meant to increase the recipient's luck."

"Well, yes, sir, I know, but what about bad ones?"

"I've never heard of bad chain letters."

"Not until now, maybe? So they hadn't existed in the past; it's not to say they couldn't eventually. Those boxes Pensee and Desta got acted as such, don't you think?"

On contrary of Ambrielle, I'd have to think otherwise. Normally an individual receiving a chain letter acquires that, nothing more. Depicted in their note is simple instruction, usually incomplex direction asking the receiver to write a copy of the text. It's then mailed to another awardee, along with money or tokens, should it be required.

In regard to what Ambrielle spoke, my intellect has me believing no individual, not one, would receive ritual supplies as part of a chain letter. In lieu of the contents, of the box I refer, would alternatively be viewed as instructions for magic.

I abandon my silence to speak. "Nowhere in the letters I've read was anything stating the copying of text. Second to that, there was no direction to any part of that box saying mail it to another person. How do you get your presumption?"

"Strangely, sir, I view it as this. The first of three pages stressed the attempt for action. I see that being no different than a chain letter. Each contain directions. When a person's curious enough, you'll be surprised what she'll try."

"That's what happened with you and Pensee?"

"We gave in to curiosity and followed every instruction. If I could stop that mistake now, I would. Those boxes cause death to all who act upon their direction."

Ambrielle's last statement's filling my mind. I sense the rise of curiosity intruding my thoughts. I turn in my seat and spy the girl lounging comfortably. "Don't take this the wrong way, but how is it you're still alive?"

"Do you not think I've asked myself?"

"Maybe you're lucky?" I turn back in my cushion.

Marin stumps to my car. I know because I see him topple, losing his balance. Lovely, the old lug's gone and done something. He pulls his door as I'm yelling aloud, "That injury better not be serious, 'cause you're out of luck for a first aid kit."

"Idiots and their damn beer bottles. I stepped on a damn piece of glass."

"You bleeding?"

He shouts, "Yes, I'm bleeding," while descending to his seat.

"Get out, Marin."

My brother glares. "God forbid I wouldn't want to wreck your damn car." Marin backs up from the door. "We're in rooms nineteen and twenty. Cruise down, you jerk."

"Detective Biertempfel, I know it's not my business to get in the way of you and your brother, but, sir, he looks hurt."

"Marin's a sissy. He sobs at small sores."

Ambrielle says nothing more as she steps from my car. I watch as she wanders away, chasing my brother. That's real original, chase the whiney fusser. Someone's always bound to.

When I get to him, all Marin will have's a slight scratch. He can whine when his wound's an inch deep. All I want now is a bed to fall back on.

I gather everyone's luggage from the trunk, then take it to door nineteen. I lean into the room already occupied by my travelers when I plop Ambrielle's crap along the side door. As I attempt to step off, Ambrielle calls my attention.

"Might you have something for pain? Sir, your brother, he's hurt." I become flustered. I don't care. I know the dumb lug's okay, but anyway, to show my concern, I ask, "How bad's he?"

"It's not too deep, but it's bad enough. I washed it as best I could. He'll need something to cover it. I can't find anything here. I've looked."

I hadn't thought about walking toward my brother till now. Ambrielle directs me to the bathroom. Inside, Marin's sitting upon the tub with his back to my ventral. "Water won't cut it. You need disinfecting."

"Well, you got something, 'cause I sure in the hell don't?"

"I'll check the car. I might have peroxide."

I step to Sable and unlock her trunk. Then, tossing my belongings around like rags, I find the bottle buried within a small box. In a plastic bag I find strips of torn cloth. I carry the bag along to the room where I pace toward the lavatory. "Get that foot of yours over the tub," I'm telling Marin.

Ambrielle stands in the doorway as I'm attending my brother. "You want me, I'll do it."

"Don't matter who does it, just pour the shit on," my agitated brother's directing.

Turning his foot aside has allowed me to view the incise. Between Marin's first and second toe is an inch-long gash, dividing his flesh. Blooded water runs from the wound and is passing the drain.

"This don't stop bleeding, I'm taking you to the hospital."

I pour peroxide onto Marin as the weakling blares, "Ah. God. Jesus."

Momentarily, I pull back and refrain from flowing the bubble maker over his wound. "Prepare yourself. I'm coming with seconds."

Marin takes a deep breath. "Do it!" He cringes.

I pour the solution over his foot as it's erupting once more.

"Ah. God. Jesus."

"It ain't that bad. Suck it up and dry yourself. I've got you these cloths to wrap on it. I'm going to bed." I exit the room with Ambrielle trailing aside me.

Marin shouts, "Don't lock me out. I haven't any key." "Sir, your luggage," Ambrielle tells me.

I linger near the door. "Run Marin out. You need your rest. Tell him I'll leave the door ajar. One of us will wake you tomorrow."

I step aside to room twenty. After unlocking the door, I step through the frame and, as quickly as I'm in, I fall to my bed. At this moment I couldn't care being in my clothes. I undo my watch and let it drop to the stand. I loosen the shoes from my feet, letting them plummet to the floor. Oh yeah, yap. That's it. This buck's had it. I'm off to bed.

Chapter Twenty-Four

It's the following morning and I'm awakened by the noisy blare of the alarm. Damn this arresting raucous. I hate the sound of rise and shine signals that rouse me from sleep. I look to the adjacent bed and find my brother still conked in his sheets. Inertly the dullard lays, stimulated not by the bellowing clamor filling our room. You've got to be kidding. How's he not affected by this, this beep, beep, beep, beep? In my annoyed choler I slap the dinger, ceasing its fussy furor. It was Marin who'd set the clock, not me, yet I'm the one awakened. Dissatisfied my brother's not up, I conjure an evil plan sure to raise my snoozing bunky.

I remove the clock from the stand and place it near Marin's ear. All I'm left to do is swat the button and the thing can blare. Ready, set. I push the catch. Suddenly it goes off in Marin's sound sensor with the blatant pitch of bleep, bleep, bleep, bleep. His attention's now kindled.

"Christ, Satordi. You've damaged me. Get that thing away."

"You'll live. Pull your ass up."

Marin grieves to his pillow, "Another hour, please."

"I want to be gone, so up with you. Up!"

After jumping into my clothes and brushing my teeth, I head next door. I knock upon the barrier loudly enough to rouse Ambrielle. After a brief wait, the young maiden greets me.

"We're rolling out soon. You be ready?"

"I'll start getting dressed."

"I'm next door. Come knock when you're through." I trail back to room twenty. "Marin, where're you at?" I then spy the bed. "That better not be you relaxed in those covers."

Suddenly I realize my eyes were mistaken when the bathroom door opens and Marin comes out. "Gees, brother, can't a man take a piss?"

"I'm taking the luggage. Got anything you need to throw in?" Marin shakes his head, so I toss him our key. Ironically the plastic top piece has landed perfectly between his fingers. "Don't forget Ambrielle's, and walk the keys to the office." I remember to say as I'm on my way out, "Don't close this door. Hey. Okay?" I depart with our luggage, carrying it to Sable.

Rather than casting our things to the trunk, I situate them neatly. Behind me I hear Marin at Ambrielle's door and, from her, he gathers her key, then trails to the lobby.

Ambrielle remains at her door. She catches a glimpse of me through the frame before deciding to stroll toward my cruiser. Alongside her she schleps her luggage. She hasn't the muscle to be carrying it. It's a poor sight, I realize.

"Let me get that," I offer.

Ambrielle smiles with sincerity.

"If that's it, you can get into the car."

I now see Marin as he's holding the news. "I grabbed us a paper. You don't have to thank me."

"Flash through. See if the Ladous' made in there." Marin consults the articles.

"Keep looking. I've got to get my watch." Seconds later I return. "We set? Everyone got their shit?"

Marin nods and is pointing to a headline as I'm shutting my lips. The caption holds my attention and silently I'm reviewing its write-up.

> *Late yesterday three bodies were found at*
> *a residency in Bordeaux. The victims of*
> *this blight were immediate relatives.*
> *Among the deceased was Odo Ladou,*
> *forty-four, his wife, Reinella Ladou,*
> *forty-one, and the couple's only child,*
> *Pensee Ladou, seventeen. Their cause of*
> *death is currently unknown. With a lack*
> *of information, authorities contest to*
> *disclose any presumptions of what may*
> *have taken place at the home. The only*
> *response by the commandment in charge*
> *was the scene had been unsettling and*
> *freakish. The crime had been tipped off*

*by an unknown caller. Whether this person
has anything to do with this atrocity,
authorities don't know or aren't saying.*

Following my completion of the text, I scan through the paper, hoping to find any exposition concerning the death of Miss Desta Zerbib. To my astonishment, no story's shown. Okay. Give it till tomorrow, I think.

I raise my eyes to the rearview and spot Ambrielle. "Don't know if you care to or not, but there's an article of your family." I slip it behind my head to Ambrielle, allowing the decision to be decreed in her mind.

My wheels hit the road as I pull from the parking lot. We're about to embark another long day.

Chapter Twenty-Five

My passengers and I've been on the road at least five hours since leaving Biarritz. Except for the occasional break to relieve our bladders and stop for food, we've remained within Sable. During most of the drive my commuters have been snoozing quite soundly. Like the hours before now, Marin and Ambrielle are again both asleep.

I'm alone to myself, my thoughts, and the freedom to turn on my radio. No longer can I contend with the silence. It makes me feel crazy. So to save myself, I'm turning the receiver on low and unwind to the songs of today imagining, decades from now, these tunes will be classics. They'll remind people of what music really was in the time of rockabilly. Way down the line, like many generations before it, this will be an era once lived. Though, it's barely fifty-two, only dual years into this decade, I can see myself enjoying what these years have to offer.

I light a smoke and roll down my window. A humid breeze is gusting through Sable, stirring my stolid drifters. "Well, finally, I was beginning to grow bored without company."

Marin stretches. "The blowing wind cast your smoke to my face."

"That's your complaint?"

"Had I complained, the clamor of my voice would have been set at your ear. Sort of like what you'd done with the alarm this morning."

I grin ear to ear. "Why didn't you punch me?"

"Wouldn't want that ugly mug getting uglier." "You wouldn't have had the nerve to hurt me."

"Maybe not punch, but I kick."

"But you didn't." I glance to the rearview and see Ambrielle. "Be glad you don't have a brother." She returns a smile through the mirror. I'll take that innocent acknowledgment as yes.

Before returning my gaze to the road, a heedful sensation directs my eyes to the fuel gauge. Thank God I'd done this. I'm well below half a tank. Soon I'll be on fumes. I see an upcoming sign. Five miles more and we'll be in the next town. There we'll stop for gas and stretch our limbs a short bit.

Chapter Twenty-Six

It's 9:10 when we've returned to Annecy. I do miss Biarritz, but I'm content being home. I'm exhausted after succeeding an eight and a half hour drive and I have nothing more than rest on my mind. I plan to drop Marin home. Knowing she's usually there, I pray Deja will be attending the kids and Cerissa. I've missed my future spouse. It hasn't been long, but I'm eager to return to her arms.

I stretch along Marin's street, searching for a place to park. I spy an opened space four cars from his house and decide to pull in.

"You got a few minutes to visit?" my brother asks.

"I'll swing through a minute." I find Ambrielle in the back. "Come on, let's introduce you to everyone." I watch her face droop, so I'm eas-ing her abraded mind while luring her from the car. "No need to feel sheepish. You'll fit in just fine."

My brother's first to the door, yelling ridiculous speech to his wife, "Cerissa," he shouts. "The love of your life's returned. Come give me warm welcomes." But the arrival greeting his ululation are his two tiny moppets.

Running to his legs, Paien and Zuri scream in unison, "Daddy's home! Daddy's home!"

"How're my rascals?" Marin grasps Zuri, while keeping an arm around Paien. "You been good squirts, tell me?"

"Daddy!" Zuri teehees.

"What's that, giggles?" He begins chasing her side. "The tickle monster's getting you!"

Zuri blares in cackle. "Daddy! Daddy, that tickles!" She continues crowing.

"What about you, Paien? I think this monster's got an eye on you!"

Laughing aloud, he runs to avoid his dad's twittering fingers.

Marin releases Zuri before taking off through the room. "Paien? Paien!" He spots the child hidden behind a recliner. "Hey, tadpole, how do you expect I get back there?"

The adolescent laughs. "You're not supposed to!"

"Well, I'll say. You're a bit out of reach, son. Say, where's mom?"

"Upstairs, gathering our jammies."

Marin's daughter walks to her father, tugging his trousers. "Daddy. Daddy, who's the pretty girl with Uncle Tordi?"

"Well, baby, that pretty girl's Ambrielle."

"Oh." Zuri tugs her father toward her, whispering, "Is she going to replace Aunt D?"

"No-no, course not, baby. She's not taking her place. She's needing help from your uncle is all."

"Well, then, that's okay."

Marin begins to laugh. "That's honest. Come on, let's have you say hi." Marin strolls his young daughter along, while Zuri stares keenly.

Sauntering slowly, Miss Biertempfel paces toward Ambrielle, then is standing below her. "I'm Zuri. I'm seven. How old are you?"

"Seventeen," Ambrielle announces, shyly.

"Want to be friends?" Zuri questions.

"I would."

"Do you have sisters and brothers that'd want to be friends?"

"I have a sister, Holland. I bet you'd get along."

Zuri's eyes widen as she grows with excitement. "Really?" She then inquires boldly, "Why isn't she with you?"

"Holland's with our mom."

Zuri smiles warmly. "Can I meet her?"

"Hopefully."

"I'd like that." Zuri lightly chews her upper lip. "I have a brother. He's older. His name's Paien. He's nine. That's him over there." Zuri points. "He's rotten, but mommy and daddy love him."

Ambrielle was unprepared for the nutty remark. "Rotten, but why?"

Zuri's quick to offer her comment, "Paien's a boy. He's rotten and smelly. Want to know a secret? It's about him." Zuri gets on her tiptoes and whispers to Ambrielle, "He stinks. He farts like my dad and has smelly feet."

Ambrielle barrels with laughter.

"Do you like my Uncle Tordi? He's smelly, you know, because he's a boy, but he's nice. He don't fart."

Ambrielle peers to me, cracking a smile. All the while she continues to speak with Zuri, "He's not too smelly."

Ambrielle doesn't know I hear, so I decide to tease and joke, "That ain't what Zuri thinks."

Ambrielle blushes, but regains her composure.

I peer at my niece. "I still smell better than your dad, don't I?" Zuri flares her little nostril while her cheeks puff with laughter. "Say, squirt, had Aunt D stopped in?"

"Yeah. She's here." "Where, kiddo?"

"Upstairs. She has a toothache. Mama put her to bed. Want me to wake her?"

"Let her rest."

"Can't I just tell her you're here?"

"Whisper then, but don't be loud."

While hastening the stairs Zuri runs into her mother, who's wearing a satin robe tinct in red. "Whoa, whoa, baby, slow it down. Why the rush?"

"Daddy and Uncle Tordi. I've got to get Aunt D!"

"Zuri, no. Aunt D's resting."

"But Uncle Tordi said I could."

"You be out then after. And mind your scamper. I don't want you falling. And put on your jammies."

"Awe, momma, must I?"

"Mind your mother and don't fuss."

Marin finds Cerissa as she descends the last tier. "There's my gorgeous honey."

"Ah, dear, how are you?"

"Tired, definitely."

"Mmm, too bad. We could have made up for lost time." Cerissa tassels his hair.

"Did I say I was tired?" Marin pecks his wife's lips. "I slept enough on the way here."

"Then don't conk out when I need you."

"Not me, cookie. Get the kids to bed. I'll toss my brother out."

Cerissa spots Ambrielle as she trails toward the room. "You didn't say we had a guest." Walking to the living room, Cerissa acknowledges, "If I'd known we had company I'd have dressed properly. I'm Cerissa," she tells Ambrielle.

I speak up and respond, "I see you've met Ambrielle, my client's daughter."

Cerissa tells the timid maiden, "How rude these men, never regarding a guest. Would you care for a drink? Something cold while you're here?"

"Yes, ma'am, please."

Cerissa nods, then spots her son in a sofa chair. "Why aren't you upstairs? It's bedtime, young man."

"But, mom."

"Paien, now. Upstairs with you. I'll be up to tuck you in."

"What about Zuri?" he complains.

"She's already gone. Now go. I'll be up in a moment."

"Awe," he grumbles. "I'm not tired."

Cerissa raises her brow. "I don't care if you aren't."

"Mama, please, can't I stay, just for five minutes?"

"You want me calling your father to race you up them stairs?"

"No."

"All right, then. Tell everyone goodnight." Cerissa turns around. "Satordi, you want a drink?"

"Always," I tell her.

"It'll have to be whiskey. I'm out of pommeau."

"Damn Marin, he drank the last, didn't he?"

Cerissa smiles before traipsing the kitchen.

Marin sights me and comes my way. "Slam it quick. Cerissa wants to play," he whispers.

That's Marin's way of saying get the hell out. "All right, all right," I relay.

"Make yourselves scarce. Get out in good time."

I know nothing more than to smile and poll, "Haven't had any hanky-panky lately?"

"Ha," he expresses. "It's been a long while."

"Well, sir, I won't stand in your way."

"Good words, brother."

Upon the stairs I spot Deja, looking worn. Her face appears dull, without color. In her hand's an ice pack filled with chilled water. "Zuri said you'd been sick. I'd ask how you're feeling, but I don't think you're much better."

"I'm not. It's still achy. I'm ready, Satordi. I want to go. I feel I've got fever."

"I'll get you home shortly."

"Would you, please?"

"Yeah, honey, sure. I'll put you to bed." As I'm answering, Cerissa comes with my drink.

My lovely but ill tootsie rests her head on my shoulder. "Honey, please, take me soon. I really feel bad."

"I promise, soon. Let's get you sat down."

By then Deja spots Ambrielle. "Who's the girl?"

Looking to speak boldly, I throw down my whiskey. Whoa. There's the kicker. "Dej, I've ah, got a favor to ask. Could she stay with you, would you mind?"

"What? You haven't even said who she is."

"A client of mine who's got some troubles. Please, kitten, let her stay with you awhile. I wouldn't have asked, but it's important." I take Dej by her hand and politely introduce them. "Ambrielle, this is Deja, my gal."

My love stretches her hand and greets the young girl. "It's nice to meet you." Through her pain Deja smiles as she tries to be genial. "Satordi says you're needing a place to stay?"

Softly, Ambrielle replies, "Yes, ma'am."

"If you like, I have a guest room."

"Thank you. I appreciate your offer. Whatever you need, chores, cooking, I'll do."

I interrupt the conversation, "I think it's time we scoot along." I turn to my brother. "Gather your wife. Carry her on up to your chamber."

My brother smiles, embarrassedly. "No need you go blast it." I return a cheesy grin. "I'll be seeing you. Enjoy your night."

It only takes moments before I'm arriving at Deja's. She lives no more than two blocks from my brother. "I've got another run, so I'll be dropping you off."

"Oh?"

"I'll swing in tomorrow, see how things are."

"You won't be back tonight?" Deja asks.

"It'll be too late."

"Why am I not surprised?" Deja steps from the car. "I'll just see you whenever."

"Dej? Ah, come on." I slap my hand on the wheel. "Not a hug? No kiss?" I pull from my car, raising my hands to the air. "Sweetheart?"

"Satordi, I'm tired. I don't feel good. Please, let me go in."

I hurry alongside the curb to stand by my lady. "Don't think me an ass. You know I've got work." I kiss her gently upon her crown. "Rest, okay? Tomorrow you'll feel better."

I grab Ambrielle's luggage from Sable's trunk and carry it to my beloved's door. I then peer upon the young woman before leaving. "Make yourself comfortable, all right? I'm ah, I'm heading to the tavern. Haulmier and I have some talking to do."

"Mmm." Ambrielle grows concerned.

"He won't know you're here." I hand her the trunk. "Whatever you do, don't stay awake worrying. Get some sleep."

After the door closes, I head on my way. Shortly I'll be at Frenchman's, conversing with Haulmier, who, I'm led to believe is a filthy, rotten scab. Should I catch him in lies, I'm liable to whack him. I'm in no mood to be led a fool. In prior days he may have falsified claims, but let that bastard see I won't go for that now.

I head into Guloe's, composed and walking tall. The atmosphere's always the same and so are these stiff-necks, these men all apprehended by an immediate group of caroused souls. Quietly they converse. They pay me no heed. I hail noiselessly; it's how I like it. Without them noting my stride, I'm detecting no troubles.

As I'm moving to the counter, the drink slinger spots my advance. Nudging his head, Artus affirms, "You're alone."

"That's the reality. Where's Guloe? He around?"

The man picks up the dialer, pushes some buttons, and, in a sealed adjacent room, I'm hearing a toll. The bartender relays several words as the receiver picks up.

I'm now directed to the room where I heard a phone ring.

"Knock once, go in," the barkeep's commanding.

I do as advised. Stepping into the room I see Haulmier at his desk. The place is small, with a meager window behind the jerk's back. Beside the work desk, there're two bookshelves and an extra seat for sitting. Not being able to contain myself, I hear a sarcastic set of words release from my mouth, "Nice space."

"It's not much, you see, but it serves its purpose. Have a seat, Detective. What news have you for me?"

I manage my brain, determining where to start. I then settle my thoughts. "Have you spoken with your sister recently?"

"Reinella? Well, no, but I've tried phoning her. Why?"

Hmm. Mmm-hmm. Guloe has no discernment. I see I'm the one who'll convey the unfortunate. "Well, as unsought as this is, I must make a report."

"Oh? And what's this you must tell me?"

"It's obvious you don't know."

"Has something gone on?"

"Mind you, I dislike being the bearer of bad news here." I don't restrain the truth, be it crude or direct. I'm just stating situations. "But Reinella was murdered along with her family."

Shock fills the lunkhead's face. "But how did this happen?" Guloe takes a belabored breath. "Are they really all dead?"

"I'm afraid so."

"Well, how? Here you are in my presence, telling me my family's slain. What man could have done this? Tell me you found him."

"Maybe."

"Maybe? No, I want yes. Not maybe. Not no. You tell me you've found him."

"Someone was seen."

"He's been arrested, though, right?"

"No, sir. It's impossible, by me or anyone."

"You could have done something. Why didn't you get him?"

"She took off. Got away."

"A woman? You're telling me a woman's responsible?"

I decide to pull the spattered papers from my pocket. "I found these by your niece." I toss them to Guloe. "There're two names. Yria Dane and Guillaume Rhoe. Who are they?"

Haulmier reads the papers, then looks to me dully. "Guillaume Rhoe had been a cousin of mine."

"Had been? What is he, dead?"

"Yes, killed during a boating accident in forty-one. It was quite tragic, his death."

All right, seems that's cleared. "Then you care to explain Yria Dane?" "I can't, no. I have no idea." He returns his gaze to the papers.

"So you never met the woman?"

"I haven't a clue who she is."

"Well, I consider she's someone we need to look at. Whoever she is, she's scouting your kin."

"Then, by God, Detective, find her. You've got rights being who you are. Take it upon yourself to stop this."

"It's out of my hands. The woman's dead. I don't deal in corpses."

"Nonsense. You're off your rocker. You're insane. Listen to yourself. Clearly, you've been drinking."

I become angered. "Do I look smashed, tell me? I'm completely sober, I'll have you know."

"I'm not badgering you. I just want the truth."

"You want to speak of truths? Then tell me the real reason why Ambrielle left."

Guloe sits firm. "We've gone over this."

Yeah, figured I'd hear that. I'm starting to feel indignant. I'm intolerant to the words this flake's directing. "I've enough information to put you behind bars."

"You're threatening to throw me in jail? But for what?"

"Oh, don't play me those words."

"Apparently you're thinking you have something on me."

"Ambrielle informed me of the rapes. And don't say you hadn't done it."

"My own daughter? Is that what you think? Well, I'll have you know you're one perversely sick man. How dare you come into my business, alleging me of such disgusts."

"Defend yourself. Go on."

"Where is that conniving fabricator? That wicked child shall be punished."

"Nah-ugh, no," I respond. "This damn goose chase you've had me on's returned nothing. Wherever your daughter's gone, I don't care. I suppose it's clear. Ambrielle has no desire to be found. I'm done. I've gone all over for you. I'm through."

"You can't quit."

"I just did."

"Seeing I can't count on you, I'll hire someone else."

"You do that then, 'cause like I said, I'm through."

"Least tell me you checked Biarritz."

"No one there except Miss Zerbib and her little dog."

"And you were allowed to check the house?"

God, this guy just doesn't quit. "Yes, I was allowed entry. I searched all the rooms. I didn't come across your daughter. You can go yourself and see."

Haulmier stares me down with beady eyes. "That's it? You've officially removed yourself from this?"

I glare back, tired, but pestered with gall. "It's not my intention to be endlessly searching. I'm not up for that. Whatever you do now, that's your call." I step from my seat.

"Are you so eager to leave, you don't want your pay?" Guloe shoves forth an envelope. "Take it. Be gone."

I'm nodding. Feels good to get out, but before leaving, I'm filled with a remark, "Oh, the woman you say's your spouse, she's not your wife, but I'm sure you know."

"What kind of fool are you? You're meddling in my life?" Guloe half grins. "Go, Detective. Go to my home. My wife will be there. Have a cup of tea. Chat. Stay awhile. I won't stall you. When you're through, come back."

I mosey to the door with my back to Guloe and shut the entree before I creep through the bar.

Yasmina Guloe. Haulmier claims she's home. I believe I'm about to go see. Is the woman an imposter? Surely so, but to know accurately, I'll take Ambrielle. By the time I've reached her I'll have figured some scheme so the girl isn't seen.

Time to cruise back to Deja's. Told her, I know, I wouldn't be back. What a misinformant am I? Oh, well. I've never claimed to know the future. I just journey on. Destination known, destination unknown, that's how it goes, so I'll settle with that.

I arrive at the steps of Deja's chateau and, not wishing to knock or toll the bell, I ease a key from my pocket. I saunter in where I find my drift on the second floor. Quietly as a mouse I stall before my darling's room. Giving way to the ingress, I study my sleeping dame, making certain she's okay and recessing with comfort. Once concluding her tranquil state, I pull the door, then step away to the guest room.

Inside, Ambrielle lies hushed in her bed. I feel bad having to wake her, but I must. Foolishly, I stand, considering how I'll not jolt her by the sight of my presence. Pondering my approach, I heedfully realize it's probably not possible. Merely I'll startle her, causing whatever shock I may. I'm praying I don't force her reaction into wanting to beat me.

Taking my chances, I whisper lightly as I roam toward her bed. "Ambrielle. Don't be deranged now. It's me, Satordi."

Her response snaps quickly, though I hadn't figured it. I imagined having to put my hand on her shoulder where I'd rouse her from somnolence. I'm seeing now it's no option.

She rises, keeping the sheets tucked beneath her. "Sir, is that you?"

"Sorry. I'm sorry to wake you, but I need you dressed now. I've somewhere to take you."

"It's the middle of the night, sir. Can't your implore wait till morning?"

"It can't. I need you to identify the woman at your house. We'll need to do this now while it's dark."

"What woman?"

"Come with me. Come on."

"This isn't some scheme to leave me there, is it?"

"Surely not. No. But I'll need you to hurry."

I leave, closing the door behind me. Downstairs, I tread to the living room where I proceed to the couch. Ambrielle appears after no more than five minutes. "We'll keep this quick. Ready?"

Chapter Twenty-Seven

Ambrielle's directed us to her father's and, in thinking, I know to hide her before I'm to approach the front door. I direct her between thick shrubs and towering bushes, where I have her settle before the house. My plan's to conceal her, to keep her low-key and, however, not seen. Upon her stance, Ambrielle's allowed enough crevice to spy through the hedges.

I carry myself to the porch where I'm trying to develop proper dialogue. Unfortunately, it doesn't come to me easily. I haven't a clue what to say. My only thought's to make this play smoothly. I step aside the door, allowing Ambrielle sufficient sight. After a much needed breath, I rap on the frame. The imposter then shows. I keep her stalled at the entree, all the while hoping Ambrielle's seeing clearly.

The woman peers to me, recollecting my image. "Detective Biertempfel, isn't it?"

"Yes, you remember?"

"Of course. We'd spoken a few days ago." The spoof then steps through the frame and closes the door. "Is there something I can do for you?"

"Well, I'm here to let you know my attempts to finding your daughter have now been defeated. After some retrospect, I've decided to relinquish the case. Understand, please, I've done all I can."

"Is my husband aware?"

"I've just come from the tavern."

"Could he not persuade you in continuing? I'm sure you realize we want our daughter."

"This was a personal decision, ma'am. I ask you respect that. I've given my best, but through my efforts, I've gotten nowhere."

"I can't say I'm receiving of this. It's not what we wanted."

"That's why I've come. I wanted to apologize."

"Least you're respectful enough to do so. I suppose I'll have to accept your decline. Very well. Thank you for coming."

"Ma'am." In respect I nod, then tread from the porch.

Ambrielle creeps along from behind the bushes as she comes into view.

As we're heading to Sable, I ponder, "You get a good enough look at her face?"

"I'm sure that was Azure Cashlousier. Her twin Sylvie Molière owns The Spice Box."

"How do you know the woman's Azure, not Sylvie?"

"The beauty mark near her chin. Sylvie doesn't have one."

Ambrielle's right, the woman had a mole. "Who's Azure's husband? Is she married?"

"Not that I've heard."

"But Sylvie, she is?"

"Her husband's Corbin Molière of Molière's Auto Shop."

I take this all down in my scratch pad. "I may need to speak with them. For now we'll focus on Azure. You have any idea why she'd be posing as your mother? Are she and your father in cahoots? Help me, Ambrielle, I need some info. Do you know anything of this woman? Who she is? Think, girl, you must know something."

"I've caught Haulmier conversing with her several times on the street. Eventually I found out she was Sylvie's sister. She and Haulmier were friends from way back. How long he's actually known her, I don't know."

"Not saying you do, but you know where she works?" I'm asking as I pull before Deja's.

"I've heard rumors was all. Sketchy ones. Supposedly she worked at a clinic."

"That's it? That's what you know?"

"Will you be inspecting her?"

"Eventually. My priority right now's Yria Dane."

I notice movement upon the street as I peer through my windshield. On the sidewalk's some stewed scum staggering along his way. An unease creeps over me. I don't like the looks of him. If I'm any kind of man I won't allow Ambrielle to stride solo. I walk the girl toward the chateau, making sure she gets inside.

Approaching me in his wobbling fashion, the man comes upon me, mumbling speech, "It's begun, hasn't it? She's extracted blood and taken life."

I try to ignore the man as I step to my car, but insistently he chases me.

"I knew him, her murderer. Knew him well, I did."

"Who're you to be talking to me? Brush off, you drunken fool."

"It's me, Detective, me. Ghislain, remember?"

"What the hell do you want?"

"I can help. But I'll need your trust first."

"You're a street rat. What trust could you get?"

"I oversaw this town as did he. I was somebody once."

"You're a crazy loon. Go home to your streets." I ease to my seat and pound Sable's lock. Outside, Ghislain stalls beside my door, still rambling his words. Angered, I yell, "Move, fool, or you're going to get squished."

"Give me a chance. Listen! Give me a chance. I have the answers, Detective."

"I don't associate with street scum. I'm pulling out, so move your ass."

"Detective, please. Detective. Detective! Please, I'm begging you, listen!"

"I run you down, you'd be one less lout on these streets." I pull off, screeching Sable's tires. Screw that man and his speech. He's no one. One day someone will off him and Ghislain will be found in a dump- ster, deader than a bloated coon, that foolish creep.

I'm on my way home. The hour's late, my eyes are heavy, and I've been yawning like a drowsed chap and am ready for slumber. I'll start the day fresh tomorrow when I trudge from my bed and drift to the shower.

Chapter Twenty-Eight

Mornings; I hate them, but I've got to do work. I arrived at The Bier-tempfel Brother's business roughly twenty minutes ago, sucking down coffee and munching on biscuits. I've been lounging in my chair, stag-nantly sitting. I can't seem to kindle my senses. As much caffeine as I've had, I figured I'd be pumped on energy, but not so as I find myself stalled, doing nothing. My day can't continue like this. I must get on track, not later, but now. I've wasted time, an act which can no longer succeed me. It's work time; time I start doing.

I look around my desk, hunting for a phonebook. I search the top, then take to drawers, unceasingly questing. I'm sure I had one. I know I did. Crud. Where'd the damn thing vanish? Unbelievable. When I need something, I don't see it. Hopefully Marin's got one, so I tread to his desk.

Through his drawers I go, tearing them apart. I flop stacks of pa-pers and other crap onto the counter as I frenziedly quest a directory of numbers. Ah-ha, yap-yap, found it. Bless Marin for having this, 'cause I sure in hell didn't. At my side I carry the book to my station. All right, I'm looking for Laroque. Orisia Laroque. Let her be listed. I scan the column of names, then come upon hers. Time to extend my call. I draw forth my ringer.

The line resounds as it breaks in my ear. After four rings a woman picks up. Kindly, she answers with a soft voice and speaks. I explain who I am, then inquire whether she's the sister of Yria. To my happi-ness, I'm descrying her answer.

Without second thought, I offer assistance to help find her sister. Orisia beholds my proposal and is agreeing contently.

"The police," she says. "Those men, them fools, they never helped me. They closed the case because they couldn't get any leads."

"Well, I'd be glad to do all I can. Eleven years of not knowing your sister's fate is agitating, I understand. You need answers. You need clo-sure. And if I can–"

"You don't need to say it. It's been too long, these years. One more, I'd go insane, if I hadn't already."

"I'm sure, Miss Laroque, you're completely together. Nonetheless, I acknowledge the amount of stress this has put on you."

Orisia breaks down. "It was no one but us." Orisia sniffles when crying to the phone. "My sister and I were the closest friends, and now I don't have her."

Her words bring me grief before I jump into question, "Would you be free now or maybe in a bit? I'd like to swing by."

"Come when you'd like. I've nothing to do."

I agree to leave soon as I'm hanging the phone. "Whatever you have pertaining your sister, have it handy. A diary, pictures, articles, whatever." After closing my statement, I head to the door, then lock it behind me.

I set off, cruising through streets. What a perfect day. The sun hanging high sends warm rays upon me. After eight blocks I come to Orisia's. I spot her humble chateau, a paltry building, not over enormous, nor fit for a queen. Instead, it's ideal for a couple who's raising a lone child.

The place is pretty; nicely kept, with trimmed lawn and stationed flowers. Everything's abloom in lustrous color, even the Kel- ly green grasses.

I park Sable and am now treading toward the hearth. I stride upon the only step when finding myself graced by the polite smile upon Orisia's face.

"Detective Biertempfel, hi. I appreciate you coming. I'm Orisia."

Va-va-voom, what a looker. I impulsively scan her while remaining discreet. Tall, she is, and petite, with brown hair and dark eyes. Like a giddy schoolboy I feel a crush coming on. Settle yourself, or I fear I'll start blushing. Don't just stand here, you fool. Pull yourself together. Say something, man. "My pleasure. It's nice to finally meet you, Orisia."

"I'm glad you could come. I've made us coffee. Let us go sit."

I trail behind, watching the brim of her dress as it wavers the air. My eyes then fall to her shapely, slender ankles as I'm watching her walk. What're you doing, idiot? You've got Dej. No room for another.

Refocus. Refocus! But I find that I can't. "I understand you go by Laroque. Are you not married?"

"No, sir, Detective. I've had many suitors, but never a spouse. I suppose it's too late in my life."

"Why say that? I'm sure many men would enjoy you as his wife." Oh, I caught myself. Was that too forward? I wasn't referring to myself, but she could count me on board.

She laughs, then hands forth my coffee. "I'm raising an eleven-year-old child. What man would want that?"

Her response stuns me. I hadn't figured Orisia to have a child. I now find myself heedfully gazing the room, searching for pictures. On a mantle I spot the black and white photo of a little girl graced in a gilded frame. Her hair's fair blonde, long and flowing, and her eyes, either faded blue or light green. "Your daughter's pretty."

"Mira's a sweetheart. She's inherited her mother's beauty and heart. She's Yria's only child. My beloved niece."

A turn of events. This is a turn of events. Mira's not Orisia's, but instead she's her sister's? I hadn't seen this coming. This development has undoubtably overcome me.

"Mira was just a baby when my sister went missing."

"How is she, the child?"

"Just as lively as any. She's a good student. Makes A's and B's. Is well liked. Has many friends. My sister would be proud."

"You want to talk about Yria?"

"How loved she was by me and by others. At seventeen she was happily married. Yria and Matthias had trouble conceiving, but by twenty-one she was graced having Mira." Orisia stops a moment to dab her moist eyes. "Three months before Yria's disappearance, Matthias was killed in action. He'd been in the army seven years and was proud to be serving. My sister hated it. Devastated by her loss, Yria sank to depression."

"Well, of course, I imagine."

"Tragic, it was, certainly. And Yria's sadness, unbearable. She wouldn't leave home, no matter how I begged her. She stayed dressed in her husband's shirts. Said it gave her comfort. Yria longed for Matthias, she did. Said he lived in his clothes, but I knew it'd been his essence she smelt. To her, that's what kept him alive."

"Had you tried helping her?"

"Endlessly. We shared the same friends. Hung with pretty much the same people. We made constant attempts to lure Yria from home."

Orisia eventually explains there'd been two men who cared for Yria in their circle of friends. One was a childhood sweetheart she once dated by the name of Basile Devereux, the other, a familiar name I've seen and heard, Guillaume Rhoe. My interest heightens. Orisia had known Guillaume, but not just known him, she saw him, they spoke. Maybe now I can get some information on this spoof.

"Who's Guillaume Rhoe?"

"A man. Someone who'd been madly in love with my sister. Besides Matthias, no gentlemen could have loved Yria more. He gladly proposed marriage. He wanted nothing more than to marry his love and support baby Mira."

"But it didn't happen because she went missing, that right?"

"Well, Yria wasn't ready to remarry. And I logically agreed. How could she consider? She just lost her husband. As much in love as he was, Guillaume respected her. Said he understood. After having turned Guillaume down, Basile figured he'd attempt that second shot."

"Basile? That was the man she dated?"

"Hmm, yes. And just as she'd done Guillaume, she denied Basile, too."

"What was his reaction to that?"

"Anger. He was heartbroken and hurt. Before Yria met Matthias, she was going steady with Basile. Yria had some seriously deep feelings for him."

"What age was that?"

"Well, it must have been two months before Yria's fifteenth birthday. My parents weren't happy. They wanted Yria to wait till she was fifteen before she took a suitor."

I shrug. "What's two months?" That's pretty much fifteen, right? Then again, maybe I'll better understand when becoming a father?

"What it was to our parents? It was to show respect of what they had asked. She would have been allowed to date him soon as she turned fifteen, but Yria wouldn't listen. She was rebellious, did what she pleased. Our parents couldn't stop her."

Orisia fills in more of the story saying her parents tried, but got nowhere. Yria was seeing Basile secretly when her mom and dad had found out. There were no means to ending what the pair had already begun. Orisia says Yria would have seem him anyway.

"She loved Basile, you could see. Her fondness was, well, obvious. She talked day and night about that boy, to the point I'd be sick. He was all I heard. Basile this and Basile that. She just rambled on."

"Orisia; you said she loved him, but I'm guessing something happened?"

"Well, yes. A year after them dating, Basile had to move. His grandparents had been in an awful accident. A fierce storm rolled in. The rain came in sheets, too thick for their eyes. Control of the car was lost and they hit a lamp. Both Basile's grandparents were seriously hurt. One left paralyzed, the other, blind. The grandmother passed thirteen months later. Three years thereafter the grandpap died."

"Gees, poor guy."

"That was only the start. At nineteen Basile came back to Annecy. He returned to the one he loved only to find her married to another man. As much as he tried, he couldn't get Yria to betray her vows. She was happy, in love. Following her husband's death, Basile again pursued her, but my sister wouldn't have him."

I've taken notes of all Orisia's said. Now it's time I ask questions. "You don't suppose Basile would have harmed her?"

"Oh, no. No, he was too mild a soul. He could barely smash bugs."

"What about Guillaume Rhoe? Was he capable, you think?"

"Guillaume was a respected gentleman of the law. Right straight and honest. A good, simple man. Like Basile, Guillaume was swept deeply in love."

"Correct me if I'm wrong, but you said *lawman*?"

"Yes, an officer in town. Quite a good one, too."

"I don't suppose you'd know if he was still around?"

"Mmm, no. Sadly, he's not. Guillaume was killed in a boating accident. To this day it's hard to believe he lost his head. He had such a handsome face. Sad to think he'd been buried without it."

"Huh?"

"Strangely it was never found."

My thoughts scream. Haulmier had actually been telling the truth, but he hadn't told of the missing head. "No one came across it?"

"Ugh-ugh, no."

All right, apparently the man's dead, this much I know. Moving on; "That's an odd shame, but back to your sister. I'd like you to backtrack. Run me through the day, the final day when Yria went missing."

Orisia's face sinks in sadness. "We were together that night. Our favorite performer was scheduled to sing at a local joint. Our father agreed to watch Mira so Yria could come and she met with me and our friends."

Orisia explains Yria had gathered Mira, then drove her to her dad's. Gabriel was already a widower by that time. He was by himself, lived alone, so having Mira for a night brought him comfort. Mira was almost a year. It'd been the child's active energy which kept her gramps going.

"It was a good thing. It's what dad needed. It wasn't like father was ill. He'd been healthy except for an occasional sore throat or runny nose." Orisia then returns to her story. Apparently, Yria parked her car at home, then simply walked to their nightspot. "We were all there, me, Guillaume, Basile, Adora, Tayce, Gaston. It's like yesterday I'm remem- bering this. I recall Yria having kept her distance from Guillaume and Basile the times they drew near. She wished to avoid all conversations and just have a good time."

"I guess her reason was blatant?"

"My sister was tired of being chased. She wanted time to mourn Matthias." Orisia wrings her hands and continues, "Yria left on her own following the night's end. Said she wanted to return home by herself. She was supposed to call the next morning. I never heard the phone."

I take consideration. "Evidently she was followed. Had you no-ticed anything the time you all left?"

"All was fine. Yria gave me a hug, then took off down the street. Everyone broke separate ways as we all did before."

"Had you noticed anyone strange on the street?"

"No, but frankly, I can't say I was looking. We were all pretty tired."

"Hmm. So you can't say whether a stranger was near? Even with the amount of people leaving the club, had nobody lingered?"

"I can't say, really. I don't know."

"Yria's home, then? Had there been signs of forced entry?"

"My sister never made it home, Detective. Her bed was still kept."

"Oh, I see. Well, is there anyone, anyone you suspect to have taken her?"

"Some street lout, maybe? That's the only thought that's made sense."

A street rat; Annecy has lots. And Ghislain; well, he's one of them creeps. Chances are Orisia's right. Some lout may have snatched her. Maybe Ghislain's that guy? I never envisioned the thought of speaking with him, but I'm beginning to now. I could analyze his statements and keep his composure in check.

I confess, "There's someone I'm vaguely familiar with. Some homeless clod. By his looks, he's been one for some time. If your suspect's someone of his status, then he's liable to know."

"Whatever could help. I hate to sound simple, but that's all I can say. Besides these years since Yria's vanished, I've found me no clues." Orisia leans into her hands, crying. "It's been horribly distressing. I feel she's dead. All I want now's to bring her home."

"Hopefully I'll help you do that."

Orisia nods slowly. "Will you, please?"

"I'll work my ass off to find her, be it on bright roads or dark streets. Anything I hear, I'll let you know."

"I just need her found. That's my baby sister out there. Do me the greatest honor; bring her home."

"I've got enough information to give me a start. I'm pretty sure I've an idea where to begin." I pull a vocation card from my wallet. "This has my business address and number. Use it when you have to."

Orisia walks me to the door. "Be careful out there. Those streets aren't tame, nor are the people."

What a sweetheart she is. Had I not been keen on Dej, I'd be trailing Miss Laroque like a smitten runt. To be a youth, freshly in love; I remember those days—how bittersweet those times. I leave now before impulsive action takes over, leading me on driving lust.

From Orisia's I steer to Deja's. At the door Ambrielle answers.

"Good morning." I nod. "Is my honey bun up?"

As I stand stalled, the maiden acknowledges, "We're in the kitchen, finishing breakfast."

Inside the cook room I see my beloved at the sink. "You up to par now? You look a lot better."

"I slept it off. I awoke with no pain."

"What are your plans? You heading to Marin's later?"

"Thought Ambrielle and I could go to town, do some shopping. I'm broke, though, hon. How about you fork me some cash?"

"Stay out of Annecy, I might. Sticking in town's too risky. You shop some place else." I grasp my wallet. "This is the last of it. You've bled me dry."

"For now. You know more will come later."

"The way you spend, I'll be bankrupt."

I know, though, Deja's not a gold digger. After putting away dishes, she takes to my side. "You going to be around awhile?"

"Probably not. Got some business here and there. I wanted to see you before my day becomes hectic."

"You have time for breakfast, though, don't you?"

"I'm ahead of you, babe. I already ate. Just save that for later."

"It'll spoil, then I'll have thrown away money."

"Fine. Hand it here. I'll pick at the plate."

Women always gripe about money. They go to the store, buy food, and if what's cooked isn't eaten, they'll fuss about that. Here's a good example. I've slaved away at this stove all day cooking a meal. I want- ed you to have something you liked, something good, and something that fills you. I've made enough, that we'll have leftovers tomorrow. The next day comes and goes and the remainder of food sits in the fridge. Another day passes and the same has gone on. Food sits 'cause it's not getting eaten. Eventually it's taken out and the sight of mold's already been growing. That's when you get fussed at, but, of course, when a woman shops for herself, say for clothes, and she buys things that re-main in her closet, never once to be worn, she don't fuss; but when it's food, and she's cooking for you and that grub goes to waste, better know you'll hear about it.

Enough of that vivid accession; it's time I hunt for Ghislain, a man I'd never considered seeing. Funny how things change.

Chapter Twenty-Nine

To find a street rat, you must think as one. Therefore I've contrived a list of places to check. These locations include bars, alleys, and booze stands.

I head first to taverns, inspecting every last one known to this city; the good, the bad, the terrible, and in my pursuit for Ghislain, my scouting's become futile. No sign of him is seen, not even one report.

Following my final investigation of taprooms, I review the few alky stores offered by Annecy. Still, to my avail, no Ghislain. Only places left are alleys. If I can't find him, I'll have met my defeat.

I don't like failure weighing me. It hinders all progress. How could it have been so simple in Ghislain's quest to find me? Had he stalked my steps? Had I coincidently come upon him? All I know's I need to find him.

I drift down Annecy's alleyways to the homeless locality. The first is the rocky passage behind the street of Harbour Ridge. I see tattered boxes of cardboard serving as makeshift shelters. Trash fires burn for suppliance of heat. The shoddy folks remaining here, men, women, and children alike, call this sullied stretch their home, people, people who may have been like you and me, but are now forced to live on streets, some having lost their homes, many others, runaways. Then there're those born into this beggary life. Whatever their stories, this place is plain sad.

I slowly skim the street, inquiring for Ghislain. Oddly, these folks have no clue who he is. They shake their heads when I'm passing by them. I'm gaining no help, then again my roam's hardly over.

Decidedly, I now travel to South Road, looking, searching, desperately eyeing for any likelihood of Ghislain. Akin to Harbour Ridge, this street's much the same; sad, dirty, pathetic, and stinks to high heaven. Stopping before some shelters, I gaze a homeless horde. As before, I'm requesting help, "You know Ghislain, any of you?"

An unkept man, with snaggy beard and frizzled hair steps to my door. "What's it to you?"

"Don't know yet, but I need to find him."

"Who's asking?"

Really, this chum's grilling me? "I am. You've no need for my name."

"Well, mister, understand, you got no name, you get no answer."

Feeling fed up, I force a blade through my sleeve and allow its silvery glint to reflect the man's eyes. "The name's Cutter."

"Nice. Oh, that's nice. You going to use that, I suppose? Go ahead. Introduce me to your pointy little friend."

This guy got a death wish? "What's wrong with you, fool? You begging to die?"

"I'm without fear, man. You do as you feel. Take that shiv and shove it through me. I want to meet my maker."

Holy crap. Never have I seen a man more out of his mind. Something's seriously wrong if he's requesting death.

I screech my wheels and haste off. Screw that bromide. I'll not be coaxed into taking his life. No. I'll not have it. I ease a little farther, then spot a congenial woman, mid-forties, sweeping dirt from her makeshift shelter. "Miss." I divert her attention.

She steps to my car. "Couldn't quite catch that. My hearing's gone absent."

"Ghislain, ma'am," I talk ever louder.

"Huh?"

"I'm looking for Ghislain."

She thinks momentarily. "Duplessey?"

"No, ma'am. Ghislain."

"That's who I said."

"He reeks of whiskey," I explain.

"Mmm-hmm," she replies. "East Grove; he keeps an apartment. Fourteen-eleven, second floor, door three."

Whoa, okay. The scum's got a place? I make sure I respond the address, keeping certain I've heard correctly. Following her acknowledgment, I jot it onto paper. "What was that last name again?"

"Duplessey. D, u, p–"

"That's all right. I can spell it." I reach to my wallet and toss her some francs. "Here, to make sure you and your family have food."

"You're generous, sir. Very generous. Bless you. Oh, bless you." I hear her as I'm driving forth.

Time of truth; is this Ghislain guy the one I'm seeking? It's now I'll find out. I breeze through the streets, then drive upon East Grove. I spot fourteen-eleven along the left side.

It's somewhat favorable, this place, a brick home with flared eaves. The moment comes, I tread inside. I surpass the burly, dark alder door, heading to the second floor. Down the hall I find room three. After knocking loudly, a man answers. He's a familiar face, thankfully.

"Detective, finally, you've come to visit. Come inside. Come inside." "So, this is your place?" I look around.

"I get by here."

"I didn't imagine you having a room, or a home for that matter."

"You don't know me's your reason. Seeing me on the street, you automatically fathom, it's there I belong. In truth, well, it's quite opposite, what you figured."

"So you're no rat now, I see."

"I'm pleased you finally see I'm not homeless. Rather, I'm a drinker who prefers the company of night. But as I appear, you see I'm not sloshed. The moon is my mistress. I only drink when she visits."

"Don't we all?" I saunter around the room, looking things over. Upon a chest of drawers I eye a frame. In it's a man posed in coordinat-ed attire. I take closely to it while regarding the fellow inside. "Who's this guy here?"

"That uniformed man is myself." I stand shocked. "You're a cop?"

"Had been. I was removed from the force."

If this is true, I'd like to know, "For what reason?"

"Oh, let's say I got to meddling too deeply in things others thought I had no business attending."

"What sort of meddling?"

"My partner. The man was crooked. I knew. I tried exposing him for what he was and he had me expelled. Told our captain I was going mental, seeing things, crap like that."

I scratch my head. "This was when?"

"Forty-one. Not long before he had a run with bad luck. He'd been killed, you see."

"Who?"

The man states, simply, yet boldly, "Guillaume Rhoe."

I titter my head. "Rhoe was your partner? Is that the truth?"

"I told you I was a cop. Shouldn't be hard to believe. You've seen the proof there."

"He's dead, are you sure?"

"Boating accident." He then stands silent. "Despite it, I could never grasp how his head was cut off. It seemed fishy to me."

Ghislain tells me the boat Guillaume was in had been non-motorized. So, if falling from a boat, how did Rhoe lose his head? "What'd you say happened?"

"Me? Nothing. I'm stumped, to say the least. I could produce speculation, but I know it'd be wrong."

I ponder, what did happen? Could Yria have been the cause of the mishap? Time comes I inquire the no nonsense bullshit, "What sort of crooked deal had Rhoe been in?"

"It all involved a girl. She'd been missing prior months to his death. I know, I'm certain, Guillaume killed her. Yria's blood was on his hands. I know it was."

"If you're certain as you think, what'd he do?"

"That'd be a thought to ponder." "You're saying you don't know?"

"Clearly."

"Then you have no real knowledge of Yria being dead?"

"But I do. Don't dispute me, though, because it's odd, but a pair of doves gave this assumption."

"Excuse me?" I ask, not understanding.

Ghislain calmly remarks, "There were two officers working Yria's case from the time she went missing. Hadn't Guillaume been in love with her, it would have gone to us, but it was our captain's decision to pass the case to other members of the force. Though, I hadn't worked it, I got to know Yria's family through visitations at the station."

He relays that he and Yria's dad had became close in that time.

"Probably about, oh, say, three weeks after Yria's disappearance, her father experienced a vivid dream. Gabriel confided in me of what he had dreamt."

I continue listening, but I'm not hearing about doves. Maybe he'll get to it.

"I agreed and listened to Gabriel, who told me he dreamt of his daughter in a dimly lit room, where she was standing in darkness. As I recall Gabriel having said, Yria had stated something close to these words, my image, daddy, is not for your eyes. Turn around not, as you heed what I say. You shall know him, father, when you've seen the white doves. It'll be then you've found him, my killer. Gabriel's conscience alerted him Yria was gone. Thereafter, he had no other dreams."

"Where's the claim in that? It don't mean she's dead."

"It couldn't have been closer to the truth because Gabriel found the white doves."

I'm becoming agitated, I feel. White doves? Come on, really? They're everywhere. "I can walk outside now and I'm bound to see many."

"Gabriel thought the same. But in truth they had been revealed to him differently."

I know Ghislain reads the perplexity on my face, and if he doesn't, then simply, this man is quite dumb.

"Guilluame and I had desks back to back. Between us, we shared a bookcase. Rhoe had been an avid collector of porcelain birds and, among his assembly, had been a pair of white doves. Noticing, Mr. Laroque asked whose they were. When finding out they belonged to Guillaume, Gabriel then divulged me his dream."

Okay, so I'll admit it's ironic. "But it's not proof."

"Well, that gathered over time."

"With hard evidence, I presume?"

"Strangely, in a sense. See, Guillaume had done something which implied him a suspect. The day after Yria vanished, he wrapped a woman's necklace around one of his doves. Laroque recognized it quickly. Said it belonged to his daughter."

Ghislain tells me it'd been a birthday gift Yria had gotten from him years earlier.

I clarify my following statement, saying, "Rhoe having the necklace couldn't have automatically made him a suspect. It wouldn't have been regarded as a substantial evidence; you see where I'm getting?"

"Trust me, Detective. Gabriel spotting that necklace around the dove was plenty proof. Yria never took that pendant off. Her father and sister confirmed that."

I find myself reneging my earlier statement. Seems Ghislain's validating Orisia and Gabriel's testimony with legitimacy. If the Laroques' said Yria had the pendant on at all times, then she damn well did.

Ghislain continues, "Curiously, here's where things go bizarre. Over the weeks following, mysteriously, somehow, that dove took to different colors. First, soft pink, then blushed rose, by week three, scarlet red. Week four crept about and the damn thing was black as ash. It appeared burnt, is simple to put it. The following morning the dove was gone. A pile of soot stood in its place and, within it, the pendant."

How crazy. This is crazy, but could these events have actually transpired? Before having knowledge of Yria Dane, I'd say it wasn't so. "Had speech transpired between the two men?"

"Oh, Gabriel asked questions, all right. Made many accusations, but Guillaume denied him."

"Did Rhoe explain the pendant?"

"Yeah, the bastard claimed Yria left it at his home during a visit."

"He claimed that, had he?"

"No one believed that, of course. Not myself. Not the family. Yria's necklace belonged with them, not Guillaume, so Gabriel demanded it be returned."

"Where's it now?"

"With Orisia."

All right. All right, I'm now thinking. "What current help have you been to her?"

"Lately we met with a columnist, pleading to get Yria's story back in papers. With enough imploring, it worked and, Yria's article was written."

"I suppose there haven't been any leads?"

"Nope. In all these years, zilch. Yria's case went cold. That's why myself and Miss Laroque requested the press. As of now, we've nothing to go on. But we'll give our last breath till we do. As for you, well, I knew Yria would guide you to me. It was just a matter of time."

"And to think I supposed you were scum."

"As you've learned, we've walked the same shoes. You and I, we're no different." Ghislain leans forth in his seat, stretching his hand to a clasped box of cigars. "Hopefully you'll acquire information that myself or Orisia haven't. A fresh take is greatly needed. You care for a stogie?"

I nod no as I draw a pack of smokes from my pocket. "I prefer these, but thanks."

"It's in kindness to offer."

"The cops have given no assistance, right?"

Shaking his head, Ghislain announces, "Them station boys don't give a rat's ass. Had they, they'd have done something long ago."

I hear mentally, my mind, steering off subject, and while I'm unable to control my verbalization, I find it's utterance instantaneously seeking release. "Hey, Ghis, you mind I call you that?" He nods to my request. "First time I saw you, you spoke of something in the air. What did you mean?"

"The cold stir of some shadowy figment. It looms near. It's around you, but always one step ahead. It knows, like I do, where you'll be, where you'll go."

I laugh modestly. "How could you know where I go?"

"I've seen your face many times in dreams."

Nonsense; is this a load of bull? "How? Doing what?" I ask the one-time cop. He explains his subconscious upheld my image. Really? Come on, how's this true? Does one dream of an individual he's never met?

Ghislain relays a vision he'd had of me conversing at a bar with some fellow. The man, though, unable for Ghislain to describe, makes me think of Guloe. Ghis then says the dream suddenly shifted when he viewed me above bodies; one in a bedroom, he tells me, two in another. His recounts quickly capture my interest. No doubt it'd been the Ladous' he'd seen. "How long ago was this?"

"Oh-ah, about a week before I saw you." Ghislain grows quiet, then begins pointing at my pocket. "I recall you taking something. You held it. You put it into your pocket; I saw."

All right, Ghis knows something. I feel I've been shoved to a corner as he's awaiting some truth. Time to fess it. I pull the spattered papers from my coat as I'm tossing them forth. "These are what you saw."

Ghislain peers upon the tainted leaflets. "I have, yes. Be it true then, the prediction was real. Did it happen as dreamt?"

"You seem to know something. Admittedly, however, that dream of yours wasn't completely clear. I'll have you know there are crucial details missing throughout your account."

"Well, certainly, of course. Dreams are weird. Mine was scattered. Even at that, in a wakeful state, could one fully recap impressions made while sleeping? Could he, Detective? Be yourself an example." Ghislain stretches forth his hand while passing the papers back.

"Not so fast," I say. "You hadn't bothered to read those. You wish to know more, you'll unfold them."

Ghislain follows my incentive, and as he's reading, I reveal my following disclosure. "First fact's first. Yria's dead, as you figured. Just for the record, the bodies you saw, those I came across, they'd been relatives of her killer."

"Relatives?"

"Relatives. And if you wish to dig deeper, I'll tell you something else, something I've seen, some phantom thing, something not human."

"So you've seen her?"

"The glimpse caught was a woman, yes."

"She's visited me twice. Both times at night. She whispers softly and touches my arm. I dreamt of you after her first sighting. She always leaves a bloody print on my skin before departing my room. The visitations are real."

"Well, I've no doubt the Rhoe family's cursed. Guillaume's brothers, sisters, cousins; everyone."

"Have you notified Orisia, told her of this?"

"Of that, no. Guess I want Miss Laroque to know certain truths."

"The longer we go without recovering Yria's body, the lengthier the list of victims become. Innocent people will die, Detective."

"That's already contemplated."

Ghislain rubs his chin while musing. "I can't help wondering if this is out of our hands."

"We'll get this figured out. We have to. People's lives are at stake." "We have no gallant solutions, Detective. Three people are dead. It'll be a long road till we uncover the body and, unless she's at rest, we won't save a soul."

I hate saying it, but, "By the time this is finished, Yria will have claimed many."

"Yes, I agree, and soon there will be another body."

"This vision, too, come in a dream?"

"I remember an apartment. I saw you and I remember a dog."

"Biaritz," I quickly envision.

"Then you've already encountered this?"

"The event's transpired, yes. There was a fourth victim. Have you seen anymore?"

"I'm sure they're coming. As long as I dream, Yria will show me."

"Ghis, these glimpses you're having, you see for a reason. Your foreknowledge is useful. It might help us."

"Useful, it might be, but I don't enjoy it one bit. Nonetheless, Yria chose me, just like she chose you."

"If we're to work together, Ghis, I'll need you onboard."

"Oh, I'm already on."

"Then let's put this together. Guillaume's friends; did you know who they were?"

Ghislain shrugs. "Outside work, we weren't what you'd call buds. It wasn't until Guillaume's death when I met all his pals."

"You were hoping someone would point a finger at him and say he killed Yria?"

"I prayed, but nothing developed. It pissed me off, let me tell you." "I imagine."

"All I needed was one person, one person to crack. Someone who'd say Rhoe wasn't the proper nobleman everyone said. Orisia, too, that sad, stupid girl, thought greatly of him." Ghislain breathes with disgust. "I just want to shake her so badly for still thinking that way. Least her father, God rest him; we were on the same page."

Though I've heard titles, I have to ask, "Who were Rhoe's friends?" I'd gotten a list from Orisia, but I want to be certain Ghislain replies the same names.

"Oh, gosh, it's been so long. I'd have to think who I'd recall."

Leaving Ghis to his thoughts, I stretch to my pocket and grasp around for my tab. Opening it, I scan several names which had been relayed from Orisia.

Ghislain then breaks his silence. "There may have been a fellow named Basile."

"Devereux?"

"Yeah, that's him. And Gaston, I'm remembering."

I hand him my notebook. "Check these. See if they strike you."

Ghislain reads my scribble and speaks, "Tayce and Adora. Ah-huh. But there's someone else. A woman. Her name's missing." Following a few moments, Ghislain remembers. "Rousseau. Oh, what had been her name? Oh, damn it."

"It's all right, Ghis. You'll remember later."

"No, I know it. Her name was, was, I know it. Damn it, I know it. Who was she?"

"Ghis, it's okay."

"It's not. I know her name. Callia, Soleil? Hmm, Clairese? No, no, ah-ugh. She was ah, oh, Charlize." He snaps his fingers.

"Charlize Rousseau. Okay, Ghis, who was she?"

"Only woman to have been involved with Guillaume, as it was said."

"Where's she now? What happened to her?" "Eh,

left, I heard. Just picked up and moved."

"There must be more, something else you can say?"

"Orisia said Char kept her job at the hospital. She was a radiographer outside of town. During the war many male radiologists were shipped overseas, therefore a slew of women had been trained to replace them."

"And siblings?"

"Maybe? But, hmm, you got me on that."

I want to learn about Char. "You have any thought on where I'd find her?" I have her questions, I'm thinking.

Ghis tells me, "If anyone knows, it'd be Orisia."

"Then I'll have to drop by Miss Laroque's again." I scratch my neck to relieve an itch. I draw my eyes to my notebook and gaze at the names. "The other people on this list, I want them found."

"I haven't got last names. You'll have to check with Orisia. But be- fore you leave, I have something else I should mention." Ghislain claims to have seen a fifth victim. "It's not happened yet, but this death will come soon."

Apparently, he dreamt this last night.

"What do I need to know?" I hold a pen to my scratch pad, pre- paring to write.

"There was a young man, about twenty or so. He was fishing for mail when I saw his name on a box. It was Marpuis, or something close."

Marpuis, I'm thinking, as it absorbs in my brain. "I'm not familiar; however, I'll find out."

I realize the longer I sit, the more time I'll be wasting. If I'm to know who Marpuis is, I'll have to address Ambrielle. "I'll buzz around and get back to you." As I'm on the verge of standing, a question unex- pectedly strikes me. "You got a car?" I pray he answers. It's important should any distance be traveled.

He comes back, "An old beat up clunker."

"Make sure it's got gas."

"It's no good. My rear tire's been flattened."

Christ, is he kidding? "Let's get your spare. We'll put it on."

"It was my spare."

I'm realizing this is going from bad to worse.

I realize Ghislain will need my number should he have to make calls. After digging for my wallet, I throw him my card. "We'll keep in touch." I pick my ass up and head for the door.

Chapter Thirty

I'm back at Deja's, and after coming inside, I find the house empty. The girls, well, I'm unsure when they'll come back. Once Deja steps foot through a store, there's no way of talking her out, and if Ambrielle's the same, then they're an absolute pair.

With the twosome absent, I decide to search for a notepad. Within a drawer I come across a near empty tab. Attached to the cardboard are two lonely leaflets. When they're gone, that's it. I'll be left with a depleted square, amidst the remembrance of pages that filled it. So, to the trash I'll throw it, just as soon as I'm through.

Following an addressed letter to Ambrielle, I compose several paragraphs detailing my visit at Ghislain's. I explain who he is and why I had seen him. I go on to reveal his divining dreams and how they've proved valid. I then disclose his most recent impression, Ghislain's precognitive recollection concerning Marpuis. I finish my concluding lines, saying it's imperative we talk. This person Marpuis; this person's in danger.

I leave the note in sight on the table and, upon it, I station a glass, hence the breezing fan above. I'm now out the door, locking it, and off to my business.

The avenue where my building stands seems quite populated in this downstream hour. Given the dawn-to-dark time and, depending on the day, the street could see its suppliance of people, or perhaps it will no, but today's an exception as many folks stroll about, either succeeding their errands or enjoying the fine weather.

Before my establishment, two boys hop along, pouncing on pogos. I'll admit I've never seen Paien or Zuri with one, but I'd imagine they'd like some.

I call the boys as they leap my direction. "Those as fun as they look?"

"Ain't nothing better," one tadpole responds. "Want to give it a spring?" The kid hands me his stick. "Go on, mister, jump!"

I guess this rascal has no patience. "I'm getting there. I'm getting there."

"Yo, old man, don't be forgetting your balance."

"Hey, I ain't ancient," I imply to correct this blustering sprout. "Say, kid, how do I get on?"

"Plop your feet on the rest. Come on, mister, it ain't hard. There, see? You got it." He starts laughing. "Hey, guy. Guy, you gotta bounce. You not hear me, pop? Gee, old man, you're gonna fall on your ass."

Already this kid is envisioning me falling? Some support he gives. I continue springing in motion while I chat with the kid, "Aren't you a bit young for that word?"

"What, ass?"

I cease my hippety-hop-hop. "There, you said it again."

"Oh, hell, pop, my ole man says it all the time. It's regular in my house."

"What are you, twelve? Your mouth should be washed with soap."

The second kid starts laughing. "He's barely eleven."

"Then he's closer to ten." Oh, to hell with it, I won't continue my hassle. I had a mouth like his when I was a youth. "Say, how about you boys pick me up two of these?"

"You got cash, mister?"

I toss the kid a few francs. "Keep what's left. Share the rest with your friend."

"Boy, mister, it's an awful lot; you sure?"

"Take it. Shut up. That's easy enough, right? Anyway." I turn around. "See this building?"

The kid scopes my sign. "Yeah, Biertempfel Brothers? That there?" "I'll be inside. Drift through when you're here." I dawdle to my door, leaving the kids to my back. Inside, I take a seat near my desk. I should manage it better; the thing's a damn mess. Oh, well, I'll do something later.

Against my phone I spot a note. It's Marin's handwriting, I know. So I pull a cigarette and fire it up. Tugging a drawer, my hand frisks around, grasping my only bottle of pommeau.

After abducting a few swigs, I read Marin's scribble. I scan it throughly, but admitting now, its contents have shocked me. Marin claims of his most recent client's return. The man pled to my brother, asking him again to be in search of his wife, Mrs. Audric Badeau.

Hell, I thought this case was tossed? Apparently this guy's persistence has deteriorated my brother's will. Doing so, Marin subsequently consented his request. Gosh damn. This ruins my day. I had hoped for my brother's help, but as I see, my plan's gone to shit. Marin, the old chum, is en route to Savoie, knowing that's where Christoph, Mrs. Badeau's *au courant* flame derives.

As I sit shaking my head, I hear the toll of my bell. Looking, I see the two youths I'd spoken with. They come, wagging the pogos to which I'd requested.

The one kid I talked with steps forth, speaking boldly. "You're lucky, pop, you got the last two." The half-pint peers about. "Say, mister." Now concentrating sharply upon the inward conditions of my business, the stripling questions firmly, "You work here or something?"

"Well, I'm here, aren't I?"

"Yeah. Well, yeah. So you're a PI? You sneak around and trail people's asses?"

"It's what I do."

"Seems swell enough." In a hey pal sort of fashion, the kid waggles his head. "Say ah, ah, what would my friend and I have to do to become one?"

I respond quickly, "Be an excellent snoop, that's the start. You want to go pro? Wait a few years, learn the ropes. Make sure you get a license. You'll be nowhere without one."

"That won't be hard, right? Is that it?"

"In a nutshell. Be good at what you do and have the attitude that goes with it. Be hardboiled. Have that tough exterior; it helps."

"I've already got that, mister."

"Don't lose it. Get tougher as you grow. You'll save your ass. Now I've got work, boys. Time comes, you be leaving."

"Ah, gee, mister."

"Sorry, kid, but I'm busy."

"All right, well, maybe we'll catch you around?"

I watch the two leave through my door. The one talker reminded me of myself. The other kid, well, he didn't have much to say. Alone now, I imagine what suggestion comes next. Smearing my butt in the ashtray, I slam the last of my pommeau. Pulling Sable's keys from my shirt, I head to my door, carrying Paien and Zuri's pogos. Sometime today they'll be getting these, but I envision it'll be much later; much later, indeed.

Chapter Thirty-One

I find myself back at Miss Laroque's, where we sit at her couch. Further- ing our earlier speech, Orisia treads into areas not previously mentioned.

"Your father and Ghislain seemed to think otherwise of Guillaume's innocence. Why hadn't you?"

"My father had a dream. Poor man figured he had it thought out. When he told me of his so-called vision, I was quick to deny him. Guillaume was a good man, I told my father and Mr. Duplessey."

"Even after having found evidence in Rhoe's office, you remained unchanged?"

"I spent much time with Guillaume, me, Yria, the gang; we all did. Rhoe's nature wasn't boorish. He was much too kind to have had a wicked bone in his body."

"And seeing your father finding the doves meant nothing?"

"Finding them, no. But what happened to the one over following weeks was peculiar."

"Still, you didn't take that as a sign?"

"I don't believe in ... not in mysterial occurrences. They don't exist."

"How would you explain what occurred in his office?"

"It's logic, Detective. Someone replaced it every week. On account its color was different each time."

"Who'd have had the sense? Only person near Guillaume was Ghislain. That collection of birds belonged to Rhoe, you do know?"

"Others working my sister's case may have very well deceived him. Them hotheads were stony; they lurched with ill mean. Guillaume was nothing like that. The clash was from personality differences, nothing more."

"Let me ask, had anyone besides your father or Mr. Duplessey have knowledge of those doves?"

"Father only confided to Ghislain. Ghislain didn't tell."

"Then how'd anyone but them have known anything? What your father shared had been kept in secret. Only person to have pulled such an intellectualized stunt would have been Ghis, since he already had knowledge."

Orisia speaks softly, "I don't believe that."

"Then take a moment to tell me, why can't you?"

"My father trusted Ghislain. In these years since my sister's disappearance, Mr. Duplessey's been the sole person committed to helping me find her. I couldn't imagine him to have been involved with Yria's disappearance. They weren't acquainted. They never met."

Veritably, she's wrong. Here's why. An abductor doesn't need to know his victim to take her. Had Ghislain, indeed, been the culprit, he could have easily gathered the girl at random. Killers do that, but more so on ole Ghis. I know he hadn't been Yria's abductor, so I'll release my claim now. "Suspecting Ghis as the only person who'd have tinkered with the dove, I'll sensibly declare he did not. I believe there's fact in the story he and Gabriel shared."

"You're like them. Just like them. You suppose Guillaume, that innocent man, having been responsible for what happened. I knew him, rest his soul. Guillaume couldn't have done what you think."

"And Guillaume having personally seen Mr. Duplessey be removed from the force, wasn't enough to grasp your concern? Could Ghis have meddled enough, he may have found something."

"Listen, Detective, I appreciate you trying to help me, I do. But Guilluame, he'd never have done anything to Yria."

"Miss Laroque, your sister's necklace was found with him. He had it."

"And it's with me now. Father got it."

Oh, no, no, no. I say, "I don't think you're understanding. Guillaume had her necklace. How'd he get it? Was she ever at his house?"

It seems my question's challenged her. She reflects, "Yria hardly went anywhere following the death of Matthias. Though, I never asked, it's possible Yria may have gone to his home."

"How often was that pendant on your sister?"

"It wasn't something she took off. It clung to her like skin."

"And your last day with her, I suppose it was on?"

"I'd imagine it was."

"Then case settled. Rhoe got it when he took her."

"What if he didn't?"

"I'm asking, divert your previous presumptions. Face what's feasible, I'm telling you. We'll get nowhere if you don't."

"I'll tell you exactly as I've told Ghislain. Until you have evidence, my beliefs remain firm."

Maybe Orisia's in denial and can't accept the truth? "You had evidence. Rhoe sealed his fate by having her necklace. He screwed himself, the dumb fool. Guillaume hadn't fathomed the possibility of your father seeing it. Think about what I've said, Miss Laroque."

Orisia's spaced out as she's thinking. The leer of an empty gaze is now filling her eyes. "It was always on her."

"Your sister kept it close at all times. Why would she, without reason, suddenly take it off?"

"She wouldn't."

"Then that should make you aware of the fact, it'd been her killer who removed it. He wouldn't have hesitated. Why would he? She no longer needed it. Her life was gone. The pendant was taken as a token. It was a remembrance of the crime he committed. Wake up, Miss Laroque; her killer was much closer to you than you realized."

"You're speculating. What you've said is a contemplative thought made by your mind."

"Answer me this, would you find peace in knowing your sister's fate? Could you accept whether she's alive or dead?"

"I need facts. I've lived too long without them."

All right, then. Orisia wants palpability, she'll have it. "Excuse my being blunt, or better yet, insincerity, but your sister, Miss Laroque, is no longer among the living. This I know as fact."

A look of inconsolable despair reads clear in her face. It's as though I'm detecting her thoughts. My greatest fear's confronted me, a cli- ent lost in pain, but the words from her mouth arise otherwise as she speaks, "Where's your proof, if that's so?"

Reaching to my pocket, I toss forth the spattered papers. "Your proof," I say.

Orisia reads the letter, along with the poems. "How'd you get these?"

"Never mind it. But people are dead because of that mess. Did you write them? I request an immediate response."

"That's a farcical question. You know I did not."

"No, Miss Laroque, I don't know that you didn't."

"What would have been my motive? The wording's incongruous. Besides, this handwriting; it's nothing like mine."

"I want you to write the top letter in its entirety."

"Have mercy, Detective. Can't you believe me?"

I hand forth my pen and scratch pad. She'll take my incentive, rather she likes it or not.

"You're serious; you're really having me do this?"

"Understand, I have no choice."

"I don't get why you can't take my word?"

"Please, just copy the paper."

"Fine, but then you tell me where these came from."

"I shall, once I conclude you're not the composer."

Moments pass as Orisia scribbles the letter.

She turns her copy over. "You'll see I've had nothing to do with the original."

Luckily I'm educated in handwriting analysis. I bought many books on the subject when Marin and I first went into business. Though I have no degree, I am accomplished in detecting the signs of forged documents. Additionally, I've trained well enough to interpret various writing styles, too. I'm cocky when I say I know it all. I can analyze the depth, darkness, and thickness of one's scrivenery. I know the interpretations of size, spacing, slants, and loops, which reveal truths about the composer's personality and character. In my field, yet less than often, it's applied. Be it for what it's worth, it's a good tool I possess. I never know when intelligence such as this will be needed.

I draw Orisia's copy before me, along with the original, then prepare my inspection. Quickly, I'm noticing the size and spacing's drastically different than that of the primary draft. I highly doubt Orisia was the creator of these pages found at the Ladous' and Miss Zerbib's.

"Well, Detective, you still think it's me?"

"Hardly. Your longhand's not matching."

"I tried telling you."

"I had to be sure. It's part of my job."

"So, who wrote it? Who'd have written about my sister and shamed Guillaume's name? Tell me where you found these."

I go on to tell Miss Laroque, "Those pages were found at a crime scene. The victims were of Rhoe's bloodline. As for the writer, well, I'm supposing your sister."

"What a farce assumption. You said—"

"There's no assumption."

"You said she's dead."

"I did, and she is. I'm sorry."

"Then find her, Detective. Bring her home."

"I'll just need to search. It'll take time. She could be anywhere." "I have nothing but patience anymore. All I ask is you find her. Now, a few months down the line, I don't care."

My mind's stuck in thought of finding Yria. It'll be a long shot, because it's been more than a decade, but if I'm to figure out Mrs. Dane's last moments, maybe it's best I start my search in the former home of her killer. I'm hoping to find clues, something to go on. So in an attempt to learn more, I request the old address. It's worth the inquiry and Ori- sia better give it.

She doesn't hesitate a moment as she's divulging the street. "Grange Road, 1002. It's a stone Tudor, with dark timber."

I'm curious. Might something be found there? "Would you be against me going?" I ask Miss Laroque.

"Suppose not. Course you'd ultimately go had I spoken otherwise."

"You're right, I would."

So in saying that, I believe I'm ready. I'll journey to Rhoe's former home, talk my way past the current owner, and tour the place, if allowed.

Chapter Thirty-Two

Here I am upon the steps of 1002 Grange Road. It's taken no more than eight minutes to arrive. Thank God the home's in Annecy, not miles away in some city, which could have taken hours to drive. This is about the only good thing I could say about Rhoe; the damn rotter lived local.

Before tolling the bell, I plan my words carefully. I want to avoid any pronouncement that might force the owner to utter scram at my face. Feeling I'm prepared, I draw forth my finger and I'm pressing the buzzer. A rhythmic toll chimes the house, summoning forth its chieftain. I stand alone in wait of an answer. Finally the door gives as some elderly gent peers upon me.

He inspects me calmly while I'm addressing my name. "Hi, sir. Good day. I'm Detective Biertempfel."

He stretches his hand to mine. "Pascal. Pascal Cartier. I thought you'd be the man from the market, coming with my produce."

Pascal Cartier is an elderly widower, at seventy-two. Eleven years ago he lost his wife, Claudine, to a massive heat attack. After her death, Pascal could no longer remain in their home, despite all their memories. Eventually he found Guillaume Rhoe's home for sale and chose to move here.

"No, sir, Mr. Cartier, I'm not from the market. As I've said, my name's Detective Biertempfel." I consider my thought up speech from earlier, but professedly I realize, forget beating around the bush, screw conceptualized lies, I'll just keep it straight, my reason being here. "I'm working a case for a client. She mentioned a name, a man, Guillaume Rhoe. He used to live here."

"That's a name I haven't heard in awhile. Guillaume lived here some years back. I purchased the property after his death."

"Was anything left here?"

"Odds and ends. Hats, clothes, things like that. I have them boxed in the basement."

"Would you mind if I checked that stuff out? It'd be a great help."

"No, sure-sure. My stairs to the furnace room are rather steep. Prepare to watch your step."

Mr. Cartier leads me into his home. Behind him I journey through the parlor. At the end of the room we hang left, where we pass through an opening leading to a hall. Farther down I spy the gleaming light of the kitchen.

Pascal unlocks a door positioned at the rear of the room and, with his feeble right hand, he attempts tugging it. "Well, gee whiz. I'm afraid I haven't the strength, young man. Maybe you'll try?"

Poor fellow's a string bean. He lacks the performance to struggle with a hefty frame such as this. Should it come off its hinges, it'd crush him, no doubt. I hassle with the knob while I tug and pull the ingress. Nothing's happening. I can't get it to budge, the damn door. Maybe I've underestimated my strength? Have I become week all a sudden? My toilful efforts are defeating me, and to my back I hear him laughing.

"A tough one, she is. This door's always been the same, I remember; stubborn to move."

"Well, I say. When's the last time you had her open?"

Pascal gives not a moment's thought. "Seven, eight years. I've avoided the basement. Don't like it much there."

"Seems whatever moisture's in the basement's gotten into your door." I continue my fight. Ain't no way in hell I'm leaving and giving up. I won't allow it. I want to know what's down there. What's hiding? My frustrations are weighing, flustering my physical potency. "Well, gosh dang." Never have I seen one so stuck. It's just ridiculous. I feel like a fool.

"I'm sorry, young man. Maybe she's meant to stay closed."

I hear Pascal, but thankfully my response comes as this. "I'm getting it there. I'm feeling some effort. Maybe another tug or two?"

"If you get it, you'll have to venture on your own. My knees are shot badly. They'll lock up if I go."

"She's coming along. Think I just about got her." I release my grip as the door swings toward my chest. "Bout time." I turn to Mr. Cartier. "My arms were getting sore."

"Those stairs now, they're onerous, so you be careful. Turn right when you land at the bottom. Against the wall's a box labeled junk. That'll be it, what you're searching."

"Just one?" I query.

"Mmm, yeah."

One's certainly better than none, no argument. I'm hoping the box contains something significant. I simply need evidence, however small, to show Miss Laroque.

"I have a flashlight. Should be on the first step. Maybe it works? And check for dangling lights off the ceiling. I'll be up here."

Pascal flips the switch going down the flight of stairs. Overhead a pale bulb emits its glow. It's not much brilliance, but I see and, in seeing, I spot the creepy crawlies, up high, down low, and appearing at each corner. "You've got spiders, I see."

"Oh, those are harmless web-spinners, son. They won't mind you if you don't mind them."

"I'll consider it a fair shake."

I journey on through the stale air, down into the bleary footfall, then come to a halt as I'm arriving at the end of the platform. This room feels cool, damp, and creepy, but I shake away my sensations as I tread forth and step right. My sight's obscured by the block of darkness before me, but still I walk. Grappling the flashlight within my hand, I search for a button. I give up when feeling nothing. To hell with this. My patience falls short. There's no switch, latch, or clasp.

I gather myself, then consider a new attempt. I give the thing a good twist, but get zilch. Maybe the darn light's without juice, or could it be the crappy thing's defective? Perhaps it's been stripped of batter- ies, or unfavorably, the lousy thing's just broken. It's done diddly squat considering I've engaged all my efforts. I no longer wish to fiddle with this doggone searchlight. It's out of my mind and away from my cares. Instead, I decide to search for a drop-light. Cartier says they're down here, so I quest about. Granted, the room's dark, therefore I acknowledge this shall take time.

I saunter through the hushful expanse with a few thoughts in mind. Where's a pull string? Why aren't there pull strings? Then, smack,

I whack my head. It doesn't hurt, but whatever's hit me keeps clouting me up side my crown. Back and forth it sways, while me, I hurriedly grasp my hand through the air. I'm now feeling an object within my palm. What do you know, it's one of umpteen drop-lights. To my merriment I've obtained one. Thank you, God, it hit me. Anyway, I pull the string and, spark; illumination.

Presently having a sufficient, well, near sufficient amount of light, I can meddle through the box, which is stationed just before me. I've read the bold large letters that've grasped my awareness and, so, in viewing it, I know that casket of crap's the one I've been searching. I waste no time in treading forward. At last, Rhoe's shit is in my reach.

I tug the box, situating it below the ceiling light. If I'm to browse this mess over, wouldn't it be fair to view it clearly? Upon the box I spy a knotted piece of string. Its usage was assigned to keep the flaps from flipping open, but also it's a disadvantage for irksome bugs and stinking moths which feed on things like garments. It's food for them; they don't care. Myself, well, I've had many shirts and pants cast to waste as a result of those beleaguers.

Reaching to my pocket, I search for a knife. I slice the string, cutting its threads in half. The remains of twine drift down to the floor as I'm tugging the cardboard flaps.

Now, staring me in the face are a pair of trousers and, below them, several more. I take each out, then check the pockets for notes or forgotten cash.

In my digging I find they're all bare. So I move to the next collection, which are shirts, mostly fashioned in white, cream, and tan colors. Below are a meager amount in green, yellow, and blue. Seems Rhoe stuck to solids more than stripes and batiks. As I did with the trousers, I'm doing the same with these shirts, checking for simple jottings or neglected loot.

As before, nothing. I return to the confinement, digging from end to end. I spot suspenders which I toss to the floor, not giving much care about them. I'm now pulling forth shoes, stinky, smelly shoes, that once fit on Rhoe's feet. I hate touching other people's footgear. There's just something about it that simply disgusts me. Call me strange, if you will, it's how I am. I disregard the loafers as I'm drawing forth flattened hats. No use for them now; they've been squished beyond wear, as if Guillaume's actually in need of toppers, the dead louse.

This box is boring me, but now my curiosity spies an immaculate mahogany caddy, with crafted ivory inlays. Could it be something interesting's inside? I open it to several tie tacks, a couple rings, and tarnished cuff links. Even after removing all this shit, I still feel the box is heavy. Wooed by my instincts, I begin to shake it; somewhere within, something moved, an object slid. The sound's impossible to deny. Undoubtably, I heard it, so I jolt the thing again. As I'm doing so I check for hidden compartments. I try along the bottom, pushing each side to see if something loosens. No luck. My hand then wanders to the top, repeating the same motion. I don't understand, not a damn thing's come unearthed. Why? Am I working this wrong? This caddy should have been a cinch.

I deliberate my next thought of inspection. In an effort I tug the front, expecting an unseen drawer to spring forth. I attempt pulling along the back, thinking a trap might release. Apparently, however, I can't make sense of what's to be done. I'm no puzzle genius, but I wish one was beside me. I suppose I'll have to accept being useless. In reali- ty these matters beckon folks with more brains than myself. Instead of giving up, I badger my dim-witted mind for further solutions.

I rub the caddy's top, tracing its inlays with the stroke of my finger. As I'm drawing the already etched details, my index comes across a small piece of raised wood. I continue when another releases, then finally, one more. To my surprise the box top lifts, exposing a disguised cubical. While yanking back the cover I reveal a tooled brunette journal, dinky in size, with leather ties.

I'm undoing the straps as Pascal calls to me. "Young man? Hello? You all right?"

"Just fine, Mr. Cartier. Still going through stuff."

I draw my attention back to the journal. The first page describes Rhoe's affection for Yria. As he goes on, I'm detecting the fixated desires of Guillaume's polluted mind, both profane and explicit. One verse states his animalistic urge of wanting her strapped in bondage, all the while ramming her with his manhood. He visualizes her climax, then writes his desire to choke her as she's peaking. Rhoe additionally states his aspiration for seeing Yria pass out. When she does, he discusses the menacing attributes he'll contrarily inflict, which will rouse her from somnolence, while additionally adding to Rhoe's perverted excitement. One calamity mentioned is sticking steel skewers into her suckling sites. The rest is too nauseating to mention, so I'll bypass the succeeding paragraphs.

Forth on in the journal are records pertaining to days and times Guillaume saw Yria. Knowing somewhere within these pages are implications to the murder of Yria Dane, I decide to shove the journal into my pant waist for disguise.

I return once more to the box of Rhoe's shit, seeking anything extra that might be of use. At the very bottom I spy the coordinated attire of an ex appointed cop. I'm drawing the uniform out when my hand comes into contact with something furry, alive, and rushing past my wrist. I pull back when spotting a fully grown mouse. It begins to scram once catching my sight. Through a hole chewed along the box's rear corner, it scurries forth, leaving me to inspect its course with my eyes. "That's right, rodent, run for your life," I whisper. Had it been found in the alley of Harbour Ridge, it might have been skewered and devoured for supper.

I return Guillaume's belongings to the box, flip down the flaps, and knot the twine just as it had been before. After pushing the cardboard against the wall, I decide to look around. Don't know why, just feel like it. I suppose I want to nosey my way through the basement. I do, then I stop, because something's fallen. I heard the direction of the crash and go to it. Cast to the floor, I see a brick. It had somehow descended the wall and, just a step from where it lay, I spy a door. Beside the barri- er, a few spaces left is a four and a quarter inch by three and a quarter inch hole. I stall as the crater peers toward my face like a large dark eye. A strange question nags me. Had this fallen brick been some sort of strange sign? It's led me here, after all.

I return my gaze to the mysterious door. A determined sensation requests me to open it. Where it'll go, I have yet to perceive, but I be- lieve once my reach takes that knob, I'll be sure to find out.

This door, like the basement, hasn't been opened in years, and I'm certain this stupid thing's going to be stuck. I've only my prayers to as- sist me. So to God, I am asking, let it release. I'm not in no mood to fight the darn thing.

After two hefty jerks, the frame complies and swings to my chest. Presently, looking into the space, I'm presented with disappointment. I had hoped to see a room, either small or big, but instead I spy an en- casement of shelves, counters containing garden instruments, hand tools, spackle, and paints. I view a can, then tip it forward. Inside are a mess of nails and small traps used for catching mice.

Immediately I stall my contemplation. Right away my attention's directed to a noise just beside me. Upon the ground floor's another brick, same in size as the first, yet this one's cracked into three separate pieces. I wonder what'd been the cause of them falling? In all ableness they could have tumbled to the ground last week, a month ago, or even a year, but instead they've dropped now? On thought, seems the con- crete's giving away. Then again, as odd as I find it, the blocks have pref- erably collapsed while I'm here. I gaze at the two holes while stretching my hands. I hope Pascal doesn't mind me fooling with his wall, on ac- count I'm about to tear the shit up.

I dust away excessive debris before sending my hand through the cleft. In me I possess hope of grasping sheltered objects which had purposely been sealed in this breach. With every effort I stretch, extending my fingers, and straining them as far as they'd reach. Sad- ly, I've come across an empty space. Should I remove a third brick? I don't think it'd do any harm. I consider my prevision and take my chance.

Momentarily, I return to the bordering door, probing its shelves. My eyes then fall upon a chisel. Stepping back to the wall, I start stab- bing cement. Thankfully it's freeing as it descends to the floor. All right, great. Keep crumbling like this, I'm sure to stay happy.

I further go, pursuing my mission. After scraping an outline around the block, I ease the thing out. As it falls to my hand, I'm im- mediately spotting something strange. From the top of the stone loaf, drilled straight to its base, is a cylinder rift. Through it, direct down the middle, I see a piece of tied string. Only reason for doing this was so an individual could conceal money, or perhaps a reticent note.

I flip the stone over and, carefully folded into a pocket-sized square, I find an entry of some kind. The tips of my thumb and index clinch the article and, slowly, very slowly, I tug it along. It releases from the string, then slips to my hand.

Traces of citrus presently advance to the air as I'm unfolding the paper. I draw it closer to take a breath and, in doing so, I've made a mistake. I choke and begin coughing. The essence of lemon lingers within my breathing spouts, tingling my nose and trailing through my esophagus. After gaining myself I commence to undoing the paper. It appears at this moment I'm observing more than one page; but just a minute now. Something strikes me. No words have been jotted; well, not visible, anyway. On the contrary, I realize a pronouncement's been written. It was composed, however, to deceive the claimant's sight. One just needs sense to understand this.

My knowledge tells me these entries were written using the juice of a lemon. Ultimately, what had been produced was invisible ink. The solution's to hold a page before a candle and, in doing this, the scribble turns brown before sullying the paper. It's an approach to a centuries old trick to employ secret messages. Thankfully, as it just so happens, I possess the discernment of recognizing confessions that are trying to cheat me.

Rhoe, as slick as he was, figured in doing this, he'd stay ahead of the game. To him, no soul possessed the slightest understanding on how to view these words he obscured. The dumb idiot, had he not imagined the possibility of these being read? Too bad for him I smelt the redo-lence of citrus.

I haven't time here and now to decipher these notes. The analyzation will have to take place at my home. I decide to stuff the leaflets inside my pocket. I wouldn't want Pascal finding me with these things I've discovered. Legally, these belong to him, but if they contain evidence of Yria's murder, well, then, I'd already have them.

It's sad, I think. Taking from an elderly man's merely wrong, but to protect what I'm doing, you see, I must oblige to this act. I don't want any part of this case being leaked, even if the jabber's an aging old man. Should things reveal themselves later, I'll deal with it then. For now Cartier can remain without knowledge.

I abandon the basement as I'm returning upstairs. Pascal's seated at his table with a mug of Joe and a plate of galettes. "Find anything you want?" he asks.

"Ah-ugh, no. Just junk, like you said."

"Oh, 'cause I'd have told if you wanted that box, you could have it. It's done nothing but sit in my basement."

"I'd have no use for it, really."

"Well, if you change your mind, come back and get it."

What a kindly guy this man is. In some respects he reminds me of my uncle. Maybe his mannerisms, or the way he sweeps his fingers slowly? I suppose he unconsciously does it, as did my uncle. What a great man he was, my father's brother. He's journeyed on to heaven now and had done so years back. I wept hard for that man, I had. He meant as much to me as my father, and I was rueful in the way God took him away. Having been a fireman, he was out on a call. The building he was at collapsed with him in it. I'm happy, though, he saved many lives that day. If only God had granted his own, but, as not to dwell on sad moments, I snap forth from retention. I'm hardly sure whether I'll be coming back to this house, but likelihood always looms.

Chapter Thirty-Three

I'm back at Deja's, where I find her minding our evening meal. I sneak behind her, then leaning in, I kiss the back of her head. "How's your day been?"

"Enjoyable. I found me a bracelet. I didn't buy it, though. I knew how you'd get."

"You didn't or you did?"

"I didn't, I swear. But, Satordi, it was so pretty. I might have bought it if the jeweler hadn't been asking so much."

"Stay patient. Maybe one day he'll have it on sale." I peer behind me. "Ambrielle around?"

"Upstairs. I bought her some dresses. She's trying them on. Hope you don't mind. It's just, I felt bad. The poor girl barely had money."

I mumble, "Blame her father for that."

"I'm sorry?"

"Never mind."

Deja turns into me. "You going to be around for dinner?"

"Should be, if I'm not working."

"Can't I just have a straight answer?"

"You know how it goes. And your expensive taste, Dej, well, you wouldn't have it if I was broke."

"Don't throw the blame on me. You're a slave to your job, you know that."

"I can't help being addicted to work."

Deja hints softly, "It'd be nice if one night you stayed busy with me."

"I'll be around for that, kitten."

"You men and your lines."

I heard her say something, but I don't know what she said. Rather, I progress to the table, where I lounge in my seat. I then grasp the salt shaker and spin it around. I let it dance in four circles, but now its whirl's slowing down.

Ambrielle soon emerges as she trails through the kitchen. I grin, but say nothing.

The maiden beams modestly when returning a smile.

My darling Deja glances upon Ambrielle with a seraphic gaze. "The other dress; I suppose it fit?"

"It was perfect, ma'am. No loose ends."

"Oh, good. I was worried it'd be a little big, like the other. If we find time tomorrow we'll stop by the seamstress."

"I could do the work myself."

"Absolutely not. We'll get the altercations done professionally."

"Ma'am, don't be obdurate. I could manage."

"It'd been my choice to buy you those dresses, and it'll be my choosing to pay the adjustments."

Ambrielle bows her head. "You're too kind. I appreciate everything you've done. Detective Biertempfel, too. You've both gone beyond your means and you've hardly even known me."

I watch the smile form on Deja's face as she's shaking her head. I know she wasn't compelled on taking in some strange girl, but she did as a favor. She could have simply said no, but instead my babe didn't. She's a good woman because she has a good heart, then there's me, I'm thinking. I'm still not understanding how such a darling gal could love some noxious creep. I know to say quickly, we're two different people. So how is it we get along when we, as individuals, are completely dis-similar? Obviously Dej is a countess of conduct. And me, yeah, well, and me. I was bred for the streets, but forget this jumble; I have im-portant terms to pronounce. "Tomorrow, if the two of you make plans, make sure they're out of town. I don't care where you go, but stay out of Annecy."

"We already know," my honey tells me.

"All right. Well, you mind making some coffee, then? I need to speak with Ambrielle." I smile, then turn to the courtesan who's sitting quietly. "You got a few minutes? We need to address some things." I settle my notepad on the table, then flip the thing open. "You've any relation to a man named Marpuis?"

Ambrielle thinks, then shakes her head. "Marpuis, no."

"Do you know someone by that name, then?"

"I can't say I do."

"Something close to it, then?"

"Well, there's Dupuis, my cousin. And last I knew he lived in town."

"His first name, I need it."

"Marcel."

Marpuis. Oh, I see. Ghislain had it, but he had the names combined. "We need to find him, call him, something."

"I'll have to check my black book."

"Find it and come back."

I send Ambrielle off as Deja rises with questions. "Who's Marpuis? Marcel Dupuis?"

"A dead man, if I don't find him."

"Wouldn't that be an issue for the cops? Let them handle it."

"Too risky, I can't."

"Too risky? Satordi, hey, don't turn a deaf ear."

"They'd know about the other bodies, then take me to jail. I can't risk calling."

"What bodies? Where are there bodies?"

"Never mind what I've said. It's best you not know."

"Jesus, Satordi, you're talking about jail."

"'Cause they'll think I did it, then go after Marin."

"Marin? What's his role in this?"

"He was with me. Cops know what happened. They'll charge us with murder."

"You're scaring me." I watch her step from the table with fear in her eyes. "Did you do something? Was there an accident? Satordi, tell me."

"We didn't do anything, promise. Trust me, I haven't killed any people."

Ambrielle returns, then quickly notices Deja stalled before the cabinet with a note of dread upon her. Instantly she becomes worried. Ambrielle rushes beside her, prepared to help whatever way. "Miss D, whatever's wrong? It looks as though you're wanting to cry."

"I spilt coffee. It spattered me," Deja lies. "I'm all right, though. I'll be okay."

Her words floor me with shock. Whatever her reason, Dej refrained from the truth. It's not that it matters. Ambrielle knows what happened, but Deja doesn't know that.

Ambrielle makes her way to the table and, like a true lady, tucks her dress beneath her before sitting. She then stretches her arm before me where, within her palm, rests a small ebon book.

"Marcel's number's on the left."

"Give him a call. Do it now. I'll advise what you say."

My aim's to get Marcel on the phone. Both cousins can shoot the breeze, I don't care, but after awhile I'll interfere and cut in.

My purpose is to write simple inquiries, flash them to Ambrielle, then during her discussion, she can present all my questions. Finishing my announcement, she agrees to the terms. I point her toward the phone as I'm preparing requests.

I write thoughts pertaining to strange packages, odd sounds, and strange smells. Some of my jottings might come across weird or out of place; then, on second thought, truly it'll depend on Ambrielle's fluidity of speech and how she'll direct it. I persist with what I'm doing when Ambrielle returns to the table. "Why'd you get off the phone? I have questions."

"No answer, sir."

I shake my head. "Let's just hope he's gone out. I'll have you try again later."

"He should have answered, though. He never goes out. He suffers from anthropophobia."

"Huh?" I'm unsure what she means.

"He has a fear of people, sir."

"Seriously? Well, okay. Okay, we're going to him. Get your shoes."

Deja overhears and soon interrupts, "What about dinner?"

"Honestly, dear, we won't be forever."

"This is what tires me. We're hardly together."

"Don't be mad, babe. I'm still coming back."

"Well, I won't be here. I'll go to Cerissa's."

Deja already holds x's against me and I've added one more. "We'll come there, then."

Dej, choosing to ignore me, says not a word. Instead, she gathers whatever's made and takes it from the kitchen. Maybe, hopefully, she'll have stewed in her anger and it'll have left by the time I'm there.

Already Dej has passed through the ingress and is leaving the house. From the front step I watch as she leans to her car, followed by the clangor of her door as it smacks shut beside her. Normally, she'll have jerked the door lightly, but that's not the matter I'm seeing today.

"She'll simmer down, give her time," Ambrielle assures me.

"She usually does."

"She always goes to your brother's?"

"'Cause Cerissa's there. I think if she had the opportunity, she'd probably move in."

Believe me, I want to be with Dej more often. Beside her, all I have's Sable who brings me joy, but to a certain extent. Deja has the capabilities Sable's lacking. When's the last time Sable's cooked me a meal? She's a machine, so it's never. My regard for Sable's different. I'll say it; if I had to choose between my two women, God, tell me I wouldn't, but if I did, Dej would own my vote, completely.

I replace my thoughts with my work. "Where's this address we're searching?"

I hear Ambrielle, "3244 Dauphine. It's an apartment. Door ten."

"Dauphine's, ah, a block from Canal Street, right?"

"Mmm-hmm. Then turn left and drive a little way down."

Though I was born and bred in Annecy, there're some streets that lack my awareness. A number of them I haven't traveled, others I'm not keen on their names, or maybe I never paid attention? Anyway, we're still in Annecy, so thankfully I'm home. Well, not in my place of shelter, but you get what I mean. "Should we expect anyone with him, your cousin?"

"His mom, if she's there."

"No one else?"

"Mmm, last I saw him's been more than a year, and it was only his mom living with him."

"How's he related, I've been meaning to ask?"

"Marcel's mother, she's Haulmier's sister."

"Does your dad have no brothers?"

"Please, I dislike that man. He's no father to me. But answering your question, he has only sisters."

"Reinella and who?"

"Adelisa and Laina."

Sometime during our conversation I pulled along the curb of 3244 Dauphine. "I'm guessing we're here? Anyway, let's get moving. You said apartment ten?"

I follow Ambrielle along the stairs of the adobe, then into the scarcely lit space. You'd figure these people would know to change light bulbs. If not them, at least the repairman.

"Watch your step, sir. These stairs are rotted and coming loose."

"The whole building looks dead. I'm wondering if we should leave?" "It's how it's always been," she tells me. "Half the tenants are mid-aged or diseased."

We rise through the stairs as I'm peering round. "This a nursing home? Place smells strange, unwashed and old."

"It's not a ranking hotel, but it's the best he could do. We're here, sir."

Directing the girl's stance before me, I then command my instruction and tell her to knock. Whoever's inside should be coming shortly, but time passes and, for the moment's we've stood here, we've begun to feel worried. I give a few breaths before I direct her knock again. I've got that feeling in my gut, that bad feeling. You know that sensation you get when you've eaten things you shouldn't mix, or the thought of things that make you sick? I listen to that inner guide in my belly, to that which never fails when I've given care to listen.

I place my hands upon Ambrielle's shoulders. "You should wait downstairs."

"I can't stay here?"

"I'd rather you stay on the steps and wait there."

I make certain the girl does as I've said and, after watching her disappear at the landing, I make my attempt at the door. There's a fifty percent chance it'll open, and happily I find it comes free without hassle. I ease in when coming into a small den. A gush of stench comes upon me. I know that smell; its funk is familiar. Now all I got to do's find the body.

My investigation leads me through the house. While scouting rooms, I've come upon Mrs. Dupuis in the kitchen. She's chest down on the table, with her face a front to its surface. Her arms reach forth as she was trying to stretch, and from my stance I sight the marks; fissur- ing holes and overhung veins, their appearance, identical to the before- hand bodies I've seen. Damn. I look closer. No way she had a chance. Those things, these holes, they're everywhere. Her color, or lack there of, is blanched like the others. All I can do is credit Yria for gaining the blood she so desperately wanted.

I'm in no doubt after finding Mrs. Dupuis that her son will be here. I leave the body as I exit the kitchen. I check bedrooms and, within the last, upon a bed's a pair of poodles. Fluffy one lies to its side, frozen in death. Unfortunately, Fluffy two's not as tranquil. It respites upon its back, with fours straight and its face looming forward. Sad sight, them poor pups. Prior to closing the door, I wish them off to doggy heaven.

I gain my bearings to continue my search. Upon a minute I've come to the bathroom. It's taken less than a second till I've spotted Marcel. He's slumped in death much as I figured.

Through a whisper, I speak, "Jesus, kid, why'd you open it? That box and its crap, and you had to get tempted. Now look, your breath is gone and so's your mother's."

Without warning, Marcel's body tips back. It's like someone's pur- posely knocked this kid over. Apparently, many hours ago, rigor mortis kicked in. Marcel's legs and feet are now risen, with knees slightly bent. His spine arches upward, all the while keeping him supported by the lowest part of his back.

In contrast to a letter, he looks much like an ill contrived Z, or maybe my mind lacks reflection? Anyway, his sight is abnormal, and it's his look that appalls me; not just the body, but that contorted fear in his face which screams silent clamor.

What more could I do than stare at the dead? My arrival's come late, and in my shame I was unable to grant help. I gaze one final glance when something jumps out; a pen. I see a pen not more than a foot from Marcel. Why's it here? I know the reason the contents of the box are out, but a pen? I hadn't seen a pen within the grasp of the others.

I tread carefully around the body and pass by the John. On the farthest side, which was once out of sight, I spot what looks to be a letter or written account. The paper doesn't belong with those from the box. This one's different. It contains Marcel's writing. In my disbelief I scan through it. The letter reads as follows.

> *Within a trunk, within his house,*
> *contains the head of a man from Spouse.*
> *It was kept, and it was safe, so no one*
> *knew the man's real fate. Beneath the dirt,*
> *within the ground, the bones remain without its*
> *crown. Only one may know this truth and, as it*
> *goes, I've chosen you.*

Quickly I stuff the letter into my pocket as I'm about to rush off. I then stall when considering something doesn't add up. Whose head's in reference here? Guillaume had a second victim?

My curiosity's got me. I'm running downstairs, expecting Ambri- elle, but the girl isn't here. Hadn't she realized I had things, important things to attend? I haven't the time to locate this missing chicky. This puts a damper on things and screws me all up.

I trail to Sable in anger and, as much as I'd like to yell, I can't. People will hear, then know I was here. I continue while drawing Sable's key from my pocket; then, leaning into my car, I slip my key to the fixture. Click, I hear the lock. I slide my hand to the door's release and tug it open.

While lowering myself to my seat, I spot Ambrielle. Sometime during my investigation, she returned to my car. She let herself in and now the girl's sleeping. But how? Oh, God, she left the door open? What's it take for people to know Sable's got to be locked, she's got to. Gee, I think, I'll get her ass up. "Hey. Hey, you." I snap my fingers. "Come on, wake up. What, what're you doing here? How'd you get in?"

"The door. Oh, I'm sorry. I'm sorry, sir. Please don't be angry."

"I thought you knew the rules?"

"It won't happen again. I'll remember next time."

"You better swear."

"Sir, I'm sorry, really. It was an accident."

"I'll let you off now, but don't do it again."

Ambrielle acknowledges, but is almost afraid to ask, "Did you find Marcel?"

"His mother, too. Police should be finding them soon. Someone will call after smelling the odor."

"Could you be a tad less insensitive? It's my family you speak of."
I apologize, but Ambrielle says, "It's just, it's not something you say."

"Hey, I said I was sorry."

"Fine, sir, but say it no more."

In due time I pull to my brother's. I grab the pogos from the back seat of my car, then carry them to the house. Not knowing if Paien or Zuri will answer, I put them behind me. Ambrielle and I are waiting shortly when Cerissa decides to answer.

My sister-in-law presides her glance. "Don't think about stepping inside if you plan to leave quickly."

"Deja still mad?"

"Heated."

"Oh, boy. Couldn't you have talked her down?"

Cerissa allows myself and Ambrielle's entrance as she continues to speak. In the house, against the wall, I prop the pogos.

Cerissa acknowledges, "I don't think she cared to hear what I said."

"I prayed she'd simmer down, but, really, she knew what she was in for when we consented to date."

"She's lonely, Satordi. I understand. So should you."

"She won't like it, but I've got places to be later."

"I understand you and Marin. I understand all your work. But Deja's a little younger. It may take her more time."

"I just wanted the road to be a bright and happy one."

"There's still plenty time. Come on, Deja's in the back yard catching fireflies with the kids. Sorry, Ambrielle, for having you stuck in the middle of this."

The young maiden and I speak in unison; however, our responses are different.

She goes to say, "It doesn't matter, ma'am. We've all had our troubles." While my replies comes as this, "I suppose I'm ready to get clobbered, but it'd be nice if you women stood in my way."

"Don't rouse her and I'm sure you'll be fine."

"That might be less easy than it sounds."

I advise Ambrielle to go on, fill her plate. By now I know the girl's bound to be hungry.

Cerissa overhears. "Satordi, that's not the way we treat guests. Come on, Ambrielle, I'll get your food."

"You don't do that for me. Then again I'm no one special. I need a candle. You got one to light?"

Cerissa's nodding. "Ah, check the mantle in the den. But don't be burning my house."

I saunter through the living room and I'm eyeing the fireplace. There a candle sits upon the broad slab of teak. I grab the rushlight, then walk to the couch. Before me I slide the bougie along the table. Now I'm searching for matches. In my attempt to find them, I draw forth the papers I'd stuffed in my pocket. Oh, gee, and I've almost forgotten Rhoe's diary I'd hidden within the waist of my pants.

Anyway, gathering myself, I light the wick and, bam, there's my fire. Such a beautiful flare, this yellow-white glow. If I go off and I'm gazing too deeply, I'm liable to find myself induced in trance, but why would I care? It'd bring me some much needed peace. Aside from that, I need to decipher these papers and I realize I'll need help. I'll need someone to write.

I shout to Ambrielle when she appears at the doorway, "You finished eating?"

"Almost."

"Finish, but I'll need you here when you're through." The young maiden does as advised, then returns to me later. Eventually she stands before me as she awaits my instruction. "Whatever I say, I want it written down. Got that?"

The girl nods as I'm holding the first page before the stretching flare. After giving it a minute, I see a disclosure of words spread through the paper. I go on to read.

> *The 2 of August, 1941*
> *For the last time Yria's dismissed me.*
> *I can no longer handle these rejections she's so*
> *easily given. I've told that woman many*
> *times how I've felt, but she discomfits my*
> *feelings as though I weren't human. I may not*
> *be Matthias, but I'm deserving of Yria*
> *as much as he'd been. I've requested her*
> *companionship for the last time tonight,*
> *but like earlier times, she regularly*
> *denied me. I know Basile wants her just as*
> *much as I, but I won't let him at her. If I can't*
> *have Yria, no man ever will.*

"You getting all this? You want me to stop?" I see Ambrielle nod, so I know to continue.

> *Remaining firm on my word, I've brought her*
> *here to my home. I obtained her after*
> *the local joint had let out. It had been a*
> *flawless opportunity, because I caught her*
> *alone. I pressed the rag to her face,*
> *forcing her to inhale ether. I thought Yria*
> *was dying when I'd done it, but I later found out*
> *she had only passed out a short period.*
> *She awoke on the table as I was bisecting her*
> *skin. I'd already split her flesh in two when I*
> *was attempting to extract it off muscle.*
> *She'd awakened with the most horrible screams. The*
> *sight of seeing her alive had jarred me.*

*Stupefied and hardly thinking, I drove my knife
into her widened eye. Not once did it freak me,
what I did. My trepidation deserted me and that
fear became madness. I twisted the blade, I
whirled it around. That's when I recognized how
much I'd enjoyed it. Eventually, I popped back
my blade and out sprung her eye. It soared
across the room and slapped the stone wall. I
was along with enjoyment when that damn bitty
cursed me. That's all it took. My anger set in,
joined with my madness. I picked up the nearest
tool, a blowlamp. I turned to Yria and, in her
face, laid my torch. She screamed and screamed,
and for my reasons, disturbing as they are, I
ate it up. I wish she hadn't died so quickly,
because within seconds, that damn cunt had checked
out.*

"You get that all down?" I'm asking Ambrielle.

"Almost, sir. Is there more?"

"Nope, girl, that's it." I got what I needed and Orisia can know.

"What are your plans now that you have this confession?"

"Probably, I'll have to speak with authorities."

"You still believe she'll be found?"

I reach to the table and grab the tooled journal. "I'm hoping this says something or gives an idea. I've much to do, though, and I'll need to make time." I sit silently while trying to think.

"Is there something I can do?" Ambrielle's inquiring.

I continue my probing. How'll I sort out my time for that which draws my attention? I've entirely too much to do and many places to go.

I'm feeling flustered before a lighted idea presently persuades my attention. I look to Ambrielle as my consideration emerges. "How'd you like to make money? You know I haven't the time to read this, but it has to be done."

"Hand it over, then."

"Think you can start tonight? We're in bit of a cramp."

"I can read now, sir; it don't matter."

"Might be better. I just need it read, long as it's before the week's up, okay?"

I feel a grumble in my stomach, an evident sign telling me I must eat. I snuff out the candle and, once the wax has cooled, I return it to the mantle. I now head to the kitchen with Ambrielle at my back.

The kitchenette's empty, so I step to the window. Peering through, I see Cerissa, Deja, and the kids catching bugs. With my back to Ambrielle, I say, "I know you'd like to be with them, so don't worry about that journal just yet."

"I agreed to start now."

"You deserve a little fun. Go on, girl, scram."

"I won't be out long, then."

I saunter to the oven where the food still sits inside a great big pot. I don't know what Deja made, but I'm sure it's good. I draw back the lid and I'm staring inside. Looks like French onion soup. I'm not a huge fan, but it's something to eat.

I set the burner on medium flame and let my food heat, then, as I'm waiting, I decide I'll pop my head through the back door. I'm spotting Paien on a bench nearby, holding a jar of insects, which he shows to his mom. A little farther I see Zuri in the dark, performing somersaults. Aside Cerissa, Ambrielle has her hair braided by the hands of my gal.

"You look pretty," I relay to the young maiden. "I've told Dej she should be a beautician. All right, well, I'll be inside now."

So I sat alone and ate my soup, which had been sort of sad on account people were here, but I had no one to eat with. I'm used, though, to eating on the road by myself. A lot of my life has been lived in this way.

Cerissa enters the back door with the kids when I'm hearing them whine.

"I want to stay in the yard," Paien pleads.

"Me, too. Just a little longer."

"Zuri, you're overdue for a bath. Now run up stairs. I'll be along to draw your water."

Paien leans into his sister, laughing. "Ha-ha, mama's gonna make you wash."

Cerissa overhears and adds her expression, "Why're you laughing? You're next, young man."

Zuri, at the same time, squints at her brother. "Shut up, Paien."

"Mom! Mom, you heard her. She told me to shut up."

"Zuri, apologize right now to your brother."

Paien laughs again. "Ha-ha, mom sided with me."

"Paien, stop nagging your sister."

I intervene, "Won't you let me handle this?" I peer to my young niece and nephew. "You know good children get gifts when obeying their mom?"

Paien ponders, then asks, "Mom got us gifts?" "I want mine," Zuri exclaims.

"Then take your baths," I simply direct them. "Me first. I'm going first," Paien's screaming.

"Listen to your mom, then. Get your baths and, when you're out, I'll have something waiting."

The kids exit the room, chasing each other up the stairs.

"Well, you've handled that nicely, but you realize I've nothing to give them?"

With a sly grin I peer to Cerissa. "I might have a surprise."

"You bought things?"

"Well, just wait."

"Great. Now they'll be expecting stuff every time you're here."

"Maybe we'll get lucky and they'll both forget?" I smile.

"Children don't forget, Satordi. Sit tight. I'll be back."

After several minutes, Dej and Ambrielle return to the kitchen. Deja sees my empty bowl and draws it forth from the table, then steps to the sink to finish dishes.

I get up from my chair as I'm traipsing toward Dej. "You and Ambrielle going to be ready soon? I'll follow you home, make sure you get in."

"Let me finish these, then I'll tell Cerissa goodbye."

I wander off to make a call, to phone Ghislain and fill him in on my finds. I tell him about my journey to Rhoe's former house on Grange Road, where I found his journal and some papers he'd hidden.

"The damn bastard wrote a detailed report. We've got him, Ghis. We have his confession. Now to tell Miss Laroque."

"I can't believe you did it."

"Beside Guillaume Rhoe, had any headless bodies been sent to the morgue, do you know?"

Ghislain responds, answering, "Back then? Oh, I'd probably think not."

"Someone you can't think of shortly before, perhaps even right away following the abduction of Mrs. Dane?"

Ghis reaffirms his answer, telling me there'd been nothing similar to that I'd described.

All right, it's true. "We've got another body out there. Rhoe killed someone else. I don't know his identity yet, but we'll need to find out."

Ghislain's quite shocked by this news. He tells me, "What if Yria's husband was never killed in the war? Guillaume served the same time as Matthias. He'd been an MPO."

"I can't exactly say," I tell him. "What are you thinking, Matthias could have been the other victim?"

Ghis responds, telling me he hadn't actually known how Matthias Dane met his fate. His funeral was closed casket, so it's quite possible, still, Guillaume's victim had been him.

"In that case, we'll need an explanation of death document. Can you get it?"

"It'll probably be hard," he reacts.

"Do what you can. It's imperative we get that. That document's important to us."

Ghislain says he'll try tomorrow, and I hang the phone.

Sometime during my conversation with Ghis, Cerissa returned and, so, during my absence, she'd accompanied my lady and the young maiden girl.

"Hey, ah, I'll be out of here soon. Have the kids gone to bed?"

"Paien's drying off. Zuri's combing her hair. I'll have them down in a minute."

"Good. I don't got much time to be staying."

I wander toward the front door, searching for the pogos I staged near a wall. I hear the children's feet scrambling as I rush to approach the back kitchen.

I return to my seat in time, dropping the pogos on my lamp. Then, shoving my knees up, I hold them tight to the table.

In unison, I hear, even before they've reached the kitchen, Zuri and Paien, "Mommy! Mommy, we want our gifts!"

"See Uncle Tordi. I think he's hiding something."

"Come on, Uncle Tordi, we want our surprise!" Zuri squishes her palms together as though she's praying, but rather she begs, "Please, please, please, please."

"Yeah. I haven't nagged Zuri no more."

My nephew makes me laugh. "Come here, you two."

Their little faces fill with the brightest of smiles, and a glint of light shimmers in each of their eyes.

"Close your blinkers now. You shutting them tightly?" I hear their response when they both react, "Ah-huh."

"All right, no peeking. Hold out your hands." Before positioning the spring toys into their runty palms, I declare, "Don't be opening your eyes till I've said." They obey as they serve my direction. I'll no longer force them to endure their suspense. "Open your eyes!"

Their opticals widen, while apparent excitement radiates from their young, tender faces. The incorporated image has overjoyed these two kids. I'm happy to brag, saying it was me who'd done this.

Zuri blows her top. "Wow-wee, a pogo! Uncle Tordi, thank you."

"This is the best," expresses Paien. "I'm flipped, Uncle T."

"Glad you like them, but mind your mama, kids, and don't be springing these things in the house."

They then lean to me and embrace me with love.

"It's bedtime now. Set them away. You've got all day tomorrow to be playing."

"We just got them. No fair. It's not fair, Uncle Tordi."

"Zuri, shh. Say goodnight to Ambrielle and Aunt D. They'll see you tomorrow." I step from my seat and walk to Cerissa.

"Thanks for thinking of them. You mean a lot to the kids. They think the world of you."

"It's no problem." I turn to my darling Dej and the young Ambrielle. "Girls, ready?"

As incentive, Cerissa walks us to the door. I depart to my car while Dej and Miss Guloe step to hers. My darling pulls out first, then stops alongside me. I hint to Ambrielle to lower her window.

"I'll be behind," I say, "following you home, then be on my way."

Dej wonders, "You can't park and come stay?"

"Over?"

"That's what I'm asking. Whatever, Satordi. Decide what you want. I've got a car coming on me." She drives away.

In all truth, it is somewhat late, and I realize I never spend enough time with my gal. I'm sure I could abandon my work this one night. It's already too late to drop in and visit Miss Laroque, knowing she has Yria's young daughter to raise. I've already called Ghislain, having updated him on the conditions of our case. There's not much more I could be doing tonight. I guess instead of abandoning work, I'll just not have any.

I'll settle on going to my kitten's, where I'll remain till tomorrow. I realize, yes, if I'm to make this relationship work, I've got to apply effort. Lord knows she can't say I'm not trying.

Chapter Thirty-Four

I awoke at 7:20, leaving Dej to rest, as I had no intention of waking her. I peered on Ambrielle as she soundly slept, then made my way through the door.

Currently, I'm in Sable as we're heading to Ghislain's. I had spoken with him five minutes before leaving my gal's. As he directed, I've come to his house.

I'm now standing at door three, Ghislain's entrance. He's invited me in, so I head to his couch.

"I got in touch with a few of Rhoe's acquaintances last night. Adora and Gaston agreed they'd meet us."

I ponder, "And the others?"

"Well, Tayce moved to Quebec, Canada, as of forty-eight. No one's heard from him since."

"What about the other guy?"

"Basile. As Gaston informed me, relocated to Cherbourg, in lower Normandy."

"All right. Write them off. I don't know about you, but I'm not traveling to Canada. And Basile, well, forget, he's just a little, too, far."

"You're not wanting to talk with him?"

"Not unless we have to. Anyway, you have any luck finding, ah, hold on a sec." I forgot the name, so I'm having to check my notes. "Charlize Rousseau?"

"Not so much. Neither Gaston or Adora knows where she's at."

"We'll be speaking with them, though?"

"Yeah, boss. I'm just waiting to arrange it. Gaston's in Meythet and Adora, Rumilly."

"They're not far. Set up an appointment. Have them meet us at my building this evening, around six. I'll come back tonight and pick you up. I'm on my way to Orisia's now."

"You don't want me with you?"

I shrug. "If you're coming, better hurry."

"Yeah, I mean, I'm ready. You're bringing those papers you found, right?"

"What's that, Rhoe's confession?" I pat my pocket. "Got them right here."

We then exit his place.

I'm wondering how hard it'll be to convince Orisia these truths. The girl's so hardhearted when it comes to disclosing Rhoe's facts, even when it's right here in my hand, what he'd done. Watch, she'll try to claim me as the one who wrote these. I'm going to get my message across as boldly as possible, and if she has to hear certain disturbing details, well, course then, she'll hear.

Chapter Thirty-Five

I took time cruising over to Orisia's. I hadn't been much in a rush. I explained to myself, I'd get there when I could. So, going off course momentarily, I drove to the donut shop and got Ghis and myself a few patisseries and Joe. After leaving, we came directly to Miss Laroque's.

Of course, just as imagined, Orisia's not happy with the confession I've presented. As to console her, Ghislain has her in his arms as she cries.

"Guillaume loved her. I can hardly believe this. I trusted him." Ori-sia continues sobbing.

"It's hard, I know," Ghislain's saying. "But at least you've got the truth."

A young girl appears beneath the corridor, adorned in a simple blue jumper. Her taupe hair casts to her shoulders, where the tips have curled under. Her light green eyes trace the room and fall on Orisia.

"Aunty, are you okay?"

Miss Laroque looks up, wiping her flow of tears. "It's all right, Mira. Honey, I'm okay."

"But I see you cry."

Orisia looks to Ghis and me as she stands from her couch. "Will you excuse me just a moment, please?"

Miss Laroque then walks to her niece and slowly bends to the floor. She places her hands upon Mira's frail shoulders and is rubbing them softly.

"I'm just a little upset right now, sweetheart."

"Why, Aunty? Are they taking you away?" "No.

Oh, no, honey, they aren't taking me."

Across from me Mira raises an arm to her aunt, brushing aside Orisia's tears. "It's all right, Aunty. Don't be crying, please."

Orisia embraces the girl in a firm hug. "I'll try not, sweetie, I promise."

"You'll be okay. You will, won't you?"

"Of course, honey, of course."

"Then could I have permission to go next door?"

"Did Cordella's parents say it's okay?"

"Yes, ma'am."

"All right, but be home before noon."

Mira gives her aunt a kiss, then strolls to the door.

As Orisia returns to the couch, she asks, "How'll you find my sister? Do you know where you'll look?"

I confess, "Guillaume hadn't left any details to that. I'll do everything, though, to find her."

Orisia again breaks into cries. "This is just so hard. So very hard."

"I promise, Miss Laroque, I'll go all the places I can."

"I'm having a time accepting Guillaume as being the one who'd done this. It just shakes me up so."

"I know, ma'am. I know."

"You couldn't understand what I'm going through. After all these years and now knowing it'd been someone close to me. I'd not wish this upon anyone."

"If you'd prefer, we could come back later. Seems you might need some time by yourself."

"To cry more? Forget it, Detective, we'll finish this now."

I look to Ghislain, then return my gaze to Miss Laroque. "In respect to you, would you be fit to answer questions?"

Orisia breathes with much stress, then settles her propensity as her breathing's less tense. "Okay. Go on."

"You were familiar with Charlize Rousseau, is this correct?"

"Somewhat. I didn't really know her. I met her four times. It was quick hi and byes."

"Guillaume liked her, didn't he?" "I

suppose he had mild feelings."

"But they became a pair?"

"More like snuggle buddies. They weren't very serious."

"But Char, she was present that night your sister went missing?"

"For about twenty minutes. She was there, then gone before Yria arrived."

"She hadn't stayed?"

"Well, no. She was feeling sick. Had a stomachache, I think."

"You ever see her again after that?"

"Only once. She'd been a mourner at Guillaume's funeral."

"And that had been it?"

"Yeah, ah-huh."

"So you have no way of contacting her?"

"Never did. We had no friendship. Following Guillaume's death, she moved. She's kept contact with no one."

It's a shame, I think. It might have proved favorable to talk with her. If anyone knew Guillaume, it was Char. Had he confessed killing Yria to get it off his chest? This is a question that'll remain unanswered.

"Guillaume have any enemies, you know?"

"Besides myself?" Ghislain interferes. "Ghis, quiet. It wasn't directed to you."

"The cops working the case, they weren't fond of him. Then again, they'd been a pair of asses. They hardly liked anyone."

"So what happened with them?"

Once again Ghis interferes, "Ambroise Gravois became lieutenant and is in charge of the homicide unit."

"The other?"

"Retired, far as I know." "His name?" I ask.

"Pierre Dubois."

"I guess myself and Ghis will look into these men, see what we can find out, Miss Laroque."

"They'll be no help, but go on and try."

"I'll see to it they cooperate."

"I know you as a man of your word. I can trust what you say."

"But your displeasure with them?"

"They're imbeciles. I believe you'll see that. Let them endure what I and hundreds of others have. They'd change if tragedy hit close to their home. Not that I'd wish it. But, really, they could have taken better care of Yria's case."

"Some cops are just bad at their jobs. Guess those were, too."

Thankfully, Miss Laroque knows now the fate of her sister, and though she was displeased hearing Guillaume had been accused, she had to accept it when reading his own implications. It was then she conceived Guillaume had indicated himself, guilty. I hated her having to read chronicled accounts of her sister's last moments, but I had no other choice than to make her believe.

Chapter Thirty-Six

I've dropped Ghislain at his home to set up my evening appointments. Later I'll return to his place and pick him up, but now, for now, I'm head- ing to Pascal Cartier's, hoping I'll find a missing head in his basement.

After arriving at his residence, he allows me inside. I tell him, "I apologize for my being back, but I fear I've overlooked something."

He leads me through his kitchen, where the basement door awaits my return. It hasn't been long since I've seen the hatchway, but unlike before, I know what I'm seeking.

Should I find the head, it'll be taken to my friend, the doctor, that he might rule out any visible injuries which may have attributed to death.

I step through the basement, searching and thinking. For some reason my instincts return me to where I found the papers. The dark- ened space in the wall exhales a cold breath, making me suppose there might possibly be something back there. Drafts don't rush through an open breach for no reason. The air rushes from somewhere and it's my duty to find why.

My hand enters the hole and I'm now feeling grit. It's attracting particles to my skin as I stretch my arm along. I expand far enough that my head now rests upon the wall.

Against my lone extremity I feel myself brushing planks of wood. I suppose these are part of the home's frame? Anyway, I pat along, hop- ing to feel anything unusual or out of place. I endure this thirty seconds, then my fingers sweep across it. I'm unable to see, but the icy cold pat- tern I trace feels much like a hinge or bracket of some sort. I'm now realizing there's a hidden door aback to this wall and it'd been placed here for good reason.

I retrieve my arm so I may inspect the extent of space before me. In my observation I conclude that behind the ingress, near the four and a quarter inch by three and a quarter inch hole, is where the now known door lies in disguise.

As much as I'm wanting to tear things apart, this isn't my house. I return upstairs and, in a gentlemanly manner, request to excavate the site of the door.

Pascal accedes my implore as I'm promising to make the least mess possible.

I return to the basement where I get down to work. I fling open the door to the mini shack where the collection of garden instruments and hand tools remain. As promised, I'll keep to making the least mess I can. Only way to maintain that's to gently set this crap to the floor so I can uncover the shelves.

I sit the last of the junk beside me. Luckily, I'd come across a hammer. Seeing that the shelves are now cleared, I begin busting wood. I tear the planks away and let them fall to the floor. I go on to do this four times before the last piece gets broken.

Facing me is the back panel of the shack, nothing more. With my trusty hammer, I begin clobbering wood. I bust away and am ripping it forth just as quickly as my hands work. Finally, I'm left with nothing to do. All my labored attempts have come to an end, least for hammering, I think. Could be too soon to know; I'm merely guessing.

A front to my eyes I view the hidden door about a foot from my stance. Happily I am to see it. Silently, I praise, time I tear this shit open.

I place my hand on a clear crystal knob, then twist the thing slightly. Jovially I feel as the door's coming open. A raunch rush of air breezes my face as the door's swinging freely.

Beyond my sight's nothing but darkness. At the back of my pants I pat for a flashlight. I direct its range into the shadowed room ahead. I step through, barely able to discern any detail. If I find no light, how'll I illume the space? I decide to start searching for a switch or pull string.

Without luck I find nothing and my light hardly works. How ironic it is I step to the room and my flashlight decides to start failing. I have matches, however, but sadly they'll not last long before their flames creep down and burn away at my fingers. At that, my matches will be a last resort. I beat my flashlight onto my palm, praying for better lighting. Thankfully it's worked and I'm in view of things now.

Seems I'm standing in a fifteen by fifteen foot space, with a ceiling height of barely eight feet. Beneath my soles lie distressed boards, scuffled with wear that's worn out its stain.

I shine my light to the walls and glimpse the cinder blocks composing this place. They've been painted moss green, maybe as an act to beautify the place, who knows? I decide to shine my light toward the ceiling when, thankfully, I spot a drop-light overhead.

I pray the thing words.

I carry myself to the bulb. Along its side, just at the top, I find a twist switch. Apparently the bulb still has some juice as it brightens the room.

I return my gaze to the space around me. I hadn't spied it before, but I'm attempting to now. Toward the rear of the room's a hackneyed table that's endured all its time. A haggard slab of hard maple rests atop four cold metal posts. A rusted away shelf, the length of the counter, lies just below the maple slab with a pile of dried blooded rags. Above it are two metal drawers, which I decide to pull open.

Within the first are various sized knives that have seen better days and a sharpening stone with oil. Inside the second drawer's an empty butane torch, a spool of thread, and a pincushion containing assorted needles, ranging from small to large.

I'm remembering the deciphered notes I've read. As Rhoe stated, his utensils for killing Yria sit somewhere in my sight. Now finding this, I wonder, where's her body and the man's severed head?

I peer below to the shelf just beneath the table. Could the fluid on those rags have been Yria's blood? Or could it have been from Rhoe's other victim? I'll have to gather them cautiously and put them into bags, but for the moment I'll forget them that I may continue searching the place over.

Roughly five feet from the table's a sort of large steel medical cabinet. Why Rhoe would have one's beyond me, but somehow he got it.

Upon shelves, behind glass, are every medical instrument imaginable, forceps, clamps, retractors, distractors, dilators, scalpels, lancets, injection needles, tyndallers, scopes and probes, suction tubes and tips, measuring devices, even electrical instruments.

There's several trays resting behind the doors I've now opened. Also, I spy things like alcohol, mercurochrome, ether, and iodine. At the lowest shelf are half used jugs of formaldehyde and peroxide. Beside the bleaching agent I'm spotting a heavily wrapped object veiled in cloth.

My curiosity excites me as I'm grabbing the item. Whatever it is, it's at least two pounds.

I'm unwrapping the layers of cloth when I reveal the object I'd hoped to seek. Finally I've found the missing head.

I'd say it's been cleaned with bleach to make it bright after inspect- ing its whiteness. Some hobby of Rhoe's, maybe? Too bad he's not here to ask.

I'm unsure how any doctor could attempt to identify this victim. Unless the skull talked, I'd say we're without luck, but anyway, I have it, whoever's head this belonged to.

I wonder now, could I find the body upon which this head resided? Time's on my side and it'll make its way with me. I step to a suspicious large trunk constructed from metal. Inside I'm hoping I'll find the bones of Rhoe's victims. Eagerly I'm opening it, but am confronted by dissatisfaction. No bones here, not a damn one. Instead, there's a half dozen metal skewers, some long lengths of chain, a few shackles and cuffs, then several strange looking devices, probably crafted by Rhoe.

My anger takes me as I slam down the top. Where're the bones, Rhoe? What'd you do? I'm running out of areas to inspect in this shed.

With determination, I waddle around, attentively scouting more places to check. I eyeball the floor, then study the walls. Something's here. It's my stomach which tells me, but I can't find hide nor hair of it.

As I survey the space, I find myself coming back to an object, the cold metal cabinet, but there's nothing in it I was wanting to find. The items it holds weren't things I was seeking.

I'm wondering if my instincts mean to tell me there's something behind it; the cabinet, that is?

Only one way to admit curiosity.

I lean against the towering storage, pressing the full force of my body upon it. After exhaustively shouldering it a foot, I rest on my laurels. I readily turn to the wall behind me when I view the outline of a door. To open it I must shove the cabinet several more inches. I had done it before without busting up jugs. Let me hope this second time around those liquids stay safe. Indubitably, I'd be wise to remove the harsh chemicals, but admittedly, I'm much too lazy. I'll just pray that I encounter no spills.

Currently I've shoved the cabinet eight more inches from its preexisting position. No clanks or bangs are heard as I moved it. The opportunity now presents itself to open this second undisclosed door. Who else could accomplish what I have in just hours? There's a reason I'm a PI; it's 'cause I'm damn good at what I do. Anyone wants to object me, I'll be ready to fight.

I'm just moments away from knowing what's behind door number two. Could it be the bones I've been seeking or something less vile? My interest awaits me and I open the door.

Holy Mary, mother of Christ. I ogle the upset before me. If ever I've had reason to regard something horrific, it couldn't have existed till now. The sight on my face must show my expansion of horror and look of disgust.

Before me, no more than ten inches, the chilling sight rests, pinned at a hanger. It's no fake, this five foot, eight inch clad of Yria's skin; and her face, I imply, has been fully included.

The body's unclothed, the way it'd been kept. Amber hairs still cling to the head. Evermore shocking's the hollow eyes peering through a blind gaze. Upon Yria's fingers remain the red polish she'd painted. Not one flake or flaw has displayed its result.

The condition of flesh, no doubt, is superb. With great skill it'd been taken care of. Rhoe, beyond question, used a preservative agent to treat Yria's skin and keep it intact.

Why had he done it, though? Killing Yria was one thing, but saving her flesh? Maybe he was more insane than I thought?

What type killer keeps the hide of his victim inside a sealed closet? This is ungodly, if not completely deranged. In all my years of working undercover, I've seen nothing, honestly, that'd compare close to this.

Who was Rhoe, really? That devilish brute lived here in my town. We've walked the same streets, have breathed the same air, even seen the same sights, but between us, he was the one who'd been bread of ill means. Maybe so, he was a lawman, but that stinker was foul, not honoring his code. He deceived the general public, the people of my town. I'll make sure that dead churl gets exposed for his deeds.

With a pen, I poke the pitted flesh which had once remained Yria's. It starts swaying when each visible suture grabs my sight. The meticulous needlework's successfully kept Yria from coming apart. The crafty labor begins at the left of Yria's head, down the outlining direction to her sinistral foot, then up into her inner thigh, rising farther into her crotch, then joining her central right flank, reaching along onto the dextral exterior leg, up into the torso and arms, extending upward into her neck, then finally stopping upon the right side of her head.

I poke the flesh a second time and, upon this turn, get a view of her back. It's been exceptionally kept, like the rest of her. Prior to seeing, I'd have simply concluded that.

Rhoe wanted Yria's remains to be perfect, and because of his labored efforts, he proved himself that.

Just to the right of Yria, I spot a small chair. Upon it sits a mason jar filled with clear liquid and an uncanny round something. It can't be? I'm almost afraid to lean in for fear Yria's flesh will brush upon me, but I do. It can't be, I think again. Is that her peeper leering back?

It rests at the bottom of the glass, where it peers directly upon me. Eerily, I feel, being confronted by a fair blue eye. Rhoe really was a morbid freak.

I won't have the cops involved with this shit till I've found Yria's bones. There's no way I'd let them take credit for my work. Hell, I won't even tell Pascal about Yria's stretch of flesh till I'm damn well ready, though, I admit, I'll let him in on the skull. It's not something I could easily hide. It'd turn out unsuccessful if I tried. He'd see the wrapped cloth I'd carry and bug me for answers.

I guess my business is done, except for the blooded rags I'll need to gather. I suppose those will need an explanation; just something else to consider.

I prepare myself to go upstairs. The kitchen's empty, so I roam the house in search of Pascal.

"Mr. Cartier, sir, you here? Mr. Cartier? Mr. Cartier?" My luck the old man's shuffled to a room where he's had a heart attack.

I continue walking when a door unexpectedly swings forth in my face. Pascal drags his old limbs from the room and is now moving toward me.

"Thought I heard a faint call."

"Yep, you heard me."

Pascal crinkles his nose when he's squinting. "You say something, son?"

I'm preparing to speak when he says, "Wait, wait. My old hearing aid needs some adjustments. Probably why I can't discern you."

He pulls the device from his ear and, now, fidgeting with it, it makes a loud shrill. Though the noise hasn't seemed to affect Pascal, it has me. I still hear the high screech as though it's still faring.

"Now I hear better." He grins.

"I was just wanting to tell you I've finished my work in the basement."

"Well, good. You come across hidden jewels or coins?"

"Wouldn't that have been nice?"

"It could have made us a lot richer." He laughs.

I then follow Mr. Cartier into his den, where I'm taking a seat in a comfortable large chair as he aims for the couch.

"Well, if you didn't find treasures, what have you found?"

I explain the door I found and what it revealed. "It may have been a medical examiner's office." I don't want to scare Pascal by, indeed, tell-ing him the true intent of the room. I am honest in revealing what I saw, but I'll limit my sayings.

"I came across a skull. It could have been there for craniology purposes, I'm not sure; but to get answers, I request it be sent to my friend who's a doctor."

"All this time there's been a head in my basement? I admit that has me unsettled."

"It's most certainly male, from judging the cranial mass. There's also some rags beneath a table. With permission, I'd like to gather those as well."

"We don't know what's gone on here. I should probably call the cops."

"I'd like to know more about these items before any branch of law gets involved."

"You'd be capable of handling this?"

"Absolutely, unless you object."

"I'm an old man. I've worked and retired, but you're still fit to get by. You have your forte. I'm sure I won't mind."

"I appreciate it and I'll have this handled."

"If there's anything you need and I have it, let me know."

I don't have to think when I reply, "A few paper bags."

"Groceries bags, sure. You're welcomed to them. Look by the fridge."

I trail from the room and return to the kitchen. As Pascal mentioned, I see what I need.

After reeling back to the basement, I clear debris from the floor and toss it into bags. I had to employ two with the amount of mess that was sitting. The remaining pair will service the nasty rags, which I'll take.

I know I haven't any gloves to protect my hands, so I'm trying to figure out what to work with. The thought of the cabinet comes to mind. I spot forceps and decide I'll transport the blooded cloths with their use.

Thankfully they work like a dream and keep my hands from touching evidence. I set the bags near the door, alongside the others.

What I'll do with this skin, I've still not determined. I suppose it'll remain in the closet, safe, least for now. Should it not, I better devise an idea.

I return the burly medical cabinet to its spot, to hide the door. Since I'm now done, I can boogie out of here; just have to gather the bags, collect the clothed skull, and shut out these lights.

I trace back upstairs, secure the door, then revert to the den. "I've got some garbage. Figure I'll save you a trip and run it outside."

"Oh, just set those alongside the house. My son comes tomorrow. He'll see them to the trash."

"All right, sure. I'll set them where you said. Most likely in a few days I'll be back."

"Sure, son. You know me. I'll be here."

I exit the front door, then make way toward the exterior part of the home. I see a laced gate, then drop the two sacks of wood, dust, and grit. After getting out of here I plan to head to my friend, the doctor. He keeps his office on Rosebud Road inside the hospital where he works.

Chapter Thirty-Seven

Well, I've made it. I'm at New Hope Hospital. What a surprise when Dr. Ignace sees me. If I'm concluding right, we'd last been acquainted at this year's New Years party. I'd taken Deja to the ever popular Aqua Room, where we saw Roman and his wife.

We shared bottle after flowing bottle of champagne, enjoyed the entertainment, and counted the last few seconds of midnight. It was a damn good night, I remember.

A year prior, Dr. Ignace's daughter ran away. Feeling she was contending with the likes of her younger sister, young Angelique decided she'd had enough and, while her family was sleeping, snuck away through a door.

Roman petitioned me, asking if I might find her. That commenced the start to our friendship. After returning Angelique to her home, Dr. Ignace said there's nothing he wouldn't do should I ever need help, and, by God, I did thank him, and as you see, I need his aid now.

I wander through the long stretch of New Hope's never-ending expanse. I pass through a few of its many halls, then find the elevators. As its doors open, I see a doctor standing inside. He looks to me, saying hi, and respectfully I return my acknowledgement as I'm standing alongside him.

I search the button panel, looking for the basement dial. I then exit the elevator quickly as the doctor and I depart separate ways.

I walk down two fairly long halls, then find the medical examiner's office, where I tap the door before walking in. I see a man with blond hair presiding over a body, with a tray just beside him.

I ask, "That you, Roman?"

The gentleman turns around at the drop of my voice. "Well, Satordi, how've you been? Better you walk here than appear on my slab," he jokes.

"Wasn't sure I missed you or not. Guess I came the right time."

"Except for lunch, I'm always here. Well, don't just stand there. Come on in. The dead don't bite."

"Well, when they do, you better say."

He smiles. "But anyway, how've you been?"

"Eh, better not ask," I say as I eye the cold stiff on his slab. "What happened? He eat too much lead?"

"The old bull snatched seven shots."

"I'd sure say so. What've you got there, different bullets?"

"A couple. Should say there were two shooters. He came here a bloody mess."

"Well, I bet."

"So, what's bringing you in? You just come for a visit?"

"It'd be nice to say. However, no, I've come seeking help."

"Needing my expertise, are you?"

"Well, yeah. I've brought you a skull. I'd like it examined. You up for the task?"

"You robbing graves now?"

I flash a cheap smirk. "Well, it'd be like you to think that."

"So where'd you find it? Or had it somehow appeared?"

I hand the crown to Roman, explaining, "A house on Grange Road. There was no body, though."

While unveiling the cloths covering the head, Roman declares, "Let's see what we've got."

"It's male, am I right?"

"Viewing the shape and size, I'd say so. It's quite clean, isn't it? Someone likely boiled this, or if they were lucky enough to use them, had flesh eating beetles. I imagine it was then placed in a solution of peroxide and water. And whoever kept this had high regard for this skull. Their concern for it, Satordi, took great time and care."

"Can you check for trauma that might have attributed death?"

"You know I can, but appears it's a collector's piece, Satordi." "What a way to fool you, 'cause this person was murdered."

"Well, telling you now, if this doesn't show signs of trauma, I'll not be able to determine a cause of death."

"Guess you'll have me out hunting the body, then?"

"Probably don't want me saying it, but it'd help. How bout you check back tomorrow? I'll give you my report."

"You're a good man, Doc."

Really, I do appreciate him. Roman's a busy man. In and out each day are bodies he's having to examine. It's a good favor he's giving me considering he'll have my report tomorrow. That's quicker than I thought. He's going above and beyond his means to assist me. Granted, I'd have completely accepted if it took a few days, even a week to get back to me. But a day? Well, I jolly am happy.

Chapter Thirty-Eight

Currently, I'm at my business. I've tread here 'cause it's quiet and I'm hoping to gain thought to what Rhoe had done with the skeletal re- mains of his sufferers.

Clearly, I know Yria had been killed at his home. To what, though, had he done with her body? If he'd been ill enough to retain her flesh, wouldn't he have kept the bones?

And who was his male victim? It's got me puzzled. What had Rhoe done to him and why did he do it? These are questions which fill me.

Imagining, if I'd been Rhoe, I'd have buried the bodies behind my home, considering it would have been the choicest place. In doing so, I'd have complete supervision over my property. If I wanted my victims to remain from being found, that's the way I'd have done it.

I suppose I could survey Pascal's property, and, if I want, I could inquire people who'd been neighbors of Rhoe about any strange dig- gings that took place at his home.

I write notes to myself of things I'm to do; return to Mr. Cartier's, question the neighbors, drop by and get Ghislain.

My head's down as I continue jotting my important summary. Be- fore me I hear the clink of my door as I happen to look up.

Oh, brother, I mumble when spotting Guloe. Why's this fool here? He remains quiet till he gets to my desk. "Nice place you've got here."

"What do you want?"

"To talk."

"'Bout what? I've no business with you."

"I'm not here about Ambrielle."

"Figured by now you'd have hired someone else."

"And, so, I did."

"So why're you standing here?"

"'Cause, Detective, I fear for my life. My family's being murdered, and today, the last of my kin had been killed."

I snicker modestly. "And you suppose I'll help you?"

"Show some respect and don't laugh in my face. All my family's died, have been murdered; my sister Reinella, her family; another sister, Adelisa, and her son; my niece Desta, then today her siblings, mother, and Laina's spouse. Whoever's killed those closest to me will be coming for me, my wife, our daughter."

He's still hiding the fact he has another child, but I won't disclose any truth of my already knowing.

Haulmier continues, "For the sake of our lives, the person must be found."

I grab my pack of cigarettes from my desk. "Sorry you're in a fix, but I can't help."

"Bullshit. I want your help and I'm needing it now."

"Forget it. I'm not available."

"Apparently, you are. You're here on your ass," he shouts to my face. "You need to get out," I tell him, sternly.

"What sort of treatment is this? I've come proposing a job, and you turn me down? Well, I'll make sure to tell folks never to come here. I'll ruin you, Detective. You'll never get another case, Biertempfel, not as long as you live."

"Keep your threats coming. You're not scaring me. Your smack has no effect."

"You won't think twice when it does."

"You're like a clingy mutt at a kettle. Don't lose your place in line to be euthanized. I'll call the morgue and tell them you're coming."

"Take your business and shove it."

I stand from my seat. "Hey, you came here, but I'll be glad once you're gone."

Happily I am as I'm seeing him go. That damn prick overstepped his boundaries coming here. How dare he. The full stretch of his stench is still filling my building. I'll need to aerate the place and breeze his funk out.

Guloe coming here has upset my current state of mind. I'm hoping to redirect my thoughts and get on track.

I relax in my chair as my breathing winds down. I peer back at the notes I'd previously written. Five-thirty, maybe even a quarter till six,

I'll travel to Ghislain's and pick his ass up. From there we'll return here to my place and prepare for my appointments.

It's currently a quarter of two as I'm checking the time. I guess I'll cram in a visit and see Ambrielle.

Chapter Thirty-Nine

Ambrielle and I sit upon the couch while my kitten's at work. This gives us much needed time, with no interruptions, to converse by ourselves.

"To put it on the line, your father stopped by my business. I didn't like it very much, but he was there. He says your Aunt Laina and her family had been discovered today."

"Not them now. I can't go through much more. My mom, me, Holland, that nasty filth; we're all that's left. He's not still wanting me to be turned over to him? Please, sir, tell me not."

"He's hired someone else and, believe me, he'll never find you, but that man will be looking. Just keep hanging here, you'll be safe."

"Sir, I can only think sooner or later he'll learn where I'm at. I can't live like this. I have no freedom."

"Would you rather go with him?"

"Why even ask that?"

"Ambrielle, listen, I'm doing my best, you know, to keep you away, but you make any slip-ups, you'll ruin your stay here. It's imperative your independence be limited. I'm not being cruel. My controlling your actions isn't meant to be mean. I'm merely trying to look out for you the one way I know how."

"I'm only wanting my life."

"And to live it, you will. We've got to get him off your back first."

"He'll not stop as long as I'm breathing."

"You never know, we're liable to read about him in tomorrow's paper. It's a matter of time now. I know you don't care about him. Undoubtedly, his death would be a blessing to you. The only matter's keeping you, your mother, and sister alive." That brings me to Rhoe's journal. "Have you read it?"

"Entirely, sir. And I was just about sick."

Ambrielle now explains that every page had been filled with precise accounts concerning days and times Guillaume saw Yria. When he wasn't at work, he was undoubtedly stalking the young widow. Whether he was scouting her steps at the market, following her and Mira, or sitting before her house, Rhoe was, as he's evidently put it, there.

Ambrielle also alleges Rhoe of fanatical desires; fixated propensities to which he wrote in regard to abusing the body. Sick, deranged obsessions, the young maiden tells.

"I'll not repeat what was read. As a lady, I'd not feel right quoting those statements."

"I won't force you, but had Guillaume made any account of Yria's murder? Any mentioning of where he took the body?"

"There was no chronicle of that. I'm sorry, sir, it seems we're on our own."

"God, I was sure it'd be in there. I have so little to go on and, still, there's so much to be gained."

I haven't felt more crazed by a case since I was working LeMire's in forty-three. I sink into a grody laugh. And I thought that case diminished my sanity? If I could have prepared myself then, I'd have warned myself of the doozy heading my way.

"I just need things to fall in place."

"It will."

"Maybe, I don't know? But I've got to be going. You be all right on your own?"

"Mmm, yeah. I'll be fine, sir. And I talked to my mom. She's been worried sick I haven't arrived, but I informed her of the situation and said I was safe."

"I'm glad you spoke to her."

"As great as it was, it'd been hard. I cried. And she tried not to squall, but I could hear her voice break."

"I know it's rough and I apologize."

"It's not your fault, sir. None of this is."

"You're strong, you know that?"

"I have hardships to bear. What you call strength, I refer endurance."

"You're getting by, and better than I could, I'll add." "You know, sir, you're much nicer than you think."

"I suppose I could be." I humbly laugh. "But don't go telling no one." "I wouldn't ruin your image. But, really, I owe you more than I own."

"Now don't you be thinking that." I stand from my seat, smiling. I stretch a minute, then crack my stiff neck. "If you're not wanting to stay here, I could take you to Cerissa's. It'll be awhile before Dej gets home."

"In all honesty, I've wanted to visit Lady Ancelin. You think I'd be safe?"

My brows rise as she's confronted this question. "You're wanting to go to The Blossomed Rose?"

"If you'd allow it, that is."

"You understand that could put you out on a limb? The possibility of having you exposed is a risk."

"It would be. And since you're advising me not, I'll respect that."

"I'm worried of someone recognizing you, especially after your father's hired some goon. Unless? Hmm, hold tight. Write a letter to Dej saying I've taken you."

"But you told me I can't. Where're you going?"

"Just stay there. I'll be back."

I race upstairs where I search through some clothes. I've got an idea and most often it happens.

After three minutes I go to the living room where, on the couch, I'm throwing a suit, along with a shirt, hat, and a pair of my shoes. I rush from the room and head to the front.

"Sir?" I hear Ambrielle.

"Hold tight."

I've left her alone in the house as I've come to my car. I'm undoing the lock, then, for a moment, I reach to my glove compartment and remove several things.

Upon returning to the house, I meet Ambrielle, who remains on the couch, looking upon the stack of clothes.

"I'm going to turn you into a gentleman."

She begins laughing. "Are you mad? There's no way this could work." I flash a sly grin. "You're not familiar with my skills. Go on, throw this on. Meet me here when you're dressed."

"I'll look a fool."

"Nonsense. You want to visit Lady Ancelin, that's what you'll wear. Come on now, we haven't much time."

"Don't be laughing, then, okay?"

I set my things along the table while Ambrielle remains absent. If I'm to make her a man, she best look the part.

She returns a while later. "I can't wear this. Your clothes are too big."

"We'll make it fit. Stand straight."

I cuff the pants outside each leg, then secure them with the use of pins.

Ambrielle peers down to my work. "The waist, sir, keeps slipping."

"Tuck in your shirt. I'll look for a belt."

"Please, because if I walked in these, they'll fall to the floor."

"I wouldn't have you risk the embarrassment."

"What about the shirt and blazer? They swallow my hands."

"We'll get them, too."

Ambrielle looks to the table when spotting my things. "Why's there makeup? Is that something new you play with?" she jokes.

"Well, we've got to hide your girlish features."

"I can't believe I'm allowing this." "Oh, stop. You know it's all fun."

Ambrielle giggles. "Least one of us enjoys this."

"Hold still, please." I hold an eyebrow pencil to Ambrielle's hair. "Too light. Need something darker."

I ogle the others which sit on the table, then grasp the one I'm assuming will work.

"That, sir's, not it. May I please advise you grab the last one?"

"You're right. This is too dark."

I grab the remaining pencil, using it to make short marks on her chin. I continue this until crafting a beard. I bring the marks down just beneath her mouth, then blot the specks with an eye shadow similar in color.

To keep it from smearing, I apply translucent powder, which I've dusted on, but in doing so, I've lightened the beard.

I pull Ambrielle's hair toward her face and I'm comparing the color. "Actually, this looks pretty good."

"And you're through now, right?"

"Golly, girl. Be patient."

"Haven't I?"

"You're becoming restless, I hear. You're not liking this, are you?"

"Let me dress you as a woman. I'm sure you'll complain."

"Thankfully it's not me who needs the disguise."

"Maybe one day, though? But, sir, if you don't mind, I have to use the lady's room."

"Well, I wouldn't make you hold it. But come back, we need to finish your face."

I wait on the couch, then fiddle through my pocket. Pulling forth my shiny, plated watch, I ogle the clockwork. Time's wasting quickly, the hour's 4:20. If I'm to get Ambrielle to The Blossomed Rose, it'll have to be in the next forty minutes.

The young maiden resurfaces as she comes to the room. "You've proved your talent. I'll admit, sir, you've done well."

"Told you I was good. Now bring your butt here."

After sitting, I hold two mustaches above Ambrielle's lip. I decide on one, then with glue, it's applied to her skin.

"Ugh, it's too bushy. I've got to trim this. Where're the scissors?" I search. "You see the scissors?"

Ambrielle helps me look on the table. "Did you have them?" She even searches the floor.

"Yeah. Yeah, I laid it right here. Did it fall to the floor?"

Ambrielle spies around. "Well, hmm, maybe check under the table? You know, I bet that's them there." She points.

"Good eyes, girly. I'm going to trim this right quick, so don't move, or you'll have me mess up."

"Try not to snip my lip, please. That's all I ask."

"I won't."

I trim the bulge and am thinning it out. As I'm doing so, I use the outline of her lips to shape the stache and barber it to the width of her face.

"There. Perfect. Don't touch. Don't monkey with it. Don't pick. Same for your chin. Don't be messing with that beard. Now." I'm looking around. "Where's that hat?"

Ambrielle's laughing, purely. "On top of the couch."

"Oh, so it is."

Ambrielle smiles to me and is raising her brows.

"Got any hairpins?" I ask. "Nope," she's insisting.

"Damn. Great. I don't think Deja does either. But you've got a rubber band, don't you?"

"No, ah-ugh."

"No? Ah, okay. Give me a moment while I go look."

I check the kitchen, hoping I'll see one. Dej, come on, don't you have any? I sift through her drawers. I find a bunch of twist ties, but no rubber bands. Who doesn't have at least one in their house? That gal's got everything else, but the one thing I'm needing, my lady's without.

I'm about to walk off, then I spot one stretched upon a cabinet handle. How wise of her she have it here. It was so out of sight, in a place I'd never considered. Thankfully my eyes caught glimpse of it before I was leaving.

"Look what a little searching brought me," I tell Ambrielle while I circle back to the den. "Why don't you pull your hair up as high as it'll go and arrange it into a bun?"

Ambrielle finishes fumbling with her locks before I plop the fedora on her head.

Ambrielle peers to my imperial, brown, wingtip loafers. "Guess all I need now are those?"

"I've stuffed them with socks so they'll fit. If you feel they're too loose, I'll stuff more in."

"They feel pretty snug."

I step aside. "Try walking."

She shuffles across the floor with some difficulty. "Pick up your feet and walk right. You can't drag them on the floor."

"I'm trying."

"No, you're not. Bring your feet up. You got it. Okay, now keep going."

"I can't. These pants are falling off."

"Come here." I loosen her belt, then adjust it to fit. "That should do. Try again."

This time I spot no struggles as she's striding through the room. "Better?" "Much."

"All right, call Ancelin, let her know I'm dropping you off. Hurry now. I'll be in Sable."

I step to my beautiful black car and rest on her seat. As you're probably aware, Sable's the hottest wheels on the road, and I bet if I placed her in a show, she'd be taking first prize. Fortunately I'm not one of those conspicuous young fools who thinks he owns the best. I'm a seasoned exception. What I own's superior rate, and if you don't agree, then, boy, you better damn well flip that hood and check her engine. My girl's a hemi. Dropped it in myself. Took it from of an abandoned Saratoga. The owner won't miss it. He probably don't know I ripped his ass off. Who knows why the dumb idiot dumped his car? Later the Saratoga was found and repossessed. It now resides in a lot while Sable attains its fast engine. My, how life is good.

Chapter Forty

I pull before The Blossomed Rose where I'm parking. "I didn't even think, how're you getting home? Will you need me here later?"

"I'm sure if I ask, Lady Ancelin will take me."

"Call if she can't and I'll get you."

I now pull from the alley as I soar down the street. I steer through each avenue while flying to Ghislain's. Deliberately, I'm reducing my speed when I come to East Grove.

He better be home. It'd be a waste of gas if he's not.

I stretch from my car and race to the stairs. Inside I head to the second floor where I go to door three. I knock loudly to gain his attention and in seconds he answers, as the door's pulling open.

As quickly as I've come, I plan to be leaving. I tell Ghis to get his coat, that we're heading out, and like a good sport, he listens.

Chapter Forty-One

It's been a hell of a day, I'm telling old Ghis. "But I'll report, I found our head. Yep. Not like it's major, so don't get excited."

"You lucky bastard. You actually did? But how?"

"Oh, I found a lot. But the head, I took to a friend."

"He better be a good friend."

"I trust him. He's a doctor. I'm having him examine the skull. He said he'd tell me something tomorrow."

"You know yet whose head it was?"

"Well, no, but it'd be unreal if it turned out being Matthias Dane's." "That reminds me, that explanation of death document, I have you the info. The person I spoke to wouldn't allow the original, but he gave me the cause of death."

"And what have you found out about Matthias?"

"Shrapnel. He endured a lot. Especially to his neck and face. And among the other casualties, he was taken to a field hospital in Dorset, England."

"That explains why his casket was closed."

"I'm sure Rhoe had nothing to do with his death, boss."

"Nope. Me either. I need coffee. Want some?"

"Sure, okay. And when you're done, I've something to show you." "Yeah, what's that?" I await his answer, but instead he shoos me off. I fiddle with the parts of my percolator, lining the basket with a filter, then adding in grounds. In a back room I spout the pitcher with water, then I'm bringing the pot to my desk where I fasten its cord to a socket.

I relax to my seat as Ghislain's forcing over some print. "Take a look at this."

I'm seeing a photo of several guys at a Christmas gathering. "It's a bunch of party people; so what?"

"That photo was taken at my department's annual Christmas party. The man you see on your left's Guillaume Rhoe."

"Really? That dark headed man's the egregious brute? Didn't look very frightening. But, then again, he'd been a beast."

I lean my head to the picture to absorb his image. He seemed average height, probably six foot tall. His frame appears thin, yet wiry. His hair, as I'm looking, had either been black or dark brown, and his face, though, not most attractive, had been sharp with good features.

"I wish that dick was alive to be thrown into the slammer," I'm hearing Ghis mumble. "If only them inmates could have torn him a part."

I hear the clamorous bell jangle upon my door as I'm raising my head. A woman, my age or younger, glides across the floor and is coming my way. She wears a tightly fit dress, in black, with a fichu on her shoulders. She's quite attractive, but it looks like she knows it. Her chestnut hair, she has drawn up, and above her eyes is a thin spread of black liner.

She gets beside Ghislain and tells him hello.

He responds to her greeting, "Well, well. How've you been?"

"Hadn't quite figured I'd grace this lovely city again. But you called, Mr. Duplessey, and I've come."

Ghislain pulls her a chair. "Adora, I'd like you to meet Detective Biertempfel. He's the reason I called."

"Ah, you're the one deciding to work Yria's case? Well, I'll say, it's about time something's done."

"Miss," I'm extending my speech.

"Adora."

"I want to thank you for coming on such short notice."

"I'm here for Yria." Adora's pulling a silver cigarette case from her clutch. "You mind?"

"Not at all."

"So, where shall we begin?"

"Ah, your first time meeting Guillaume."

"Well, I'll have to backtrack, then." She takes a puff of her smoke. "Whatever you hear, don't think me bad." She laughs vociferously. "It was an early day in late thirty-nine. I was, course, booked one night in the city's cold jailhouse. It was a little thing, really. A sort of minor offense. Anyway, I'd gotten out about the time Guillaume was leaving work. It was on the street, I met him. Clumsy me dropped my purse and Guillaume picked it up."

Knowing my pronouncement's false, I declare it anyway. "He was a real gentlman, no?"

"Course. He was finer than most."

At this time my bell clings again. I lean aside in my chair and, by my door, see a tall man, in casual dress, with blondish-brown hair and blue eyes.

"Oh, I'm terribly sorry. I'm not interrupting things, am I?" "You Gaston?" I'm asking,

"Yes. Mr. Duplessey called at your request for an interview."

"Well, bring yourself in. We've just gotten started."

Ghis, out of view, is now standing. "I'll get you a seat."

"Well, Officer Duplessey, hi. I wasn't sure you'd be here." "Have a seat," I advise the tall man. "You care for coffee?"

"Ah, yeah, please."

"You, too?" I look at Adora.

"Well, if the Joe's piping hot."

I pour four steaming mugs and pass them to my guests. I then grab cream and sugar from a drawer and place them on top of my desk.

Gaston's removing his jacket and hangs it along the back of his chair.

"How long's it been?" Adora requests him.

"A good while, I know. You still living here?"

"No. No, I got out when I could. It's my first time being back."

"Is that the truth? Well, then, where're you staying?"

"I have a home in Rumilly."

"So close you are still, but you've never come back?"

"No." She laughs. "It was never my agenda."

"Well, whatever the matter, it's good to be seeing you."

"Like old times, isn't it? We're just missing the club and being in-veigled by the tunes of Ramilla."

I interrupt, "Sorry to be frank, but you mind revisiting your days on your own accord? My time's precious; I hope you'll understand."

Adora's putting out her smoke and is remaining silent for the time being.

I look to Gaston. "Tell me about Guillaume and how you both met."

"Didn't Adora say I met him through her?"

"No, sir, she did not."

"Well, I did. Must have been around New Years 1940. We met at a joint."

"It was Satin, Gaston, that's where we went," Adora informs him.

"Yeah, Club Satin. We met after he and Adora came in. He was an interesting fellow, had a lot to say."

"Aside from being interesting, what else was he?"

"You know, he was one of these easy going guys. Easy to talk to. Never boring. My interest in him was Guillaume had been a cop. I my-self had been wanting to get into that line of work," he says, modestly.

"You ever see him lash out? Had he ever been mean?"

"Not Guillaume, no. That man was too nice."

As I had with Orisia at the beginning of this, I find myself hearing the same shit all over again. Just as Miss Laroque, these people were led to believe misconceptions produced by one deceivingly, willful man. I won't waste time trying to convert their thinking. I know the truth. I've found evidence. Knowing I have that, I haven't an hour to battle with Gaston or Adora's impressions of Guillaume. Instead, I'll move to my present inquiry.

"I like to hear about Charlize Rousseau. What kind of person was she?"

Adora's rubbing her hand across my table. "An on again off again girlfriend of Guillaume's. Although they'd been romantically inclined, I couldn't understand the attraction. Charlize was, well, not very social." Adora crosses her legs while smoothing the trim of her dress along the edge of her knee. "She could have been shy, I suppose, but even with him, I found her timidity strange."

"Might her reserve have only been displayed with the public? Generally, how well had she known any of you?"

Gaston responds to the inquest, "I believe the true question's how well we knew her? Char kept to herself, mostly. I recall my attempts at conversations, yet her answers were less than lengthy. It wouldn't be wrong saying it was hard to lure that lady into simple discussions."

"She was private," Adora adds.

"I remember, during our meet, and it was only that time, I learned she'd been working in a hospital."

Adora looks to Gaston. "As a nurse, wasn't it?"

Ghis remarks quickly, "Char worked as a radiographer, according to Miss Laroque."

"Sorry to inform you, but she was neither. Miss Rousseau was receiving practical training at the time for her to redeem a full medical license," Gaston explains.

As am I, Ghis seems shocked by this as he's scratching his head. "You're sure?"

"She told me herself."

Adora's commenting, while removing lint from her threads, "It never would cross me, Char being smart."

Finding Charlize might prove an easy task since I'm now learning these truths, I scratch this note in my tablet.

"Had she completed her internship?" I wonder.

"I wouldn't know." Gaston now reminisces, "Soon after Guillaume's passing, Char packed her things and fled town."

"Then you don't know where she's at?"

"I know nothing after that. Why would I? We weren't close."

I inquire, "Were any of you?"

"I know I wasn't," Adora adds. "And I don't believe any of the others were, either. We were an easy going, social band of friends. That wasn't part of Char's makeup."

"Simply, then, she didn't fit."

"Had she not acted aloof and attempted friendship, Detective, we would have gladly accepted her. We tried. We extended ourselves, but she never did," Adora's admitting.

It's as the ever celebrated motto says, to have a friend, you must be a friend. In respect to the willingness of others, friendships are met with full heart. To exercise a friendship in whole, one must extend themself fully; as for the second individual, that person should employ the same figure.

I understand Adora's frame of mind. I'll not sit here and defend

Charlize's misgivings. She acted on her own accord. If she didn't want to extend friendship with any of those people, it was her own business.

"I'd have gone about things in the same sense. You weren't wrong trying to act kindly to that woman. But soon as you realized you were getting nowhere, you let it be, I understand."

Adora comments, "She was one of those people you had to pass up."

"Maybe she thought she was too good for you all?" I lean back in my chair. "Well, ah, besides Char, were there any others who immediately left Annecy following the death of Guillaume Rhoe?"

Gaston declares, "I can't think of anyone."

I peer to Adora and Gaston. "Was Yria involved with anyone either of you knew?"

Bewildered, Adora stares forth, answering, "Yria dating? Please. You really think she'd have jumped the gun to be with some clown?"

"I have to ask. These questions come with the job." I move on, holding my pen in hand. "Guillaume have enemies?"

"His father," Adora states. "Jehan was crazy, Guillaume said. He once described his youth as aphotic."

"Explain."

Adora merely laughs in revolt as though she's insulted by my request. "Jehan was a drunk. Liked to beat his son."

Guillaume's hatred for his dad could have caused him to kill his old man. Will it be his head Dr. Ignace examines?

I'm quick to inquire, "Jehan Rhoe, is he alive?"

"You really suppose I'd know, Detective? Please, honey, check your phone book."

"When all else fails." I smile. I then draw my notebook toward my lap. Continuing to grasp my pen, I inquire, "How about an address?"

Adora sneers as I'm picking her brain. "Look, all I know's he lived on Spouse Road. Info's scarce, so I suggest you stop asking."

"That the truth, or are you trying to haul me off subject?"

"I've answered all your requests. Whatever input I had on Jehan, I've given. How could I respond to further questions when additional knowledge is lacking?"

"Impossible," I mumble.

Adora sits her coffee mug upon my counter. "Does this conclude our meeting?"

"If you don't have some reason to be leaving, no."

"Look, I don't know what else there is to tell. There's not much left."

"What about Basile? He had a thing for Yria, isn't that right?"

"They dated in the springtime of life. What youths hadn't? He and Guillaume were in the same boat. They'd been in love with a woman they couldn't have. Yria was done with Basile the instant he left her and, as she wanted it, had nothing to do with Guillaume. It would have been illogical had she. Yria just lost her husband in war."

"Where's Basile?"

"Probably off somewhere, married."

"I need more detail than that."

Gaston breaks forth in response, "He was residing in Cherbourg, last I knew."

"How long ago was that?"

"It's been years now."

"How'd you know he was in Cherbourg?"

"He up and wrote one day. It was unusual. We hadn't had any contact since Yria, and it might have been a good year later when he decided to write."

Quickly, I ask, "What was his reason for contacting you?"

"He was wanting to know how things were. He'd asked if there'd been any leads to finding Yria and, strangely, he was asking about Guillaume's house, wondering if it sold."

"What's strange about that?"

"Basile left Annecy before Officer Rhoe was killed. I wasn't sure how he knew Guillaume died. See what I'm saying? How'd he have known the house was for sale?"

"A newspaper, maybe?"

"The *Cherbourg Press* carrying Annecy's news? It wouldn't seem possible."

"You kept writing each other, though, or had you not?"

"I mailed a response, but never heard back."

"Well, I wonder why?"

"I left it alone after realizing he wasn't going to follow up on my letter. I figured I, too, was done writing."

"So it was a closed book after that?"

"For lack of better words, yeah."

"Concluding that, I haven't anything else to ask. Should an additional thought come to mind, I have both your numbers here. And if either of you come up with something not presently mentioned, try reaching me at this number." I pass them my calling card.

"Sure, no problem," Gaston adds.

Adora smiles, while fanning her face with my card. "This a twenty-four hour number you've given?"

"If the line's not pulled."

"Well, then." She's giggling, childishly.

"I'm not always here, so keep trying till I'm caught."

"Well, I wouldn't mind that."

Oh God, gee, who is this woman? I've had my fill. She needs to go home. "My fiance's expecting me shortly." Maybe having said that will deter her sprightly tongue? "Ghislain will see you both to the door."

I walk from my desk, taking the once-filled coffee pot to a back room. I toss the used grounds and filter to the trash, then clean the pot for its next use.

I hear the closure of the door as I'm making my way toward the front. I see Ghis trailing to my desk when I decide to tell him, "Couldn't have lent some form of warning, or at least prepared me for little miss sassy ass?"

"She's quite the character, wasn't she?"

"Something. Don't think I've met a woman quite like her."

"That's Adora. You either love her or you hate her." "Ha," I express. "She's different, that's a certainty."

"Was that all you thought?"

"I'd imagine she's a lot of things."

Ghis grins ever slightly. "So, boss, what's next in line?"

"Not sure I've got thought. What's your call?"

"Not sure I have any. What do you think, want to swing by a café and grab dinner?"

I ponder, "The Sandwich Shop on the main strip?"

"That's good enough."

Thankfully, it's good enough. My belly pleads for a roast beef sandwich and an jus on the side, and The Sandwich Shop's the best place to get it. They've got a line of other grinders to chose from, but I like that best. There are a few things I enjoy, but their roast beef's just too good to pass. It's something that, once I've tasted it, I always want more, and right now that urge is pestering me to go eat it.

Chapter Forty-Two

Ghis and I finished our meals no more than ten minutes ago. Instead of picking up to leave, we've decided to remain and discuss my earlier conversations with Gaston and Adora.

"You know, I'm wondering if our head belonged to Jehan Rhoe, due to something Adora said."

Ghis rubs his chin. "You want, I could check around, find out if he's alive."

"Sure, 'cause I've no other thought to whose it could be and, should we get screwed, it'll be the end of this case."

"Just for thought, but, ah, there's a man I'm acquainted with, big into skull reconstruction. In his spare time he sculpts. Has done some outstanding works, I remember. I wonder if he'd be able to do something for us?"

"What, sculpt the face?"

"Why not? I'd bet anything he could do it. It'd take some time, of course."

"Impossible. I've never heard anyone sculpting a skull and revealing a person's identity."

Ghis shakes his head at me. "Doesn't mean it can't work."

"This sounds like futuristic science. This isn't of our time, Ghis. You're years ahead of the idea."

"Time allows the formulation of ideas, right, boss?"

"There'd be only one attempt at doing that. One shot, my friend, at getting it right. We can't have your man tinkering with things when he's not sure what he's doing. He could permanently destroy the skull, and it's over."

"Well, I think it's worth the effort."

I pull my tablet from my pocket in an attempt to scan my notes. In doing so, the paper found near the body of Marcel Dupuis has glided to the table. I unfold its creases to again view its length of words.

Within a trunk, within his house,
contains the head of a man from Spouse.
It was kept, and it was safe, so no one
knew the man's real fate.

Ghis is watching me scan the text as he asks, "What's that?"
"Something I found." I continue the text.

Beneath the dirt, within the ground, the
bones remain without its crown. Only one
may know this truth and, as it goes, I've
chosen you.

I say aloud, not even realizing, "Hmm, I missed that before."
Ghis snaps his fingers. "Hey." He whistles. "Eyes up here."
He's distracted me. "Huh?"
"I can't help if you don't fill me in."
I explain that the body had somewhere been buried by Rhoe, but its exact location's still unknown.
Ghis holds forth his hand. "Let me get a look at that."
I push the note across the table where it meets his hand. He's drawing it closely as he prepares to read.
He speaks out, "Within a trunk, within his house?" His eyes rise to mine. "I assume this refers to Rhoe's home?" He redirects his focus and continues the text. "Here's something else you've missed."
I peer upon Ghislain while awaiting his response. "Hadn't Adora said Jehan lived on Spouse Road?"
"Yeah, why?"
"Says the trunk contained the head of a man from Spouse."
"Guess I hadn't paid attention."
Ghis returns the paper to me. "First sentence. It's clear as day. If it hadn't jumped at you then, it should now."
Had I actually overlooked this? "How was it I missed this?"

"You're seeing now."

"The body, then. Rhoe had to have buried it near his home. Back yard, maybe?"

"Or in the basement, even."

I'm thinking, my God, this is going to suck. "Suppose the new owner would let us dig?"

"He'll have to."

"Looks like we've got us a job tomorrow."

"Yeah, a long one. We'll be busting our backs."

Probably best I stayed with Dej tonight. I don't want her mad 'cause I didn't drop by. My babe gets pretty upset if I don't check in. Okay, I suppose that's a lie, really. The genuine truth, Dej would rather have me check on her. She says a gentleman looks after his lady, even those who live apart. Instead of speeding to my home, I could quickly dash to hers and be settled. I wouldn't have to worry about shifting be- tween chateaus or having to hear her complaints of living solo.

Chapter Forty-Three

It was a hell of a night. I hadn't gotten much sleep. Usually I'm out like a baby. Last night, though, I had an irritated throat and pesky cough. At one time I thought I was coming down with something. I think the room was just dry, even a little too hot for my comfort, and Deja wasn't much help. Every time I began to doze, she'd start talking in her sleep. When her giggles started, I had to leave the room and move to the couch. I got a tiny bit of rest, but not much.

At seven o'clock, I accidentally rolled off my nest. I crashed to the floor with a loud thud, but thankfully I'd been downstairs, so no one heard. It was after my ordeal with the floor that I decided to rise.

Currently it's a quarter of eight. I'm on my second mug of Joe, with a few swigs to go. After it's gone, I'm heading through the door. I'm not sure what I'll be doing first this morning, head to Ghislain's or see Dr. Ignace? I assume I'll have that figured when I'm settled in Sable.

I finish the last of my brew and head upstairs. I sneak through Deja's room and whisper at her ear, "I'm off now. See you tonight."

I pull to leave when hearing her drowsy voice, "Don't I get a kiss?" I retract my previous steps, then lean into her head.

"What time is it?"

"Almost eight," I say softly.

"Is Ambrielle up?"

"No. But I've got to go, honey. I love you."

I trail through the front and pass several steps till I've made it to Sable. I begin driving when deciding I'll journey to Ghislain's.

Hope it's not too early for the man. I won't be happy having to wake him, but if I do, I'll have a few ideas in mind and, like me, he won't be happy.

I get to his place where I'm ascending the stairs. One-one-thousand, two-one-thousand, three-one-thousand, four. Eight more and I'm up. I get to the ninth and I hear my knees pop. Had it been Marin,

I'd have cracked a joke. My poor brother; I think he'll never get home. I'm sort of missing that big slug. My days seem sad without having him to laugh at. Oh, well, I suppose Ghis could temporarily take his place.

I'm standing before door three and knocking loudly. Come on, man. I knock again. I hear the patter of feet as they're making their way to the entry. Bout time, I consider.

The door swings and there's Ghis standing in the most outrageous attire. "What the hell, man? What are you wearing?"

I begin laughing, for his sight's too amusing to behold a straight face. Here before me he's wearing a white undershirt, yellow boxers, brown knee socks, a green apron with white dots, and an oven mitt upon his hand.

"I'm making breakfast." "You cook in all that?"

"Oh." Laughing, he looks at himself. "Yeah, well."

"It's unpleasant."

"I've got grub. Come on in and eat."

"If it looks half as bad as you, then, no thanks."

He questions me, "You know what I do to people like you?"

"Throw 'em out?"

"No. I put them in my blender and make protein shakes."

I barrel into laughter. "Well, you better chop me up."

"A mess you'll be, but I'm fine with that."

"You know I've got a knife?"

"I've got plenty in the kitchen. I'm afraid you're outnumbered." "I suppose I am," I realize.

"Have a seat. Sorry, I haven't any orange juice. I've got grape-fruit, though."

"Eh."

"It just needs a little salt."

The idea of grapefruit juice makes me cringe. "Ah, think I'll pass."

"Suit yourself. You want coffee instead?"

I move to the stove. "What's this you've got cooking?"

"Crepes."

"You make crepes?"

"With apple cinnamon."

"What are you, the good housewife?"

"If I didn't have my dick, I'd be. Go on, sit down. I'll come with your food."

"Sure thing, toots."

Ghis laughs. "Ah, so the apron turns you on?"

"That ugly thing?" "I like

my apron."

"Mmm." I shake my head. "No."

"Nonsense. I'd seen you eyeing it the second you came. So you ready for today?"

"Aw, if I had more sleep."

"I thought you looked pretty dead."

"I am."

"Well, what are you doing here?"

"Had to be up. I can't cast my day aside 'cause of no sleep."

Ghis expresses, "In that case, I better put on a whole pot of coffee."

"Nah, I'll get by."

"You won't be much help digging later."

"I said I'd get by."

"Yeah, we'll see." His eyes fall to my plate. "So I figure you enjoyed your crepes?"

"Wasn't bad, man. You've surprised me." "Get

another. There's more on the stove."

Don't mind if I do, I tell myself. "I'm thinking we'll make a run to Mr. Cartier's when we get through. I'll leave you there to start work."

"Leave me? You got some plan or something? Where're you going?"

"I've still got to meet with Dr. Ignace."

"Oh, your friend?"

"I'm just trying to think of time."

"Guess I'll put some clothes on, then. You'll be ready when I'm back?"

"Mmm-hmm," I say through a stuffed mouth.

I really am surprised by Ghis. A man looking as bad as he did when answering his door cooked this awesome breakfast? He genuinely stuck it to me, him being able to fix up grub like this. He'd even gone as far to cook down his apples with butter and cinnamon. Well, hell, he throws it up like this each morning, I'm liable to start coming here. The food is damn good.

Chapter Forty-Four

Ghislain eyes Mr. Cartier's house from my car, realizing, "The man don't know me, Satordi. What if he won't let me in?"

"Are you daft? I hadn't planned to send you solo. Now get out. I'll handle things; let me talk." I approach the house with Ghis at my rear. "Just stay behind me. I'll introduce you come time."

I ring Pascal's door, waiting for the feeble man to answer. To my surprise, he comes sooner than expected.

"Mr. Cartier, good morning."

"Well, I hadn't been expecting you."

"Yeah. Well, yeah, but I'm here."

"Well, you know I'm always happy when you come."

"I've brought my partner this time." I introduce him to Ghis.

Pascal looks him over with inspecting eyes. "Ain't you Aubin Du-plessey's boy?"

Ghis is stunned. "You knew my father?"

"Knew him? Boy, we worked together."

"At the fire station?"

"Sure did. How's that old boy been?"

Sadly, Ghislain shakes his head. "He's no longer with us."

"Heavens, I'm sorry. Aubin was a good man. A good man. And a cut-up, always pulling pranks. I'm terribly saddened to hear he's now passed."

"That was my pop."

"You're here to attend work, I presume? Well, can't get far if I don't let you in."

My response is honest. "Recent evidence has indicated a possible burial here at your residence."

"My goodness. All this time I've been living with bones?"

Ghislain adds, "It's no fact, but the possibility looms."

"Do I call the cops?"

I act in answer to Pascal's question, "Well, because we have no physical body at the moment, we'd like to do our own search before having the police involved."

"Have you an idea where to look?"

"We're requesting permission to dig in your basement and back yard, if necessary."

"This is a mighty big decision. I've worked hard getting my lawn green and pretty."

"If this wasn't needing to be done, we wouldn't request it. But as situations go, it's important."

"I suppose I'll agree to digging, then. But may I suggest, to ensure an easier search, you try dowsing rods? It eliminates chances for having to dig my entire yard and basement."

"Ah," I think. "Neither of us know how that works. You'll have to say how to use them."

"It's simple, son, nothing to it."

Pascal informs Ghis and myself the proper way of making rods. As Mr. Cartier's directing, we start with two metal hangers. They should be cut at the neck, then straightened. Afterward, a ninety degree bend's applied to what'll become handles, four inches in length.

Pascal comments, "You boys don't worry about hangers. As many as I've got, I'll give you some."

I say in response, "How'll we use the rods?"

Pascal's direction continues as he communicates his classical knowledge. Apparently, according to his advice, the rods should be held slightly, keeping our hands set in loose fists. Forearms will have to be parallel to the ground, while our elbows remain near our waists. The rods are to be held straight while parallel to each other.

"You'll have to walk the property slowly and, where the rods cross, you dig." Pascal now laughs full heartedly. "Watch for waterlines, though. Rods have been used to indicate sites of water."

"And we'd be digging for nothing?" Ghis questions.

"I guess you'll not know till you've dug through the soil."

"Don't get me disheartened now."

"Hope not, but I'll get you those hangers."

I suggest Ghis start in the basement. "I expect you'll have some work done upon my return."

"How long till you're back? 'Cause I'm not taking on this entire job, just myself."

"Do what you can. I shouldn't be long."

Pascal's returning to the room. "All right, boys, I'll show you how to make these."

"Pardon my hustle, but I've got to take a run somewhere. I'll be back when I've finished."

"Oh, but your friend?"

"I was going to leave him, if that's fine? I'll do my best and return before noon."

"Sure. I'll show him to the basement and get these rods made."

I'm grateful he's allowed Ghis to stay. By doing so, it grants us more time to be getting things done. If I'd taken Duplessey along with, it'd been that much longer till we'd begin digging. This way's more suitable. I can be off tending to business and Ghis can be here starting this other. I always think to work things out as best I can.

Chapter Forty-Five

How relevant it is to be hunting the hospital halls in search of a doctor. I've passed many, I'm sure, but the one I seek's several steps from me, through a door, should he be there.

My fingers are crossed and I hope to acquire some news regarding Jehan Rhoe's skull. Could blunt trauma have been his cause of death? I'm eager to find out.

I pass through the door of Dr. Ignace's office where, as suspected, I find him minding a stiff. I'm strolling toward his direction while watching him plop the muscular mass of some woman's heart upon his scale.

"You always throwing around people's tickers?" I laugh.

Roman turns to me. Upon his hands are gloves, wholly soaked in sanguine fluid.

I eye the still pumper lying upon the cold metal scale. "You know if that was mine, I'd expect you be gentle."

Roman grins. "What care do the dead have for organs?"

"Ask your stiff, she's liable to say."

He peers at the woman before spotting the curious grin crinkling my lips. "Cut that smirk off your face."

Roman removes his gloves as he's pacing toward a counter. Upon it I see the veiled crown of Jehan Rhoe concealed neatly by the use of several cloths. Considerably, he's taken good care of it; least, I suspect.

"Got my report?"

"He was male, all right, between twenty-five and thirty-five years of age, with no unusual mutations sighted, and no visual indication of fractures. The specimen was noted unremarkable."

"Between twenty-five and thirty-five? Is this analysis considered accurate?"

"The estimated range was based on cranium fusions and the man's teeth. Though, estimates are only that; approximate calculations are hard to figure. Knowing the quoted age is based on my rough impression. I can't say it's exact."

"He could be older?"

"No more than thirty-five, I suspect. In validating this, understand, as we age, our skulls increase in size. Another indication of older skulls are smaller cranial sutures, but none of this was evident during my inspection. Of course, the only way to broaden this analysis would be in viewing his skeletal structure and we don't have that."

If, as Dr. Ignace has informed, the man was between twenty-five and thirty-five, then Jehan Rhoe couldn't possibly have been the skull's owner. If this is fact, then who am I left to consider?

Currently, we have the unknown skull of a young adult male. No visual signs of trauma were indicated anywhere on his head and, basically, as Roman advised, the skull was unremarkable.

"You don't seem too thrilled by all this," Dr. Ignace responds.

"Well, no, Roman, I'm not. I thought I knew who that belonged to. You've just proven me wrong."

"With a little more work, you should figure it out."

"I'm not sure I'm wanting to."

"You're no quitter. Besides, someone's depending on you. Don't let them down."

"It might be too late for that."

"Think things over; that's what your mind's for. And in time you'll find answers."

"I'm feeling sort of stuck, like I'm in quicksand and sinking."

"It's only temporary, you know? It happens to people all the time, even me. You're a better man than the one who stops what he's doing. Don't lose your direction."

"I just need some time, I suppose."

"We all do, it's natural. What'll you do now?"

"Hmm, head to the office, probably. See if I can't gather clues as to whose skull this belonged to."

"If there's anything more I can do, I'm here, always."

"Help me figure out whose this is."

"If only it was simpler."

He's right; if only this was simpler, but it's turned out to be a burdensome chore, trying to figure out who this man was. It seemed plausible, after learning of Jehan Rhoe and easily I assumed the skull had been his. Before him I was considering Matthias Dane, but Ghislain got the evidence we needed to prove it hadn't been him.

I feel I'll never be able to put this to rest. I'm going batty. When considering I have a good hunch, that I can clarify certain elements of this complex case, the damn mystery decides to become more polemical.

Chapter Forty-Six

Flustered, I'm feeling, as I sit at my desk. This whole case was over before it began. To think I had most of this shit figured out; then again, that's what I was figuring. Considering Rhoe killed his father and the skull belonging to Jehan wasn't so far-fetched, but now, after speaking with Roman, I see my hypothesis proved wrong.

There is one thing, however, one fact I know certain; Guillaume Rhoe murdered Yria Dane. Besides that, I'm still without her body and I'm liable to never find it.

How do I piece things together when additional evidence is lacking? I have the skull of an unknown male sitting before me, the victim whose life was taken by the hands of Guillaume Rhoe. Who the hell was he? I thought I'd gathered most the facts. Where did I go wrong? What am I missing?

I remove my notebook and set it upon my table. Carefully, with a keen eye, I review all my scribble. I flip through till I've come upon my references pertaining to Yria's circle of friends. Gaston's the first name my saucers are drawn to. I've seen him; he was present, so I know he's alive.

My eyes now narrow upon Tayce. Says here he relocated in forty-eight. The information given had tied him to Quebec, Canada. Is this accurate? Having moved so far away, how can anyone be sure the man's not deceased? I hereupon think, only way to know certain is to take a chance in calling him, then there's Basile, who, like Tayce, decided to move from Annecy, and since not having contacted him, how can I be sure Basile wasn't the man sentenced to death?

My ideas are expanding, leaving room for additional thoughts. I'm now considering Guillaume Rhoe himself, wondering if the skull could actually be his? To speak precisely, after all, it's been missing since the report of his death.

I realize this case thickens. My educated guess leads me deeper in thought. Could Charlize Rousseau have heard from Rhoe what he'd done to Yria? Shocked by his confession, Char became disturbed by her lover. Realizing the same could be done to her, Char decided to put an end to his madness. She killed Guillaume Rhoe to protect her own life, could it be? Maybe I've finally got it? That's why she left town following his death. If this isn't the truth, I don't know what is.

I must phone Ghis, tell him to get here. We've new developments to discuss. I search rigorously through my notes, searching for Pascal Cartier's number. Crap. I realize, to my mistake, I never took it.

In deciding, I'll contact the operator, get her to connect our lines. Thankfully, I know Pascal's address, so I won't have her phoning the wrong guy.

I hear Pascal, so I report who I am before requesting my pal Ghis.

I'm now hearing Duplessey at the receiving end as I ask, "What're you doing, old boy?"

"Digging the floor as you asked."

"Put it on hold and bring your ass to the station."

"It'll take awhile, boss. I'm on foot."

"Jesus, get a cab. Make sure you're here quickly."

Really, must I think for the man? I get back to my notes. If I'm to try contacting Tayce, I'll need his last name. Thankfully, when it comes to Basile, I have his already.

Once again I find myself pestering the operator. This time I say I need information for Basile Devereux in Cherbourg.

I await her at my end.

"Sir, I'm not finding any listings for Basile Devereux in or around Cherbourg. Shall I check somewhere else?"

"I suppose not. Thank you anyway." I hang my phone while feeling perturbed.

I suspect Mr. Devereux could be anywhere, and trying to find him will be a less than simple task. For the matter, I'll let Ghis have the pleasure of searching.

I rejoin my review of notes. I unfold the pages taken from the Ladous'. In scanning them again, I admittedly confess not finding one lick of useful material.

My next brush up and, likely my last, is the paper I'd snatched near the body of Marcel Dupuis.

I read his final words once more, those to which were dictated from none other than Yria Dane, herself.

I speak aloud, listening to the sound of my voice. "Within a trunk, within his house, contains the head of a man from Spouse."

Upon my desk I unveil the cloth layered crown to view it. Stirred with a pivotal question, I ask, again wondering, how's this not related to Jehan Rhoe? The man lived on Spouse Road. It'd only seem reasonable to say this was his. The clue's in the sentence. Who else might have lived on that road? I wonder if Orisia could say? I believe I'll phone Miss Laroque to find out.

After a short-lived conversation, I get me a name. Though, I haven't spoken with him, his name is familiar. It's one I've heard in previ- ous discussions. Orisia tells me the man was Tayce Rosin.

"What's this about?"

I'm telling her, "There's not much to go on now, but a second victim."

"What do you mean, second victim?"

"We'll talk when I've filled in more facts, Miss Laroque. I'll keep in touch."

Though I still hear her voice on the line, I hang my phone.

Blasted, where's that darn Ghislain? Couldn't get a cab, is that it?

I walk to a back room and begin prepping my coffee pot. As I'm returning to my desk, the jangle of bells begin their toll at my door. There's a man standing tall, but looking all too tired as he comes through the door.

"Well, well," I say. "Another day absent and I'd think you for dead." "I should tell you I'm worn," Marin grumbles.

"Well, I'm just starting some coffee. So, what's your news, brother? You wrap up that case?"

"I'm catching dead ends. I've got nothing, Satordi. Absolutely nothing and I'm tired."

"That's how it goes sometimes."

"I'm wondering if Mrs. Audric Badeau changed her name? I can't find hide nor hair of that woman. It's made me sick."

"Christoph, either?"

Marin makes a strange face. "I never knew his last name."

"Have you spoken with your client?"

"Told him I'm hanging my coat and staying in town." My brother then asks, "You finish that weird case you had us working?"

"Don't have me answer."

"Why won't you toss it? Be done, Satordi, it's wearing you out."

"You know I won't quit."

"It's become an unhealthy addiction. Deja worries you'll work yourself to death. Don't force her to bury you, brother."

"I can't leave work. It's my job to make money."

"Your girl's strung out, she's worried. She's at the house now."

"I'm swamped, Marin. I can't be leaving. There's too much work." The jangle of bells are once again tolling. Through the breach I spot Ghis slowly entering the building.

I yell out, "You know what time I called you? And you're coming now?"

"No cab; had to walk, and it's raining. Where's the sympathy?"

"I'll show you sympathy. Walk on back to Pascal's. I'll see you tomorrow."

"You serious? Come on, boss. Give me a break."

I look to my brother. "You hear something, Marin?"

"Boss. Boss, come on. I got here quick as I could."

"I'm jerking your chain. Take it easy. Oh, and while you're here, this guy's my brother. So you don't confuse us, take note; the man's sloppy, he's fatter and, oh, he don't wear the best threads."

"Don't listen to a word of that. Satordi's way off on all he says. I'm Marin by the way." He's extending his hand. "I'm the older and much wiser of the two. Satordi hasn't graduated from textbooks, but with hope I believe he will when he's forty."

I shake my head for Ghis to see. "Marin's lies. He always does."

Ghislain grins. "Seems more like friendly sibling battle."

My brother says, "Welcome to brotherly combat. It comes in stride, so I'll aware you now." Marin steps from my desk. "Well, boys, I'm off. Take it easy."

"Just another dog in the rain," I say as he's leaving. "Your turn's coming later," I hear him shout back.

"So, that's your brother?" I'm hearing Ghis.

"Yap. Now come on, have a seat."

Ghislain gets a whiff of air. "Am I smelling coffee?"

"Want a cup?"

Ghislain nods. "Why're you needing me here?"

"Got some news."

"This couldn't have been done on the line?"

"Will you shut up for one minute? Jesus, Ghis, please" .

"All right, boss."

"Because the skull was estimated between twenty-five and thirty-five years of age, we can't suspect Jehan Rhoe. Additionally, Dr. Ignace couldn't find anything wrong."

"That puts us back with an unknown."

"Well, not necessarily. I've come up with a few random thoughts. Just hear me out." I explain my first theory pertaining Tayce Rosin. "If he's alive, then good. But if he's not, that could be our break. Oh, also, I heard he lived on Spouse Road. It was a stroke of luck learning that."

"It could mean something."

"Hopefully. Anyway, I figured I'd leave you to making the call."

"Apparently, what you don't want to do, you dump on me. Okay, I get it."

"I knew you'd be handy."

"Cut the crap. What's next?"

"Basile Devereux. He and Tayce moved. No one hears from either one. In comparison, both are speculated to be alive, but in certainty, no one knows."

"Considering you're right, our focus should be Tayce."

"Not so fast. I've got another thought."

"Oh?"

I fill Ghis in on my theory for Guillaume.

"You can't possibly think that skull was Rhoe's?"

"Yes, I can. And if you listen, Ghis, you'll hear why." I finish my statement from where Ghislain stopped me. "Char may have killed him. Huh, what do you think?"

"I don't know? Really, a woman, you think?"

"Let me put it this way. Why, following his funeral, had she suddenly skipped town?"

Ghis admits, "I always felt there was something funny about the way he clocked out. It hardly made sense."

"The boat incident, I know. I've considered it, too."

"I still, I don't know, Satordi? While what you say makes sense, I still find myself challenged with questions. Let me see your notebook."

I slide it across the table. "Have at it. I'm taking a run to the pisser." I remove myself from my chair and step from my desk. In a back room I hurry along to the toilet, where relief quickly beckons as I channel my stream.

Moments later I'm back at my desk. "This head," Ghislain mumbles.

"What of it?"

"I don't think, I don't think it's Rhoe's." "Are you challenging my assumption?"

"Don't get me wrong, boss, I liked your impression, but I'm not sure it's right."

"That sets us back to Mr. Rosin."

"Only one name belongs to that skull and I'd imagine it's Tayce."

"Very well. If we're right, our chances for finding bones at Pascal's is still likely, let's hope. I want to test my luck and go searching myself."

"I thought we were working as a team?"

"We are."

"I hadn't finished Pascal's basement. I left the dowsing rods on the stairs. There's a shovel, too."

"Lock the door when I leave. I'll flip the sign to closed. I don't want anyone in, unless it's my brother. You got that?"

Ghis nods in agreement.

"Pascal's number's on my desk."

"Right, boss. Now get out. I need my concentration."

"Keep talking like that and I might add your name to my business." I tread to my door, flip the sign to closed, and exit my building. A light drizzle speckles the ground and cars as I'm stepping out. I peer toward the sky when noticing several somber clouds moving slightly.

They'll be gone in no time, and these showers will stop. It already poured, according to Ghislain, at least.

I step forth to Sable before flopping inside. I peer to her gas gage, noticing she's low. I'll make a run to Bellamont's Service Station and get her filled up.

I travel on down the road a ways, then hang a left and continue straight. I pass eight blocks before I come upon my destination, Bigler Road. To the right I'm turning and continuing my pace. I drive farther a little more and see Bellamont's to my left. I pull in aside a pump and await the assistant.

Skippy, the owner, comes out within seconds. "Hey, Biertempfel. Just gas today?"

I nod as I peer toward his shop. "That's a fine looking ride you're working on there."

"Oh, the Roadmaster. It's a beaut, ain't it?"

"What's that, a forty-nine?"

"Well, I'll be, you know your years."

"It's sure a looker, all right."

"It surely is sweet. Hey, you want me to air up these tires? They're looking low."

"Might as well. I wouldn't want an accident."

My eyes fall back to the Roadmaster. That baby's slick. Whatever lucky bastard owns that's having fun.

"All right, bud, $5.40."

I dig a wad of cash from my pocket and find exact change. "Thanks, Skip. See you next time."

I head out and hit the road. I make it to Mr. Cartier's and head up his stairs. He allows me inside, then we tread to the kitchen.

Pascal acknowledges, "Your assistant left everything on the stairs. Said he hadn't found anything."

I head on down and, upon the last step, see the rods where Ghislain had left them. I pick them up, wondering how'd these work again? Point them to the ground? I'll try that. Nah, nope. Nothing's happening.

"Pascal!" "Hmm?"

"How do these rods work?"

"Hold them straight, but loose in your hands. They'll cross when you've found something."

"By themselves? How do they cross themselves?"

"Son, you need me to come help?"

"Oh, no. Uh-ugh, sir. I'll get the hang of these."

I begin walking the room and see several places Ghislain's previously dug. I want to check the farthest sides of the room, rather than directing my focus within the center, as he's done.

I walk to the farthest left corner and begin my dowsing. Slowly, I'm walking, step by small step. I take twelve paces before my rods begin intersecting. I'm bending down now and shoving the rods through the soil as markers to symbolize where I'm to dig.

I return to the stairs in search of the shovel. I race back to my post with the excavator in hand. I lay the first blow into the ground as a commencement to digging. Before long I've dug a deep hole. Sadly, no bones have beckoned my sight.

I gaze into the pit and am noticing nothing more than a water line positioned deeply beneath me. Its extent feasibly spans the range of the room, so I'll have to be careful as not to be fooled and dig in areas it's likely to rest.

After packing the dirt back, I follow the pipe above ground. With my foot I scrape a line through the soil straight across the room to mark the line's position. After doing this, I go back to the room's corner, where I begin to dowse again.

Thirty minutes have come and gone and, during this span I've dug two other areas. I did come across bones, though not human, as I'd been seeking. What had been found were the skeletal remains of a cat. Why it'd been buried in this basement makes no sense, but someone had done it.

I finish my inspection of the room and, with a lack of additional sites, I realize nothing's left to uncover. I'm done here.

I return upstairs, taking the shovel and rods with me. I find Pascal in his den where he's listening to a radio.

"Well," I say. "There weren't any remains down there. I suppose I'll be going to the yard now."

"I know how eager you were to find something, but I'm relieved you hadn't found bones in my house. I assume what wasn't here could be found out back?"

"Well, yes, possibly."

"Do let me know if you come across anything."

I nod in agreement, then ask, "You got a back door?"

"In the kitchen."

I chuckle at my stupidity. Probably should have known that, right?

"Just be careful. One of my back stairs has come to start rotting."

"I could fix it if you've got any boards."

"My son's supposed to get around to it. You've got enough work of your own. Thank you, though, for your offer."

"Well, if you change your mind."

I make my way to the yard where I'll begin my timely chore of dowsing. By the time I finish, it's liable to be dark.

I wonder, as I stare upon the stretch of ground before me, why have I gotten myself into this? This one man task I see will be taxing. Am I stupid thinking I could do this alone? I'm an idiot.

Chapter Forty-Seven

Meanwhile, at the business, old Ghis tries hard finding a number for Tayce, but every chance he's gotten has brought him nowhere. Not even the last known city of Quebec, where Mr. Rosin was said to have moved, can't provide a listed address or number.

He's thought what to do, but finds a lack of ideas. He peers to the clock, thinking he's been at this for over an hour. He pulls himself to his chair, then stares to the ceiling, knowing Satordi's going to be displeased. He's given Ghis this simple task which he's been unable to complete.

Ghislain contemplates his next move. When in desperate need of help, there's no one to call but Orisia, so he picks up his phone and is dialing her number.

"Hello?" a youthful voice answers his call.

"Mira, honey, can I speak to your aunt? It's Ghislain."

"Aunty!" He hears her scream. "Phone."

Orisia answers, "Yes? Hello."

"I don't mean to bother you, but you got a minute?"

"Of course."

"Does Tayce Rosin have any family here in Annecy, you know?"

"Well, I should think. I know his mother passed a few years back, and he has a sister, Eleta Lefèvre."

"Eleta's all?"

"As far as I know."

"Okay. All right. Thank you."

Since learning Tayce's sister may still be local, Ghis decides to contact an operator in order of retaining a possible number for Eleta Lefèvre.

Following his call, the line's connected to some hopeful whose ti- tle was listed beneath the same name.

The ring reverberates through Ghislain's end as he waits ever patiently, then, following the fifth toll, communication is made.

A woman picks up her receiver while her tone rises softly, "Hello?"

"Eleta, please." "Yes, I'm

she."

"Mrs. Eleta Lefèvre?"

"Mmm-hmm, yes."

"My name's Detective Duplessey. I've been issued a case regarding Yria Dane, and your brother was mentioned. I've news his last residence placed him in Canada. Could you tell me, is this information still current?"

"My brother relocated to the states. He'd taken a job in Maine some six years ago as a fisherman."

"Oh, okay. You, ah, happen to know his number, then?"

She stresses. "Well, my brother and I haven't kept much in touch. I have no way of reaching him."

"You don't?"

"No. No, I'm sorry. Tayce isn't in trouble, I hope?"

"Not at all. I'm only needing to speak with him. Might you know which harbor your brother's working?"

"Forgive me, mister, I wouldn't know."

"Then the name of his captain, maybe, or the ship, even?"

"The ship I know was the Slania Marie."

"The Slania Marie?" That's some information to play with.

After connecting with a local Maine piscator, Ghislain finds luck contacting a man, Spencer Finnie. He learns the Slania Marie is captained by Dakota Cooper, whose boat keeps dock in Camden Harbor. Following a brief absence, Mr. Finnie returns to the line, conveying contact information for Capt. Cooper.

Chapter Forty-Eight

So I've been in the back yard too long now. My back aches and my hands, sore. I've given my best at searching for bones, but like the basement, there's nothing been found. I'm feeling worn and weary, and in need of much rest. Since nothing's uncovered, it's best I retire.

I guess I'd been wrong supposing there'd been bones on this property. At least I'll admit it and without hesitation, I'll say, I'll easily accept my miscounted assumptions. It's true, however, even the most seasoned detectives make their mistakes. Like all people we learn and we live by our lessons.

Currently, I finish packing the last shovel of dirt; and being honest, I'll tell you, I can't wait till I'm within my business and settling my ass at my comfortable seat. This physical labor has taken its toll. I wasn't cut for this mess, this job, these somatic encounters. Hopefully this'll be the last time I'll do it.

I step back through the door of Mr. Cartier's house to tell him I'm finished. There's just nothing there. I imagine for him he's relieved. However, I'm extremely dissatisfied. I know there's a body somewhere; I'm just not sure where to look.

"Could it be, son, you were simply mistaken?"

"I don't want to argue that saying, no. But it could be I was."

"Every good man has to do what he can."

"Guess then I've given my best. Anyway, thank you for allowing my inspection of your property."

"Oh, well, you seemed up front with your facts. And having been sincere with your intent the moment we met, I felt most obliged on letting you in."

"And that's been more than one occasion." I laugh. "We never know, I may always return and, if I'm back, then by God, my friend, please open that door."

Pascal smiles warmly. "Maybe have coffee sometime, or a drink of rotgut? A vintage Bourbon I've got, I've kept for some time for some special occasion. I've been eager, as you'd imagine, to split that dam seal."

"Tell you what," I say. "I'll crack this damn case and come back. We'll be tipping that bottle."

"I'll certainly be ready."

"Well, my friend, if I continue my keep here, I'll never be going. I've got more work, so I'll be leaving you now. I'll see myself to the door." I shake the man's hand before I exit his house.

It's been a long day, and since I started this case, I've seen myself work harder now than I've been in the past. Of course, many times I've said my work's tiring, but now I've got the arete to boast about it.

Chapter Forty-Nine

I step through my business as the sight of Ghis stands clear in my eyes. "What on earth you doing, fool?"

I shake my head while watching him sweep the length of the floor. Not Marin nor myself have had enough moxie to clean when we're here. Call us lazy, but it's true. I hope Ghis doesn't think he'll be paid for his time; then again, having a butler might be an idea. I take this thought into consideration as I envision my musing. Mind you, this representation plays in my head and I think it for laughs.

Marin's at his desk and I at mine. The eager thirst for a kettle of coffee is minding our urge. Feeling my laze, I turn to Marin and plead with my eyes, but just as myself, my brother's lethargic and unwilling to move. I spin in my chair as I look through the room, then there near the shelves of books on the wall I spot Ghis with a rag and dusting the spines.

We need coffee, Duplessey. Come fill us a pot. Ha, I think, that's a good start. I then draw my eyes off him so I can peer to my brother and I envision my speech; hey, it's near lunch, you getting hungry?

My brother acknowledges with the tip of his head. Put me down for a sandwich, a Croque-Monsieur. Get our servant to fetch it.

Oh, I like this idea. I'm really into it. So, thinking, I look through the room in search of our server. When you finish that pot, run to the bistro. We're ready for lunch.

Yeah, so I heard, would be Ghislain's reply. One Croque-Monsieur.

No, make it two; and don't keep us waiting as you'd done us before. Hurry back when you have them. You're cleaning the bathroom upon your return. Scrub the toilet this time and get rid of that ring! Don't forget the floor either. It'll need some grease work. Have it glis- ten. That's what we'll expect.

I find myself laughing aloud. I've nearly forgotten I was caught in a mind trip.

Ghislain stares at me strangely. Seems he's bothered by my comical burst. "I've got news to respond."

"Suppose we both do. I'll let you go first."

"I tracked Tayce Rosin to Camden, ME, where he was working as a deckhand upon the Slania Marie. I spoke with the vessel's captain, who told me Tayce returned here to France eight months ago. I've also spoken with Tayce's sister, but the news I got was hardly receiving. I've tried locating Tayce, but I've been unable to find him."

All right, could the man really be dead? Possibly. Someone may have stolen his identity and is living his life. On the other hand, just in theory, Mr. Rosin's alive. If so, the man's evasive. What's to say he doesn't wish to be found? It's like he's fallen off the face of the earth and has erased his name completely.

Let's say he's alive, again just in theory. I'm wondering could he have done something wrong? We all know unlawful incidents force peoples hiding. If this is true in Tayce's case, then I'm bothered with questions. What sort of crime or erroneous act was committed? And had he really returned to France eight months back as Ghis stated? These thoughts now concern me.

"So what's the word, boss? Should I abandon search?"

"We've no evidence proving him to be alive or even dead."

"You know, boss, I still have that buddy of mine, the guy who does sculptures. It wouldn't kill us to give him a shot."

"I told you how I felt on that."

"But we've hit a dead end. Only thing left is to take a new road."

"The idea still refrains me, but I'll give it some thought."

"You would, really?"

"Don't push it, slick. You'll have your answer tomorrow. Now don't bug me no more."

He shakes his head as not to annoy me. "So what's your news? You got some work done?"

"I finished the basement for you and found a dead cat. I hit the back yard, supposing I'd find something there. But you know, all that stinking work, I didn't find nothing."

"Don't josh me, boss. You're joking?"

"I'm not happy, slick."

"We know whatever was done with the body, the possibilities are endless."

"For the time I say we draw our focus to the skull. It's all we've got. Might as well deal with it."

Ghislain thinks and comes with a thought. "Would you consider digging up Guillaume's bones? And maybe after talking with your doctor friend, he can tell us whether the skull's really his."

"Exhume his remains? We'd need permission, not to mention a judge-issued warrant and proper permit."

"You know, Satordi, I'm here 'cause you requested my help. The ideas I've been giving, you seem not to like. What can I do when you won't consider my thoughts?"

Maybe he's right? Could I have been jealous when told of his conceptualizations and knowing they weren't mine? Probably so.

Sensibly thinking, how're we to work as a team when all I do is scorn his ideas? It wouldn't be fair to Ghis if I continue acting this way. His thoughts have been good, I might honestly say. It's been me disagreeing because I was feeling upstaged.

I find myself asking, "You going to call town hall tomorrow and get in touch with the judge?"

"Does that mean you're on board?"

"You're my partner, right?"

He nods with a smile. "I'll see what strings I can pull."

"I don't know about you, but I'm starting to get hungry. So how about it, want to grab dinner? I know a wonderful cook who'd be serving good supper. If we make it in time, we'll be dealt a hot plate."

"Well, all right, then, let's you and I go."

"Just let me close up and we'll be on our way."

Oh, food. Glorious food. What'll Cerissa have prepared? I won't even ask that 'cause I imagine something good. She always knows how to please my belly. Unlike Dej, Cerissa's a much better cook. I'm not saying my kitten can't make a good meal, she can; but if I had to chose between her and Cerissa's cooking, my sister-in-law's got my vote. Course, I'd never tell Marin his wife's better than my gal when it comes to the kitchen. I'll just keep that to myself.

Chapter Fifty

Just as promised, I've brought Ghis to the best place to get food;
Marin's, of course. We all know he's not the designated cook of the
house, so don't get confused. Rather, it's his wife, who, every day, per-
forms her best when she's minding her kitchen.

I introduce Ghislain to Deja. They meet, greet, and are shaking
hands. I'm now directing my focus a few feet from the floor. "And those
two heydays would be Paien and Zuri, my nephew and niece. Don't be
shy," I tell them.

Ghis, whom I suspect isn't accustomed to children, tries his best to be
cordial. "Lay it there." He extends his large hand.

The children look to him oddly.

"Lay what, mister?" Paien unknowingly wonders.

"Why, your hand, little man. Haven't you heard? It's an expression
of greeting."

Paien laughs. "I thought you wanted my yo-yo."

"You, kids, you like tricks?"

They answer, "Yes!" They're joyously beaming.

"So imagine your uncle having two francs. You doing it? Imagine
clearly. As clear as you can. Now go to the sink and put your hands beneath water. Then, stay and say, money, money, come to me."

Ghis blushes while my niece and nephew move to the sink. With
their backs to us, Ghis quietly asks I remove the two francs from my
wallet. Apparently this trick of his is including my money, not his. How
genius, that scheming con.

Paien and Zuri return to his side. "What now?" They're harmoni-
ously questioning.

"You did as said. Now run to your uncle and blow soft on his
hands."

As directed, the kids charge upon me. Paien, acting too eager,
blows with such force, he spits on my shaker. Aw, really? This wasn't
what I wanted. Couldn't he have taken enough directive to listen?

My nephew remains at my one hand while Zuri keeps herself at the other. "Oh, what's that? A bit of tingling in my hand? What's this?" They spring open. "Will you look at that!"

Two faded bills lay crunched in my palms.

"Zuri, it worked! Look now, we're rich!" Paien screams.

"Let's do it again!"

I look to Ghislain, sort of feeling provoked. My eyes widen, and within my brain I hear my thought bark, oh, that man! He better listen when my lips tell him, no. In a voice spoken silent, I form my command.

Seemingly, Ghis understands. In his made-up approach, he tells the kids firmly, "It was fun, I know, but it only works once."

Zuri slightly pouts. "It's not fair. I wanted to play more."

"I know, little doll, but even tricks have their rules." He tassels her hair and cossets her crown.

I leave Ghislain with the kids, that he may befriend both the children. It's an inventive scheme I've prepared to spare my kitten. Usually she's their run to when they're wanting to play. So, rather, I'll just tinker with things so they're left with old Ghis. He'll be a fool not to know I've set his ass up.

I step through the house, searching for Deja. I find her lounged on the couch, reading some paper.

"You look exhausted," she tells me. She pats the near cushion along the side of her seat. "Come rest yourself. Prop your feet and get comfortable."

Undoubtedly, I do what's advised. I take the open space nearest her and sink to the couch. Attentively, Deja's eyes get drawn to my shoes and, like a good dame, she glides them right off.

"I was in town today," my lady, she's telling me.

"You? Just you? You know what I've said, so you best have been solo."

"It's okay. Ambrielle stayed home. I couldn't help it, though. I passed a bridal shop and was looking at dresses, wondering, will we ever be married?"

"I've told you, when the time's right."

"I never thought I'd become impatient. I guess I'm eager, Satordi. I've wanted so long to be your wife."

I draw my hands to her face and kiss her lips softly. "I promise, kitten, it'll happen."

"Don't keep me waiting."

"But, dear, you realize you'll have to?" Oh God why'd I say that?

"You'd marry your car if you didn't have me."

"Honey, Sable will become an old beater. And ten years from now, she'll probably be gone and I'll have a new car. A good thing for you, there's no one in this world who could ever replace you, ever."

"You see us together ten years down the road?"

"Yes, I can. Don't you?"

"It makes a good dream."

"Right." I kiss her crown, then peer the room. "Well, Marin's not around. Has he picked up and left?"

"He's napping upstairs."

"Oh. And Ambrielle?"

"In Zuri's room."

I figure I'll sneak upstairs and drop her in a quick peek. I make it into my niece's chamber, where I see Ambrielle sitting upon the bed, straight. Before her's a scrapbook and some loosely cast papers.

"What's going on? Working on something?"

"Mmm? Oh, I'm gathering my family's death notices. Thought I'd have their obituaries kept in something." She makes a long face. "It's sad, sir, knowing my name could be added here soon."

"You've better thoughts to be thinking. Lay off that, huh? Let me take you downstairs."

I coax the girl on and we exit the chamber. After heading to the kitchen, we're greeted by Cerissa and the kids, who are coloring on paper.

"Ghislain?" I look around. "That old fool, where's he gone?"

Cerissa speaks, "Your friend ran bags to the trash."

The good housewife, I think; and it's not the first time I've thought this. Said it before, he'd make a good servant.

I hear him returning through the back and, as he's coming inside, I see he's removing his shoes. "It's terribly muddy out there."

I make a quick paced remark, "Well, bless you, dear man, you're more thoughtful than I. Heard you were taking out trash. What a nice thing you've done." I grin. "Does Cerissa have you for hire?"

"What are you, a comedian?"

"You saying I am, 'cause I never knew." I foolishly laugh.

Ghislain sees Ambrielle and masterfully asks, "Who's the pretty gem beholding my vision?"

I look to the young maiden, saying, "Hey, girl, I think you've caught his eye." I send her a wink. "Meet my partner, Ghislain Duplessey."

He's asking her softly, "You're related to the family, I take?"

"Oh." She laughs, as any girl would. "No, sir, but they're good friends."

"That's swell to hear. Say, I can't help but wonder, have I seen you somewhere?"

Ambrielle's hesitant, but decides on her line. "I don't suppose."

"I could've sworn I've seen you around on the street. Maybe I'm wrong. It's just you look so familiar."

I speak and I'm talking to Ghis. "As many women as there are in Annecy, you've probably mistaken her for some other lass."

"Wouldn't have been the first time. Anyway."

I make an angular face while shaking my head. "Anyway?"

Cerissa zealously interrupts, "Anyway, men, supper's ready. Someone get Deja. Tell her it's time to come eat."

"Mommy, I'll get her," Zuri suggests, sweetly.

I hear my name being called. "Grab six plates while I'm filling these glasses."

The instant I see my sister-in-law, I bust forth with laughter. "Cerissa." I can't control my amusement. "Cerissa! Woman, that ain't sugar you've got!"

By now Ghislain shrieks with hilarity. "Can't she read? My God, Satordi, can she?"

Cerissa realizes what she's done. Instead of adding sugar to the bottom of each glass, she's mistakenly plied baking soda. "Good thing I hadn't added tea," she facetiously admits.

It's these simple slip-ups that make moments pleasant.

Say you're having a terrible day such as mine and you're needing some bliss, some good humor to get by, then pay heed to your family; they're liable to arouse you with their artless faux pas.

Following Zuri, Deja comes to the room. We all settle ourselves as we prepare to scarf dinner. Following this and, depending on how we're feeling, we'll either stay a short bit or drag on through the night.

Conversation starts as usual with Cerissa's habitual questions about dinner. Common point of issue, to which all should respond, begins, food okay? Then, as she receives praise, Cerissa joyously beams. She adds a note of content when regarding our homage to the work she's contributed. Additionally, her eagerness to provide more viands kicks in when she asks, "Seconds anyone?"

Anxious to not decline, Ghislain speaks, "I wouldn't mind getting more."

Thrilled to hear his response, Cerissa gets up to flow his plate with more fare than before.

Again, as she gets to her seat, Cerissa's enthralled and starting to speak. Her curiosity to how Ghis and I met begins her next question.

Not holding back, I tell her the story. "I had no idea he'd been an officer of the law," I say. "I mean, I thought he was scum. First time we met, I easily disliked him. Then, all a sudden I learned he'd been a more decent man than I knew."

"See, working together, you've taken some chances." Cerissa looks to Ghislain. "How're your experiences so far?"

"Well, if it hadn't been for that man there, I'd still be drinking my- self away every night. I hadn't had stable work other than side jobs. So it's great getting back to my field and having a newly acquainted partner to work with."

"Well, then it's a blessing."

"Absolutely is."

Ambrielle becomes curious. "You're working the Dane case?"

My partner's responding, "Mmm-hmm, and the suspect, Guillaume Rhoe, had been my partner, but the instant I felt suspicion, the man had me fired."

"Why, sir, would he get you fired?"

"Simple, honey. He knew I was onto him."

"Couldn't you have done something?"

"I tried, little lady, but I just wasn't heard."

Cerissa, sitting next to Ghis, shakes her head. "He continued to work while you lost your job? What's he, still working there?"

"No, ma'am, the guy's dead."

Deja's confused. "How do you continue a case when your suspect's deceased?"

I add my two cents. "Dead or not, it's still a case. Everyone has a right to know who Guillaume Rhoe really was."

"Everyone?"

"We'll have his misdeeds printed for people to read. And when it's time, we'll discuss it together, but now, I'm feeling pretty beat. Won't you help Cerissa with dishes so we can get out of here, please? Ghis, you bout ready?"

I don't know about everyone else, but I'm ready for bed. Tomor- row will be a long day and, with the shit we're to do, my exhaustion might kill me. I know with all the crap I'd done today, I'm needing to bathe. I don't much feel like it, but I need to get cleaned. My hair's look- ing nasty, my skin's dowdy, I reek of sweat, and my clothes appear grimy. There's no sense in even asking; there's no way in hell Dej would allow me in bed while looking like this.

"I'm about to fall out to the floor. We need to get going."

Feeling sorry for me, Cerissa tells Dej, "Go on, get him home. I'll get the dishes."

"Ghis, your shoes, and grab your coat."

"You don't have shoes," my young nephew says, staring at my sock-covered feet.

"I do; they're just in the living room." I hush for a second as I have an urge to start yawning. "I'm tired here, people. Let's get a move on."

"We know. We've heard," my Deja advises.

I plead to Zuri, "Grab my shoes, please." Respectfully, she listens and, in moments returns dressed in my peddlers. I can't help it to laugh. "A little big, aren't they?"

"They're mighty large, Uncle Tordi. Mine are much littler."

"Be thankful for that. A girl with large feet would be hard to imagine."

"You're just saying that."

"I bet none of your little girlfriends at school have shoes big as mine."

"Not even the boys."

"See, then, aren't you glad you've got little stompers?"

I give the kids hugs and kisses and, after telling their mom thanks, I'm officially ready.

I know before even reaching my bed, I'll have to journey to Ghislain's and drop him off there. What's five more minutes? Doesn't sound like much, but when I'm tired as hell, I want to go home.

No one better fight me when we step through the door. I've dibs on the bathroom and I'll appoint my insistence. "Shower's mine, ladies. Just let me get cleaned, then the place is all yours."

Following my pronouncement, Ghislain polls, "What time do I expect you tomorrow?"

I pull upon his place. "Don't know. Maybe eight?"

"Ladies." Ghislain nods before leaving my car. "All right, boss, eight tomorrow."

Finally, I can go home and prepare for my shower.

"I mean it, ladies; bathroom's mine."

My doll face acknowledges, "Honey, we're as tired as you. We just want our beds."

My day ends after my cleansing wash. In Deja's room, I fall to the bunk. She's off brushing her teeth as I'm inducing my coma.

I'm turned on my side and, in less than five winks, I get taken by slumber. I'll probably be snoring when she comes to the room, and if she be smart, she'll know not to wake me.

Chapter Fifty-One

All morning I've found myself considering Ghislain's request for professional aid from his friend, the sculptor. However, I still find I'm somewhat fearful. If an attempt such as this fails, then the state of skull would forever be wrecked. I'm sure any agile yet tense individual would share this disturbance, but, thinking expansively, any clever human would also find himself examining the pros, not just the cons, to determine his course.

To consider the pros, I'll have to concede with the thoughts in my mind possibly saying the artist is well-trained and highly skilled at his craft, and that his learned genius has supplied him enough cleverness to appoint a well reached decision, that, in turn, will accomplish his course of action. In simpler terms, it's better he takes enough time to mull over an appropriate solution in relation to what we expect from this process.

Ghis and I are looking for a realistic face, one that is three-dimensional, that is smooth and free of flaws.

If this guy has no confidence to do it, I'll not let his hands near the skull.

Deciding to call Ghis over, I lean in my chair and stretch toward my desk.

"Yeah, boss?"

"That guy, that buddy of yours; I've been considering you call."

"Yeah? Yeah, no bull?"

"Set us up with the earliest appointment, then come talk to me."

Turning away, I step from my seat, determined to walk to my cork board. It's here I post a collage of notes relating to the additional proposal Ghislain made, exhuming Guillaume Rhoe, which I've ironically entitled the task.

The first of many steps is to find reason for request, and as Ghis and I would put it, the skull, which we hold in possession, is believed to have been Rhoe's. Second, make our argument agreeable enough to obtain a judge-issued warrant. From there I'll request Dr. Ignace for his scientific involvement. Lord knows I'd not have someone else.

Following that order, we'll apply for an exhumation license with the Department of Health, and the cemetery in which Rhoe lies must be informed and an exhumation date be scheduled. Also, proper machinery for digging and lifting will have to be rented.

I'd say that about sums it up. I return to my seat and am looking at Ghislain, who smiles as his serving me nods.

He withdraws the phone from his ear as he eagerly hangs up. "He requests us there now."

Anxious to leave, we gather our coats and, in good stride, we're speeding away through the door.

Chapter Fifty-Two

Jourdain D'Anjou, otherwise known as the sculptor, is a rather regal gent, standing steadily at six foot, with ashen hair and piercing eyes. His attire is simple; a pair of navy slacks upon his legs and, covering his chest, a soft-hued shirt, with sandy stripes, rests beneath a ginger-toned cardigan.

His home is beyond all neatness I've seen, with a lack of dust and soiled floors; makes me think I might be in an exhibition room or much more, a museum.

Considering his taste, which I view in my eyes, D'Anjou enjoys the finer things, from the furnishings so stunning to chandeliers and crystal fixtures, to the Persian rugs grandiosely guarding the floors. Even the couch and upholstered chairs stretch beyond perfection.

Thankfully Jourdain calls Ghis and myself into his lofty workroom where we rest our rears with ease.

I look around. "You've done all this yourself?" I'm referring to the superb tract of sculptures. "Outstanding."

I inch closer to gain a better view.

"These pieces," D'Anjou acknowledges, "I've prepared for my clients." This guy's absolutely something. To have a talent like this and have a buildup of clients is a reward in itself. I imagine D'Anjou has banked some sweet doe.

"I'm noticing you only sculpt people."

"It's what I prefer."

Jourdain shows Ghis and me a newly finished piece. He tells us he works mostly with pictures. "Many times clients bring photos of a person so I may rely on the visual aspects of that individual when I'm doing my work. Like this last piece, Mrs. Lavernia wanted her late husband's bust. She came with several photos, which I used."

For my reference, he hands me the pictures. I find my eyes darting between them and the bust he's presented. The resemblance I find is uncanny. This shows D'Anjou's exact with his work; he knows what he's doing.

Ghislain looks to me, smiling. "You blown away? You should be. I told you he's good."

"I'm seeing. He's got some damn good skill."

"I'll show you other things," Jourdain says. "A collection of re-articulated skulls. Between these and sculpting, this is all that I do. Some find it morbid, but I've many clients with special interest in osteology."

I don't know if I'm fascinated or weirdly put off by these things. It's not every day I stare at re-articulated skulls. Though it's D'Anjou's hobby, I'm a little disturbed; then again, it's for him and not me.

"You ever sculpted someone's face using only their skull?" I ask.

"The idea rather fascinates me, yet I've made no attempt. Largely, it's a challenge, though I'm sure there're ways to achieve such a goal. So if you don't mind, I'd like to examine the prospect."

I unveil the skull before handing it to Jourdain. "From what we know this person was male, between twenty-five and thirty-five years of age. The consultant I spoke with reported no visual fractures or unexpected mutations."

"So what sort of questions might you have for me?"

"I've seen your skills. No doubt do I think you can't do this, but I better ask."

"Work like this comes at a price. And, like you, I'm not lacking my belief. I'm more than certain I could produce your request."

"But could you make it dimensional?"

"The thickness of soft tissue from man to man's different. To acquire dimensions, I'll have to apply dense material. For example, a man's cheeks have more stratum than his chin, therefore his cheeks must be built upon to supply the affect."

Jourdain looks over his room as he searches for something. He reaches to a pack of smokes which rest at a table. "This'll be a good idea to show. Having broken the butt off this cigarette, I can apply it to the skull in an act to determine the depth of the soft tissue involved."

D'Anjou briefs Ghislain and myself with an example. He takes the cigarette butt, sticks it upon the skull, then finds the thickness of the cheek.

"This'll be the first of several markers I'd have to apply. Because lay- ers of tissue differ from different points of the face, the markers would be cut strictly to size. The use of these butts make a perfect example; however, I'd need something denser, but still easy to cut."

Ghislain suggests, "Straws, maybe?"

"Well, I don't think that'd ever work, simply for the fact the centers are hollow," Jourdain tells us.

Ghislain again adds suggestion, "Say then you soaked cigarette filters in liquefied wax. They'll toughen; maybe then they'll be put to use?"

"Well, hmm. The thought could reasonably work. Of course, to do that I'd need more cigarettes, then a chunk of beeswax to establish this process."

I began wondering about the financial value of the skull once completed. "Mr. D'Anjou, considering the time you'll have invested in this, what sort of appraisement would we be talking about?"

"Talking about time, skill, and perfection, somewhere around two-hundred francs. My re-articulated skulls sell for one-hundred, so a skull having to undergo the process you're asking would be a bit more."

"Is that including supplies?"

"I've got most of what I'm needing, except a few things I don't have on hand. The cigarettes and wax, furthermore, it'd probably be best to use an oil-based clay. Unlike water-based, it wouldn't harden and may be continually used."

"If I pick these things up, would you consider lowering your price?"

"I could, but it wouldn't be much."

"Maybe knock it down to one-fifty?"

"I'm considering more around one-seventy-five."

"All right, then, you've got a deal. How many packs of cigarettes and how many pounds of wax and clay?"

"Smokes, roughly two packs. Oil-based clay, I'm supposing two pounds. And the wax, well, I won't need much."

I've scratched this all down in my note pad, but since I'm unfamiliar with where to buy this variety of stuff, I have to ask Jourdain. His reply fills me in on one shop, a small building along the main street that's simply called Aucoin Crafts.

"I could start right away when you get the tools to me."

I nod in agreement. "Give us about forty-five minutes. You'll have the supplies."

I like this guy, Jourdain. I know how I earlier felt about coming to him, but now seeing his work and viewing his skill, I've got to say I'm completely astonished. Ghis had been right all along. This guy knows his stuff, and his forte is that, without doubt, Jourdain's strong point. I'm considerably happy I chose to give this man a chance. I'm even hap- pier Ghislain knows him.

Chapter Fifty-Three

As any good chap would imagine, I've directed Ghislain to the smoke shop while I remain at Aucoin Crafts. The game plan, as I see, is to save time shopping. Knowing my duration here will be spent longer, the ole bloke knows to return.

Instead of wasting time, I walk straight to the man employed at the counter. "Hey, could you help me? I'm needing some things," I tell him, "but I'm not sure where to look."

"Sure, I can help. What're you hunting?"

"Two pounds, oil-based clay and a pound of wax."

"What sort of wax? Paraffin, palm, soy?"

"Beeswax."

"Okay. Well, let me see. Don't seem to have nothing out. Let me check the stock room. It's a pound, you said?"

"Yeah, and two pounds of clay, but not that water-based stuff." I wait near the counter as the man walks to a rear room.

Ghislain appears through the door, gawking at me as I silently stand.

Holding the packs of cigarettes, he inquires, "What do you want done with these?"

"Hold them." I toss him my keys. "I'll meet you in Sable." He leaves, and again I'm on my own, waiting.

Come on, bud, I think in regard to the clerk. My eager request pays off as he strides through the room.

"I'll get these wrapped and have you set."

I fiddle in my pocket with intent to draw forth my wallet. I have no idea what this'll cost, but I should have it covered.

Regardfully, I watch the man finish wrapping the last package, and like the other before it, he's tied it with twine, having bound it together.

The gentleman then asks, "Anything else you'll be needing?"

Shaking my head, I indicate no, while handing forth the owed cash.

"You have a good day now." The man smiles.

I'm exiting the door. A few steps away rests my lovely wheels. I see Ghislain through the window, returning his gaze, and I shout, "Roll her down."

Though I can't hear, I see he gives question, 'cause I'm reading his lips.

"Roll her down," I say again.

I see the window lowering as Ghis sets forth his speech. "It's airtight, I can't hear."

After laying the small load of supplies upon him, I step to the driver's side, where I ease to my seat.

I explain to my partner he'll be running the things to Jourdain while I wait in the car. There's no reason for both of us going. Jourdain has a burden of work ahead, which I know will take time. He doesn't need us distracting his progress with our inquisitive probes to what he'll be doing. Rather, like him, we've got work, too. It's better our attention is directed on that, not suspending our time to question D'Anjou.

Having sped through town, I now park my car along the curb and kill the engine. The sight of Jourdain's pad reflects my vision. Wholly, I remain in my seat as Ghislain steps out and, slowly on foot, he traverses toward Jourdain's.

Through the windshield I watch D'Anjou appear at his door. His arm is outstretched, with his hand mildly wavering the air. A minimal amount of words have likely been spoken, but now Ghislain steps forth and joins him inside.

I look to my clock to make note of his time. Ghis better not once think to remain with his keep over the pass of five minutes. I should have told him before that would not make me happy; however, instead, for some reason, I didn't.

Time's winding down. Five minutes pass and my passenger seat remains empty. My eyes have been fixated and glued to the clock. It's now forty-five seconds past Ghislain's stint, but now, from the side of my eye, I spot the swing of a door. Quickly, my eyes are drawn to the porch. Jourdain, positioned to the side of his hatchway, waves Ghislain goodbye.

Well, I earnestly consider, I'll not give him hell when he arrives at my car. For now he'll remain safe from my temper.

Ironically, of all things, Ghislain asks, "I haven't kept you, have I?" I ignore his question and rise one of mine. "What's the word? You went inside."

Ghislain says Jourdain believes his work could take several weeks and, to that I'm okay; we all want perfection, not flaws. I'm completely understanding since I know a job such as that requires time to complete. Moreover, I realize this assignment accompanies an entirely new approach and philosophy to executing a proper job. I'll trust my faith in Jourdain, that he knows what he's doing.

Ghislain and I are now entering my business. I land one step through the door when hearing my brother.

"Guess you boys been out?"

"Had errands. But, really, Marin, had you wanted to come?"

"Would have been something to do. But, whatever."

"I don't get it; why're you here? You were taking time off, I thought?"

"That's what I said, but apparently I've grown bored. Figured I'd see if you boys wanted help."

I respond to him quickly, "I'll give you work."

Though I didn't want to go into details, I know it's best. Marin needs to know where the case stands, what's happening, and what Ghis and myself have done. Instead of laying out the foundations, I decide to submit Marin to our current concerns. I begin with the discovery of the skull, to where it's led us and what we've planned next.

My brother ponders. "You're wanting the judge to issue a permit?" "I'm assuming we'll get it. If not, we'll figure another way around it."

"Illegal?"

"You insane? I'm not trying to lose my license. Anyway, I'll tackle the call, see what can be done. So keep your fingers crossed, boys. Ghis, what cemetery's our murderer in?"

"One of them here. Don't curse me for that line. I can't say where he rests. Give me time, I'll find out."

"Well, I'll need to know soon."

Ghislain uses my phone to call Orisia. He's not on long when I hear him mentioning Sainte-Croix Cemetery.

I tag the name in my notepad, then pen a note for reference.

Marin's at my ear, asking, "What can I do?"

"Sit tight. I'll let you know."

I look desperately through my desk drawers, searching for my phonebook. Apparently, where I placed it's unknown, so in good thought I'm requesting my brother's.

"What're you needing? I'll just read you the number."

"Town hall."

I dial the number as Marin gives it. The line rings, then the receiver is answered.

"I need to speak with an attending judge regarding an exhumation permit. My name's Detective Biertempfel. Yes, sure, I'll hold."

After five minutes the man returns to the phone. "Could I get your information for the judge? He'd like to call you back."

I give the man my number and tell him again who I am.

"And the name of the deceased?"

"Guillaume Rhoe."

"And the reason for request?"

I'll have to be blunt. "It's possible I'm in possession of his head. I'll need a medical examiner's opinion to know this for certain."

"What's the cemetery?"

"Sainte-Croix."

"Please, sir, verify yourself using the number on your license."

"Ninety-five-eighty-one. Expiration, ten-twenty-nine-fifty-five."

"I'll get this on Judge Boucher's desk. Your response should come within the hour."

"All right, sir. I'll be at my phone."

Ghis overhears. "They're making you wait?"

"Not too long, hopefully. Anyone for poker?"

I've nothing to do but wait around. Least if we're playing cards, we'll be busy. The boys agree, so I'm setting the table. I wonder how much of their money I'll be taking? It's always fun to find out, and the game's now beginning.

Chapter Fifty-Four

Ambrielle realizes dinnertime's usually spent at Cerissa's, so, slightly feel- ing shamed for eating there always, Ambrielle believes Cerissa deserves a break and, therefore, suggests requesting the Biertempfels' for dinner.

Deja confesses as she's sipping her coffee, "It'd be a nice change. I think we should. We'll do dinner. Something good." She smiles warmly.

Ambrielle's eyes twinkle when asking, "Even dessert?"

"Mmm, you know, strawberry cream cake? That would be great and, ooh, we can use my mother's recipe." Deja looks around. "Gosh, I've got to look. It's here somewhere."

Ambrielle's anxious and asks, "Can I be the one to call?"

"Number's by the phone. Tell her seven, for her and the kids to be here at seven."

The young maiden expresses while she beams ever brightly, "Can you see I'm excited?"

Seeing Ambrielle happier than she's ever been brings elation to Deja. This joyous sensation shall ever lastingly be remembered by the fact she's made someone happy.

A year ago Dej would have never envisioned the cheer she'd bring one single girl, all because a sincere act, something as simple as a dinner party.

"We're set for seven," Ambrielle responds after hanging the phone. "Marin might be a little later. He's working."

"I'm sure he'll arrive here sometime. Found my recipe. Let's get dinner, then we'll start this cake."

Ambrielle suggests, "I'm thinking we could make *Coq au Vin*."

"Ooh, and have *Grantin Dauphinois*," Deja acknowledges.

"With a simple green salad, maybe?"

"And vinaigrette dressing." Deja then says, "But I'll have to stop by the market. I'll have you stay here. Satordi well, he'd kill me if he found out you'd gone with me."

"What can I start while you're gone?"

"You can make *Gratin Dauphinois*. You know how?"

"Yes, ma'am, ugh-huh."

"There's Gruyere, chives, and cream in the fridge. Salt and pepper, well, it's on the stove. What's missing? Oh, garlic. Check the stoneware canister on the counter. That should be it, unless--"

"I'll find everything, ma'am, and have those potatoes cooking by the time you get back."

As Deja's preparing to leave, the phone tolls. She rushes to the receiver, picks it up, all the while supposing it's Satordi.

"Sweetie, hey, where are you? Oh, forgive me, I thought you were someone else. Yes, she's here." Deja's handing Ambrielle the phone. "For you. A woman. Maybe your mom?"

Through overjoyed eagerness Ambrielle rushes to the phone and snatches it from Deja.

"Mom! Mom, you okay? How's Holland?"

"Fine, sweetheart. We're doing all right. You okay, honey?"

"Yes, mama. I miss you. I miss you and Holland."

"Oh, sweetie. We want to come visit."

"What about dad?"

"He won't be with us, honey. The way things are, I don't want him in trouble. You understand, don't you? Your father misses you a whole lot, Ambrielle, he does. He's hoping to see you here soon."

"Tell him I love him, mama, please." A single tear trails down her face.

"Honey, I will, you know. But if your sister and I come, we'll need a place to stay. The lady you're with, can I speak with her, please?"

"She's gone now, but I'll speak with Deja about you coming."

"I don't care what time you call, make sure you just do. Holland's wanting the phone now."

"Sissy! Sissy!"

"Holland!"

"I miss you. When will mama and I see you?"

"I'm hoping soon. Won't that be great?"

"Ugh-huh. Mama wants to take a train and ride where you're at."

"I know. I can hardly wait."

"Me either. Mama wants to talk again."

"Ambrielle, you're sure you're okay?"

"I'm fine, mama, really. I'll call you tonight."

Before the phones are hung, their final annotations are spoken and the last utterance of *I love you* is shared.

Ambrielle sits at the table doing nothing. The unexpected call has disrupted her state of mind. She's forgotten what it was she's to do. Instead, the idea of her mother and sister visiting has her worried. One worriment, fortunately the least of them, has Ambrielle wondering, is there enough room in the house to fit two additional people? An issue she'll have to take up with Deja.

Chapter Fifty-Five

I look to Marin as he studies his cards. Just as the prior game, I'm sure he's got nothing. My eyes now switch to Ghis. His deadpan impression's more likely played as a shield 'cause he's got a bad hand. He's done that before, showed an expressionless face, which has cost him the game. Had he been a great player, then his expression would have been hard to determine. However, Ghis plays his hand the same way each time and the man hardly wins. To me his game's set in stone, therefore, it can't be read an alternative way. He thinks he's got it, but he doesn't get it at all, the poor bloke. A dead giveaway to him when he's got a good hand is he fidgets in his seat; something he does rarely. I've seen it, though. I pay attention.

Marin's turn arises and, thinking he's got the right hand, tells us to, "Read them and weep, boys."

"Too bad, my friend," Ghislain advises. "I'm running a flush. That beats your straight hand."

"Then, boy, pull some tears. I'm sitting with four of a kind," I burst with cheer.

"Should have known it'd be you. Why can't I just win me one hand?" Ghislain questions.

"You're lacking your game. You haven't no luck." "I don't. I'm done. You've robbed all my money."

"Thanks, Ghis, you made me quite rich. Whenever you boys are ready for a round, I'm eager to play."

Ghislain's quick to respond, "Not on my money."

"Cheer up, sad man. There'll be games you can win."

"Then we'll play something and I'll win back my doe."

"It's sad seeing you so determined. Especially when you know you wont win."

"You make it sound like a crime."

"When you have nothing to play, it is. You're out of cash. Said it yourself. And you can't borrow from Marin. He doesn't want you losing his."

"I've got a few coins, unless you're too cheap."

"Then I'll take those away like I did with your cash." My eyes begin to narrow as I peer upon Ghis. "What's your game, slick?"

"Darts," he responds simply.

"Could be your lucky day. I've got a board back there." I point. "You're sure you're game? I'm notorious for kicking asses. You ready to get beat?"

Marin begins laughing. "I'd like to see our friend kicking yours."

"You want in on this? I'll take you both, no prob. Ghis ain't got but a few coins, but you, brother, have cold hard cash." I smell my won doe to provoke his response.

"Nope. Nope. This is between the two of you. I'm out."

"You're part of this. Nonetheless, you can serve both our darts."

"Couldn't you allow me to sit back and enjoy this?"

"Hell no. You're the foot man. Now round them up, brother."

"Ah," Marin sighs. "The abuse. It's do as you say 'cause I haven't my rights."

He trails toward a filing cabinet to collect our tossers. While doing so, he passes Ghislain, then draws his eyes upon the unlucky dope. "Beat my brother," he says. "And I'll give you an additional chunk of doe."

"Oh, I got this." Ghislain smirks. "That brother of yours better worry for what's coming."

I answer back with a few words, "That's challenger's speech, Ghis. Don't think you've got me. I'm the dart master bad ass. I'll kill it, you watch."

"Oh, buddy, it's on! The best of twelve and you'll see who's the winner."

"I'm looking forward to taking that measly bit of change you've got. First shot's yours. How much you betting?"

Ghis lunges his hand into his pocket. "This entire chunk of measly change." He draws forth his coins and smacks them upon a table. "You match it, we're on."

"Match that? That's easy." My eyes then chase the room to find my brother. "Marin, serve him darts."

My brother walks to Ghislain and supplies him with thrusters. He then takes a step back to explain the game. "Three darts per round, boys. Best of three gets a scratch on my board. Winner's revealed at the end of round twelve. May the best man win."

"Game on," Ghislain acknowledges. "Where do you want me to stand?"

I respond, "Trash bin. Take your stance."

Marin, standing stilly, serves as announcer. "Ghislain's first dart lands him one-hundred. He prepares again and, oh, takes another hundred! Will his last shot pull off? Satordi nervously stands as Ghislain throws his final dart. He lands at seventy-five. Pretty damn good. Satordi now prepares for his round. With his view on the bull's-eye, he shoots for one-hundred, oh, but instead he lands in at fifty. Will his second toss be better? He shoots and, oh, comes in at fifty. He prepares his final throw. What will he hit?"

"Marin. Marin, put a lid on it. You're not helping my game."

My brother speaks softly as I ready my toss. "The dart spirals to the board, but misses its mark. No points. What a shame."

"Marin," I say his name again.

"Tone it down?"

"Just stop talking, period."

"And at the end of the first round he's already annoyed. Game two's beginning with Ghis at the mark. Ghis has the floor. Oh, he scores a one-hundred! Will shot two serve well? It does! One-hundred again. This man is on fire! Toss three's now coming and makes it as well. Satordi steps up, hoping to tie the game and match Ghislain's numbers."

That brother of mine just won't stop. "Marin, find some peanut butter. I want it shoved into your mouth."

"You're looking red there."

"Keep it up," I say. "My veins might start showing."

Marin throws his hands to the air. "I'm going to take my seat, be out of your hair."

"About time. And keep your views to yourself."

The game continues and my throws are much better. All I needed was a little peace. Thankfully Marin's shut his mouth. I've got this now.

If before my brother, the disturbance had been refrained a bit sooner, I would've had Ghis, but instead I've been forced to catch up, and I pre- sume that I'm winning. It's not like I'd be trying to make Ghislain angry, but won't he be shocked when the winner's announced? It's good to be bad. Better yet, it's great to be good.

The final round's in order. Ghis finishes by shooting all his darts at seventy-five. My game comes to play. I hit one-hundred back to back, then finish with fifty. Not bad for a last round.

Marin nods. "And taking the win at seven to five is none other than Mr. Ghislain Duplessey."

"Don't be joshing me, brother. Confess you're lying."

"It's no lie. You simply got beat."

"Don't relish in this, Marin. Wipe that smirk from your face."

"I've tallied his wages."

"Forget it, I don't want to know what I've lost."

"Gees, brother, you really that bitter?"

I look at the clock. "If that call doesn't come in the next fifteen minutes, I'm gone."

"I'm not letting you leave. You sit yourself down."

To ease my frustration, I pour me a glass of pommeau. These fools would be dense had they thought that I'd share.

Ghislain stands in the room and appears to look bored. "Anyone for dominos?"

"I'm game," Marin announces.

"Satordi?"

"Nah." Instead, I nonchalantly ease a pencil into my hand and be- gin sketching a gnarly tree upon a pad of paper. I shadow in various areas and gently smudge different parts of the picture. My digits are covered in graphite when my phone makes several tolls. Quickly, I'm grabbing a Kleenex and removing the smear from my fingers. In a rush I catch hold of my phone.

"This is Judge Boucher returning your call regarding an exhuma- tion at Sainte-Croix Cemetery. You're wishing to disentomb Guillaume Rhoe as stated by my clerk. Will you reiterate your concerns?"

"Your Honor, while attending an investigation concerning this man, Guillaume Rhoe, I came across a skull. I'm requesting his body be exhumed and analyzed by a medical examiner, preferably Dr. Ignace of New Hope Hospital, where he can inspect the skull alongside the remains of Mr. Rhoe."

"Request granted. I'll draw a permit and have that prepared for tomorrow. My clerk will inform the cemetery of this exhumation and supply them the date of this undertaking. I'll authorize an approval on your behalf request for Dr. Ignace as Chief Medical Examiner. However, proper machinery required for this task will be left at your convenience. Your permit will be ready for pick up tomorrow at nine in our building's Health Department. If you have further concerns, please contact my office."

I hang the phone, then peer to my comrades. "Permit granted. I get it tomorrow. Either of you know where we can rent a bulldozer and coffin hoist?"

Marin explains, "A crane and hoist company for your coffin lift. And if you're needing a bulldozer, then a construction equipment rental."

"Where's that phonebook of yours?"

"At my desk. Here, Ghislain, pass this over."

I scan the text searching for a local construction rental, then find Steele-Clave Construction Supply. Within my notebook I'm taking their number. Tomorrow, after finding out when the exhumation will take place, I'll give them a call.

My last engagement will be to find a crane and hoist company. Following that, I'm out of here. Marin and Ghis can stay if they want, but I've had my fill of this place. It's a quarter till seven, as I'm checking my clock. I'm needing a meal, then my bed to lie down in.

Chapter Fifty-Six

Standing before the stove, Ambrielle peers through the window at the last risen cake, then turning to Deja, her friend now acknowledges, "Golly. I've nearly forgotten it. Please say it's not burnt."

"No, ma'am, it's fine. Ice the others. I'll let this cool."

"Our guests, they'll be arriving here shortly. Has the vinaigrette been made?"

"It's staying cool in the fridge."

"Then would you mind dicing carrots and lettuce, then slicing some onion to have for our salad?"

From inside the kitchen the creak of a door is detected, followed by the shuffling of feet.

"In here," Deja's yelling.

I follow her voice to the scullery. "Hi."

"Hi, honey." She smiles.

"Ladies, my, what's going on here?"

"Getting things ready for our guests."

"Guests? And who might they be?"

"Just be useful, dear, and get us some glasses."

"You care to tell me who's coming?"

Just then the front door bell tolls and, here I am, standing. I don't know who's come, but instead of answering my question, Deja continues her business while leaving me hanging.

I decide to answer the door, but before I get there, the bell strikes its toll again. "All right already. I'm coming. I'm coming." I reach to the knob and twist gently. The door swings back where it rests at my heel.

"'Bout time, boy," delivers a most familiar face.

I'm shaking my head. "Jesus, not you two." It's Duplessey and Marin. "What's brought you idiots here?"

My brother chimes, "We've come for the food."

"Just when I thought I'd gotten away. Now you blokes stand a foot from my face. Well, come on if you must. Girls are in the kitchen. Head on through."

Marin grins. "Don't mind if we do. So I guess you'll wait here?" "For what?" I question.

"Cerissa. She's bringing the kids. They're out on the lawn, trying to look for some rabbit."

"Must have seen Baloo. The neighbor boy's got a pet."

"God forbid Zuri gets her little hands on it. She'll try everything to get it home," my brother's explaining.

I envision my niece's perseverance as I laugh through my lips. "Head back. I'll join you boys shortly."

I hear Marin as he lands in the kitchen. "Hope you've got enough range for the two of us men."

Deja's voice follows, "Plenty enough. So you better have come hungry."

I question myself as I walk through the lawn, had Deja planned some party to which I'd not known? Apparently everyone, including the kids, were told to come by; and where was I during all this planning? Why hadn't I been informed of this plan? For whatever reason, I'm sure Deja had several.

Cerissa spots me as I'm approaching her side. "You've come to help, have you?"

"Well, if forcing Zuri's squalls can be viewed as help, I'm sure we'll have problems."

In Cerissa's eyes the uncertainty of what I meant is seen as she stands puzzled before me. Therefore, to gain understanding, I'm patting her shoulder, while relaying my speech, "That rabbit they're chasing belongs to the neighbor. I'll gather Baloo and take him back over."

Cerissa watches her daughter as she runs through the yard. "That's going to break Zuri's heart. She wanted the cottontail taken home had she caught it. Now I know why she'll be squalling."

In the distance I see Paien squatted in the grass with Baloo in his arms. Aside him his sister sits, stroking the fuzz ball. There'll be a certain pain I'll encounter when I take it away. Unhappiness will surely inhabit my once joyous runts, with a hatred for me which could cost me their love. This is one aspect of being an uncle I dislike most. The sight of squalling kids does something to me. I'm bothered intensely when feeling that sadness. I guess I'll prepare myself now before it gets underway.

I'm telling Cerissa, "If I didn't have to do this, I wouldn't, but real-ities like this, Zuri needs to be told. I suppose I'll deliver the news. She may hate me an hour, but that trial I'll take."

Cerissa understandingly smiles. "You've always been a good sport."

"If it betters the situation, I'll let you tell."

"Backing out? I supposed you would. Don't sweat it, Satordi. I'll prepare her the shock."

Cerissa calls to the children and requests them beside her. In the kindest way possible, as only a mother can do it, Cerissa delivers the news, and as I imagined, Zuri's eyes swell and are filling with tears.

"But, mommy, no. The little bun-bun loves me. Please, mommy, please. Don't take him from me."

"Zuri, I'm sorry, baby. He's not yours to keep."

"He is. I found him."

"Zuri."

"Mommy!"

"Honey, don't yell. I'm right here."

"I can take care of him, promise." Zuri's eyes then shift my direc-tion. "Uncle Tordi, tell her I can."

"I'd like to help you, little spud, but Baloo's already got a family. We need to take him home. I'm sure you understand."

"I'll miss him, though."

"You'll be sad for a while."

"For the rest of my life. But if you bought me a bun-bun, I'd no longer be sad."

Ooh. Ha-ha, I laugh in my head. The girl's good. She's trying to coax me. "I don't know about that, kiddo. That's a concern you'll have to discuss with your parents."

"They won't care."

Cerissa speaks up, "Zuri, quiet now. Don't pester your uncle."

"Then you and daddy get me a bun-bun."

Paien breaks his silence. "Like that'll happen."

Cerissa peers to her boy. "Son, go inside. Your father's there."

"No. I don't wanna."

"Do as I say." Cerissa waits as Paien disappears into the house before casting her gaze upon Zuri. "I imagine if you asked your uncle nicely he'll take you along to the neighbor's so Baloo can go home."

"Then we'll talk about getting me a bun-bun?"

"We'll see. Hurry on now. Aunt D's got us dinner."

I see it now, my niece will want to stay at the neighbor's 'cause Baloo's there. Hopefully they'll be kind and let her come visit. If she's lucky, maybe Marin and Cerissa will allow Zuri her own bun-bun, as she calls it.

Chapter Fifty-Seven

A long awaited stand of silence fills the house following our guest's departure. I've decided to spend the night with my gal rather than retreating to my home. Though I live a short distance away, I'll admit I'm much too exhausted to embark on the trip.

As I'm passing the hallway en route to my bath, I encounter Ambrielle. She postpones my duration momentarily by requesting my attention.

"Give me ten minutes," I tell her. "I'll find you when I'm through." I get to the lavatory and quickly undress while the tub fills with water. Caught in a gaze, I watch steam rise from the surface of the tempered pool. I figure for most people this fifty gallon mouth of sweltry Adam's ale would be far too torrid for their sensitive skin. Unlike them, I enjoy the scorching touch of singeing aqueous as I soak away stresses.

More than ten minutes pass, but I don't seem to care as I'm enjoying my lax. Ambrielle will just have to wait as I'm in no mood to abandon my souse state of pleasure.

I apply a parched rag to my face, forcing my skin to absorb the heated moisture. Following my excessive span of blissful refreshment, I decide to get out.

I dry off, then put on a change of fresh clothes. It's nothing major, just a clean pair of boxers and a simple white tee. I am at my second home, after all. Be that as it may, there're a majority of people in this day and age who'd consider me indecent. Why, you might ask? Well, the answer's simple, really. Decent folks, as they call themselves, think non-hitched couples aren't supposed to see each other's nightly apparel till marriage betides them. Same goes for sex. Copulation, as it's religiously insisted, should be reserved for marriage. Though it is currently 1952, the same's stated now as it'd been throughout earlier decades. What people do behind closed doors, be them married or not, is solely their business. I do believe, nonetheless, a day will come when beliefs and circumstances change drastically.

In addition to my reference above, there'll be no more sleeping in separate beds, as married couples do these days. A change will come and, when it does, the world shall be rocked; but enough mentioning of today's practices. I've prearranged a gathering with Ambrielle to dis- cuss whatever matter she has on her mind. It's about time I set out to find her. I've cost her enough time due to my sluggish bide and enjoy- ing my bath.

I follow my feet where they lead me downstairs. In the room I find Ambrielle and Deja both viewing some show being played on the tube.

"You still want to talk?" I ask Ambrielle. She

nods to my question.

I take a seat in a chair where I'm peering toward Deja. "Could I ask you go upstairs? I'm not sure what this discussion pertains. Could be business?"

"It's all right, sir. Deja and I've already spoken."

"Then you don't mind she stays?"

"No, I don't mind it."

"I hope this isn't bad, what you're about to relay. With everything going on, I don't have the mind to merge in more news. This brain of mine's already been flooded."

"I understand, sir. But I hope what I'm to ask won't bother you."

Bother me? Oh boy, should I have reason to worry?

"It's my mother, sir. She's asked to come visit, she and my sister. I know the situation, how it is; it could be a huge risk."

"More like jeopardy," I state. I continue my speech while noticing Deja, who seems to be rationalizing my every stated thought. "Consid- er them getting caught. That's my concern. It's better they stay far away from Haulmier as they possibly could."

Deja soaks in my assertions before responding an accession, "You know, Satordi, it's not fair Ambrielle continues to lose time with them. I'm sure we could figure some way around this."

"Probably, but where'll they stay?"

"Here. We've kept Ambrielle safe all this time."

"How'll you expect me to safeguard more people? I can't be around 24/7."

"Ambrielle and I've been fine on our own."

The girl then speaks, "My mother and Holland would commit to your guidelines. Anyway, mom has no wish to see Haulmier."

"Then call. Tell her to depart on the earliest train."

Ambrielle grins from ear to ear. "I can't wait till you meet my mother and sister."

"Yeah, well, call now before I'm changing my mind."

Deja attacks my final pronouncement. "You'll do no such thing, changing your mind. Phone's in the kitchen, Ambrielle."

The young girl exits the room when Dej steps from the couch. She trails my direction as I express my discourse. "Better start clearing rooms to appease these new guests."

She bends to her knees where she's sitting before me. "There's plenty time for that. I want to thank you for saying her mom and sister could come. It means a lot to her."

"I know."

"You saw her face, that excitement. And you put it there, that happiness. That should make you feel good."

"I enjoy it, I do." I'm now yawning. "Honey, my brain's fried and my body's beat. I'm thinking of turning in."

Deja smiles slyly. "You know there're ways to correct that?"

"If only I could stay awake, that's the problem."

"I hone enough skill, I'll shake my man up."

"You're killing me. There's not enough fuel to kindle this engine. My tank's set on E."

"Fine, you ole fuddy-dud. But when you're waking me later, I'm turning you down."

"Ouch. That stings."

"You had your chance."

"Tomorrow, kitten. Just wait till then."

"I'll have wine and melt us some chocolate."

"Wear that sexy little number, you know the one. I'll get berries. Oh, those sweet, juicy ones they've been selling in town."

"You don't bring them, you can forget your sweet pie."

"Oh, I won't. Tell Ambrielle good night. I'm heading upstairs."

"Nite, hon."

Finally my deadbeat body can be off to bed. I'll have another long day tomorrow, as I so often do. Though it's early for me, I hear myself begging rest.

Chapter Fifty-Eight

Currently I'm standing in the Health Department, waiting for the attendant to fetch me my permit. Law says I can't attempt an exhumation without one. I'd be in deep shit had I not obeyed rules. I may be stupid to risk things at times, but regarding this prospect, I'll keep it conventional. For now I'll hold this thought in my head, no skipping rules and disregarding commandments.

The man at the desk finally locates my papers. "You've checked out, sir. Here's your ID. I just need you to sign these two papers."

"These lines here?"

"And date them also."

"When I spoke with Judge Boucher, he said someone would inform the cemetery. Has that already been done?"

"It's already documented in your papers. The date and time's previously been scheduled. You're to be at the cemetery this Friday at noon. Judge Boucher has appointed Dr. Roman Ignace as Chief Medical Examiner to be present at the time of excavation."

"I didn't know this would be scheduled so quickly. Well, all right, sir. Let Judge Boucher know I appreciate his action in regard to this matter."

It's been a long ride, but finally I can say this is going somewhere. Rhoe will be dug up soon, and Roman will look at his remains in comparison to the skull. Once doc affirms the crown's belonging to Guillaume, I'll have part of this mystery externalized.

Chapter Fifty-Nine

I'm two strides from stepping into my business. Inside's Marin and Ghis, behind the closed door, but tracking through the entrance I find Ghislain lazed back and reposed in my chair.

My eyes narrow upon him. "Don't you know you're not supposed to be swiping my seat?"

"And a good morning to you, boss."

"Move it, slick. I want my chair."

"Ey-yi, Captain Cranky. Shall I fetch you some Joe?"

"You should've had that prepared. Listen here, if you care to work for my team, you better learn the ropes and learn them fast. You'll not last a week if you don't."

I fear I may have overwhelmed my friend due to the bewilderment I read on his face.

He quickly speaks, "You're playing me, right? This is all in good fun?"

"Well, I've been stuck with Marin all these years. It's time someone else gets ribbed."

"You had me going for a sec." Ghislain laughs lightly.

"Hold up now. I'm not letting you off easy. I still want my coffee."

"How about a donut, boss?"

"You wait to ask now? Come on, hand some over."

A back from me I hear Marin's voice, "What's going on with that permit? You get it or not?"

"Got it here in my hand. We're to be at the cemetery Friday at noon."

"This Friday?"

"What? You got some place to be?"

"No. Just you better get your rentals in order. We don't want it to be Friday and you without the equipment."

I step from my seat and I'm trailing toward Marin. "Hey, call this number. Get us that coffin lift."

He questions me, "Whose pocket's this coming from?"

"Yours, for now. I'll pay you later."

"Well, you better."

"I'm good for my word."

"Yeah. Ha." I hear him snicker. "If you're not, just buzzing, but will you be giving me Sable?"

Had he really asked that? "Dream on, brother. That metal baby's mine."

"Hey, you slip on your promise, then that pretty car comes to me." I pass back to my desk as I'm forgetting his speech. I search for the number to Steele-Clave Construction Supply, but damn me, I don't know where I wrote it. Finally I've found it where it's been scratched into my notebook.

I'm reaching my phone when Ghis and Marin both take to my side.

My brother stands close. "We're taking a run to pay off that rental."

"They're making you pay now?"

"Something about reserving equipment. You need anything before we head back?"

I don't have to think. "Pack of smokes. A bottle of booze."

Marin waits as I cough up his doe. "How about extra to fuel up my car? I haven't the cash to fill it myself."

I'm shaking my head. "What're you, broke?"

"Sort of. I came here last night and played some darts with our friend."

Ghis laughs. "I told him no, but he insisted we bet."

I peer to my brother with a smirk. "So, Ghislain robbed your monies, too?"

"Yep. Yep, sure did."

My head shimmies as my laughter breaks.

Aside me Ghislain pats upon Marin's shoulder. "How about I save your brother the funds? I'll throw you some cash."

Looking to me, a mammoth-sized smile takes Marin's face, forcing his grin to stretch ear to ear. "That's a good friend we've got here."

My answer comes betwixt and between. "Eh, sure, whatever."

"Well, don't sound supportive. God forbid you'd ever be. Guess we'll see you later."

With Ghislain in tail, he and Marin disappear through the door. I can now return my focus to the phone as my finger weighs in on the dial. At the receiver's end I hear the raspy voice of some grumpy man.

"Steele-Clave," his indelicate tone receives me.

All right, so what, he's going to be shoddy; fine. I'll just do him the same. "I'm needing a bulldozer available Friday no later than noon."

Croup, hack, whoop, he coughs to the phone. "I've got three on the lot. I'll set one aside. You picking up or having this thing dropped to you?"

"What's delivery?" I question.

"Frank and a half for each mile."

All right, let me think here a minute. The cemetery's what, eight miles from here? Delivery ain't bad. "Drop the thing off."

"Where's it going?"

"Sainte-Croix Cemetery." "This for an exhumation?"

Duh, I want to say, but instead I answer, "Yeah."

"Give me the lot number and section, then."

Great, the man requests answers I'm unsure I know. Lord help me 'cause the attendant at the Health Department didn't say. Pray. Pray the info's somewhere on these papers. I quickly scan the documentations. Thankfully the reference is noted. "Section E," I say. "Lot thirty-six. I need it–"

The crank cuts me off, "Yeah-yeah, I got it. I know. Friday, no later than noon."

God this gripe's a real piece of work.

"What's the name?"

"Satordi Biertempfel."

"You ain't one of them private detectives? I see your business when I pass it in town."

"I'm the bad half of us boys."

To my surprise, my swollen-headed remark has forced him to laughter when he says, "The devil done bless you."

"Nah," I say. "I'm as God made me, except I've got flaws."

"You ain't so bad to admit that. If you're like me, I'm sure you've got many."

"Who knows, we were probably cut from the same cloth?" Though he didn't see, I smirked to the phone. "Anyway, do I head there now and come pay you?"

"Eh, pay the man when you see him Friday."

With that our conversation's concluded. Though the man had been a crank, I soon found he wasn't so dreadful. It only took my tact of strange humor to turn him around.

Now that I'm off the phone, I've nothing to do. There's no sense phoning D'Anjou. The man's needing time before discharging the skull, and moving on to Pascal; well, I dare to not think of bugging that man. Poor guy's put up with enough from my end. I've ripped up his house. I've torn up his yard. So in good thought I know it'd be proper to give him some time. Don't get me wrong now, he's always been nice, but I've bound to upset him one way or another. It only takes a split second for well-bred manners to turn adverse.

Since I've nothing to do, I've grown bored with displeasure. The silent stand in this room's just making me mental. Thankfully this isn't a nut bay, where I'm confined to a ward with no one but me, but if I was there, which I'm not, I'd sure in the hell wouldn't want to be repressed by the tightening straps of some jacket. Being alone in this place does enough to my mind. Least here I still have my freedom.

To pass time I'm counting ceiling tiles. It's what I do when things get dull. I've done it hundreds of times in the past, and I always end up with the same tab each time. Really, I must find myself some other form of amusement.

To my satisfaction I hear the drone of a phone. It's not mine, but so what. The thrum comes from Marin's ringer. I roll my chair to his desk and answer his call, "Biertempfel Brothers."

I'm hearing a man at the other end. "Marin?"

"No. This is Satordi. Marin's out."

"I'm needing to speak with Marin."

"I can help. What's this about?"

"My wife. Mrs. Audric Badeau. I need Marin. I've got work."

Christ, not this man. Come on. My brother's done stopped. He's not helping this fool. What's Marin got to do to be rid of this clown?

I decide on saying, "Marin's not available to work your case. He's currently assigned to another."

"You don't understand; I'm needing him. I'm needing help now." "There's nothing I can do. Marin's a busy man. The least I can say is I'll have him call you."

"Would you, please?"

"Yeah, sure. He'll give you a ring when he's back."

I can only envision Marin's words when I tell him who's called. I tried to deter Badeau the best I could, but apparently my attempt was no use.

Once again I'm off the phone. I return to my dull state and it fills me with boredom; then it hits me, some spontaneous surge. Like a flippant child, I race my chair throughout the landing, where I find myself spiraling out of control. Any onlookers peering from outside might consider I'm smashed, but why should I care what they think? Instead, I persist in wheeling my chair across the wooden planks beneath me. Dizziness is now taking my head. I decide to cease my motion just before the front door, where I'm obtaining my breather. The oxygen hits my brain and my lightheaded mind begins to clear.

My spontaneous surge revives its command when seeing my hands push off the glass door. My chair journeys backwards and is traveling across the laid boards below me. I'm about to tilt into the grandest whirl when I see Marin and Ghislain both standing before me. Their laughter, so obvious, it escapes their gut.

"This is what you do when we're gone?" Marin polls.

"How much did you see?"

"Enough to form an idea."

"Don't act like you've never let loose. Give me some slack. I was bored. Anyway, you get me my booze?"

Marin hands forth a bagged bottle. "Coffee, Satordi's, much better for you."

"Don't want none. Just a swig of this devil's piss shall suit me just fine. Either of you boys care to gulp?"

"Ah, no," Marin answers. "I know better than to be drinking this early."

Should have figured. My brother's a killjoy, but forget him. I've still one other person to pester. "Come on, Ghis. I know you're wanting this."

He just looks to me plainly.

Marin tosses forth some paper. "Here, your bill. I expect you'll pay me."

"You'll have it by Monday. Where're my smokes? My change, too, before you forget."

"God forbid I'd steal from you. Wouldn't be much anyway."

"Smartass." I smirk.

"Seeing you've been lazy, did you not rent our machine?" "No. It's handled. Oh, but before I forget, you had a call."

"Who?"

"Audric Badeau. He wants you to call him."

"Oh Lord, you're kidding, right?"

"Wish I was. Listen, I tried talking, Marin, but the fool wouldn't hear it. Sorry, brother, he's your grief."

"You didn't think to tell him I died?"

I respond, "Why, so he'd look through the paper?"

"That man's done drove me insane." My brother shakes his head with displeasure.

"As I see, he wants to continue."

"Ain't no untruth in that," Marin mumbles.

"I said to him you were busy, figuring that'd get him deterred, but that damn turd's a darn hardhead."

After listening to mine and Marin's conversation, Ghislain begins, "Who is this guy?"

My brother's face turns red when he speaks, "Some stupid loon I had the displeasure of serving. That man had me roving all throughout France in search of his spouse." Marin continues, "She left his ass for some younger man. That's all it took. She was gone."

Ghis shakes his head. "Women these days. Soon as some lusty stud comes along, they're pitching their rings."

"She sure in the hell did. Anyway, boys, I've got to call that blockhead and get this shit settled."

Marin trails to his desk while Ghis remains at my side. "Take a chair," I've directed him. "Sit awhile."

He squats to his rear. "Hey, so, I've been wanting to ask. Why hasn't a man like you never married?"

"You feeling some need to nose in my business?"

"Well, yeah."

I answer honestly, "I never liked the idea of getting hitched."

"You still feeling that?"

"Well, I'm realizing things I hadn't before."

"I suppose you have to. You don't want to be an old man without someone beside you."

"Well, between us, I worry about Dej up and walking out. I couldn't imagine starting over. Especially this late in my life."

"Trust me, boss, you ain't old till you feel it. You'll know when time's right for you both. Just wondering, though, how long you been going?"

My reply comes, simply, "Eight years. Imagine that."

"I guess I know now why you're feeling that way."

"I remember three years into the relationship, Deja wanting to be married. Course me, I just wasn't ready. But I'm considering I am now."

"Go for it, then. You've nothing to lose."

"That's why I bought her this ring." I pull it from my desk and show it to Ghislain.

"Sure is pretty."

"Would you be a groomsman should I decide to propose?"

"Well, I'd be honored. Sure. Have you made any mentioning to Marin?"

"The day I came in with this. I told him right here."

"You planning this soon?"

"Wish I could now, but I'm wanting this case finished first. I guess I'm needing time to figure things out. I've an idea how I'll make my pitch, but I'll need to work through the kinks."

"Well, when you do, make it grand."

"It'd be great if things could run smoothly. What about you, Ghis? What's your story?"

"Ain't much to tell. I had a girl. Esme. But that was awhile back."

"You never married?"

Ghislain's mouth tightens as he totters his head. "Due to my drinking. She's lost to me now."

The words, "What a shame," spill out through my lips.

"That's what happens. When we don't mind our priorities, we lose out. It's a bitter truth, but I chose my grief, sadly. There's no one to blame but myself. It's no one's fault but my own."

"How're you getting along? Apparently that's had some affect upon you."

"I get through my days. Like everyone else, I eat, sleep, and bathe."

"I meant emotionally. Are you getting along?"

"Pain never goes away; it only lessens."

"Well, then, let's find you a date."

"Dating's for kids. Besides, I'm halfway through life, Satordi. I'm an old man at fifty-six."

"Forget that. I'll take you out. Get you cleaned, have you shaved. Not to mention that hair of yours needs a good trim. How bout it? We'll find you some snappy threads, then roll to some romp room and find you some tail."

"I'll think about it."

Behind me I hear Marin's voice, "I've made it off the phone. Either of you care to applaud me?"

I spin in my chair to peer at my brother. "Not really. Did Badeau blather your ear?"

"In no short stretch."

"What's he wanting? Why'd he call?"

"Eh, he declares having obtained new details concerning his wife."

"Yeah, so?"

"A friend apparently told him she boarded a train and is en route to Meythet."

Meythet's not a far stretch from Annecy. It's only a few miles, so say, "Tell that dunce his friend can go find her. You're working, I hope you informed him."

"He knows."

"Yeah, but? I feel you're hiding something."

"He offered to double my pay."

"Christ, Marin. You've better said no."

"I told him, but then he offered to triple my wages."

"Jesus, you answered him, yeah, didn't you? Why would you? The man's done drove you insane, I've heard you complain."

"It's money, Satordi. I've got mouths to feed and bills to pay. Sorry if my choice here upsets you."

"What of our case? You think turning your back's any help to me? You know what?" I throw my hands into the air. "Do what you want. You plan to anyway."

"Satordi, don't be against me."

"See yourself, man. You're as much a fool as him. Just tell me when you're leaving."

"Train won't arrive till tonight. I won't leave until later."

"You doing this has screwed my plans. I devised to send you out later."

"Nice you're finally telling me. You never made any mentioning of this. So explain where you were having me go."

"I was going to ask that you pick up Ambrielle's mom and sister."

"So what do you want? You want them picked up?" "I'll have to, you idiot. You've got that stupid case."

"So? I can still pick them up. You want to ride with me?"

"I wasn't planning on going to Meythet."

"Fine, then. Don't come."

"Might be better to pick them up there." I take a deep breath before thinking. "Call the station. Ask when they're expecting that train."

"Audric said it should be expected around nine."

"Audric said." I'm raising my brows. "Tell me, is Audric from here?"

"Well, yeah, I suppose."

"Why don't he just find his wife, then? Let him wait for her train. Meythet's, what, a few miles from here?"

"I'll give you his number. You find out yourself."

"I'm serious, Marin."

"I don't know, okay? He gave me orders and I plan to do as he asked."

"Have you any idea what she looks like?"

"I'm supposed to get a photo. Just got to stop by his house."

"Well, then, I'm done here," I say. "Got errands, then I'm heading to Deja's."

Ghislain questions me, "Seeing I've nothing to do, you mind me heading with you?"

I agreeably nod, then look toward my brother. "We're leaving. I'll expect you at Deja's, so pick me up there."

"I'll roll through around eight."

"Remember, we're taking your car." "I

know. I know. See you guys later."

Ghislain disappears with me through the door. We carry ourselves to Sable before resting our rears upon her fine cushions.

"I've got to run to the market. It's up to you if you come, otherwise I'm taking you home."

"I'm in no rush," Ghislain tells me. "I'll come along."

I pull into Beaudry's Market a few minutes later. Thankfully I've found an empty space along the curb where I park.

Ghislain stretches outside about the same time I do. He follows me into the harvest shop, where we're eyeing several bins, filled to their masses.

"Them apples look tempting," Ghislain adds. He points to paper bags. "You hand me one of those?"

Aback to us we hear Mr. Beaudry, "How's it going, guys? Doing some shopping, I see."

"Oh, yeah," I say. "How've you been, Isaac?"

Isaac Beaudry is an old school mate of mine. We've known each other, well, most our lives. Later in age Isaac became a local landscaper, but eventually found love in growing produce. Following that, Isaac opened his own produce stand and, for the last several years, has been supplying Annecy with the best fruits and vegetables around.

"Good, Satordi. Doing good. How's business? You staying busy and all?"

"Pretty much." I laugh. "But I still need that vacation."

"You mean you haven't taken it?"

"Haven't had time."

"I'm sure Mr. Duplessey wouldn't mind keeping a watch on the place." Isaac fixedly peers to my cohort.

Ole Ghis smiles and beams ever brightly. "That's if he trusts me. So, how's your boy? Been well?"

"Ah, Garner's home with a bug. Doctor said he's got the flu. It's been my refrain to not get it."

Ghislain questions, "When you taking a day off?"

"Oh, heck, who knows?" Isaac shakes his head as he's unloading some crates.

I continue to look around, and either I'm blind, considering I can't find what I need, or they're plain out of stock. "Strawberries? Where're the strawberries?"

Beaudry responds to my poll, "I moved them to make room for these pears. I have them here, though."

I follow him down an aisle, where we're tracing our way toward a passel of berries.

"They look small," I say.

"Well, they're wild's, why. Here, try. You'll see they're sweeter than those you've been eating."

Without hesitance, I pop one in. An explosion of sweet juices are bathing my tongue. "Hmm. These are great."

Isaac smiles. "Anything else, or shall I ring you up now?"

"This'll do." I turn around as I'm calling to Ghislain. "You bout done?"

I await my partner no more than three minutes after footing my bill. He comes to the counter lugging sack after brown sack of what I take to be fruit.

Beaudry gently places each bag upon scales and determines the price. After calculating the total, he states the amount. Patiently he waits as Ghislain potters his money. It takes him a moment, but Ghis turns up the exact change and is handing it over.

Issac speaks humbly, as the man usually does, "Thank you, gentle-men, and enjoy your produce."

We nod goodbye, then advance on our way. My plan's to see Deja and hopefully surprise her. I didn't have to escape work, of course, but there was nothing to do. I hadn't planned to waste my day under the aegis of poking around that damn office.

I decide to take Ghislain home, but as I relay my intent, he asserts his reluctance when showing a pleading face.

"Couldn't I stick with you for this while?"

I hadn't wanted him to, but I'm having to agree since he begs.

"I'm not meaning to be pestering you, boss. It's just, well, I get bored by myself and, unlike you, I'm without family."

Not too many things make me feel blue, but him having said that, quite frankly, makes me feel sad. I mean, here's a man, he's fifty-six. He has no wife, no kids. He lives alone and probably he's depressed all the time. To put it on the line, if I were him, there's no doubt I'd be feeling that doleful submission. I'd be pinching for friends every second I had. The prose to having at least one living soul in your life makes your existence feel richer. So, if I was put here to help him along, I suppose I'd better.

"You've got my family and me. We don't mind you coming by," I decide to answer. I advance toward the curb and position my wheels, where I park before Deja's. "Bring them bags. You don't want your fruit to sit here and sweat."

The front door opens as we're approaching the stairs and Cerissa steps through. At her heels, Paien and Zuri both draggle behind.

Zuri's shouting, "Uncle Tordi!"

Paien reacts, "Shouldn't you be working?"

I josh him by saying, "No, kid, I quit."

He looks to me with disbelief, then slants in his step. "Yeah, right."

Oh, how I love razzing this kid. "What, you not believe me?" I keep a straight face, then, turning my attention toward Cerissa, I tell her hello.

Ghislain, who's stalled at my back, fixes the kids in conversation, giving me time to talk with their mother.

My sister-in law speaks, "We just stopped for a visit. We're heading to the parlor so the kids can get ice cream."

"How bout coming back later? We'll do dinner or something."

"Well, all right. That'd be good."

I look around, but I'm not seeing her car. "You on foot? You need a ride?"

"We're fine walking. Besides, the kids could use the fresh air."

"Suit yourself."

Cerissa then turns to her youngsters. "Children, let's go."

I watch Zuri skip toward her mom. "Bye, Uncle Tordi. See you later, Mr. Ghislain."

Ghis waves. "Bye, kiddo. Have fun. Enjoy your cold treat."

"I'm wanting a milkshake," Paien tells him.

"Let me guess, chocolate?"

Paien answers eagerly, "Vanilla."

The young runt now runs from the porch to join his mother and sister. In this time, Ghislain and I are advancing our step and we're heading inside.

We find Ambrielle sprawled on the couch, engrossed in some book.

"Hey," I'm saying.

"Hmm? Oh, sir, I didn't hear you come in." Behind me Ambrielle spots Ghislain and leans from the couch. "How are you, Mr. Duplessey?"

"Fine, miss, and you?"

Before she finds time to answer, I impetuously extend an inquest, "How're things?"

"Surely, sir, I'd be dishonest if I hadn't said I've been anxious."

"You've only a few hours now."

"I know. I'm excited."

"So where's Dej? What's she doing?"

"Cleaning guest rooms and laying sheets."

She's barely getting that done now? Well, all right. "I'll head up and surprise her."

"Would you like me to take that?" She refers to the berries.

How proper she asks. "Could you? Just put them in the fridge. And, Ghis, you're welcome to put your bags in the kitchen."

I head to a guest room, but the first I find empty, so I tread to the next. I spot Dej near the closet, where she's lugging a heap of clothes to the bed.

I sneak behind her. "Jesus, the dresses. You could be clothing the poor. Give me those."

"I should probably be rid of a few."

"You'd have more room in your closet."

"Which I could use."

"But then you'd go shopping."

"Probably. You're here early. Everything all right?"

"Things are fine." I'm looking the room over when I spot a vase on the night stand. "I see you've got flowers. Looks nice."

She stands back to take a look.

"So, ah, these dresses. What do you want done with them?"

"Put them in my room." She then hints, "It'd be kindly of you to hang them."

"Thought you said you'd sort through them?"

"Well, not right now."

I highly doubt she will. Like all women, Deja's attached to her wardrobe. She's never gotten rid of anything; not her purses, not her dresses, not her pumps, nor her hose. I'm sure most are snagged; her hosiery, I mean. Often I've wondered why she hasn't bought any new? Maybe she's got some, but has them put up, tucked away in some drawer. Stockings are no different than undergarments, when worse for wear, they must be replaced.

Presently, I'm inside her room, trying to hang these dang dresses, but Deja's got so much stuff, I can hardly find room. If she doesn't get rid of things, then mark my words, I'll have these disappear.

Deja sneaks upon me with little noise. From the edge of my eye I see her pass to the closet, to the place where I stand, and hands me more garments.

"These are the last of them."

"You better hope you've got room," I'm replying. "I barely fit those others here."

"Just squeeze them in."

"Really? Have you not looked? There isn't room."

"Apparently you don't know how to work a girl's closet."

Deja uses her strength to spread space between clothes. I don't know how she's done it, but she's made enough room. She latches her belongings upon the rack, then takes a step back.

"See there? That's how you do it."

"Yeah. Now how long will they sit?"

"I don't tell you what to do with your clothes."

"Least consider the poor. You'd be helping them out. Seriously, you've got enough crap. You really think you'd be wearing all this?"

"All right. You're right. I'll make it a point to clear me some space." I'm hoping our little talk can influence her thinking. The less fortunate would feel blessed to accept her donations. I'd even pass the stuff out.

We leave from upstairs and head down to the kitchen. Inside we become completely surprised by a vision. Ghislain, for whatever reason, is behind the stove, cooking.

I ask, "What's this, slick? What're you doing?"

"What it looks like. Here, come here. Taste this."

"My goodness, Ghis, look what you've made." Deja smiles. "We'll eat well tonight."

"Figured I'd surprise everyone. And I didn't think you'd mind me here cooking."

"Sure was nice of you to make this."

"It's a little something my dad used to cook."

Deja peers over his shoulder. "Looks good."

"You like beef burgundy?"

"Honey, I love it."

"Well, all right!" Ghislain reduces the flame, then positions the lid. "It'll take at least three hours before it gets done. So hopefully no one's starving by then."

I acknowledge his declaration. "I'll carry myself through till then. But I won't guarantee you not having to battle me to get to that pot."

"You care to put a wager on that?"

Hmm, I wonder. "Should we?"

"Go on, decide, but I'll say I wouldn't want to fight me."

Wonder why? "I'd bust you all up."

"Not ole ironclad." Ghislain explains when he laughs, "I was one hell of a boxer. Believe you me, I can still throw some jabs."

I probably should believe that. I've known Ghis only a short time now and there's lots to his life I don't know, but I'm sure there've been many things which have structured his character. It's quite possible boxing had been one.

"You give yourself that name?" I decide to quiz him.

"Nah. It was my unit commander who gave it."

"Your commanding officer?"

"Ah, he was an amiable guy. You'd have liked him."

I shouldn't be surprised, but all this greets me as news. Hearing he spent time in the service draws on my respect for him. Like other survivors of that terrible war, Ghislain was lucky enough to have walked away with his life.

I don't want to upset him with questions nor attempt to pry into his trials and strife. He's seen things, awful things. In acknowledging that, I have no desire to make him relive it.

Realizing I haven't sat since I've gotten here makes me feel that's what I'm wanting to do.

My eyes fall upon Ghis as I make a suggestion. "Leave that food stewing and come have a seat."

As a matter of course, I motion his follow. We head the direction of the sitting room, where we not only find Ambrielle and Deja, but also Cerissa and the kids, who're begging to go to the yard where it's fun.

In grasping my sense, I reason, it's summer. They're out of school. Therefore, I'll reasonably acknowledge Paien and Zuri want nothing more than to be outside under the sun, basking in sweat.

I hear Ghislain's voice as he's talking with Paien. "How was that milkshake?"

My nephew answers in a near quiet voice, "Good."

"That's it, just good?"

Setting free his enthusiasm, Paien restates his expression, "It was great!"

I leave them in conversation while I proceed to a chair. I've been yearning for a cottony-soft cushion to lax my huge shank. I'm not tired too often, but I'm feeling the need to repose my debilitated limbs, so, easing astern, I sink into the mushy filler protecting my back. With my head comfortably positioned on the rest, I can now shut my eyes.

I've had no more than eight minutes rest when I feel a feather-like weight take its roost on my lap.

Slitting my eyes, I peer through the rift. I spot Zuri's saucers curiously studying my face. I sotto voce, "Hi." So she creeps toward my head.

"You sleeping?" she wonders.

"No."

"But your eyes were shut."

"Mmm-hmm."

"Doesn't that mean you were sleeping?"

"Could've been."

"But you weren't?"

"Not entirely. I was resting."

"Want to see what mama bought me?"

"You've something to show?"

"Chalk! You want to play hop-scotch?"

I'd love to shoot it down, this dreaded question, but Zuri sits here and waits for an answer.

I like to consider myself a good uncle. However, there are things I wish my niece wouldn't ask. I just can't see myself hop-scotching across the sidewalk. It isn't a game for a grown man like myself, but here she is, asking. I suppose I should be happy she requests me to play.

"Tell you what," I say to this little darling. "You go set it up. Get done whatever you need and I'll be along shortly."

Having said that, she rushes away to the door. I've probably ten minutes to spare before I join her outside. I'm having to consider, should I return my restful repose, I'm liable to get swept into slumber.

I reflect what I said, knowing I've no way to get out. Well, I think, if I have to play, you better believe it's my intent to make everyone else. I step from my seat. "Come on, people! It's gonna be fun times outside. So let's do this!"

Zuri comes back to the house, shouting, "Okay, Uncle Tordi, come on."

"Yeah. I'm up. I'm coming." I look around me. "People! People, come on. Let's get you in gear."

They sluggishly remove themselves from their seats.

Cerissa questions, "You wouldn't be a teensy bit eager?"

"Ah-ha." I smile. "You riffraffs come on now. Put a little umph in your step."

Ghislain nods as he saunters beside me. "What're we doing?"

"How're you at hop-scotch?"

"Me? Oh, I don't know. Never played."

"Yeah? Well, me either. It's time we go learn."

"We're really doing this?"

"Absolutely!" I pat Ghislain's shoulder.

"Won't this be interesting?"

Everyone heads through the door. We all make our way to the sidewalk, where we're lined in a row.

My niece begins the game. "Okay, everybody," she happily emits. "Ready?"

"Yap. Yap," I affirm. "But us guys, we're going last."

"I don't want to play this stupid game," Paien blasts. "I'd rather be hunting bugs."

"Bugs are yucky." Zuri shivers.

"Yeah, 'cause you're a girl."

"Children. Children," Cerissa says.

Zuri pouts her little lip. "He started it."

"Paien, honey, go play in the yard. But don't be bringing bugs to your sister. Keep them in a jar on the porch and play with them there."

Zuri questions, "Can we play now, mommy?"

"Of course, baby."

Zuri tosses a rock to square five where it lands. Balancing herself, she hops on one foot and flawlessly bounces her way through the path.

"Did you see that, Uncle Tordi?"

"Sure did, kid. That was something."

"Can you and Ghislain do it?"

I'm in no doubt it'll be hard.

I feel a light strain as she's tugging my shirt. Deliberately, I bend to her level as she relays some advice, "Don't fall out of the squares. If you do, you'll have to start over."

"Well, for that instant, let's hope that I don't."

"You're next after mommy."

I peer behind me and look at Ghis.

"What?" he asks.

"I wanted to make sure you're still there."

"Did you think I'd run off?"

"It could've been likely. Guess it's my turn, huh?"

I take my stone and toss it down. It lands on two, but I keep still in my tracks.

"What're you waiting for?" Ghislain asks.

"Ey, trying to figure which of my feet suits me best." I laugh ever slightly. "Seems it don't matter. I've bad balance, can you tell?"

"Just play the game without falling."

"Same to you, pal."

"What's the hold up?" I'm hearing Deja.

"Nothing, doll."

Here's to my attempt, which will indubitably be pitiful. I hop to one, then pass two to get to three and four. Here I stand, my legs are fanned. I consider the views of others. What a hoydenish sight I must seem.

Cerissa's screaming, "Sataordi, come on. Don't damper the fun."

I pull myself in gear with intentions of getting past these last squares. I hop to five and six, thinking this ain't so bad. I've gotten my- self here without falling. Only three more and I'm done. I put extra pep in my step, but I've exerted more force than desired. My feet get left behind as my upper half lunges forth. After ending up in block nine, I consider, I'll not do that again. I've made it through, nonetheless. I didn't fall. Still and all, I came damn close to kissing that sidewalk.

Ghislain comes from nowhere and is patting my back. "You might want to consider sitting out."

The man's already finished his initial round? I'm seemingly per- plexed. Considering I'd barely taken a step and was walking away when he came rushing upon me.

I carry myself over to the porch where I'm having a seat. I'd rath- er watch from afar at everyone amused by that callow game. For kids it's all right. It's something for them to do, but the amount of adults I see carousing with Zuri just seems incorrect. If you removed my niece, what're we left with? Well, I'll tell you. Four fully grown individuals all hopping around like little kids. It's off-base what I'm seeing. It strikes me as strange. Maybe it's my thinking? But not every day can someone sit on their stairs and behold a risible sight such as this.

I watch Paien scout the yard for bugs and insects. I'm unsure what he searches, but there's bound to be a collection of things in his jar.

He sees me sitting and decides to step over. "Want to see what I've found?"

"Better not be roaches," I say.

"No. No, they're caterpillars. Pretty neat, huh?" He opens the lid to his jar. "I found them on some bushes."

I peer into the bottom of the jar, beneath twigs and leaves. I feel my sight has betrayed me. I see nothing except lush foliage and small broken branches. "You're sure they're here?"

"Flip the leaves," my nephew advises.

Before I slip my hand inside, I figure I should ask, "They don't have prickly things, do they?"

"No, they're soft as skin. You won't be hurt."

Carefully, my hand reaches inside. With just a slight twist I twirl my fingers and flip the leaflet. There, resting within my sight, sits a chubby white, black, and yellow worm.

Paien pulls his head to mine. "There should be another. Oh, okay, there it is."

"They're pretty nifty, huh? You've found some plump little critters. What kind of butterflies you suppose they'll become?"

"Not sure, but I bet they'll be pretty."

"Now you know you can't keep them? You'll have to let them go." "I know. I'm just wanting to look. I'll put them back onto their bushes."

I watch my nephew as he walks to the hedges. He bends to his knees while positioning the jar atop the bice-colored lawn. The lid comes undone with Paien reaching within it. I watch him pull the first caterpillar out, leaf and all. He separates the dense twigs from the soft folioles as he sets them upon blades of high grass.

He leans forth into an overgrown briar, where he plants the caterpillar upon a sprouted growth of flowered limbs. He returns his hand to the jar where his fingers explore the glass vessel.

After gently grasping the last larva, Paien sets it upon the spray of branches resting below him. He pulls back from the bush with his arms strewed outward. Through my vision I see his little hands fiddling within a mess of brown switches. Curious, I lean forth to observe what he's doing. Appears he's inspecting the briar as a means to assure his idle creepers safety from predacious eyes.

I remove my focus from my nephew because I'm seeing my brother's car. He must have journeyed to his hearth, then, realizing no one was there, decided to swing here. Whether it was sooner or later, just as long as he made it, he needed to come.

I stand to my feet, ready to greet him. I don't have to, but I feel it's respectable.

Being the duteous man he is, Marin walks to everyone and says his hellos.

I hear Zuri calling, excitedly, "Daddy! Hi, daddy!"

"Zuri! How's my girl?"

"Good. Are you going to stay and play?"

"I can't, baby. I've got to talk to your uncle. I'll play after while, okay?"

"You mean it?"

"Has daddy ever lied?" He turns from her and is heading my way. "Satordi."

"You mean Audric didn't keep you? You got away?"

"You see me. I'm here."

Ghislain abandons the rest of the game to be with Marin and me.

An offensive comment comes to mind. "Gees, you're sweating like a fat man who's been running two minutes."

"I'm hot," he speaks tirelessly.

"Then let's get you something cold. We'll go inside."

"Yeah, please. I tell you, I'm beat. These feet of mine started aching. And my knees are shot."

"Looks like you've just stepped from a shower by the looks of you."

"I need one. I'm stinking."

"Spritz you on some linen spray." I barrel laugh. "You'll freshen that stench."

He jokes, "You want me smelling pretty?"

"Anything's better than how you're smelling now. Come on to the kitchen. I'll get you a drink."

Marin spots the fridge when it opens. "Is that lemonade?"

"That what you want?"

"Yeah."

"You fine with that, Ghis?"

"Don't matter. I'll take what you've got."

Ghislain notices napkins upon the table. Eagerly he snatches several, while using them to wipe the sweat from his body. After drying his perspiration, he carries the soiled towels to the trash, then finds him a seat.

I carry our glasses ahead to where we'll be sitting. As I do, I'm grilling Marin, "So where's this picture you got? I'm wanting to see who you're hunting."

"Why, so you can tell me you've seen her?"

"Wouldn't it be funny?"

Rather than deriding me, he disregards my assertion. "What Audric gave isn't real good." He pulls the photo from the nest of his pocket. "It's crap, if you ask."

I snag the photo from Marin to study. The depiction shows a woman standing below a large tree. In her hands she's clasping a basket of what looks like baguettes. Beneath her, poised a few inches above her knee, is a young girl, I'm figuring to be around the age of three. At a stance, near the side of her mother, is another child, with her back to the camera. Calculating her size, I'm assuming she's about twelve, give or take a year.

The problem with this photo definitely leans to the fact the person having taken it had been standing a ways from his subjects, which in turn caused their faces to appear indistinct.

"How'll you use this?" I'm asking my brother. "The clarity's awful."

"I know. I told Audric there's nothing I could do with it."

"Had you asked for another?" I ponder while passing this one to Ghis.

"I tried, but he couldn't find nothing."

Ghislain hands the picture to Marin after looking it over. Intelligently, he asks, "Couldn't he have given you a wedding photo?"

"They were put up. He didn't know where to look."

"That's got to be the biggest load of bull," I relay. "What's this guy, ashamed?" Does he dislike looking at the photo of him and his wife the day they were married? It's unheard of. Couples these days keep that memory upon a night stand, even their dresser.

"This whole situation's a mess," Marin tells us. "I should've turned away when I still had the chance."

"Well, you see, you've gotten yourself stuck."

"Satordi, please, don't. Just don't."

"I'm not bashing you. I won't do it. Since I'm going, how about I do what I can to help?"

"I'm just, I don't know, Satordi? I feel like an idiot. There you were warning me against this."

"Sometimes you've got to listen to your little brother."

"I appreciate your offer for help, but this is my problem."

Ghislain removes himself from the table as he's checking the food. "Mmm, smell that? Yep, that's good cooking," he talks to himself.

Marin leans to me. "You going to call me a jerk over this?"

"Let's just keep ourselves on cordial terms."

Ghislain returns to us as a topic comes to mind. "Why not draw upon an idea, use it to your advantage in regard to this woman?"

"If I knew what to do. It's always been Satordi who's had a mind for that stuff."

I contemplate, then speak, "Maybe we could pull off some elaborate stunt?"

"At a train station?" Marin polls.

I'm applying my mind as I'm beginning to think. Silently, my thoughts brew. I find myself hashing through each concept that regards me. I'm quite certain I've come up with a suitable means for solution. Identification cards. If we could pull something off, something genius, we could secure documented names left and right from those women on board, but what act could we use for this pretended behavior?

Marin perceives me. "I can tell by the way you think, something stews."

"We need to see identification cards," I'm explaining my previous ideation to my brother and Ghis. They nod in agreement as they mind my every word. "How'll we get them? What sort of hoax can we pull?"

Ghislain adds, "I'll have that tended to, but you agree I go along."

Ghis might be on to something, though I'm unclear what it is. To discern his plan of attack, it's important I question his idea.

He explains, "In my possession's my uniform from when I'd been a cop."

I'm liking this already.

Ghislain carries on, "I'll board the train, make up a name of someone I'm looking for, and say that woman's wanted for forgery."

I roguishly smile. "I knew there was a reason I'd been calling you slick."

"You like that?"

"Yeah," I say. "I do."

Marin taps the table to gain our attention. "You realize you're having to take your car, then, Satordi?"

I heedfully agree. "You'll not have the room. So I better get gas." I peer up to Ghislain. "How's that food coming, slick?"

"Last I looked, it needed another half hour."

"That'll give us time to run by your house."

"While the food's still cooking, you can take me by now."

I take a second, then nudge my head. Following that, I direct my eyes toward my brother. "Wait on us. Should be no more than ten minutes."

I mean, I hope it's no more than ten minutes. Any minutes over and everyone will be wondering where we are.

Chapter Sixty

I've dropped Ghis at his place to save us some time, and the reason I'd done this was so he could ransack his closet while I'm out scoring gas.

I pull into the service station and I'm killing my engine. A man's spying me from inside and trails out.

"Top her off," I convey to the worker.

"All righty, sir."

I scan through my radio and find some boogie-whop. It befits what I like, so I'll sit tight with the tune.

The man makes his appearance at the side of my window. "That all for you, mister?"

"Yap."

I pay him his money, then burn through my travel. I gad back to Ghislain's, hoping to find the chum on his porch.

Of course I get here and the flake's not in sight. Instead of marching into his flop, I remain preserved in my seat.

I consider blasting my horn, but instead, I don't do it. I've seen it before, some buck waiting around for his buddy, driver gets hasty, he starts blaring his signal. Moments later some griping grandpa springs to his door, shouting fusses from the steps of his berth, "Lay off that horn! Find some respect. Why don't you young punks show manners?"

I'll be old like that one day. I doubt I'd want to listen to the continuous bray of some idiot's horn routing my ears.

Come on, Ghislain. Where are you, man? I'm about to step from my car to see what he's doing. It would've been nice had he had his shit together and been out here already.

As before I continue to wait.

One-one-thousand. Two-one-thousand. Three-one-thousand. Four-one-thousand. Five-one-thousand. This is ridiculous. I shouldn't be having to wait like I am. What's the holdup?

Wrongly I think of just driving away, but finally I see the man coming.

He pulls himself to the car. "Whew." He breathes. "Something die in here?"

"That's me. I farted."

"God, Satordi, get us some air."

I laugh at his flighty remark. "Sorry it's not peaches you're smelling."

"Yeah, pal, me, too." Desperately Ghis holds his head through his window. "Whew. God, you're ripe."

We make it to Deja's and head to the kitchen. Ghislain makes a rush to the stove. I sit myself as my kitten strides through the room.

She tells him, "I turned that off, Ghis."

My brother comes through the back door. "Them damn birds bombed your bench again, Dej. It needs hosing down." He then sees me at the table. "Hey, you're back?"

"What're you doing, yard work?"

"I noticed a potted plant on the bench was tipped over. I set it up, but it and that bench have been covered in shit."

"Guess I'll move it from under that tree."

"I've asked for a month to get that thing moved," Deja replies. "Course you never did and it's still sitting there."

I peer around the room. "Where're the kids?"

"Gone out back. We're starting to fill plates. Will you call them both in?"

I sluggishly rise from my seat and, in undersized steps, I'm trailing the door. The screen slams my back before I pace through the yard, then I spot both youngsters stalled beside a bird bath where, within the basin, Paien tries to float his toy boat.

"Kids. Hey. You guys hungry?"

"Stupid boat. It won't float, Uncle Tordi."

"You're needing more water's why."

"Can you fill it?"

"Later, Paien. We've got to eat now. Leave your toy and come on. Zuri, you, too. Where's your mom, you guys?"

"Mommy's with Ambrielle," Zuri tells me.

"Where?"

"At the neighbor's, returning Baloo. He got out again." That
rabbit usually does.

I nudge my niece and nephew along as we're coming into the
house. "Wash up now. Get ready to eat."

Ambrielle and Cerissa walk through the door as I'm getting ready to
seat her two runts.

Zuri smiles, then asks, "Is Baloo home, mama?"

"He's in his cage, baby. He's munching on carrots."

"He was starving?"

"Yes, baby, he was famished." "What's
famished, mommy?"

"Hungry. He was hungry, baby. You going to be a big girl and eat
lots of food for daddy and me?"

"Ah-huh."

Cerissa looks to both her children. "You wash your hands?"

"Uncle Tordi made us," Paien replies.

"Just as long as he did."

"No dirty mitts on those paws," I'm telling my sister-in-law.

Behind me I hear Deja, who eyes the span of food Ghislain's
cooked. "I'm sure none of us can wait to dig in."

I watch our chef as he titters his head, then upon me he comes,
where he's taking his seat. "Eat up, everyone."

Following dinner we all remain in our chairs. Our bellies have become distended in that we've gorged on good food. Looking around, I
realize none of us have enough might to get up. Instead of clearing
away dishes and getting them cleaned, we suspend in our chairs, inert
and relaxed.

Eventually, I realize, time's winding down. I'm telling Ghis, "Soon,
slick, you'll need to be changing."

"Let's hope it still fits."

"Shoot, it better." I break a stiff lip before I peer at Ambrielle. "You
nervous, girl?"

"Anxious, sir." She breathes ever deeply. "It feels like a dream that's
finally come true. Like some wonderful fantasy."

"With fairies and princesses?" Zuri shouts in wonder.

Ambrielle beams and giggles in the way a girl would. "And a happy ever after ending, like those we all love."

"Ooh, happy endings," Zuri simply discloses.

While the girls harmonize upon their elated thoughts and flights of fancy, I tell Ghis to get dressed. He sticks behind me as I show him the bathroom. "There's the hook. You can hang your clothes."

"Yap, I see. Be out in a minute."

Upon leaving, I tell Ghis I'll be waiting in Sable. I return to the kitchen where my brother's still slacked in his seat. "Marin. Marin, get up."

"We ready?" "Just about."

"Ghis?"

"Going to meet us outside." I lurk behind Deja as she's clearing the table. "Don't forget our plans later," I've whispered to her ear.

"Don't you either," she whispers back.

"Check the fridge. You'll see a surprise."

Curiosity has caught her attention. "Could it be something red?" I crack a sly grin as it comes to my face. "I've got to run now, doll." I steal a kiss from her cheek and relay my goodbyes.

My brother and I leave as we head from the door.

I look to Marin as we climb to our cars. "When time comes to roll, you wheel away first. I'll keep up behind."

I lean into Sable as Ghislain steps from the house. Patiently I wait as he ascends through the hatchway.

"Officer Duplessey, you ready to ride?"

"Feels a little odd being back in this." He plants his rear on the seat. "Aw, whew, it's a tad snug." He straps on his seatbelt. "Guess I've got a little more gut than before."

"You look fine. Suck it in."

I put my window down as my arm stretches through. Promptly, I waver my hand as a signal to Marin and we begin to drive out.

It's taken about ten minutes to reach Meythet, and as you've learned, this journey wasn't meant to be endured very long. Meythet's just a stone's throw away in regard to Annecy. Nonetheless, we're here and we've come in one piece.

Marin pulls his car before the train station, and myself, well, I'm inching behind. He cuts off his engine, then steps to my car. I uproot myself temporarily to let him inside. He climbs to the back seat and is settling down.

He spots Ghis, who's correctly adorned in his coordinated attire and makes a remark, "Nice suit, officer."

I speak up, "We gonna ballyhoo an idea or sit here like fools?"

"This is what I'm thinking," Ghislain acknowledges. "I'll go into the station, talk to whoever's inside, tell them I've got a possible detainee aboard the next train. I'll have that person contact the conduc- tor to let him know I'll be coming on board and not to release any people."

I realize I must ask, "What's our take in this? Do we stay or come with you?"

"We can help," Marin speaks. "What do you want us doing?"

"Hold off, boys, you're getting ahead of the plan. Now, we'll board car one, with you two behind me. And you start grabbing IDs when I mention the word."

I make a remark, "Well, we've got half an hour, then that train's coming here."

Ghislain stares between Marin and me. "You act on nothing. You let me talk."

Marin nods without saying a word.

"Agreed. Now let's go," I whisper.

Keeping his lead, we follow Officer Duplessey into the train station. Attending the desk stands a woman and man. Ghislain walks to the one nearest him.

"Excuse me, miss. How's it going tonight?"

"Steady, Officer. You getting a ticket?"

"No, ma'am, not today. Rather, I'm here on leads. Got word a possible detainee might be aboard the next train. I'll need the conductor contacted soon as possible, and no one gets off that train until they've been cleared."

"Sir, I'll have that call in now."

"Very good. My detectives and I will be outside."

ed out any identification cards you have on you. Men, you're okay."

Marin and I trail through the aisle where we're being handed IDs. None have belonged to Mrs. Badeau in the few that we've seen.

I hear a woman questioning a lady beside her, "Why do they need our IDs?"

"This is absurd," comes the angry voice of a man. "My wife here's done nothing."

"People, please," Ghislain sets loose.

I'm returning an ID to a woman when a soft voice rises from behind her, "Momma? Momma, what's happening? Are we okay?"

"Sit tight, Holland. We'll be off this train soon."

Thankfully they'll be an easy snatch, so I take a step toward the lady and her daughter. "Ma'am. Excuse me. Is your name Yasmina?"

"It is," she affirms.

Yasmina Guloe, like Ambrille, is short and petite, and like her daughter, Yasmina also has amber hair, with fair skin and blue eyes. Their similarities are so striking, they resemble carbon copies.

Holland, though, unlike her mother and sister, has dark eyes and hair. It's completely apparent she takes after her father. Nonetheless, she's a pretty little girl.

"I'm Detective Biertempfel. Would you and Holland come with me?"

Marin steps over. "Anything?"

"Got Ambrielle's mom and sister. I'm taking them off the train and we're heading to my car."

Marin peers around. "I've checked nearly every ID, Satordi."

"Yeah, I've looked, too. And as far as I've seen, she's not here."

"Well, I'll be in the next vector, looking there."

I step to Ghislain. "Seems Marin was misinformed about that girl. We couldn't find her here. He's gone now to check the next car. Why don't you clear these folks out, then head there and help him?"

"All right, boss."

I turn aside to Yasmina. "You and Holland follow me. I'll get your luggage." They pursue me as we're arriving at Sable. "You have a good journey?" I ask.

"Well, it'd been a long ride, for sure, but I'd still say it was good. Holland slept a lot. Didn't you, sweetheart?"

I open the passenger door to allow them inside. Calmly, my voice comes across, "Soon as Marin and Ghislain get done, we'll go."

After locating their luggage to the trunk, I proceed to my seat where I've positioned my ass.

My eyes are in reserve of the train as masses of people emerge from the inlets. The rabble of footfalls come swiftly and quick. I envision sights such as this, of someone soon falling, but rather than comprising a stockpile, I see the crowd moving quick.

Through the dark I see Ghis and Marin step down from the railcar. They head my direction while I remain in my seat. I lower my window to be receiving their news.

Marin hangs his hand on my car as he leans through the breach. "We're too late or too early. I'm thinking I'll stick around, wait for the next train."

"That might still be awhile."

"No. Thirty. Forty-five minutes."

"Well, I can't wait around. I've got to get us home."

"I was just letting you know. But, ah, Ghis said he'll stay with. So we'll be heading back now and we'll wait at the station."

"Try not to get mugged, huh? I'll see you tomorrow."

I peel out of the lot and head to the street. A sheet of darkness wings out before me as I continue to drive. Knowing there's a woman and child aboard makes me think to be easing my haste. There's no need I act an idiot and cause us to wreck. It's a policy of mine to show I'm responsible, so, by the gleam of scattered lights beside the road, I travel the land calmly, and I'm taking us home.

I pull Sable alongside the curb as I cut off her engine. "I'm just grabbing your luggage, then I'll take you inside."

I hear Holland's excitement as she's telling her mother, "Sissy's there, momma. We'll get to surprise her."

We get to the door where I play with my keys. Soon after, we pass through and head to the sitting room. The silence is interrupted when Ambrielle's spotting her mother and sister. In a hurried rush she throws herself from the couch, and it's through her cries that she's screaming, "Mom! Momma, you're here! You're finally here." They fall into each others arms.

"Sweetheart! Ah, my baby. I'm finally touching you."

"You don't know how much I've missed you and Holland. I thank God you both made it."

Holland latches onto her sister's waist as a light flashes before them. Deja, whose had enough gumption to get a camera, begins snapping shots.

My doll comes beside me. "Isn't it great? Look how happy they are."

Ambrielle walks upon us with her mother and sister. "Mom, meet Deja. She's the lovely lady who's granted my shelter."

Yasmina speaks humbly, "There aren't enough words to thank you for what you've done. Allowing my daughter to stay when you hadn't known her touches me." She begins to cry.

"It's a privilege having her. It really is. Ambrielle's been wonderful. Just wonderful. I'm sure you know you're lucky to have her."

"Yes, I am. I'm very lucky. I, ah, well, I."

Deja begins rubbing upon Yasmina's shoulder as an act of compassion. "It's okay. Take your time."

"I suppose what I'm trying to say is, with all we've been through, I wasn't sure I'd see her again. Truly, it's been a rough road for us all."

"Honey, I've heard. I know."

"I had to get out. We had to get out. Ambrielle was going to be meeting us, but Haulmier, damn him, he found out."

"Mom. Mama, it's okay. You, me, Holland; we're safe, mama, safe."

"I was sickened with worry, Ambrielle. You're my baby. I didn't want you harmed. I'm sorry for all the years of pain you've endured."

"It's over with. We're all here. We're together."

"And probably starving," Deja acknowledges. She peers to Yasmina. "How bout I get you and Holland some food?"

"We'd appreciate whatever you'd serve."

"Except mushrooms," Holland advises. "I'm allergic."

Deja pats Holland's back. "Then we'll make sure you don't eat those while you're under my roof."

"I can have anything else."

"Well, it's a good thing you told me. Come to the kitchen. Satordi, line up their drinks."

How easily she offers my service. I guess now I'm helping. "We've got water, tea, lemonade."

Smiling, Holland wonders, "Could I, Mr. Biertempfel? Could I have lemonade?"

"Of course. And I want you to drink till you're sloshing with lemons."

Holland's smile expands as her eyes begin to widen.

"Lemonade, Yasmina? I'll get you a glass."

"Thank you, Mr. Biertempfel."

"Satordi. Just call me Satordi."

Deja takes her time at the stove. "I'll just get this heated, if you'd give it a bit. I don't want it served cold."

"We're not fussy. We'd eat it how it is," Yasmina's telling her.

"Guess I should apologize for not having this warmed. You could've already been eating."

"Don't worry about that. We'll wait here, we're fine."

"Gosh, I see where Ambrielle gets her sweetness."

Yasmina just beams. "Do you and Satordi have kids?"

"Nope, not yet. And can you believe, I'm still waiting on a ring?" She's showing her finger.

"When speaking with Ambrielle, I assumed you were married."

"No knot's tied yet. Satordi's been scared, so he's taking his time."

I say, "It'll happen one day, and you'll all be invited."

Yasmina acknowledges me, "I hope you do. You make a good couple."

"My brother, his wife, they say the same thing."

Dej comes from behind me. "Okay, I've hot plates here. Hot plates to the table. Holland, here's for you, honey. I'll get your mom's now."

Yasmina kindly acknowledges, "Aside from Lady Ancelin, we've never received such kindness. You're like an old friend."

"Aw. I don't know why I never knew you before? I'm bound to have seen you, maybe, in town? Rather, I'm sure we've crossed paths, one way or another."

"There were plenty chances for that, but thankfully now we're getting to meet."

"How long will you and Holland be staying?"

"Three days. Just enough time for a visit. I do hope Ambrielle can be coming home soon." She turns to her daughter. "Your room's ready, baby. It's waiting for you."

"I can't wait to see my old things. I wonder, could I recognize what was left?"

"You will, some of it, maybe not all. But nonetheless, they're your things."

"It'll be hard to leave this place when I do. It's been like home here." "These are good people. If not for them and the Bruels, who knows where you'd be?"

Ambrielle acknowledges, "They've sure done a lot."

"Mmm-hmm. Those women love you, Ambrielle."

"I know, mama. I know."

"It's disheartening we can't pay them a visit."

"They might could come here? If not them both, then I'm sure Lady Ancelin."

"It'd more likely be her. Voletta wouldn't make it, I have a feeling. She's got her business to manage, and she lives pretty far."

I speak, "If you're wanting to get together, you might as well should. Dej could get Lady Ancelin and bring her here to the house. That all right?"

"I don't mind doing that. Just tell me where I'm going," my sweet kitten returns her remark.

"The Blossomed Rose," I explain.

"You know, I've never been. Please tell me, it's not like those bawdy dens across the street."

"Nothing like that."

My gal angles her face. "If you're lying."

Ambrielle speaks, "Lady Ancelin runs a proper business."

"And it's lovely inside," responds her mother.

Deja breathes heavily. "I'm not used to being in places like that."

Yasmina announces, "I understand how you feel. If I'd never been to a call house, I'd likely feel bothered."

"It's my nerves, I suppose. I envision toothless lowlifes with ill manners popping in for their quickies."

"Maybe other places, but not there. Only gentlemen are allowed in the brothel."

"Well."

"Ancelin's quite a lady. One of respect is what she is. I'm sure you'll agree when you meet."

Deja peers to Holland, then in a low voice, whispers, "Poor girl, she looks awfully tired. Why don't I show you to your rooms?"

Deja's voice is interrupted by the sound of tolling bells ascending the front door.

Who's that? It's too late for visitors. I'm telling everyone, "Stay in your seats." I then trail from the kitchen and head to the entrance when I'm seeing my brother outside.

"Are Cerissa and the kids still here?"

"Nope, they're gone. Left before I even came back." I look around. "You alone?"

"Yeah. Well, ah, I suppose I'll be heading to Audric's."

"Hope he's not mad you're not bringing his wife."

"Hmm. She can't be taken when the woman's not found. Let him cast me to hell."

"You cast him first. Be rid of the fool."

"Yeah, well." He walks to his car. "See ya."

I'm returning through the house and making my way to the kitchen, where I find absolutely no one inside. Where'd they all go? Maybe I missed them when I came through the den. I go, expecting to find faces, but rather, I don't. Only one place to go, that's upstairs, so I head there.

I spy through doors as I'm passing rooms. Finally, I've come to a drifter's bunk where I find Holland being settled in bed.

"Everyone turning in?" I question.

Yasmina answers, "I've got to get my baby tucked in. That stuffed little tummy's made her all sleepy."

Ambrielle's telling her, "Momma. Her teddy."

"Oh, yes, she needs her bear. She won't sleep without him."

I stand between the frame, addressing my report, "Sleep well, everyone. See you all in the morning."

I make my exit, leaving Dej with our guests. Soon after, they step from the room and shut out the light.

Ambrielle follows her mom. "You want me to help with your things?"

"Honey, it's been a long day. I'm not about to unpack. We'll hang everything tomorrow when we're not so exhausted."

"So you're going to bed then?"

"I'd like to sit awhile. Honey, I haven't seen you. I'd like to know how you are."

"I'm fine, mama. I feel good. Things seem to be well."

"I'm happy for that."

"Daddy? How's he?"

"Misses you. He hasn't seen you in years."

"How'd you ever find him? I expected he moved."

"I expected that, too, I really did, but I found him at home, at our home. He never left. He always stayed. You should've seen him. He never imagined I'd be ringing our door."

"Did you tell him what happened? What happened to us?"

"Well, I had to. We'd been gone for so long. When he learned what we'd been through, honey, your father was sick. He's wanting to kill Haulmier. He's in war rage. I couldn't have him come with me. For that reason, I begged he stay home."

Ambrielle's shaking her head. "I was hoping to see him, but I don't want him in jail. Not now. Not when we're just getting back. We can't lose him again. So much time's already lost. Then you had to introduce him to Holland."

"Learning he's got a stepdaughter, caused him some shock. I felt bad for your father. He looked so confused."

"Mama, I'm sorry. I'll not ask nothing more. I see you're tired. I'll leave you to rest."

"Come, climb into bed. Snuggle into the covers, like when you were small."

Ambrielle ascends the mattress and is cuddling beside her mom. "I'm happy you're here."

"Me, too, baby. We'll be resting comfortably tonight and all the nights after."

Outside the guest chambers, in the dim pathway, I'm noticing, everyone's turned in, and as quietly as my feet chase the floor beneath me, I pass Holland's room en route to my bed.

I walk through Deja's place of sleep, carrying wine in one hand and a bowl of melted chocolate in the other. My saucers then fall to the bed where my love rests upon her soft sheets of all white adorn in the finest lace known to my eyes, and surrounding the room are brilliant candles lit up in a glow.

"It's a sin," I say.

"What is?" she asks.

"How stunning you are. I tell you, doll, I'm one lucky man."

I happily make my way to her where I'm pouring wine into a handsome set of crystal snifters. I present Deja a glass as we're making a toast, and beside her sits the basket of berries. Thankfully it'd been my babe who remembered to fetch them.

Eagerly, I climb onto the mattress to snuggle beside her; then, drawing in, I'm kissing her softly, all the while tasting the sweetness of wine from her lips.

From the basket, I'm grasping a plump, juicy berry and, from my fingers to her lips, it's passed to my tootsie, with a sapidity of juic- es exploding her mouth. Through her discharging regale, I hear her breathe, mmm.

She moves into me, ever closer than she was, wearing a milky kiss of chocolate upon her lips. Knowing this situation's about to get heated, I sit my snifter atop the nearest table. As I do, Dej clutches my shoulders and I fall to the bed.

Please, I pray, no interruptions. Dej is biting my chest and I'm feel- ing the sting, this wonderful sting. God, wow, what a sting! I'm clos- ing my eyes, leaving Dej to explore my whole body. I feel her slippery tongue tasting me, and now I'm sensing her lips, so ample and moist I pray she not stop.

My arousal's been fueled. I open my eyes ever quickly to be glanc- ing my kitten. She's a goddess if I've ever seen one sitting there at my waist. A surge rushes through me and I'm ready to take her. I can't stand it no more, so I guide myself in.

"Mmm," I express. "Mmm."

I close my eyes to enjoy Deja's plodding sway before she starts quicker. I love when she's slow and chokes me so tight. It makes me insane, so pleasurably insane.

As I revel in my glorified state, I feel a splatter of hot liquid pour down on my abs and, in a flash, my eyes have popped open.

I look to see Dej with a candle in her hand drizzling wax as she begins to thrust harder.

I pull from the bed, keeping her on me, and I go for her neck, her fine porcelain neck, and start kissing her wildly.

Our untamed excursion carries through the night, to the bed- immed early morning when exhaustion arrests us.

Chapter Sixty-One

Deja and I, well, we slept the whole morning. Had you actually envisioned we'd been up before eight? Us, really? Yeah, right, like that had happened. It was around 11:20 when we decided to wake. Though our wild night had set us back, we had no concerns being behind for breakfast. We ate late, but didn't mind it.

Yasmina had already been up with her daughters when Dej and I arrived at the kitchen. It was a welcomed sight when we got here. Yasmina had taken it upon herself to fix breakfast, which had been nice, very nice. She said she'd have sent it to our room had we not gotten up, but instead we made it down as she was scrambling our eggs.

After eating, we sit around, sipping coffee. Presently, during conversation, we're discussing the possibility of having Ancelin come visit, and I appreciate Dej since she'll be picking her up. I'd do it myself; how- ever, I'm needed at work.

"So I suppose I should be getting dressed? I've already held up Marin and Ghis."

Ambrielle acknowledges, "Pardon my disparage, sir. They came this morning. I let them know you weren't up."

I realize, if I keep them waiting, they'll probably be mad, so I go to Deja's chamber where I grab my duds from a chair. I'm considering now I should've had better judgment than to have thrown them here. Stupid me. Now my shirt's wrinkled and looking a mess. Least my trousers are decent. I'm not seeing signs of creases or folds.

After sliding in my shoes, I rush out the door.

Chapter Sixty-Two

My presence is signaled by the clang of a bell, and Ghislain turns upon hearing its clatter.

"Well, about time you got here. I supposed I'd have to do things myself."

I smile before responding, "Better late than never." I walk to my chair. "You alone?"

"No. Your brother's at the deli."

"How've things been here?"

"Crazy. Those phones ring a lot. Orisia called for you. She was wondering if we had any news."

I nod slowly while releasing my comment, "I'll give her a call then, later."

"She understands you've been busy. If you don't, she won't care. Besides, we've spoken."

"Who were the other calls?"

"Few riff-rafts. Not important. But Jourdain called. He's finishing things up."

I certainly feel shocked. "And? When are we going for it?"

"In one day, at least. Said he's worked his tail off to get the thing finished."

"Oh, but don't you know it'll be exciting when we finally see that face?"

"I'm ready, boss. I'm ready to see who this man is."

Marin arrives as the conversation comes to pass. "Hope you aren't hungry, brother. I haven't but two sandwiches."

"Thanks for the scoop, but I ate a late breakfast."

Marin looks to me, oddly. "You forget to iron this morning?"

"Oh, yeah, my shirt."

"I've never seen you such a mess. Consider throwing it into the wash when you're home."

My brother, oh, brother. Guess the ole boy can't recognize I have my own brain. He thinks he calls the shots and can direct me to do things, like I'm some iconoclastic child.

I leave Ghislain and Marin to eat while deciding to step out for a stroll. I don't know where I'm going, but I feel the need to wander about.

I take off down the street, passing pedestrians as I advance through my step. I'm approaching a feed house when a woman comes out. She looks familiar, and I begin to believe I've seen her before. She comes upon me, then instantly becomes aware she knows who I am. Abruptly, at once, she's dropping her head. I assume it's an act to shield her face from my sight, but what she doesn't realize is I've already copped a glance at her kisser. It takes me a moment, but then her name comes to mind. She's none other than Azure Cashlousier, Ambrielle's mounte-bank mother. I feel in this second the urgent temptation to pursue her off guard. Whatever this woman's up to, I want to know. It's my desire to see where she goes.

I stand with my back against a building, watching her walk. Not once has she peered behind to spot my location. This is good, for it shows she has no idea of my lagging behind. Knowing I'm safe and yet to be seen, I move away from the dwelling. I keep at her heels, moving in and out of a conflux. I keep with her to the next block where she's yet to discern my position. I stay with her as we continue our stride. Where she's going, I couldn't tell you, but in due time, I'm sure I'll find out.

Before long I realize she's heading to the wrong side of Annecy's tracks. It's beginning to hit me, a thought where she's going. I could be wrong, but my intuition feels right. Should she be heading to Frenchmen's, then she does so to consort Haulmier.

I follow her down South Road before making her way to Harbour Ridge Avenue, to approach the main strip. I realize things could turn bad, but what care do I have? I've walked these streets at night. I've seen all the imaginable boozers and loons who take to these paths. I can't say I'm shocked anymore by the weirdos I've seen. It's usually the same sight, speech, and acts infesting this turf, but to be honest, to relay you the truth, only one thing could make me jump through my skin, and that's the name of Yria Dane. It don't shame me saying I'm getting creeps just thinking of her. You would, too, had you seen what I have.

I shake my thoughts and drop her out of my mind. My attention returns as I focus on Azure, and sure enough, there she goes, walking through Frenchmen's.

What wonders behold me if I walked through that door?

I decide to lay low while remaining outside. I don't wish to rush in and interrupt anything. Rather, I'll snoop through a window and see what I spy.

I ease to the framework, but wisely I know to be keeping my reach. Lord knows I don't need kibitzers to discover my stance. That'd ruin my look-see and my plans would collapse.

I'm close enough to see what's occurring. Azure's at the bar with that no good drink slinger. Appears to me they're engaged in a chat. Too bad I'm not trained to read lips, otherwise I'd be trying. Her head now drops astern as she laughs. Apparently something's funny. I draw my eyes away to start scoping the bar, but I'm unable to find Haulm- ier. I'll give him a little more time to hopefully make his appearance. Meanwhile, I return my eyes upon Azure as she's taking a shot. I must admit this is boring. Had I wasted time coming here? I was sure I'd see goings-ons that I shouldn't. I guess now I'd been wrong.

I feel like walking away, but some inkling's telling me stay. I continue to snoop through the glass. It's a good thing I do 'cause there's Haulmier. He's exited the basement with a box in his hand and is walking toward Azure, who now steps from her chair. He then places the box upon the counter, then pulling Azure into him, they're beginning to hug, but it doesn't stop there. Apparently they know each other well, considering the sight that I'm seeing. Their lips are locked and they're kissing like lovers. Clearly I see what's going on; then again, I'm in a cloud and confused.

Who is this Azure Cashlousier? And who is she to Haulmier? Could she actually be Ambrielle's mother? Have I been believing in lies? I suppose I should be questioning these concerns for I see now they won't be ending for me. There's still Yasmina. Who is she, really? Have I been played all this time without having known it? Anger sets in and I start to feel mad. I exhale deeply as I begin to breathe hard. I won't be fenced out any longer. I'm going inside.

My heavy footfalls surpass the door as I'm walking inside. The look on Haulmier's face is one of shock, and I'm glad to say, I'm putting it there.

"Well, well, Detective, never figured I'd see you again in these parts. I considered our squabble had driven you off."

I slap my hand onto the counter. "Guess you'd been wrong."

Before Haulmier has his chance to answer, he's interrupted by the barman, "What'll it be?" Artus questions.

"Whatever's on tap."

Haulmier begins picking my brain. "What've you, gone soft? You've turned away from the hard stuff?"

"Can't a man get a beer?"

"I know you, Detective. You like a little kick." He draws his eyes from me to peer at the bar hand. "Artus, pour him a bourbon."

"You care to make it a double?" this two-bit slinger asks.

"Mmm, no. Keep it single."

Haulmier comes besides me and is taking a seat. "What brings you in?" He then presses for further information. "You keeping tabs on me?"

"Would it concern you if I was?"

"I've nothing to hide. You know of my illegal dealings, my absinthe, if you recall. That's all there's to know."

"And what about your wife there? What métier's she into?"

"Nothing, Detective. Yasmina's straight. She don't deal in my business. I prefer she not be busted for some wildcat act."

I see his game and I'm playing it, too. "Least you're looking out for her."

What a lying fool. Haulmier has no idea I know the woman seated to his side is Azure. If he thinks he can pass her off as Yasmina, well, let him keep trying. Maybe this guy forgets I make my living as a sleuth.

I gulp my shot and finish my beer.

Haulmier asks, "So, tell me about work. Have you had any jobs?"

"Got a job now. Then again, that's my business."

"Of course. Don't think I'm intruding." "It's confidential. I'm sure you're aware."

"I know how it goes. You worked for me, do I need to remind you?"

"Those days, they've gone and passed. I'll be out of here now." I step from my chair. "See you around."

I step through the door, leaving Frenchman's behind me. I set out through the street in steady pace while eyeing the every fool who passes aside me.

Without hesitation, an old floozy in tattered clothes walks up. "A franc, mister, just a franc. Tell me you've one to spare."

"What do I look, loaded? Get out of here. I haven't money."

"You damn sorehead. You can't help a lady?"

"What do I look like, your son? Rush along. Get to moving."

"Damn fussy-butt," I hear her rout.

If this is a sample of what I'm to deal with, I'd rather get out. I have no patience for people like that. They tempt my nerves and get my veins pumping.

After a long walk, I've returned to my office.

"You've been gone a long while," says my brother.

"I needed to get away, was all. Looks like you and Ghis should do the same."

"Well, then, we'll go. Business is slow and the phones have stopped tolling."

"And you stuck around? Shouldn't we close shop and go?" I ask.

"Whatever's your call."

"Mmm, yeah. Things won't turn around till tomorrow. And as you see, we've got no work."

"Well, we'll just finish this game and be out."

They've been at poker, probably since after I left. When business is slow, you sure better find yourself something to do.

"Go ahead, finish, but don't lose your money."

Marin laughs. "Not today, brother. I've learned a hard lesson. We're no longer playing for wages."

"Finally, you're learning."

"Well, it had to take a hard time to realize that."

"I think that taught us both." I'm beginning to laugh. "Ah, well, swing by when you're through."

I race on out to my car, then take off down the road. A few minutes later, I pull before Deja's and put a stop to my engine.

Inside, the girls sit with Ancelin. Merrily they look, sipping tea and eating pastries.

I nod. "How do you do, ma'am?"

"Fine, Detective. And, my dear, I say, it's a pleasure to see you. Why, I'm thankful, sir, you've taken care of my friends."

"Oh, ma'am, it's nothing. It's the little things that've been helping them out."

"Well, they don't stop talking about you. They tell me you're wonderful."

"Oh, yeah? Well, how bout that?"

"Oh, it's great, it really is great." She slaps her hand upon her leg. "Your sweetie told me you'd be staying at work. We weren't sure I'd get a chance to see you."

"Turned out we weren't busy."

"Isn't it funny how things just work out?"

"Yes, ma'am."

"And have I told you I adore your sweet lady?"

"Well, she is sweet. I assume she got you here safely?"

"Yes, sir. It was quite nice to have a chauffeur come get me."

"Whenever you need her, she's just a phone call away. But please, could you excuse me?" I hear the door, so I tread away to go answer. "You could've walked in," I'm telling my brother. "Door was open."

He and Ghislain trail through.

"Yeah, well, I wanted to hear you complain." "You and your manners," I tease.

He hears voices arise from the room. "Someone here?"

"Ambrielle, her mom, they're visiting a friend."

"Who?"

"Well, bring yourselves and come see."

I lead them into the room where I present them to Ancelin.

"Hey, I've seen her," Ghislain mumbles. "I've seen her, I know."

"Miss Bruel, I'd like to introduce my brother, Marin, and our good pal, Ghis."

"I know your face," she's telling Duplessey. "You frequent the street where I live, aren't I right?"

Ghis is shaking his head. "I haven't gone in awhile, but I'm known to walk there." He grins cheesily.

"And, Marin, why, I could tell by those genes, you men are both brothers," Ancelin addresses him. "Even twins, I could say."

"Oh, let's not go that far." I'm laughing.

"She's just giving a compliment, brother. Smile big and let her know that you love it."

"Well, folks, I'd like to stay and visit, but I have to get back to my girls." Ancelin breathes deep. "I worry my home's out of order."

I acknowledge, "Uh-ah, that doesn't sound good."

"I love them, but those girls go into tantrums. They'll throw things, break stuff, and scream. If you didn't know, you'd assume they were three."

"You're dealing with a bunch of children, might as well treat them as such."

"Well, young man, I think you've got an idea."

"And I've probably many more. But you must be patient to deal with them daily."

If I was Ancelin, matured as she, and dealing with damsels, I'd probably be dead.

I know she said she must leave, so like a gentleman, I declare, "Whenever you're ready, I'll take you home, ma'am."

"Honey, could I use your strong arm to help me get up?"

"Sure. Why, sure."

Lady Ancelin's slow in her movement, but gradually pulls herself from the couch. "I've enjoyed my time here, I have; and I can't get out without getting some hugs."

"We're glad, ma'am, you came. It's been a good visit," Ambrielle relays.

"Absolutely. Oh, absolutely. And, Miss Deja, it was so nice to have met you. And you come, honey, give me a hug."

"Ma'am, you're too sweet. If you have problems with Satordi's driving, just yell at him, please. Maybe give him a swat?"

Can I believe she just said that? "Dej," I say as I draw her attention. "Don't go scaring the poor woman. I promise, Miss Bruel, to have you home safe and sound."

"I'm not worried one ounce." She moves aside to Yasmina, who's a foot from her stance. "You'll see me again before you leave, won't you?"

"Yes, of course. We'll make arrangements and have you come here."

"Oh, good. I don't want you getting out of here without saying goodbye."

"We'll get together again."

Ancelin peers around. "Where's my Holland? Where's that baby girl?"

She's hearing her laugh. "I'm here."

"So you are. Come snuggle to me and give me some squeezes. Ooh-wee, those sure are good hugs." She then pulls back while patting Holland's face. "Take care of your mom and sister, baby."

"Sure, ma'am, I will."

"You're a good child, you are."

I help Ancelin through the door as we're heading to Sable. "Watch your step," I say when she's getting inside. "Here comes the door."

I trail on round, then fall to my seat.

Through a remorseful face, Ancelin's looking to me. "I'd like to apologize for my sister. I've heard she was rude."

"Oh, no. No. She had every right."

"It's because Ambrielle's safety's been everything to us."

"Well, I know. But there I was. She hadn't known me from Adam."

"She felt an obligation to maintain the girl's safety."

I explain, "Like a mother hen watching out for her chick."

"Mmm-hmm, she was."

"You wouldn't mind me dropping you off behind your house? Just, we don't know whose eyes might be watching."

"Honey, that's fine."

I pull into the alley where I'm driving slow. "Tell me when to stop."

"By those roses, you see?"

I pull along the garage where I put a stop to the engine, and after getting out, I help Ancelin from the car and assist her to the sidewalk.

"I can manage now. It's okay."

I tell her, "I'll not be rude. I'm here till you're in."

"I'll be okay. I see one of my girls. She'll get me inside".

"Then I'll stay till she comes."

Ancelin pats my hand. "I'd like us to get together again. I sure enjoyed being away from this place and seeing some friends."

"Whenever you want to come, my Deja will get you. She sure seemed to like you a lot."

"Well, I surely agree. Let's do something soon."

I leave Ancelin with one of her dames and return to my wheels. Then, in no time, I return to my gal's.

Moments pass while the day's slipping by, and sooner than later Cerissa appears with the kids. I introduce Yasmina and Holland, and happily, I see, everyone gets along.

Instantly, Holland becomes friends with both Marin's sprouts, and Yasmina, I think, seems fond of Cerissa.

Eventually dinnertime comes and the women serve grub. It's a hearty enough meal which have loaded our guts, and between all the men, we're now feeling stuffed.

An hour then passes when our guests are departing, then another attends us, and soon Yasmina assigns her youngest to bed. In short time, I realize, the rest of us follow.

Chapter Sixty-Three

Today's the day the boys and I must be at the cemetery. I'm planning to call Dr. Ignace shortly to see when he's going. After that, I'll phone Marin, whom, I'm hoping, should be at his house. If not, he's advanced to the office where he'll meet with me there.

I progress to the kitchen where I pour myself a piping mug of blackened Joe.

"Satordi, pour that out," I hear Dej from behind me. "That's pot mud; it's awful."

"You know I don't care."

"No. You wait. I'll make a fresh kettle."

"Dej."

"I said pour that out."

"Fine. Fine, here. I've got some calls I'm to make." I reach for the phone as I weigh in a number.

"Medical Examiner's Office. Dr. Ingance speaking."

"Roman, hey, it's Satordi. You got a minute for me?"

"Why, sure, my friend, sure." A thought now emerges and he comes with a question. "The exhumation's not been rescheduled, has it?"

"No. Oh, no. It's all still in order. I'm just wanting to know what time you'll be going?"

"What time?"

"Yeah. You have an idea?"

"I'll probably be arriving a quarter till."

"Okay, good. Make sure you do. I don't want this messed up."

"Well, if I'm late, you'll be waiting for me."

"Good joke, but don't try."

I hang the phone, then weigh in the next number. The line rings a few tolls before Cerissa picks up.

"Hey," I say. "Marin there?" "Hold on and I'll get him."

Eventually he answers, "Doggone it, Satordi, you've interrupted my breakfast."

"I don't want you forgetting we'll be at the cemetery today."

"I hadn't forgotten."

"Well, I'm not sure what you know. But go on and putter awhile. We're not needed till noon. I'll be heading to Ghislain's soon as I'm hanging this phone."

"Won't you be at the office?"

"Well, yeah, later on."

"Then why have me stay here?" my brother polls. "Forget it. I'll finish eating, then meet with you boys."

I get off the phone and I'm finishing my coffee. I think I'm prepared, then I'm realizing I don't know what I've done with my shoes. I gaze beneath the table, believing I'll find them there.

"Lose something?" Deja's asking.

"Yeah, my loafers."

She smiles. "Check the living room, by the couch."

I head through the ingress, then I trail to the den. After finding my peddlers, I take a seat on the couch; then, in a quickened rush, I slip both shoes onto my feet. I'm about to rise from the cushion, but suddenly I stop, for across from me, upon the stairs, I spot an image. I lean forward to discern what I see.

"Holland? Holland, hey, you okay?" I'm running to her when I see the stream of blood on her face.

"It won't stop."

"You've got a nosebleed. You'll be okay. I'll get you some tissues."

"Ugh," she expresses. "It's drained in my throat."

"I'll get you to the kitchen. You can spit into the sink."

Deja sees us as we come through the door. "What's happening?"

"She's got a nosebleed." I move Holland to the basin. "Here, child, spit into the sink."

"I'll take over, Satordi. Holland, tilt your head forward and try pinching your nostrils. Usually that helps."

"Won't that cause it to drain into my mouth?"

"If you tilt backwards. Here's more tissue. Let's get rid of these."

She takes the bloody Kleenex and throws them into the trash.

"Mommy always puts a cold rag on my face."

"Then I'll get one."

"Dej. Honey, I'll wake her mom, if you want."

"We've got it under control, don't we, Holland?"

The young child answers, "Just about."

Right then Yasmina comes through the room. "Morning, everyone." She's then seeing her daughter. "What's going on? Are you hurt?"

"I had a nosebleed, mama."

"Honey, why didn't you get me?"

"Mr. Satordi saw me coming downstairs and he helped."

"Well, that was nice of him, huh?"

"Deja helped, too."

My gal smiles. "Thankfully it wasn't a bleeding wound because I probably have fainted."

Things seem good when I'm deciding to leave. "We've got a bunch going on, so I'll be home when I can."

After relaying that, I head out to leave.

I've gotten to Ghislain's where I knock at his door. It takes hardly any time for him to come answer.

"Hey, boss."

"Slick." I'm gradually nodding.

Readily, he tells me, "Let me get some shoes and we'll go."

"Take your time. I'll be around."

I hear his voice rise from a back room, "Come on in if you want."

I stretch through the door, peering any which way. "It strikes me you keep a clean place."

"I don't care much for messes."

"Yeah, so I see."

He then emerges past an ingress. "Well, boss, you ready?" We exit his place and he's locking the door.

"Where's Marin?" he ponders. "He waiting outside?"

"Probably home, still downing his grub."

"Well, hey, I'm not meaning to alarm you, but I dreamt a vision last night and I'm needing to talk."

My gut suddenly drops and is plunging far. "I haven't heard that in awhile."

"Trust me, I thought it was over."

Though dreadfully I'm feeling, I drill his response, "Do I even ask?" We fall to our seats, then stare toward each other.

I consider, "If it's Haulmier, please blare away."

"No. It's not him."

I refrain from starting the engine. "Who, then?"

"I can't be certain, but Yasmina, I think."

"Oh, Christ, Ghislain." My face sinks to my chest. "Why," I'm asking, "are you assuming it's her?"

"I saw her, Satordi, least I think it was her. She was carrying the box."

I'm now heavily concerned. "In my gal's house?"

"If not yet, then wait and see."

"We have to go. We have to go there," I unmindfully shout.

Like a bat out of hell, I race from the curb. My wheels begin squealing and I'm kicking up dirt. In record time I've traveled to Dej's. I'm barely in park when throwing open my door. I leave Ghislain behind me as I take off to go running.

I pass through the entryway and I'm approaching the kitchen. After seeing Yasmina at the table, I breathlessly start blaring, "A package. Have you gotten a package?"

Unnerved, she looks to me and she's shaking her head.

"Did you bring something? Perhaps a small box?"

"Like what? I only came with clothes."

"You haven't received anything?"

"A gift or something? No."

"If you do, if you get a package, you throw it away."

"Satordi," my doll interrupts me. "What's this about?"

"Keep a watch on the mail. Any package comes in, I want it discarded." I see Deja is curious and, like a butting snoop, she inquires, "What is it you don't want us having?"

"Squat. So you throw the thing out."

"Satordi, I'm not a child. Tell me what's in it."

Ghislain's citing his speech, "It's nothing you need to be messing with, any of you."

Ambrielle's finally wakened and appears at my side. "What don't we mess with?" she inquisitively polls.

"Packages," I hint, hoping she's aware what I mean. "You know those little brown boxes?"

Surely enough, Ambrielle's eyes widen as she makes sense of the matter.

I pull the girl aside so we may privately speak. "As far as we know, it hasn't come yet."

"But you're saying it will?"

"Be prepared. Get it away from anyone trying to discover its contents."

"I'll make sure it's thrown out."

"I don't know when it'll arrive, but keep your eyes open. Ghis and I have to leave, but should you have reason to call me, then damn it, do. We'll be leaving the office before noon. Anytime after, we'll not be around."

Ambrielle worries. "What if I need you?"

"It's not my best answer, but let's pray that you won't." I then turn to Ghis, who resides at my back. "Time, slick. Got to go."

"That's it, Satordi?" Deja poses. "You rush in with warnings, then you decide to walk out?"

"Mind what I said. You'll be helping yourself."

"I heard. You don't need to stress it."

I rancorously imply, "Damn it, I hope not." I'm turning my back. "Ghis." I'm nodding. "Come on, man. Come on."

Duplessey makes an acknowledgment before we're to leave. "Ladies." He smiles. "Have a good day."

Chapter Sixty-Four

Delayed, we were; however, Ghislain and I arrived at my business.

Marin, as I'm looking, lays reposed at his desk. He's face-down in drool, zonked out chasing z's.

As a consequence of this inelegant sight, I overtly shudder.

"Slobber mouth," I signal. "Hey, slobber, wake up."

Marin hadn't expected my crack when, suddenly, he jumps.

"Yo! Hey," he's stridently expressing.

"Do us a favor and wipe that face. You look a mess with all that dribble."

Luckily he takes my advice and is cleaning his spittle. As I should figure, he ponders, "Where've you been?"

"Handling business."

"Gee, thanks for telling me. I've been waiting forever."

"It was sudden, Marin."

"Yeah. Yeah, sure, I bet, sudden."

"Is this how you're going to be all day, having this attitude?"

"I'm just cranky."

"Then do something about it. I'll not have you going with when you're acting like this."

"Fellas," Ghis breaks in. "Fellas."

"I'm not dealing with it, Ghis. Marin needs to behave. He don't, he'll go home."

I hear my brother, "I'll do my best. I'll be quiet."

"I'd appreciate that. Have we had any calls?"

"No. Nothing."

"Well," I think. "You boys want to take a ride to Orisia's?"

Marin, the dumb nut, questions, "Who's that, a new client?"

Him having asked that has me feeling flustered. I'm currently wondering what he knows of this case.

Ghislain sees my agitation and quickly responds, "She's Yria's sister. I don't think you've met."

Calmly, I'm telling Marin, "We'll go in my car." I toss him my keys. "Head on. I'm phoning Orisia, so she'll know we're coming."

Marin turns to Ghis as they head through the door. "You know how grand it is to be getting these keys?"

Ghislain laughs. "Sable's your brother's pride. It's best you think twice before assuming he's letting you drive."

"It's a dream, ain't it?"

"That's all it'll be." Ghislain pats Marin's back.

I step from the business and I'm locking the door. Thankfully my brother knows better than to be taking my seat. I fall in my ride, then settle my rear.

We've arrived at Miss Laroque's and we're ascending her stairs. In a matter of seconds, she appears at the door.

"Please," she's telling us, "come in."

"You know Ghis," I'm responding. "Then Marin, my brother." "Hi," she responds.

"Hi, madam."

"Excuse the mess. I hadn't expected your company."

"Mess?" I say. "I see no mess."

"The laundry, you see. I've been folding these clothes. Let me move it from your way, so you men could have seats."

"This'll do. You don't need to move stuff."

"I don't know. There's still plenty here." Orisia laughs lightly. "Hopefully this is good and you'll all find some room."

"It's fine," I'm telling her. "We've all gotten seated."

"You being here means you're bringing news, I'm hoping."

"We've made some headway, but still got a ways till we're done. I wanted you to know this afternoon Guillaume's remains get exhumed."

She makes an angled face. "And the reason for this?"

"Seems maybe we've found the man's skull. It's not for certain, but chances are likely."

"And you're doing this to determine whether it completes his remains?"

I nod. "That's the idea."

"Of course you'll be keeping me informed on all this?"

"There's no reason I shouldn't."

I withhold the fact I've currently got a sculptor preparing the skull as a duplicate of the face it once rendered. Right now my concern with Guillaume's remains are to determine what type of instrument caused his beheading. Dr. Ignace will be able to conclude whether a boating accident had, in fact, been the source of his death.

Further, following D'Anjou's completion of his craft's work, Dr. Ignace will be able to concede whether the skull truly belongs with Rhoe's body. Of this, I am doubtful. I've a good mind to know that a dead man with no head wouldn't have his own skull concealed in the place he once lived. The entire scenario's amiss. Even the dumbest of fools would conceive this.

In addition to Yria having been murdered, Guillaume had also claimed another victim, an unknown male; a man whose name I wish to uncover.

This case, as I know, started with Yria, then came an additional conclusion which expanded its context. So, the matter, I realize, hadn't involved only her. This opaque thread regards me for I've yet to confirm the identity of this unfortunate male snuffed out by Rhoe.

Orisia questions, "Have you any idea the length of time this analysis might take?"

"I don't. But as said, I'll present the finds to keep you informed."

"And my sister?" she questions sadly. "You still haven't found her?" I'm hiding the fact I discovered her skin, but not her bones, "No. But it doesn't mean I won't. I said before, I'd be bringing her home. That was a promise."

"I have faith to believe it. You've come a long way."

"Don't give up, whatever you do."

"No. No, never."

"Boss, it's about a quarter till," I hear Ghislain.

"Stay firm to what you said, Miss Laroque. Give us time. We'll bring Yria home."

She breaks forth in tears. "You will, I know. Yria's counting on you."

"She is." I nod. "I'll be in touch in a few days."

Surprisingly, Orisia stands to embrace me. "For everything you're doing, I want to thank you."

"Hey, it needs to be done. The boys and I, we're here for you."

Orisia graciously moves to Marin and Ghis and, amiably, wraps both men in hugs. After seeing her emotions settle, Orisia walks us to the door.

We'll be on our way to Sainte-Croix where the exhumation's taking place. I do hope all goes as it should, and we're not encountering delays of any sort. It'll be a real mess if we do. I'm just wanting this to move along as it was planned, with no interruptions hindering our progress.

Chapter Sixty-Five

Sable, like the reliable car she is, has carried us to the cemetery. Slowly, I cruise her glorious wheels through these dusty paths that honorably accept her.

I look around to crumbling headstones where they lie aged and withered. Most have stood so long, their engravings can barely be ciphered.

Large trees supply shade to some graves, keeping the stretch of light from reaching their locality.

There are several mausoleums cast about the grounds that strongly remain in their standing. I shall note the excellence of the monument makers who erected these vaults. Though these chambers may be imposing to most, especially at night, I still find them impressive.

I continue with Sable down a narrowed path while barely roving her wheels. About thirty yards ahead I spot a bulldozer, signaling to me that's probably our site. I maunder forth and go that direction. Now having arrived closer, I view Roman's car.

He spots me as I'm nearing in. "Pull ahead," I'm hearing him shout. "There's enough room, Satordi. Go on and park."

Graciously I nod as I'm passing him by. I pull Sable ahead and put a stop to the engine.

Roman comes alongside where he stands near my wheels. "Looks like they're digging."

"I see. Yeah, I see. But the lift?" Like a hawk, I'm peering round. "Christ, those dumb bastards. They don't show, then we're screwed."

"If it don't turn up during the time this grave's been uncovered, I suggest you go call."

"Then it's back to the office. Hell, we'll give it time," I declare. "Hopefully they come."

"Yeah, hopefully."

"Since we're waiting, might as well introduce you to Marin and Ghis."

Ghislain extends his hand. "How's it going?"

Roman laughs. "Good now, I'm around some live bodies."

"But it won't last long," Marin replies.

"Never does."

I ponder, "Guess you've brought whatever things you'll be needing?"

"Got the whole caboodle."

Marin broods, "You do this a lot, come to cemeteries?" "A few, not a lot. But I'm willing to come when needed."

"Least you're willing."

"Well, I'm appointed to do it, nonetheless."

"Excuse me," I say before walking away. I head to one of the men who came with the dozer. "I guess I pay you?"

"Yeah, I'm that guy."

I pull out a wad of francs. "Suppose this covers it?"

"Sure, man, looks right."

"Well, then, we're set. Tell your boss I said hey." "Oh, the old crank. Yeah, sure, I'll tell him hey."

"You call him that, do you?"

"Among other things." He laughs. "The man's a real gripe."

"You better give him some sugar."

"Ha-ha-ha-ha," the man barrels with laughter. "My co-workers and I want to buy a whole bag."

"So what gives? You going to do it or not?"

"Oh, we have the intention."

"Well, set it to work. Drop it onto his desk. He'll never know you all did it." I'm smiling slyly. "Well, good luck to you." I'm walking away.

I take a step toward Rhoe's grave and begin peeping in. I'd love nothing more than to spit on his casket, but considering respect, I decide not to do it.

I peer in the distance to see the lift finally arrives. I purposely gaze at my watch and spy the time. They're just twelve minutes late; just twelve minutes, no more. Still, they should've arrived sooner. What's gonna be the excuse?

A man yells through his window, "You ain't the one needing a lift, are you?"

"We've been waiting for one," I shout back.

"Hey, I'm sorry. We ended up in another cemetery. Some idiot mixed the receipts. We didn't know where to go."

"Huh?"

"Mistake at the office. But still, sir, I apologize".

"Eh, least you got here. Don't worry."

"We'll get this lift out and be ready to work."

Dr. Ignace approaches along with Marin and Ghis.

"Soon, boss." Ghislain's patting my back. "We'll be knowing things soon."

"I sure hope. This day's long been awaited."

"Look, by the end of this, you'll be resting your heels."

"It'll be a long rest I'm taking."

The four of us men stand around to watch the workers. We maintain our look-see awhile, then the coffin is lifted.

Roman raises his brow. "Guess the rest is on me." He saunters toward the men, saying, "Let's get that thing opened."

Marin rises forth with a question, "You sure you want to be doing that here?"

"Have to make sure we've got a body there, don't we?"

"Don't grow concerned when you see there's no head," I readily respond.

Roman jokes, "I ain't worried bout that. But I'm fearing him to jump out and slap me. Say, he don't got his hands, does he?"

"Got those, Doc, and he's got his feet, too."

"Don't frighten me, Satordi."

Dr. Ignace pulls a mask to his face to keep from breathing smut, muck, and grime.

I smile ever shrewdly. "Just letting you know."

The casket comes open and, with it, a heather cloud of dust.

"Good thing you've got that mask," I'm telling the doc.

"It's procedure. No casket gets opened without it."

"All right, what'd you find?"

"You too scared to move closer? I've got masks. Come over. Take a look at your man."

"Bones, Roman. He ain't nothing but bones. Besides that, how do you know that's a man anymore?"

Yria Dane

"You see his clothes?"

"Clearly. But that don't mean he's male."

"I'll know for certain when I examine the pelvis."

"Is there anything you could be saying to us now?"

"Well, visually, I see the cervical vertebrae. I know both clavicles are there. Noticeably, you'll see the shirt here is raised."

"No. I don't know."

"Well, it takes a trained eye. You do this enough, you'll see what I mean."

"What else?"

"Look there, you'll view the carpals, metacarpals, and last, phalanges."

I make a bummed face. "It's easier if you just told me his hands."

"Apparently you knew."

"Cause I saw you there pointing."

"And I'll do so again. Let's move to his legs." Through gloved hands Roman gropes at Rhoe's pants. "I'll let you in on some news."

"Yeah, tell me."

"Got two femurs and both fibulas, too."

"Well, I'm sure that's dandy. Even for a dead man like him."

"Actually is. We know he's got legs."

"Funny, Roman. Very funny. Can you release anymore?"

"You know I'll be needing to get him to the testing room. Won't know nothing more till then."

"You mind if the boys and I come?"

"You'll be looking at bones for awhile." "Trust me, we've nothing better to do."

Dr. Ignace acknowledges, "I'll load him on up then. You want to meet there? Give me about fifteen minutes."

We leave Roman with the crane and hoist guys as they finish. Following that, Guillaume's coffin will be transported to Dr. Ignace's place of work to begin his evaluation.

Chapter Sixty-Six

The boys and I arrive at New Hope Hospital less than eight minutes ago. We've come to the basement where Roman's office resides. While leaned against the wall, we're watching the hall when Roman rolls through, wheeling Guillaume's coffin upon the polyflor.

"We'll give you a hand with that." I'm moving from the wall.

"You'll be more help, Satordi, if you got that door open." I uphold his guidance as I'm shoving the hatchway.

"Ghis, go round. Help him push that thing through."

"Your hands on there?" Roman asks.

Ghislain nods. "Yeah, Doc, we're good."

"Push it on over to that table." Dr. Ignace then pulls a mask to his face. "Might want to stand back now," he states, then opens the casket.

Once again the heather cloud has returned. Favorably, this time, it hasn't released as much dirt.

"It's against procedure to ask, but I'll need someone's help."

"What you need, Doc?" I hear Ghislain.

"Can't very well take him out on my own. I'll need help. There's a lab coat behind you. Just slip the thing on."

"This?" Ghislain grabs.

Dr. Ignace shakes his head. "And grab some gloves and get a mask."

Ghislain looks into the casket. "How're you wanting to do this?"

"Carefully."

Punctiliously, Marin and I stand aside and are watching.

"Ghislain, your hands; slide them beneath the cervical spine and lift gently. I'll maintain the legs and arms."

"I got it, but he's needing support in the sternum and ribs."

"Satordi." Roman directs, "Get over here and help."

Forget the lab coat. I don't need it, but I do, however, grab some gloves.

"Carefully, men, let's pull him to the table."

Ever swiftly we guide the remains to the slab. In succession to this,

Ghislain and I have stepped back and are allowing Roman room when the undressing begins.

Dr. Ignace places the tattered belongings into a brown paper bag, then is sealing it closed.

He returns to the table to position the bones and set them in order.

He begins his analysis by examining the cervical vertebrae.

"I can tell, by looking, the man was beheaded with an attenuate knife. If you'd look, there are several cleave marks within this region here."

I see exactly where Roman points. "Could a propeller have caused this?"

"Not what I'm seeing. In fact, had that been it, we'd see one rive on the bone. In this case, that's not what I'm viewing."

Marin questions, "In other words, a propeller would have cut it clean off?"

"Swiftly and fast," Doc says. "Swiftly and fast." I ponder, "Are other injuries present you see?"

Dr. Ignace carries forth his exam. "There's definitely breaks in these ribs."

"From a fall, maybe?"

"Don't think so, Satordi. It's more like they'd been acquired from fighting, or he'd been beat with some instrument."

"Really? Okay. How do you tell?"

"People don't break this many ribs, not by accident. More than half have cracks."

"Could it have been a brick?"

"Or something else."

"Ghislain vocalizes, "How bout a billy club?"

"Possibly. Too bad, though, this man can't talk."

"Indeed," I dodder my head. "What horrors he'd speak."

Veritably I know the remains on this table by no means belong to Guillaume Rhoe, so the question comes, where's the man at? Is he living life somewhere? Or is he dead and perhaps buried in another cemetery?

This has become nothing more than a wild goose chase. Almost, I'll say, has this caused me to rethink my career. In all the cases I've served, never have I had anything like this. My mind is snowballing and about to wipe out.

Why did I ever promise Orisia the things I have? Was I over-confident, or had I purely been dense?

If D'Anjou doesn't come through with a face, I'm not sure what I'll do. This case might come to an undesirable end, I'm afraid. I'm not wanting to let Orisia down; it was never an intention, but if things don't pull together soon, I'm sorry to add, the inadmissible will happen.

"I'd give about anything to hear this eighty-sixer reveal his name," I'm speaking aloud.

Dr. Ignace looks to me. "You know what he'd say?"

I want to smile, but I can't bring myself to it. "What's that?"

"I can't tell a soul."

"Good humor, but I suppose there's no way to determine this man's identity?"

"I wish there was, Satordi. This is as far as it gets."

"Wish I could say that's reassuring."

"You have some other direction?"

"Just the skull. After that, I don't know."

"Don't give up just yet."

"That's your advice?"

"It's good enough. I just hope you'll listen."

"I'll try. But momentarily, let's get back to this head. You're sure a knife was involved?"

"I couldn't see it being anything else. The impression clearly indicates that, nothing other."

"Not a saw?"

"There'd be rigid grooves along the cervical vertebrae. Rather, these bone scars are different. I have no reason to doubt a knife was the instrument. And a dull one at that. The assaulter enforced repeat attempts at hacking. This would've been the result of a slow, agonizing death."

Following a long stand of silence, Ghislain imparts with a question, "How would you suppose it played out?"

"From what we've learned, he took a great hit to the ribs and, having suffered that magnitude of force, never got up. He'd have instantly been grounded. I suggest the assaulter sat on this man and quickly began cutting."

Ghislain frowns in effect to Roman's statement. "He suffered a great deal, hadn't he?"

"Sadly. It's not something you'd want to imagine."

"No. No, sir, it isn't."

"Give us a call, then, Doc, if you come across anything else," I'm telling Ignace.

"Absolutely."

"Good deal. You've got my number. We might have some running around, but keep calling till you get me."

"Well, you get bored, come back. Got a feeling I'll be working a late one tonight."

"We'll see." I'm patting his back.

"See you some time." Marin's extending his hand.

"Keep that boy there in line." Roman's referring to myself.

Ghislain's throwing forth his shaker. "Take it easy, Doc."

"Always. And don't shy away now. Come back and see me."

We get back to my car when I'm rising to ask, "You boys in the mood for a beer?"

Marin answers quickly, "Nah, not me. I'll probably head to the house. Maybe catch a few Zs."

"What about it, Ghis? You in?"

"Sure. Yeah, I'll go."

"I'll drop my brother at his car and we'll head on."

"You going to the office later?"

"I doubt it, Marin. I'll head in tomorrow."

I stop Sable before our business where I let Marin out.

"I'll stop by in the morning," my brother says.

"All right. Okay. Drop in around nine." I pull Sable away as Ghislain and I set off down the street. "So I stopped in Frenchmen's yesterday and was noticing something with Haulmier. He had some tail with him."

"Really? Who?"

"A broad. Goes by the name Azure Cashlousier. He says she's Yasmina."

"You've known this?"

"For some time. It was Ambrielle who told who she was."

"Is that right?"

"Makes you wonder, doesn't it?"

"Guess that's where you're heading. You're wanting to see if she's there?"

"Aren't you wondering how she plays into this?"

"Since you mentioned it."

We're passing another street when I see a familiar woman strolling down the sidewalk, so I hang my head through my window, yelling, "Miss Laroque. Miss Laroque." Finally, I've caught her attention.

"Detective. Mr. Duplessey." She meanders to us.

"You headed somewhere?"

"Home. Just home."

"You got some time? We're heading to Frenchmen's. You feel like coming?"

"I could."

"Well, hop on in. We'll give you a lift."

Without hesitance, she tells us, "All right."

I step from the car to allow her inside. After she's in, I fall to my seat, then we're off, heading out. In no time Sable's come upon Frenchmen's. Consciously, I park where I can keep her in view. However, I'm easily discomfited having her here, but on a welcoming note, the sun's shining bright. Had it been dark or starting to be, I'd never have driven my metal baby to a scene bad as this.

Courteously, I pull the seat, then I'm helping Orisia as she starts to step out. "Ever been here?" I ask.

"Not this place, no."

"Ain't no different than those you've been to. But if you're uneasy, let us know, we'll get you out."

Ghislain holds the door as we're walking, then he and Orisia follow me to the bar where we're taking our seats.

As usual it's the same lousy drink slinger. I don't think this guy gets a break, but who cares? I ungraciously crack my neck and, in an unrevealed manner, search the bar with intention to perceive Haulmier, but no, nope. As I see, he ain't here. Could be in the office. Granted that, he'll show his mug given time.

"So you've come again?" The two-bit punk stares.

"Yeah," I crudely reply. "Give me a beer and whiskey."

"For the lady?"

She gently responds, "Water, please." "Have a drink," I'm telling her.

Orisia looks upon the piddling scrub. "Just water, please."

The nitwit then hustles to Ghis. "What're you having?"

"Beer."

Wisely, I think to tell Miss Laroque about the happenings today. I'll let her how Rhoe's grave's been dug and the body uncovered, then I'll inform her of the shock, this twisted little truth in relation to the remains which were found.

I'm saying, "Guillaume's grave's nothing but an empty ditch."

"Empty, Detective? But I saw him laid there."

"No. We've got the remains. It's a ditch that's left. I'm just saying we've got the bones and casket."

"My thinking was slow, as it sometimes is."

"And you're not even drinking," I'm kidding.

"Unless something's in this water." She cracks me a smile.

I'm then hearing Ghis, "Have you told her?"

"What? Told me what, Satordi?"

"I was working my way on telling you."

The front door then opens, followed by fulminating footfalls. Obviously I turn in my chair as this thunderous stride precedes me. Well, what do you know? If it isn't Guloe.

"Detective, here again? Well, I'm starting to believe I'm being stalked."

"Not that you'd mind it."

"I've already said I've nothing to hide. Why should I worry?"

"Well, I hope you don't."

I'm now spotting Orisia as she turns in her chair, and with inspecting eyes, she studies Guloe.

"Basile? Basile Devereux?"

Whoa, wait. What'd she say?

I watch Guloe's color drain from his face. Apparently some singular induction has caused him alarm.

"Basile. Basile, it's me. Orisia."

"No. No, my name's Haulmier, miss. Seems you're confusing me with someone."

"Your resemblance is uncanny. So much, it strikes me."

Allegedly Miss Laroque failed to witness Haulmier's face turning pale, but I hadn't missed that pallid discolor resting on his kisser. Something was up when he heard Orisia say Basile. As I know, I've been unable to find him. I discover myself wondering if Basile Devereux was here all along? Additionally, I speculate, for what reason would this man change his name?

If he really is Basile, then why doesn't he want us to know? As it so seems, this is just another stickler I'll be adding to my list of things to discover.

Orisia talks me out of my trance. "What was it you were wanting to say?"

"Huh? Oh. Oh, ah. Huh?"

"The remains, boss," Ghislain's advises. "You said you'd tell her."

"Oh, yeah, right. I've a friend who's a doctor. He's helping with this thicket of mess we've come into. And he's concluded the remains as belonging to some other person. Whose they are, we're still uncertain."

"Wait. Wait-wait-wait."

"Take a minute, Miss Laroque."

"Guillaume died. I know. He was buried."

"Someone was buried. But without his name, we can't know."

"I can't even say how I'm feeling."

"I understand, Miss Laroque. It's a lot to take in. When unprepared for such news, we tend to get scrambled."

"This is getting me. I'm sorry, Detective. So much has raced through my head in this second. And I've got to get Mira from school. She's serving as tutor, helping children who hadn't passed their last grade. She'll see that I'm rued and start asking why."

"Hopefully she won't see it."

"Mira has that intuition. Not even I can get past it."

"Well, since you're needing to get her, what time do I take you?"

"About now. Do you mind?"

"You're ready. We'll go." I call down to Ghis, "Finish that beer, slick."

"Mind you, it's an empty glass, boss. It's been gone for awhile."

"All right, then, let's leave."

We head to Mira's school where we await her outside.

Orisia addresses me, "Mira won't know your car. I better get out." I'm stepping forth, then pulling back the seat before I set loose my advisement, "Meander back, then. You know where we are." I return to my car and settle my hind. "I tell you, slick, that's a foxy dame walking there. If I didn't have Dej, I'd be on her like butter."

He's laughing, go figure. "Seeing, though, you had the chance."

"In good measure, that'll probably remain a mystery."

"Yap. Yeah, absolutely."

I watch through my window at the flood of tadpoles escaping their school. I know their vamoose; I did it myself. As a youngster I hated that jail. Yap, you read right, I called it a jail. My attention was torpid, so that kept me from listening. Like most kids, I loathed homework. Really, I mean I loathed it, no joke. Furthermore, I disliked the teachers who taught me my lessons. Always ended up having the ones who were bitter. Marin, though, damn him, he always had ones who were nice.

Through a crowd of munchkins I'm spotting Orisia. I see her maneuvering about as she and Mira come to my car. I pull myself forth while leaving my door fully spread.

"Why, hey, there, little missy."

Orisia's nudging her niece. "Mira, you remember Detective Biertempfel. Don't play shy, angel. Tell him hi."

The child then smiles. "Hello," she ever so softly replies.

"How's school?"

Ghis turns in his seat. "Look-a-there. If it ain't the prettiest girl in Annecy. How've you been, sweets?"

"Fine." She quickly beams.

"I like your dress. Did your aunty buy that?"

"Aunty made it and she's sewing another."

"I bet it'll sure be nice."

I'm pulling Sable from the curb where she embarks down the street. A few minutes later I drive to Orisia's. All this trekking to and from my car makes me wonder if I'll be having sore knees. That's a moronic question, really, but still I am curious.

"Ladies," I say. "Your humble abode awaits."

Before Miss Laroque's leaving with Mira, she guilelessly asks, "You'll be calling once you've received any news?"

"Soon as the word's been delivered. We'll wait here till you've both gone inside."

"Would you care to come in? Mira and I have nothing to do."

"Honestly, Miss Laroque, I had planned to head home."

"Oh." She appears to be down. "Maybe another time?" "I'll visit," Ghislain answers.

"Stay here, please, just for awhile."

"Yeah, sure I can." He now turns to me. "Guess I'll see you tomorrow, boss. Maybe your brother could head over and get me?"

"I'll give him the word."

"Detective," Orisia voices quietly. "You're sure you won't stay?"

"I'm sure. I've things I'm needing to do."

I wasn't planning to head to my business, but I'm sensing I should. The place is quiet, no one's there. Because of that, I'll not be distracted.

I'm rambling through the door and, as desired, rove to my desk. I'm falling to my seat as I'm lighting a puffer.

I've come here to consider all discernments I may have about Ba- sile Devereux becoming Haulmier Guloe. I don't know why he's taken an alias, but since he did, he must have had reason.

I know nothing about how long Haulmier's been in Annecy. I do know, however, Basile Deveruex relocated to Cherbourg, but I'm unable to say when. As it so seems and, what my eyes saw, Basile's back.

I had no intention to find him and talk. Cherbourg's a far drive and I decided not to go. Finding out Basile's here has left me with questions.

I'm even pondering rather Yasmina and Ambrielle truly know who he is. If by some reason they don't, this shock's about to get them.

Additionally, I'm probing the thought, does Basile know anything pertaining to Guillaume Rhoe?

Had Rhoe planned to kill Basile and Basile, then knew? Maybe, just maybe, Rhoe was rubbed out before the deed could be done? If that's so, then Guillaume's body could be anywhere. This is feasible. I'll just have to wait it out to see how it unfolds.

I realize it's midday and I'd like to be out of here. I'm about to head to Dej's where I'll eat a quick bite, then probably take a long soak. I have the feeling afterward I'll be advancing to bed. I know that sounds more like Marin's agenda, but I believe his burn out acedia has passed on to me.

Chapter Sixty-Seven

Previously, Dej and Cerissa were up cooking breakfast. Consequentially, everyone beneath the roof of this house have supped up their meal. Still there's enough should Marin and Ghis choose to consume the remainders.

Fifteen minutes, after finishing my mug of hot ink, my brother steps in.

"Intruder alert." Marin's grinning. "Hi, everyone."

Peering to him, I say, "You ready, bum, or are you going to eat?"

"No. I'm ready."

With the absence of Duplessey, I'm beginning to wonder, "Ghis? Where's Ghis?"

"Home, on the phone."

"And you left?"

"He knows I'm going back."

So slick was on the phone; big deal. That don't mean Marin had to leave. He could've waited till Duplessey's conversation had come to an end. Later, they could have came here, but instead, my brother's lost his brains. Wouldn't be the first time, and it's sure not the last.

We head out front, then trek to the sidewalk. Above me I notice the patchy grey clouds ahead. The ill-lighted sky is an indication that we're about to get wet.

"Smell that?" I ask.

"Rain?"

"Yap. It's coming."

Marin, like an unnerved woman, to a coming storm, admits, "And I don't got my brolly."

"Complainer."

He just stares at me as we get to his car. The instant we're inside, the downpour starts coming.

"This ain't good," I'm saying.

"It's just a little rain, brother."

I know Marin too well. Him saying that's his way of throwing it back in my face.

Heavy droplets smack the windshield as he turns on his wipers.

A little rain, my ass, I'm silently complaining.

After getting to Ghislain's, Marin and I decide we'll remain in his car. Hopefully this storm will pass or at least decrease some degree.

After eight minutes we begin to get bored. I draw my hand to the radio and twist through the stations.

"No-no," Marin lets out. "Leave that. I like it." Before I know it, we're beginning to sing.

> *Shebang-do-bop-bop, Bonnie got, oh yeah,*
> *Bonnie got that shebang-do-bop-bop,*
> *see her swing, that dancing queen,*
> *who likes the dive on Humble Drive, yeah, yeah,*
> *bop-bop, shebang-do-bop-bop, Bonnie got, oh yeah,*
> *Bonnie got that shebang-do-bop-bop.*

"What do you know, brother, looks like the rain's letting up just a little".

I consider, "You ready to run?"

"Don't think to ask twice. Let's do it."

Like a bustling pair of idiots, we're racing to Ghislain's. Any on-lookers would more than likely be thinking we're nuts. Here we are, two men, scrambling on foot to get away from this weather.

I suppose now the last jape's on me. Before, there I was, joshing Marin. Maybe it would've been wise had we bought us a brolly. But like a dumbass, I'll admit, I was ribbing my brother.

"Oh, Satordi, you frozen bloke, am I seeing you shake?"

"Chilled. I'm slightly chilled."

We rush the stairs, soaking wet, then head to room three where I knock ever loudly.

In good pace Ghislain appears at the door. "Come! Come on!"

I'm confused by his discharged excitement. "What the hell, slick? Why're you bubbly?"

"I spoke with Jourdain. The skull's ready. We'll have it today. I'm grabbing my coat."

"You looked outside?" my curiosity wonders.

"The rain? I know."

"Hold off a bit. I'd like to rest a short sec."

"Huh?"

I'm telling Ghis, "That's some cold, heavy rain. Let's let it wind down."

"We're not leaving?"

My brother undesirably acknowledges, "Satordi won't tell, but this knothead's all chilled."

"Want some coffee? I've got coco."

"Coffee."

"What are you waiting for? Come on to the kitchen."

"So what's this, you talking to Jourdain?"

"He called when he didn't get an answer at the business. Good thing he did; I was about to leave with your brother."

"He say how it looks?"

"Remarkable. Said it's a face."

"That was the point." I then realize I'd been smart. "Sorry, slick."

"He even got glass eyes for the thing."

"What the hell, glass eyes? How'd he come across that?"

"Does it matter? We've got a face, Satordi. Finally, we'll be seeing this man."

"Let's hope to hell someone recognizes him."

"Someone's bound to. Bound to, you know it."

"You're right. He had friends and family."

"We could run an article in the paper. Maybe a snapshot included, you think?"

"One way or another, something's getting done."

"I don't know about you boys," Marin acknowledges, "but I'm ready to see what your friend's produced."

I pull the coffee mug from my lips. "Hey, I'm trying to finish this, how about you let me?"

"Down it, Satordi, and let's get going." He refrains from me to peer at Duplessey. "I've got to take a leak. Where's the toilet?"

"It's that door there."

I direct my speech, "Ghis, hey, look outside, see if it's pouring."

He draws his face to a window. "Just drizzling."

"Good. It's stopping." He then takes a seat before me while I continue, "Did D'Anjou give a time to go by?"

"Pretty much, whenever."

Marin appears through the door with a look of stupefaction. "This place isn't haunted, is it? I swear I just saw something strange."

"This apartment? No. No, I've never had problems."

"Well." He then laughs. "The ceiling light's acting stupid. Blinked on and off, then on and off. Ever happen before?"

Ghis admits, "Oh, it's the bulb's about to die. I'll have it replaced." I think to stand from my seat. "All right, boys, let's get a move on." We travel on out to Marin's car. Once on the road, he drives ever slowly. I look to the speedometer and see it's steadily remaining on five.

This, this is stupid. Is he worried the car could be skidding if he put weight on the pedal? I'd like to say something, but I know his defens- es so well, I'll tell you, I know what he'd say. It'd be, almost verbatim, something like, accidents happen. There's been a hard rain. Knowing that, I decide I'll keep my words hidden.

Following a long laggard drive, we've come to D'Anjou's. He greets us at his step, then we trail to his work room.

"I think you'll be amazed by what you'll be viewing," he tells us. "I sure was."

"It's been a long wait," Ghislain's responding. "We're ready to see it." My eyes follow Jourdain as he's approaching his table. Upon it looks to be a fashioned head, displayed with hair.

D'Anjou's got it turned so the face isn't showing. Astonished to see threads coming out from the crown, I bewilderly ask, "That it? That him?"

Carrying it with its backside to us, he's replying, "This is what you've been waiting for."

He turns it in view and we're all astounded.

"Whoa. Holy cow," Ghislain's expressing.

Marin, amazed and excited, eagerly vociferates, "Wow. Wow. Get a load of that."

"Gees. Jourdain, gees, that's brilliant." I gaze on perfection. "How'd you ever do it?"

What we see's so realistic, it's sending me chills. Here before me's an actual face; an actual face. My gosh. My gosh. A man whose identi- ty's been lost for all these years. Unbelievable.

D'Anjou's gone so far, he's given him eyes. Upon us the man stares through a pair of green scouters. The sculpting's dead on, Jourdain couldn't have done better. The man's got hair. An auburn shade of hair, but whether it's right, I don't seem to care. The sculpting's complete.

Regardfully, I discern every inch of detail D'Anjou's produced. I know this was a painstaking endeavor, but damn, what a job. I've never seen anything like this, and I may not again.

"He's kind of got a familiar look, like maybe I've seen him. But the man I know, he's still alive," Marin's responding.

Ghislain's shaking his head. "I'm not so sure."

I take a step back to take a hard glance. "He does look like some-one." I continue my rigorous study. "Say, I know. Had he had dark eyes, he'd look like Guloe."

Then again I think his actual name isn't that. Orisia recognized him as Basile Devereux. What the hell's going on?

Ghislain agrees with my thought. "Granted, this man's younger. But yeah, I see why you'd say that."

"It really looks like him, doesn't it?"

"He does, boss. I'd say it's pretty close."

"We need to get this to Orisia. We'll find out what she thinks." I shake Jourdain's hand. "I'm thankful, sir, you did all this work. Your skills, absolutely, are phenomenal."

"I'm happy to have been given this opportunity to serve you. It's been an interesting achievement."

"Well, you've sure done a job."

Ghislain speaks with D'Anjou a moment before gathering to leave. Seeing the finished product Jourdain's produced has twisted this plot. I'm having trouble simply trying to apply any thoughts. How is it I wrap my head around these relations?

Basile Devereux became Haulmier Guloe, for whatever reason. Now I've seen the face of a man who's long since been silenced, and uncanny as it is, the man looks like Basile. This is just weird, and I can't say I get it.

Every cuss word wants to run through my head since I've instantly become flustered. I'm not even sure that's the word to describe how I'm feeling. I thought I was figuring this out, but I've been slapped in the face. I know I'm upset. I'm shook, shocked, and bothered.

Finally, the man's got a face, but still there's no name to whom he'd once been. If we're lucky and have a chance of good luck, Orisia will tell us.

Chapter Sixty-Eight

The boys and I are sitting upon Orisia's couch as she's preparing us tea. A few minutes later she returns with Mira as they both carry drinks.

Orisia passes them out, then kindly requests Mira to go play in her room.

"I have to?"

"Please, angel. We've grown up things to discuss."

"But I wanted to stay."

"Honey, don't be upset. You can come back soon as we've finished." The young girl makes a saddened face before retreating to her room.

Before Miss Laroque even sits, she's affably asking, "Your tea's okay?" Ironically, we're all answering at once, "Tastes fine."

"Well, then, shall I be nervous? I know you've come bearing news."

"That, and also we've something to show you."

I refresh Miss Laroque's mind to the things which have happened; unearthing Rhoe's grave, the analyzation of the remains, then the shocking result when we heard they weren't his, but now it's time I let Miss Laroque in on some fact, something I've kept hidden.

"I've several times gone to Rhoe's former house, the one on Grange Road. And well, I never imagined I'd find what I did." I hesi- tate a second, then continue with my desired discoursings. "I found a man's skull. It'd been placed in a trunk of belongings, things that were Rhoe's. After talking to Ghis, we decided to take it to a friend, a guy who does sculpting. Jourdain, the man, he's brought it to life, he gave it a face."

Orisia peers down by my feet. "Is that what you've brought? The thing in that box?"

"I don't want you scared when I'm taking this out, but I need you to look at it. We're a little confused to who he is."

I see Orisia's nervous as she shakes ever lightly. "I don't know. I'm not sure I can do this."

"Miss Laroque, please."

Ghislain adds, "All you've got to do is look. You don't need to hold it or anything like that."

"Just for a minute, but please, I ask you then put it away."

I lean to my feet where the crown remains masked. Then, carefully, I'm drawing it forth.

Before I finally reveal the man's face, I'm admitting to Orisia, "I had, for a period of time, considered that maybe this man was Tayce Rosin. It's time we hear what you think." I'm now turning the face in view of Orisia.

She gasps, then she's gasping again. "Yes, I know him, Detective, but that man isn't Tayce."

Calmly, I'm requesting, "Whose then? Whose is it?"

"Devereux. It's Basile Devereux."

"Yesterday, though, hadn't we seen him?"

"The man looked like him. Just exactly."

"Where did Basile live? Where'd he live when you knew him?"

"Just off Resident Road, on the corner of Church Street."

I'm having to think back in time, and to help with my knowledge, I'm having to open my tablet so I can peer at my scribble.

Quietly, and with much concentration, I'm starting to read. With- in a trunk, within his house, contains the head of a man from Spouse. It was kept, and it was safe, so no one knew the man's real fate. Beneath the dirt, within the ground, the bones remain without its crown. Only one may know this truth and, as it goes, I've chosen you.

Orisia said Basile lived on Church Street, but the document says the man lived on Spouse. "Not Spouse Road? He didn't live there?"

"No. It was Tayce who lived on Spouse," she says. But now she's shut up because I see that she's thinking. "Maybe I've mixed my facts?" She's doddering her head. "I have. I had them confused. It was Basile who lived on Spouse."

"You're sure?"

"I'm beginning to think so."

I'm expanding my questions. "Did he have a twin or someone he looked like?"

"Basile was an only child. There was no one but him."

"But the man at the bar. You didn't see, but when you said who he was, his face lost its color."

"He looked like Basile, that's why I spoke."

"Except for the eyes, maybe? Did the guy, the one who says he's Haulmier, did he have any distinct features you remember on Basile?"

"He did. There was the scar on his brow."

"Something else?"

"Ah, yeah. The same tiny mole near his lip."

"You feel sure that was him?"

"That's what I thought."

"But he spat another name. Had that changed your mind?"

"It left me confused. I was certain, just certain he was Basile I saw. But his eyes had me thinking; the color was wrong."

"All right." I'm thinking. "Are you familiar with a woman named Azure Cashlousier?"

She's shrugging. "Should I?" "You don't know her, okay." "Has she done something?"

"I'm still trying to figure that out."

Another minute passes and Mira appears on the stairs. Right away I know to be hiding the head.

"Aunty, can I come down now? I'm hungry."

"Yeah, honey. Come down, it's okay."

I conclude time's come and us men should be leaving.

"You've got things to be doing, Miss Laroque, so we'll let you get to it."

After standing from my seat, Marin and Ghis do the same.

Duplessey reports, "We'll be in touch, Orisia. Get Mira fed. I'm hearing her stomach."

"You can all stay. You don't have to be leaving."

"We've got work, honey. A ton of hard work. But we'll call or be back." Ghislain speaks calmly.

Orisia shakes in agreement as we're being escorted. Then, slowly the door closes and we go on our way.

Chapter Sixty-Nine

I'm resting at my desk and, like a burnout, I'm yawning. Then, there's Marin, who, while sitting at his, attempts to do work. I can't speak for him, what he's doing, but apparently his mind's set in thought.

I'm turned in my chair and I'm watching him write.

"What's he up to?" asks old slick.

"Something. Don't know." I decide to inquire, "Marin, what're you writing? You commencing a novel?"

He's holding his hand up and it sways in the air. "We'll talk in a minute."

I know I'm being told to cease my request. So not to bother him, I simply overlooked that he's here.

I realize, pending the time we've stepped in the business, I've heard no word from Dr. Ignace. He may have phoned earlier, but, of course, we'd all been absent. So thinking impertinently, I pick up my phone.

I call the hospital with hopes that I'll catch him. Soon as the phone's ringing, Roman picks up.

"Doc, hey, it's Satordi."

"Bout time. Why hadn't you stopped in?"

"Got caught up in an additional mess of things. We'll not dwell on that. Rather, you got any news?"

"None that can help you. I've studied those bones over and over, and I can't find further evidence besides what we've got."

"This has me upset."

"I know you're wanting to compare the remains to the skull. We'll have time, but once that's completed, I'm not sure there's more we can do."

"Tomorrow, then. I'll bring it by."

"Well, okay. But anytime before noon."

Guess we'll find out whether the bones from Rhoe's casket will, in fact, sustain this empty think tank I've got propped on my desk.

Julien Kade

If it's no match, then it's just I consider tossing this case. I've about had enough. This plausibly could be the last straw. It'd thereon be up to Ghis and Marin to decide what to do.

I peer to Duplessey. "We see Roman tomorrow."

"Was there anything new he was able to say?"

"You'd see I'd be bouncing off walls if there was." "So, just another damper in the road, then, huh?"

I'm sluggishly shaking my head, then for some reason, I'm shouting, "Marin, pull away from your desk and come have a chat."

"Give me a few. I'll be along."

"No, you come now. Stop acting busy. What're you doing?"

"Anagrams."

"All this time I thought you'd been working?"

"Nope. Nope, I'm just passing some time."

Hmm, I think. Anagrams? It's a far-fetched thought, but I'm beginning to wonder, could Haulmier Guloe be one? Then I'm thinking again, there's no way it could be, could it?

"Everyone." I crazily shout, "Get paper, get pens. Write Haulmier Guloe. See what anagrams you find."

Suddenly, I'm seeing my brother's head popping up. "You're looking for something, aren't you?"

"Something. Anything."

Upon a tablet of paper, I pen Guloe's name. It'll serve as reference while I'm rearranging the text, so let's see what I get.

Aerie Gum Hullo. Loamier Glue Uh. Lame Lieu Rough. Laugh Rile Moue. Hula Rouge Lime. Glamour Eh Lieu.

Oh brother, this is bull. Absolutely, simply bull. "Marin," I request. "You getting anything, you or Ghis?"

"A whole lot of nothing," my brother's responding.

"Don't ask unless you're wanting to hear Lea Guile Humor." Ghis wittingly responds. "Or Gallium Hue Roe."

"Wait," my response is coming quickly. "Wait, what'd you say? What's the last thing you said?"

"Gallium Hue Roe?"

My mind's racing as I'm jotting those words. I rearrange them sev-

393

eral times, then finally, damn it, finally, ha-ha, I've written his name.

"Keep your shirts on, brothers. I've got him. I know who he is. Ha-ha." With release I am laughing. "Read it."

While Ghislain peers over, Marin's stepping foot to my desk.

Again, I'm saying, "Read it."

"Does that..." Ghislain pauses. "It says—"

"Guillaume Rhoe," Marin belts.

I explain, "Haulmier Guloe's a disguise. Guillaume Rhoe changed his name. How bout you eat on them apples? That quack brain's been busted."

"No. No-no." Ghislain confesses, "Being side by side with him, long as I was, I knew how he looked."

"Ghis. Ghis, Guloe is Rhoe. Look at the anagram."

"Boss. Boss, trust me. His face ain't the same."

I know it's him, granted Ghislain's doubt. I've never felt more sure than I am at this moment. I'm understanding now. Took long enough, but I've finally got it.

"Guillaume faked his death to start a new life and, only way he knew, was to bump Basile off. He schemed a plan so complex that he duped the whole town. Guillaume fled after Deveruex was buried. After having stolen the dead man's identity, Rhoe was determined he'd obtain a new title."

"Then he had to have known someone," my brother submits, "who could construct Basile's face."

My brother's right. Suddenly I'm looking to Ghislain as I'm quickly responding, "Charlize Rousseau. She was working toward her medical license. If anyone could have helped Rhoe, she'd been the one. Charlize Rousseau is Azure Cashlousier, I bet you my money."

Ghis, catching on quickly, supplicates, "Want me to see if it's an anagram?"

"Check it."

I give slick a few moments before he returns with an answer, "Mmm-hmm. Yap. Yap, boss, you're right."

"I'd have taken it all had you bet me your money."

"How'll we handle them?"

"Seeing I'm not done with those clods, I'm thinking we get them."

"Whatever you do, make sure that I'm there."

"Mmm." I nod to show I'm agreeing. "Let's wrap this shit up. We'll be back here tomorrow."

Upholding me, Ghislain adds, "Let's get this news to Ambrielle and her mother."

"No way will they be left in the lurch. If you boys ain't tired, how bout you come with me?"

As intended, we've gathered our things, then head through the door.

Chapter Seventy

I'm kicking my shoes and getting them off, then, thrusting them beneath the table before me, I push them aside.

My intention's to be completely relaxed before surrendering my voice to the discoveries within me.

Desirably, I'm directing, "Everyone, please, come take a seat." I wait till they've all seated themselves before emitting my speech. "We've had a good deal of information accede us today. Most of which has been credibly shocking." On account of what I'll be saying, I realize I'll need to report. "Before breaking in to these revelations, I'd like to ask that Holland be removed from this room."

Yasmina peers to me with a look of concern. "You want her upstairs?"

"Please."

She rubs her child's back. "Holland, baby, would you mind, just for a while?"

"Can I go out back, mama, and play there instead?"

Confused whether she should let her, Yasmina decides to put her gaze upon me. "Would it be all right?"

"She can. Just make sure you stay there," I'm then telling Holland.

"Go on, peanut. Mama will get you afterwhile."

With the room filled with nothing but adults, I decide to carry forth my delivery. "It dispirits me, Mrs. Guloe, having to inform you and your daughter of this, but in respect of you both, I know these are things which must necessarily be spoken. Therefore, I'll aware you. Your estranged husband's name is Guillaume Rhoe. It was changed sometime back. Formally he'd been a cop and was in love with a woman. Angry she wouldn't accept his affections, he decided he'd kill her."

I'm seeing both Ambrielle and her mother's mouth droop in shock.

"The woman was a young widow named Yria Dane. Before having married her late husband Matthias, Yria was involved with a man named Basile Devereux. Guillaume was extremely jealous of this man and wanted him dead."

Ghislain helps me explain, "Recurrently Basile tried pursuing Yria following her loss. Problem was, Guillaume wanted her, too. Additionally, having had his hatred built, Rhoe was determined that he'd also kill Basile."

"Guillaume did, all right; he knocked the man off. In occurrence to that, he faked his death, then used Basile's body in place of his own."

Yasmina pulls her hand toward her heart. "I knew he was bad, but to have killed innocent people? And looking back at myself and my daughter, he beat us. He raped us repeatedly. Eventually, Detective, he'd have buried us all."

"I have to ask, had you known his real name?"

Yasmina's shaking her head. "Nothing ever occurred to me. I had no idea."

"Mama." Ambrielle rubs her mother's shoulder. "Mama, don't you think it's time we should tell?"

What's she talking about? Tell what? Ambrielle's not only put me, but my comrades in a position where we're feeling confused.

"He was never my husband," Yasmina confesses.

Not her husband? "You weren't legally married? But you lived together?"

"No. Well, yes, but not how you think. A few years ago Ambrielle and I were staying with my mother, who was recovering from surgery. Our plans were to stay a week and tend to her. During that time my daughter and I noticed a strange man following us during our visits to town. Somehow, I don't know, he knew we were out, and it wasn't by accident that we'd always be seeing him. He was stalking us. Watching us, and he knew where we stayed." Yasmina breaks down as her eyes become teary. "He, ah, he came to the house one night. Everyone was sleeping. My mother, me, Ambrielle. No one heard a thing as he broke through a window. He came to where my daughter and I slept and put rags on our faces. When we woke, we found ourselves shackled to his basement wall. Ambrielle was just a small girl."

"Why hadn't you said something sooner?"

"I just didn't. Maybe it's shame that's kept me from speaking."

"But it wasn't your deeds which caused these events."

"No. But still I felt fault for not protecting my daughter."

"You've kept her alive, haven't you?"

Grievously, she wails, "Yes. But things have been stolen that she'll never get back."

"Mama. Mama, please, don't squall."

"I can't help it. For two years he kept us locked in that basement. It'll always be in my head what I saw. Handing you to those filthy men. Touching you all those times, he did. There I was screaming for him to let you be."

"But, mama, mama, you went through the same thing."

"I dealt with what he did to me. Unlike you, I'd been a grown woman. I couldn't deal with what he'd done to my child."

Meanwhile, Holland's by herself in the yard where she's playing alone. There's hardly much this young girl can do, so to keep herself occupied, she's climbing a tree.

Five feet away, Holland spots a woman strolling alone through the alley. She wears a peachy-pink dress with black trim, and upon her feet are a pair of raven-hued shoes.

Though her skin's pale, her cheeks appear rosy from a tint of pink rouge. Her blue eyes, as Holland notices, are overtly phenomenal, and Holland finds herself captured in marvel.

"Hi," the child speaks to this mysterious wanderer.

Suddenly, without warning, two birds descend from the sky, then pass to the ground.

"What happened to them?" Holland peers below to the grass. "Birdies. Oh, the poor birdies. They fall down."

"They've fallen, they have. But they'll be okay, child. God takes them to heaven."

"I don't want them to die."

"That is nature, dear child. Even birds have their cycle."

Holland tucks her chin to her chest. "But their mommy birds will miss them."

"And will be missed very much. But they're gone, child, gone. It's an operation of nature."

"I don't like it."

"I know, child. But it's how nature appoints changes."

Another pair of birds then descend to the ground once the woman stops speaking.

Holland looks upon the other two as her face extends sadness.

"How about a game, little girl? I've brought something with me. It might, if you let it, take your mind from this sadness." The woman stretches her arm and, within her hand, is a box. "Come, child, join me. I'll teach you what's done."

"Mama doesn't want me leaving the yard. Will you come through the gate?"

The woman treads through and is joining young Holland. "Make sure you're comfortable. It'll be easier for us."

Meanwhile, back inside, we're unaware Holland's made a new friend, so not feeling distraught over things we don't know, we've sim- ply gone forth to progress our discussion.

At some point Guillaume unshackled Ambrielle and her mother. As mentioned by Yasmina, they'd been kept in his basement where they lived for two years. What happened afterward? "Apparently Guillaume considered it safe and took you upstairs."

"Only for the fact we got him to trust us. Eventually we were moved. But, of course, his scandalous business remained very active. Seemed like more men than ever had come for coitions."

"When did Holland arrive through all this?"

"During the first year. I quickly got pregnant. Nine months later she was birthed in his basement. Of course, it wasn't until she was two that he allowed us upstairs."

"Is she his, do you know?"

"Yes."

"You said you were staying with your mother the time this all happened?"

"I assumed mother thought she'd been abandoned. Sadly, a week after my daughter and I were taken, she starved in her bed."

"And you know this because?"

Yasmina wipes away tears. "I read it in a paper. Haulmier hadn't granted many luxuries, but he did give us that."

"My gosh, I'm so sorry."

"Mmm." She dodders her head. "My husband was about the only person searching for us. He assumed, eventually, his wife and child were dead."

This plot just took another twist. Seems, after all, Yasmina was married. "Who's your husband?"

"Oh, a lovely man. Audric Badeau."

Taken by surprise, Marin leans forth in his seat where he listens ever providently.

"We live in Marseille. I recently returned and, after several years, found him still living in the home we had made."

With his eyes intently upon her, Marin gives question, "You're Mrs. Audric Badeau?"

"Yes."

"Your husband contacted me. I've gone all over trying to find you."

"Audric hired you?"

"I was told you ran off with Christoph."

"Ran away? No. I returned to him. Christoph's my husband. Audric Christoph Badeau."

"From Savoie?"

"That's where he hails from. His family's there."

"Why had your husband lied to me, then?"

"What makes you think you'd done business with my husband?" "He told me who he was, and that you ran off and abandoned your daughters."

"I'll tell you now that wasn't my husband."

"Then who've I been talking with?"

"Guillaume Rhoe," I'm advising my brother. "He worked us both. There he was sending you off to find Yasmina while petitioning me to search for her daughter. We didn't know, but we were working for the same man, you and I."

"You're not really thinking that? Satordi, come on."

"Try this for thought. Jourdain wondered if his sculpture looked like anyone we knew. What was it you said? Can you remember?"

"He had a familiar look, was what I said."

"Like you had seen him. Then you affirmed the man you knew was alive, wasn't that right?"

"That's what I said."

"Whose face, Marin? Whose is it?"

"Audric Badeau's."

"When contacting you, Guillaume lied and said he was Audric. When Orisia looked upon him, she thought he was Basile. But we've got the skull; it belongs to Deveruex. So, if the man you know as Audric had the same face, wouldn't that be telling you something?"

"You've just confused me to death, what you've said."

"Confusing, yes. But here's how it goes. Rhoe's been playing all these people, Audric Badeau to you, Haulmier Guloe to me, you following this?" I await the flit of his head. "Then there's the identity he'd stolen from the very face of a man he had killed. He looks like Basile Deveruex, we know, but the man isn't him. Then here I have you telling me the man you know as Audric has an uncanny resemblance to Basile. Tell me, Marin, wouldn't you figure that as evidence saying we know the same man?"

He's quick to come back, "I want to be sure."

"Then you take us by and we'll see."

"Now?"

"I don't care. But one way or another we'll be seeing him, count my words."

Yasmina rings her hands as she's asking, "Will he be arrested for these crimes he's committed?"

"Just as soon as I get him to admit what he's done."

"What if he's bullheaded? He's not the type man who admits to his faults."

"I'll press him enough. He'll be pushed into a corner and admitting his sins. No longer can he lie. I know plenty. I can nail him real quick."

"Don't hold off any longer. It's time you get him. My daughters and I, we're wanting our lives back. You can make that happen. Please, Detective, tell me you'll help us."

"We've made it thus far, we're not turning back. We'll go tonight,

Marin, Ghislain, and I. He won't know we're coming. We'll get him, I know. We'll make him confess."

"Send my regards. Tell him to rot."

"I'll give your regards. I'd be happy to tell him."

Yasmina turns to Ambrielle where she takes her in arms. "It's going to be over. We'll finally be free. You, me, Holland; we'll be free, baby, free."

I'm sure this is a moment that should be shared with them all. "I'll grab Holland and bring her inside."

"Please, Detective. Please bring me my girl."

I head to the back yard, yelling, "Holland. Holland, time to come in." But I don't catch her in sight. "Holland? Holland, honey, where are you?"

I continue through the yard where I'm yelling. However, unusual-ly, she has not answered back.

"Holland?"

I come upon a tree when I see a strange sight. Birds, birds everywhere, all dead on the ground. What's done this? I wonder.

I kneel to my knees where I'm examining each carcass. Peculiarly, as I look, I'm finding no trauma. For no real reason they just fell from the sky and have all landed here.

After seeing this, I sense something's wrong.

"Holland? Holland, this isn't time for games. Honey, where are you?" I trail the yard, searching frantically. "Holland? Holland?"

I hear the back door and, suddenly, I turn. Approaching me, I see Ambrielle.

"Mama sent me. She thought you'd need help." "I can't find your sister. I've looked all around." "Hmm? What do you mean you can't find her?"

"I can't find her. I've looked."

"She's probably just hiding, sir. I'll help you check."

Ambrielle trails to another section of the yard, but I'm shouting out to her, "No. No, I've already checked there."

"She likes hiding in bushes. But you say she's not here?"

"I can't, I don't know? I'm not sure where she's at."

"Holland? Holland?"

"Keep searching," I advise her. "I'm going to look here."

"Holland? Holland? Holland, come on, mama wants you inside."

Holland knew to stay in the yard. Where's she gone? The only thought in my mind has me thinking of Rhoe. Could he have found she was here? Yasmina will freak once she learns what's happened.

Behind me a wrenching shriek fills the air.

"Ambrielle? Ambrielle?" I take off running.

Just beside the alley, the young maiden stands near a tree. As I'm coming upon her, she points, and her screams come hysterically. "She's not moving! Holland! Holland!"

Ever cautiously I ease toward the tree where I take in the sight. "Jesus." I'm gasping. "Ambrielle, move away. Clear back. Hon, clear back."

She takes my direction, but runs for the house.

Below the prospered leaves and rejected bark, Holland's body lie propped along the trunk. Eerily her eyes are strung like broad saucers. Both appear glazed beyond their lost vision. Her slight-sized lips, as I look down to see, are fixed in the most affrighting bemoan. Above her, her tiny hands reach frozen atop her small face. She tried, she did, to safeguard herself from what was coming. Akin to the likes of her late family, Holland, too, has been riddled with holes. Not one lick of blood was spared. Much the same as all those before her, the poor child's been bled, empty. Her vessel remains dry where it rests without life.

Behind me runs Yasmina who's crying and screaming.

"No-No-No! Not Holland. Not my baby! She's not gone, Satordi, tell me she's not." She squalls uncontrollably.

"Honey, stay there. Please stay over there."

Just as quickly as she's come, I'm seeing the others.

"She can't be by herself. She needs her mother. Satordi, she needs me!"

"Yasmina. Yasmina, honey, you can't come here."

"No. No-no-no." She falls to her knees. "God, why? Why? Holland's my baby."

Ambrielle's arriving beside her as she pulls her mom in. "I'm here. Cry on me, mama. I'm here."

"Honey, this isn't happening. Tell me it isn't. I can't breathe. Where's your sister? Take me to Holland. I need to see Holland."

"Stay, mama. Please stay with me, please." My

gal rushes alongside them.

"Dej," I'm yelling. "Don't let her come, baby. Keep her with you." Marin advances me. "Jesus, brother, what's been done to this girl?" "Make sure, Marin, Yasmina don't cross here. You know well as I, she's not needing to see this."

I feel a pat on my back as I'm now seeing Ghis.

"I'll see if I can't find a towel, at least. She needs to be covered."

I notice upon the ground the empty box that contained Yria's curse. As far as I know nothing came here. So how, I ask, had this crossed to her hands? It's too late now to ask. Holland has not a breath to deliver her words.

I gather the objects that belong with the box and I return them inside it. As I'm casting these unlucky items away, I wonder how Holland could have read these cursed pages? To me that is puzzling. Could Yria have helped her? I guess I'll not know.

"Marin, get Yasmina to the house. I don't want her out here."

"We need to call someone. That child's body needs taking care of." I'm handing my brother a piece of paper containing Roman's digits. "Call Dr. Ignace. Tell him what's happened. Make sure he comes now."

"Here, boss," I'm hearing Ghislain. "I found a towel. I'll get her wrapped."

"Don't do that, no. Cover her instead."

"It sure is tragic, boss, seeing this child. She was a nice little kid. She doesn't deserve death."

"I thought she was safe, slick. I thought they all were. Cover her feet, if you can."

Ghislain recites as he abides my direction, "Lord, we send home this young soul and ask that you protect her in all the glory of heaven. Amen."

"Amen."

Beside the tree Ghislain spots something, then is bending to get it. "Recognize this?"

"Another box?"

"And unopened, too. Here, you look."

I'm scratching my head. "Why would two boxes be here?" Holland opened one. "This one's untouched." I flip it around to spy on a name. "It's addressed to Rhoe," I speak aloud. "What do you suppose?"

"There's a note, too."

Letters always have something to say, and this one reads, "Deliver to Guillaume."

Ghislain raises his brow. "Guess Yria's wanting you to take this?"

"I'll take it, all right. Rhoe will have it tonight."

"That's one way to finish it."

"It's making him do it; that'll be the challenge."

"You're smart, boss. You'll figure a way."

A few minutes later Marin walks with Roman as they come through the yard.

"What in God's name's gone on here?"

"Tragedy, Doc. We can't have the police. They won't understand."

"Who's the victim?"

"Holland Rhoe. She was right here when we found her."

Roman emits while peering upon the veiled body, "Jesus, Satordi, she's only a child. Who did this?"

I speak no words as I'm nodding.

"And you won't get the cops?"

"Can't. This was a preternatural occurrence. They won't understand."

"What happened, though? Had you seen?"

"I didn't, but I'm sure what occurred."

"I'll need a minute to examine the body."

"What you'll see will confuse you, I already know."

Roman bends as he's removing the cover; then, having unveiled the body, I see that he shudders.

"Good God."

"You won't find blood. It's all been taken."

"I've seen this, Satordi. I've seen this in cases I recently had. They all were like this. I tried, I did rationally, but I couldn't submit my conclusion. You say what happened. You tell me what made these punctures."

"It might be best you not know."

"Don't go telling me that. We're friends, Satordi. I need to know."

"This puts me in a tough spot, you realize that, right?"

"However tough it may be, I still need to know."

Though I'm reluctant, I'll admit I must tell him, "Veins, Doc. It was veins that attacked her."

"What did this, really?"

"I done told you."

"Just tell me what did this."

Marin, my savior, steps in. "That's the truth, Dr. Ignace. My brother hasn't lied."

"You, too, you're sticking with that?"

"We're not sticking to nothing but facts."

"That's fine. I'm sure to have the truth given time."

"It's the truth," Ghislain says. "What's your explanation?"

"Don't have one."

Roman's rigid, I see that. So, rightfully, it's fair for him to believe what he wants. Purely, this just lacked his belief. So, I say, "Knock it off, guys. Doc's just not ready. Give him room. Let him work."

Eventually, Ambrielle, Dej, and Yasmina come to the yard. Thankfully Holland was put away before they appeared.

I walk to Mrs. Badeau. "You holding up, honey?" I'm pulling her toward me as I wrap her in hugs.

She cries to my shoulder. "All I did was send her outside. Never did I think this tragedy would happen. I told Holland last night that I loved her. I wasn't able to tell her today."

"She knows you love her. She hears when you say it."

"You think?"

"Oh, honey, yes, absolutely."

"I don't know how I'll deal with her loss."

"There's people around you. We'll help you get through this."

"I just feel so broken."

"You're not alone. We're feeling it, too."

"Holland liked you and Deja. She really did like you."

"We may not have known her for long, but that little girl wiggled her way into our hearts."

"Mmm." She tries drying her tears.

"I'll pay for her services, whatever you choose."

"It's only right to have her cremated. In that, I can take her home."

"We can do that. Whatever you want. We'll make sure to get a beautiful urn."

"I'm not sure how to thank you."

"Dr. Ignace will be taking her. He'll prepare everything for a final viewing. Would that be all right?"

"Mmm-hmm, yeah."

"He'll let us know once the body's prepared."

Roman overhears and comes to my side. "Shouldn't be more than a few days, ma'am. I'll get in touch with Satordi. He'll let you know."

Yasmina's totters her head to agree.

Doc says, "I'm taking her on now to New Hope. I'll call when I can."

I gather everyone and take them back to the house. "I just want to lie down," Yasmina acknowledges.

Ambrielle grasps her mother's arm. "I'll take mama to her room."

"Sure. Sure, and I'm coming, too," Deja responds.

"Good idea. Stay with them. We'll be leaving soon as Ghislain comes in."

"Now? Satordi, you can't be leaving. Not with what's happened."

"We've got to find Rhoe. Baby, I've got to."

"I don't believe you, you leaving like this. But you'll do what you will. So don't be doing nothing stupid. Please, Satordi. I'm asking nicely."

"Hon, it's all right."

"Don't you lie. Please, Satordi, I don't want to hear it."

"Dej. Honey, it's got to be done."

"Then you do me a favor and stay out of trouble. I don't want to hear of you being locked up."

"I'll be good, okay? But Ambrielle and her mom, they're needing you. Go."

I trail off to the living room and see Ghis at the door.

"Roman left?"

"Yeah, boss. Where's everyone gone?"

"Upstairs. You boys ready?"

"I've gotta piss real quick," my brother's responding.

Literally, I'm unsure how this'll go down with Rhoe, but I'm anxious, I feel it. I haven't any concept to think what I'll say; it'll come unrehearsed. Whatever happens, happens. I can't predict the future nor can I imagine its upshot. All I can do is go with the order of things as they come. Thereon, may the Lord help us should this situation get grody.

Chapter Seventy-One

So, here we are. I've brought us to Frenchman's. Rather than having Marin, I decided to bring us. I know from past knowledge Rhoe's usual- ly here and, if we wanted to find him, this would be the best spot.

I'm allowing my degenerate proclivity to fully take over so my mood can be altered. Guillaume better understand when he sees me, I'm not a man to be messed with, so he better not bother.

I've brought a little gift, something I'm sure will be hanging him up, Basile's face. Let's see how Guillaume decides to escape this, should he try.

I storm through the door with Ghislain and Marin a step from my back, then, like a roaring madman, I set loose to my blaring, "Bar's closed! Everyone out. Get out!" I then spot the crummy drink slinger with Charlize and Guillaume as they stand near the counter. "Except for you three, I want everyone out."

"What do you think you're doing, Detective? You've no place rushing in and being rid of my patrons."

"Marin, lock the door. Ghis, close the blinds."

Guillaume comes around from the counter. "I demand to know what's going on."

"Sit your ass down. Sit. Sit it down! You, too, missy, you sit that little hind. You, me, the boys, we're going to have a long talk."

With a sudden lurch, the bartender goes for the phone.

"Hey! Hey-hey-hey, I didn't tell you to move. Don't none of you try, I'll stick you each quick."

Guillaume yells to the man, "Artus." He's shaking his head. Then, with calmness, he's turning toward me. "All right, Detective, you've got our attention."

"Yeah. Yeah, I've got it, all right. An hour ago Holland was killed. You like hearing that? Hurts, don't it, Rhoe?"

"Holland's not dead. How would you know?"

"Yasmina sends her regards."

"Yasmina's right here, or have you suddenly gone blind?"

"Charlize Rousseau, that's who's beside you. Don't think me as lame. I've figured you out, Guillaume. I know who you are."

Guillaume's flaring his nostril and deciding to lie. "I haven't any idea what you're saying."

"Course you do. Want me to explain how I know?"

"You ain't got nothing on me, Biertempfel."

"Marin. Marin, come on over. Get a good look at that face. Who's this you're seeing?"

"Audric Badeau, brother. That's what he said."

"Right. Right, Audric Badeau. Told you, didn't he, his wife left with Christoph."

"Audric Christoph Badeau, that's what Yasmina had told me."

"How bout cutting the crap, Rhoe? We know who you are. I know what you've done. I know how you did it." I reach for Basile's skull as I want to present it. "I've got an old friend I want you to see. You remember Mr. Devereux, this man you killed?"

Sharply, Guillaume responds when floored by this startling panoply, "Where'd you get that?"

"Ah, finally, I've got your attention. I earnestly do wonder, do you enjoy Basile's face? Looks to me, Char's done a fine job."

Again, Guillaume asks, "Where'd you get that?"

"The trunk, where you left it. I suppose it's a haunting reminder. Better be more careful next time. Anyway, how's it feel now you've been knocked in a corner?"

"Ask all you want. You'll never find Yria."

"Careful with your words, Rhoe, she's liable to find you."

"Trying to scare me, Detective, won't cut it. I have a sound mind. Nothing daunts me."

"Remember what you'd done with her flesh?" As I'm envisioning the vexation, my head begins shaking. "That was some unnatural thing you had done. I found it real trippy."

"You have no idea what pleasures I had." He closes his eyes. "I remember her skin, how lovely it felt. How soft it was and scented so lightly. And if I wasn't so crazy, I'd say I still smelt her."

"You're a sick man, Mr. Rhoe."

"Did you touch Yria? Did you grab her skin?"

"Jesus, you're not just sick; you're twisted all through".

"Guess that's what love does."

"It turned you to this?"

"That kike wouldn't have me. I merely did what was right."

"It didn't justify your situation."

"It gave me peace."

"How the hell could you be talking of peace?"

"Men. Their infatuations. I wasn't about to be dealing with that. Yria was supposed to be mine. I wanted her. As much as I tried, she just wouldn't love me."

"That's your clarification?"

"You know if I couldn't have her, no other man would."

"And Basile? He did nothing to you."

"We loved the same woman."

"Yria was gone. So why go after him?"

"Memories. I'd look at Basile and always I'd see her. I hated that man."

"He was innocent. How could you kill him?"

"To stop my torment. It had been my one option."

"And to not be caught, you faked your own death. Additionally, thereafter, you stole Basile's face. You did one final thing by changing your name. Had everything you done really been worth it?"

"I'd do it again if I had to."

"But, of course, you would. Basile's body's with the coroner. It should be yours lying there."

"But it's not."

"Should be. What'd you do, Rhoe? What'd you do to that man?"

He smirks and begins telling, "Saw him one night on his way home. Said I had something to say. So he came to my steps. Basile didn't know, but I had a rag, the same used on Yria. It was full of ether and, well, I pushed it to his face. Of course, after knocking him out, I drug him through the house and pulled him to the basement. I didn't know at the time what I was planning to do with the man. He woke awhile later and was trying to get up, so instinctively I took a sledge hammer and began socking the fool upon his stomach and chest. I could hear his pain as was I squatted on top him. I don't know what drove me to do it, but before I knew, I had a knife in my hand and I was sawing his throat. He tried to fight, but it was me who had power. I can't even say how long I'd been mowing his neck until his head had come off."

Guillaume continues the rest of the story, telling us he'd clothed Basile in some garb which was his. He wanted Basile found, so Rhoe concocted a plan. Guillaume owned a small boat which he kept at a dock. He hurled Basile into the water, then left him there, floating. Basile Devereux was found the next day. Thing was, people thought he was Guillaume.

As formulated, Rhoe went into hiding. He had one person to whom he trusted, Charlize Rousseau. It was a mighty challenge, but he asked that she surgically alter his face and prepare him to the likeness of the man he had killed.

Charlize had, and still does, a great deal of care for Guillaume. She didn't think twice before she did as he'd asked. If Rhoe's been able to control and influence anyone, it's her. I'm starting to consider what association Char's had in the disappearance of Yria Dane.

Flat out, I find myself drilling them both. "I know, we all do, what you'd done to Yria. But what had been done with her bones?"

Before Guillaume speaks, Charlize explains what she contributed, "Guillaume didn't know. He didn't know what to do. It was me who suggested Yria be incinerated. Admission to the incinerator was easy because I had access. And so it was me who took her remains to the hospital. I'd been the one to clean up his mess. Looking back I realize these were things I should've never been bound to."

"Charlize." Guillaume grabs her wrist and begins squeezing tightly. "You don't feel that. You can't. You helped. You helped me!"

"It was wrong, Guillaume. I was wrong. I loved you and that blinded me. Everything I worked for, everything, was lost because I chose to clean your damn mess. I'm done, Guillaume. I'm no longer your puppet. I'm walking away and I'm taking Artus."

"Then take your son. Get out of here."

"We're going to the authorities. Something I should've done a long time ago, Guillaume."

"You stupid witch. You go there, you know you're facing hard time."

"I'd rather do that than be stuck here with you."

I'm telling Charlize, "We'll let you out, you and your son. But you're to turn yourself in. If I learn that you haven't, you better expect that I'll find you. Marin. Marin, get that door open, then lock it back up."

"Traitor," Guillaume yells. "You ain't nothing but that."

"You shut your trap," I'm snapping on Rhoe. "Marin, let them out." "Aren't you wanting to hear what I'd done to Miss Yria? Can't very well shut my trap if you do."

"I know what you did. You took a mother away from her child and a sister away from Orisia."

"If Yria hadn't been out that night it may have not happened, what I did."

"It happened, nonetheless. I've had a glimpse into your mind, Guillaume. I know how it functions."

"Care to share details?"

"Why? So you can bear in mind what you'd done?"

"I'd like to know is all."

"You followed Yria as she was leaving that night. You ragged her with ether and, before you could kill her, she cursed your whole family. That's why everyone's died. Little Holland suffered, Guillaume. Your daughter suffered. It was horrible, it was, seeing how she was. You want me to tell, so you'll know how she looked?"

For the first time I think I'm actually seeing tears in his eyes.

"You think I'm a monster. But for the bit of hominal tenacity I have, I'd rather not know."

Marin slaps his hand to the counter. "Go on, Satordi, give it to him. I want you to tell."

"Yeah, boss. Your brother's right. Tell him."

"Let him know, Satordi. Tell him how his daughter died."

"Marin."

"Holland was horrified," my brother begins shouting.

"Marin. Marin, don't," I try to persuade him.

Willfully my brother ignores me. "I have children, Rhoe. I know what that would've done had I seen mine like that."

"Detective, stop. Stop it," I hear Rhoe's response.

"You should've seen all the holes in her body."

"Marin!" I'm shouting. "Cut it out. Will you stop?"

Of course, there he goes. "That child was bloodless and screaming for help."

"You've said enough. My daughter's gone and for me there's nothing."

I'm pulling forth the box that's to be given to Rhoe. "Make your peace, Guillaume. It's time this is over."

"What, a gift?"

"Call it amity. It's a solution to settle your errors."

Slowly, Rhoe opens its contents. "What's this mess?"

"It'd been left beside your daughter, and we're not leaving till you've done as it says."

"I'll not partake in such crap."

"Oh, you will, so you better get on it."

Guillaume sets the pair of candles upon his counter, followed by two oranges and an ironstone basin.

He then reads aloud the first parchment. "For centuries and decades, before my time and even yours, people told stories around the world that were bore from specks of truth. They reach through generations, stretching successfully along their course, but, through their reining span in time, tales often lose their trace of fact. From their retells told throughout the ages, persons find they alter stories, to declare them new or up-to-date, but there will always be one story, a bereaved tale to stay unchanged, and that's the yarn of Yria Dane."

Though he tries to retain it, Guillaume appears rattled. I'm sensing his fear as it expands through his eyes.

"There's more," I advise him. "I suggest you keep going."

"You can't force me, Detective."

"Wanna bet? There's three against one. You know you won't win."

"Torture me, then."

"You're sure you want to take it that far?"

Knowing I meant what I said, Guillaume's voice then breaks as he's upholding each word. "When the moon is high and in sight of your window, flow your basin with running water. Then, carefully, without spilling, set it upon your floor. This will serve as your doorway. In regard to the tapers, position one at each end of the dish. These symbolize the depiction of blood and flesh. Last, but important, your oranges. In front of your bowl, place them aside, leaving one with its skin, while the other, peeled. This will represent the body in its physical and non-physical form. Once your candles are lit, you're ready to begin. Read the poems supplied in the order they're given."

"Do it, Rhoe. Flow the basin with water."

"I'll not do this, Biertempfel. It's against my beliefs."

"I don't care that it is. You do as it says."

"Stop egging me. I told you I won't."

"You bullheaded snot. You're finishing this, you hear? You put this to rest. Marin, get water in that bowl, now." I look upon Guillaume and my eyes start to narrow. "You afraid you'll see something, Rhoe? Something might scare you, is that what you dread?" I draw my hand to both candles and I'm lighting the wicks. "Ain't no going back, buddy. This shit's been started. You face what you've done." I slip him the poems as they'd been given in sequence. "Read them." Then, from my pocket, I'm pulling my knife. "Pretty, ain't she? She's got a finely ground blade, with a deadly smooth point. My girl's keen." I breathe upon my cuspat- ed tool. "She's got a good shear. And, unlike the one used to decollate Basile, this baby's sharp. It'll take just a second and it'll be through your
hand. You don't get to reading, then your lefty gets lanced."

"All right! All right, I'll read the damn things. Don't stab me, okay?" The shoddy bloke's scared, it's apparent, we can see. As we listen to Guillaume, all his words emerge rambled.

An unnatural occurrence begins following the completion of the first poem. Steadily, above the basin, falling no more than fifteen inches, are garnet trills of phantom blood.

All of us, we watch forth in panic, then, thinking things can't become more dismaying, we watch as it does.

The unstripped orange gives rise to its skin as it's being shucked off, then, ascending through this rotund sweet rouse paunchy swells of fervent vessels.

I'm advising Guillaume, "The next poem. Get to it."

It's on his initial declaration that we're hearing crackles and pops set forth from the rushlights. Then, almost as though it'd been their direction, the flames shoot forth and rise to the air. As they restore their position, a horrifying sight impels its emission; from the wax, plopping down, are globs of baked flesh.

Jesus, I'm thinking, as I take a step back. My lips curve in disgust and my stomach feels sickened.

Before me, barreling down the counter comes a small dish of nuts. It reaches past Guillaume, then smacks to the floor.

In occurrence to that is an eruption of bottles exploding like bombs upon all of the shelves. Liquor pours everywhere, producing a mephitis of spirits. The malodor's so pungent its generated an overwhelming stench that's got us all gagging.

Within the air, from all directions, discharges a voice that spiels ever softly.

"For centuries and decades, before my time and even yours, people told stories around the world that were bore from specks of truth. They reach through generations, stretching successfully along their course, but, through their reining span in time, tales often lose their trace of fact. From their retells told throughout the ages, persons find they alter stories, to declare them new or up-to-date, but there will always be one story, a bereaved tale to stay unchanged, and that's the yarn of Yria Dane."

An exerting thrust then pushes upon the front door, forcing its expansion, and upon us a cooling blast circles while chastising our skin. Our steady placidity now turns to cold shivers as we're succumbing to gooseflesh.

A pair of bloodied red arms are now reaching behind Guillaume and, in the course, are stretching to his shoulders. Then, suddenly, I'm watching him stiffen.

Behind him his name is spoken through whispers.

Though he's credibly frightened, Rhoe decides to turn in his seat. It's upon this instant he's confronted by Yria, and so, peering upon her, he views her surrealistic shape.

An expansion of fiery-red muscle looms in his face, with a singular eye focused upon him. The other's nothing but a weeping socket, trilling gore and lurid horror.

Guillaume's breath surrenders at the very sight of her. He could try to fight, but his fears are too puissant, he can't even struggle.

Lifting away from Yria's body are a profusion of veins which grovel about.

With an impending whisk, her face draws to his. "Mind your blighted fact, your blood now pays for savage acts."

Dexterously, the invading vessels are clasping Rhoe's flesh and, like a drill, are digging through each tarpaulin coat. It takes Yria thirty seconds before she's bled him to death.

Now that his blood's ingested, Yria's image abruptly changes. It's before our very eyes that we're able to affirm it.

Fresh skin emerges where there'd only been muscle, and what was stripped flesh is no longer the issue of what we're now viewing.

From her scalp grows brown locks that cascade to her shoulders, and upon a short moment Yria closes her eyes, then, upon their exposure, we find ourselves confronted by two cerulean saucers. What we once viewed as grotesque and frightfully ugly now sways our appeal.

Since the Rhoe clan's gone, Yria can last find rest. It's been a long suspension that's kept her from this, but with conviction she's found it.

Rhoe remains in his chair with a look of fear suspended upon him. I knew, I had an inkling, he'd die at her hands. Yria's finally gotten what she's long since been seeking; Guillaume Rhoe, dead at last.

Remarkably, I'm trying to find enough courage to be voicing a question, but still I'm unhinged.

Yria, having ignored me this whole time, now steps in my direction. "You mustn't be afraid, Satordi. You've done your part and now it's over. The truth's been learned. Now take my flesh and have it buried. My sister's waiting."

After getting her point across, Yria fades before me.

"What do we do with Rhoe?" Ghis asks.

"We leave him. Someone else can find him."

"Drop me home, Satordi. I've seen enough tonight."

My brother's right; it's not only him who's seen things, we all have. Our minds have been marked with images we'll never forget. Hypnosis is likely our only solution to dismiss them from thought. However, as I'd acknowledge, it'd be a betrayal to Yria. Few people know the truth to what happened, and few have experienced her presence. As untoward as it was, we were, in fact, the ones who were chosen.

Chapter Seventy-Two

I stopped by New Hope earlier and spoke shortly with Roman. With me I'd taken Basile's sculpted dome. While there Dr. Ignace analyzed Mr. Deveruex's bones to that of his crown. I told him there's no reason to give his conclusion. I already figured who the body belonged to and that the head had gone with it, but, of course, Roman had to relay that it matched. Guess in a way I'm happy he did. Had Roman said no, then, like before, I'd be out trying to learn whose it was.

After arriving at the hospital last night, Roman immediately persisted on preparing Holland's body. I'm grateful that he acted so fast. He could've waited till today, but having seen Yasmina and viewing her pain, had him feel anguished. So in respect to Mrs. Badeau, Roman fig- ured it best to prep little Holland. Her wake will be held tomorrow in Deja's living room.

Yasmina called Audric this morning and told him what happened. Already he's packed his bags and is en route to Annecy. He'll be arriving tonight.

Also having been called was Lady Ancelin and Madame Voletta. After learning of Holland's death, they wept to the phone and could hardly believe it. Both sisters had cared much for the little girl, and it's in their earnest wishes they attend the wake to say their farewells.

Soon as the viewing's over, Roman will be returning Holland to New Hope, at her mother's request, to have her cremated.

For the first time the Badeau women can meander to town, but their reason for going is a tragic sad sense. I'd given money to Deja, advising she take both women to the nearest funeral parlor to acquire an urn, and if Yasmina's drawn to the most expensive they have, I recommended she get it.

About an hour ago, Marin, Ghislain, and myself stopped in to Orisia's. I told her Rhoe had been found, then explained what steps he applied to deceive the whole town. She now knows, as a matter of fact,

Basile Devereux's body being the one which was buried. All this was received as a shock.

In addition to Basile's remains, well, the city will be handling his reburial. Then, at last he'll have new ground to rest in. But evermore rightfully will be the gravestone above him, of which, shall be etched with his name.

My conversation then carried to my explanation of what happened to Yria. I told Orisia, finally, she can lay her to rest. I informed her of Charlize Rousseau's involvement with discarding the body. Sadly, the admittance of this had caused her more pain. Miss Laroque squalled upon my shoulder while asking me to disprove what I said. Learning Guillaume had an accomplice additionally proved to bewilder her more.

Hating that I had to tell Miss Laroque, I realized it was only fair to acknowledge the fact, one thing of Yria's remains to exist, the flesh which she wore. I didn't, however, communicate knowledge pertaining to the eye Guillaume stored. It was enough Orisia learned her sister's flesh had been kept.

Miss Laroque expressed she'd be buying a casket. In turn I advised having the remains sent to a funeral arranger. In addition I requested she not have the pall open. What'll be inside would more than devastate her and Mira. Having heeded my words, she revealed that she wouldn't. Concerning her procurement, I told Miss Laroque it's enough knowing your sister's come home.

With watery eyes she smiled, then thanked me.

It wasn't long after she asked where Rhoe was. Simply, I told her, your sister got even, then I left after that.

Marin requested he and Ghislain be dropped by his house. Afterwards I drove myself to Mr. Cartier's. Happily he was to be seeing me. He allowed me inside and, having gabbed over a few piping mugs of ink, we visited together.

It was time my honesty be lent to Pascal. So from the very beginning I told him the story.

I didn't want to alarm him saying Yria's flesh remained in his basement. Instead, I requested the rest of Rhoe's accouterments, so they may be rid from his house. Pascal agreed accordingly, and I nodded to that.

I'd taken Rhoe's trunk of shit to the alley. Soon as the garbage truck comes, that mess will be consigned to the dump. Who am I to care that it gets tossed to a cesspit?

I placed Yria, well, what was left of her, into a bag and, after leaving Pascal's, I'd gone to the funeral residence where Orisia had been.

After handing the undertaker the bag, I advised he call Miss Laroque to tell her it's come.

From the funeral home, I stopped by the station house to learn whether Charlize, indeed, turned herself in.

I was told she came last night and gave herself up. Charlize Rousseau's currently being charged with accessory and unlawful disposal of a body.

A few hours later I was accompanied to the train station by Ambrielle and her mother. Normally we sat till Audric showed up. I couldn't say who was more happy, Ambrielle or her father. For me, though, I'm not family, was an honor to witness.

After being introduced and getting to know the tall, sandy-headed man, I concluded I liked him. He's genuinely a great guy, and I'm glad now I met him.

Intra finishing the day, we'd reverted to Deja's and I'm now on the couch.

Deja, seeing I'm tired and incapable of beguiling our guest, took the incentive. She's made Audric as comfortable as possible, and as a fine host, she supplied him a room where he can be with his wife. An hour later they emerged after concluding their talk.

Dej offers to cook something and, even though the hour's late, she's ambitious to do it, knowing Audric hasn't eaten since he's been off the train.

I'd love to stay and chat, but I'm much too tired. My weariness has conquered me, and I prefer nothing than to fall to my bed.

No offense to those around me, but I'm barely able to keep my eyes from turning shut. I apologize, then head to my room as I relax on the sheets.

Chapter Seventy-Three

At one p.m. this afternoon Dr. Ignace arrived with Holland's body. He's no mortician, but rather a Jack of all trades and he's done a fine job. Yasmina's baby appeared like a sleeping angel. I'm thankful Roman was able to present her as that. Considering what we'd seen, it's hard to be- lieve the wonders he's worked.

Eventually, Marin showed with his wife and kids. Following him were the Bruel sisters and Mr. Duplessey.

The wake lasted an hour and a half. For the entire ninety minutes, Yasmina was glued to her child. As would be conceptualized, we all stood alongside her. More hugs than ever were remitted today, and so were our tears.

Following Holland's wake, Yasmina presented Dr. Ignace the urn which was purchased, a beautiful moss-green vessel, with gilded leaves and aurous blossoms.

The body was then taken to the hospital to be incinerated. Upon completion, her ashes will be returned to her mother and stepfather, who'll transmit her to their home in Marseille.

Though it's been a sad day, we've all agreed we've pulled ourselves through it. The loss of a child is one of the saddest misfortunes to suffer a family. Holland was an innocent youth, but it'd been her bloodline which wasn't. Guillaume Rhoe may have been the only fault in his fam- ily, but because of him, he contrived his kin's fate.

Chapter Seventy-Four

Roman dropped by Holland's urn yesterday. Yasmina was happy to get it, but still, having lost her child, remained sad. She, Audric, and Ambrielle stayed late into the night packing their things. Willingly, I offered to take them by the train station this morning. It turned out to be a grand farewell. My brother, Ghislain, Cerissa, the kids, they all followed in Marin's car while I drove the Badeaus' and my steady companion.

I must admit it was hard letting them go, especially Ambrielle, who'd become an instantaneous addition to our immediate family.

Hopefully we'll keep in touch by sharing visits and making calls. Normally clients make no effect upon me, but the Badeaus' are special and, for that reason, they've reached that result.

A few hours ago I found myself driving upon Rhoe's fallen bar. As I rode, I sighted unit cars throughout the whole street. I don't know who found Guillaume or what had gone on, but some person, maybe patron, had found him inside.

It had me floored, really, it'd taken this long to expose the dead lout. Why, I couldn't begin to imagine the stench in that place. The mephitis of alcohol coupled with the putridity of Guillaume's abasement would have the most stoutest of stomachs churned from revulsion.

Considerably, I figured his body would've been found the next day, so what happened? Rhoe had patrons who were in all the time. Had they gone for a drink, but found the place without light? Suspecting that, they'd have turned and left, not checking the door. But one person was wise and opened the hatch. Anyway, it's taken a couple days, but the bumpkin's been found. To that, I say, good riddance, damn chump.

Chapter Seventy-Five

Temporally, Marin and I decided on closing our business, but not before hiring ole Ghislain to be employed alsongside us full-time. With all the shit that's gone on, we're needing the break. Our women are happy we'd elected this choice. We now have more time on our hands, with less obligations to lure our request, and what a relief it's been to finally live without the daily grind of hustle and haste. Seriously, that was wearing me down. One day I'm home, the next I'm six hours from town. As I see, everyone deserves a breather; no matter what you do, you're still needing rest.

Now, as I may, I've been eager to mention a few words which have made me content. As of last night I've become a bound man. By bound, I'm meaning, I've gotten engaged. I'd been planning it and planning it, then the time finally came.

I had this sort of fanciful codification staged in my head. It was like a scene from a movie; it couldn't have gone better.

I stopped by the florist and bought a pair of roses. Of course, I had hidden them from Dej. I couldn't have her ruining my aspirations. It wouldn't have been a surprise had she learned of my scheme.

Since my business was peaceful and empty of souls, I decidedly figured to head over there. What it boiled down to was, I needed some time to be by myself. I had a huge obligation ahead, which required a plan, so I sorted through many ideas before the fanciful conception had finally been formed.

During my time alone I'd written a poem. It was constructed to be amorous, tender, and sweet. Plus, on the up side, Dej is keen on things like that and, I knew without doubt, it'd incite her reaction.

When time approached, it was already night. I'd taken a ladder and propped it against her bedroom window; then, with two roses clasped in my teeth, I climbed to the *lucarne bois*.

When I was finally along the edge of the frame, I tapped at the glass. Shortly after, Dej emerged in a gossamer gown and was beautiful-ly glowing. In a gentle reach she'd taken the rosettes from my lips, then smelt their scentful redolence. My heart pounded fiercely as I prepared for the poem. I drew a deep breath, then gradually recited the villanelle.

As expected, tears formed in her eyes as she smiled unto me. It was then, after finishing the quatrain, I pulled the ring from my pocket. I re-member her face when I watched it illume. I've never felt more alive in my life than I did in that instant when I made my proposal, and my doll, how beautiful she was when she answered with yes. We then touched lips as I came through the window. It'd been the most divine end to such an excellent night.

Chapter Seventy-Six

I've written my encounters over this time, and I'll end by saying cases will always come and go. Names will be different and so will each sto- ry. Between Marin and me, we've each worked our share, some having been easier than others, and, of course, there'd been a few that confused our precocity. However, we managed and got by. Adding to that, Yria Dane's was, beyond question, the most complexing we've seen.

Had we known early, from the beginning, what struggles we'd have, I'd probably asked myself, would we be capable of conquering this matter? With all the confusion and all of the lies, I'd had reasonably considered an uncertain conclusion.

Indubitably, it took time, but with Marin and Ghis, we pulled it together and disposed all the facts. Guillaume Rhoe never imagined it'd be us who would crack it. It was due to our persistence and determina- tion that we were able to succeed with our goal.

From the things we have seen, to the things we've encountered, I'm certain to say, Yria Dane's will be the most bewildering case of our entire career. Wherever she is, I hope she's resting.

CPSIA information can be obtained at www.ICGtesting.com
Printed in the USA
LVOW11s2347070316

478168LV00001B/1/P